Saving Grace

ROSEWOOD RANCH SERIES

ALEXANDRA BANKS

Book design by Alexandra Banks

Cover design by Alexandra Banks

First Edition: February 2025

ISBN – eBook – 978-1-7635496-6-1

ISBN – Paperback – 978-1-7637728-2-3

ISBN – Hardcover – 978-1-7637728-3-0

*For anyone who's ever needed a little help
to find their way home.*

Author's Note

TW –

This book contains difficult scenes and recounts. For the full list of trigger warnings please visit - https://www.alexandra-banks.com/ebook

The location and topographies of the places in this story have been fictionalized. They may not accurately represent actual location and terrain.

P.S The playlist is in the back!!

SAVING GRACE

The flat stone roof beneath my bare feet is hot. Sweat trickles down my spine, sending the worst kind of shiver after it. The air is spice, rancid, and barreling down my throat with each breath.

I've been here before.

A voyeur to this recurring nightmare, featuring my son.

This time—it's different.

Yelling in the streets drifts to the rooftop I'm standing on. Words I don't understand; the tone and sentiment I do.

Military vehicles roll into the street. Smoke follows. Like it always does. A gust wraps my threadbare cotton nightgown around, tangling it between my legs. I'm trapped.

Forced to witness this every night.

I know what happens next. The gibberish on the street gives way to English. The sound of his voice closes in. Any minute now, I will turn back to see him push through the door to the roof with weapons drawn. Every inch of him covered in camo. But those eyes are the deep blue of my husband's. That face, my own. That smile, not that it is used over here often, hidden; I know it will bloom like Harry's when he is happy.

My throat closes over, a visceral reaction to seeing my child in uniform, and I can't take my eyes off him. All business, he makes his way to the short wall at the edge of the building, his spotter close behind him.

The radio on his shoulder squawks, and he snaps a reply, head swiveling.

He's alert. Good.

His voice an altered, more velvet version of his Pa. Burning prickles behind my eyes. Wetness tracks across my temple and into my hair. This is the part of a mother's love that burns.

The brakes on the vehicles below whine and they roll to a stop. Mackinlay drops his gear and starts unbagging a rifle. I know what he's about to do. I know he must do it.

Still, heat rushes my chest, and bile crawls upward.

His spotter sets up his equipment, somewhat covered by the undulating half walls with gaps every three feet. His tripod supports a device akin to a video camera. Both boys have their faces painted. They work in silence, communicating only by looks and gestures.

Settling on his stomach, Mack tucks the rifle into his side, eyeing down the naked barrel. He plucks a smaller, long pack from his gear bag. One-handed, he pulls the scope from its nestled spot and slides it into the guard on top of the rifle.

"Gun up."

"Spotter up," the young man says behind him. I suppress the urge to look at him, not willing to let my gaze wander from my own flesh and blood.

"Hold." A harsh voice scratches back across the radio.

A soft click at the dial as his hand brushes over it, and he shuffles closer, spreading his legs wide, whispering something that sounds like a small prayer.

I clutch my hands over my chest. Closing my eyes, I say a prayer of my own to make sure my child makes it home, wherever that is for these boys this time, tonight. Knowing full well that whoever is at the end of my son's crosshairs won't.

That familiar burn flares in my core. That part of being a parent that smarts.

Selfishly, I ignore it, mesmerized by his hands that adjust the dial with soft clicks.

Gunshots ring out below.

Harsh voices echo over the radio at his shoulder. He doesn't flinch. Not moving in the slightest.

"Breach!"

More gunshots.

Screaming starts.

Women and children hurry inside. Our men file into buildings on the opposite side of the street. A tall reddish stone three-story faces Mack's twelve o'clock. He will find his mark. He does, every time this dream unfolds. Like a play known by heart.

Only seconds whip past before he tenses by the rifle.

"Now, gunny!" the radio squeals.

"Contact."

The radio whines, beeps.

He slides his finger over the trigger.

"Range two hundred," the young man at the tripod says.

Mack is still, barely breathing. "Two hundred."

"Zero-point-three right."

Adjusting his rifle almost imperceptibly, my son's words are fast. "Zero-point-three right."

"Spotter up."

His shoulders rise and still. A long breath in. "Shooter ready."

I hold my own breath, knuckles white over the opening of my nightgown.

"Send it." The young man on the tripod goes rigid with the words.

Shoulders rising and falling in a steady rhythm, Mack whispers two words. I can't make them out. His body frozen, he holds his breath. His trigger finger moves back with a precise movement.

Crack.

The window shatters on the top floor of the building opposite. Glass falls, tinkling like rain onto the sidewalk below.

"Impact! Move out ASAP."

Static on the radio washes away the next command.

The boys pack their gear. A deep drone whooshes in from the other side of the building.

This isn't right. The whoosh never comes. This isn't what is supposed to happen.

"Fuck! Now, Rawlins!" the spotter yells, swiping up his gear in a bundle.

"Calm down, Daisy, it's probably backup comin'."

The young man pauses, eyes darting as if that will produce the source of the rotor wash. Mack swings his head up as a militant helicopter buzzes overhead. My son's face turns from business to something else entirely.

His spotter runs to the rooftop door and disappears through it. A militant leans out of the window of the helicopter, bullets strapped to his cloth-clad chest. His head wrapped in bright colored fabric, he yells down. Aiming the tip of his weapon downward, he screams something like a madman. The aircraft jerks to one side.

Mack lets off a shot at the bird with the pistol from his hip and, leaving his rifle, makes for the door.

The weapon suspended in the air fires. A rocket-type round dives for the rooftop.

"Run, Mackinlay!" I claw at my throat. "Run, my boy!"

Rounds spark from somewhere close, charging for the

helicopter. They intercept before it can meet its mark. The explosion swallows the chopper. It plummets, rotors spinning, crashing into the building's top.

The old structure cracks under the weight. Stone bursting.

Tears spill, tracking into my hair as they did before.

I can't breathe.

A harsh grip clamps down over my arms. I thrash in their hold, desperate to get to my second youngest.

The roof implodes. Then caves in.

I watch, scant air burning my hollow lungs, as Mackinlay is tossed from the building like a rag doll. Sickening stone slams into the sidewalk below, and the air rumbles.

The grip on my arms pulls.

Pulls hard.

Warmth folds in around me.

I wake with a start.

Sobs choke from my taut face, my fingers curled to claws. "Mackinlay!"

The familiar scent of my Harry surrounds me. He presses me into his chest, hands rubbing my hair, running down my back. "It's okay. It's only a dream, darlin'."

The heartbreak in his voice sends fire into my chest. I shake my head.

No.

I push out of his hold and find his gaze. Within a

breath, his eyes reflect mine. Terror mixed with devastation. "Sweet Jesus, Lou."

"It wasn't just a nightmare this time." I push off the bed and steady myself on the side of the mattress. Forcing air into my lungs, I wrap my dressing gown around my body and pad into the hall. In the kitchen, I pull the kettle onto the stovetop. My hand trembles around the handle. A large hand slides over mine as I'm folded in his embrace, his chest to my back. His heart races against my spine, his stubble tangling with my bed hair.

"Let me, Louie."

I tamp down a sob and turn in his hold. Meeting his gaze, a torrent of tears cascade down my heated cheeks. "What if he doesn't come home, Harry?"

"Hey, we will find out if he's okay in the morning."

I sob into his chest. His stubble digs into my hair above my ear, his breath moving in my hair. "Hold hope, darlin'."

The same god-awful dream every night he is deployed. Without fail. My nerves are shot. My heart so weary.

I can't.

I can't do this anymore . . .

Harry holds me at arm's length. "How about I make the tea, and you find a spot on the sofa."

I nod and lean back a little. Hand resting on his weathered face, I force a smile. Where the hell would I be without this man?

I sink onto the sofa and tuck my feet beneath me.

Staring into the unlit fire, I let my mind wander back to the days when the boys were little. Mack and Reed, peas in a pod, always up to something. Up a tree. Hunting for no good. If anything happens to Mack, Reed will never be the same.

Harry settles in beside me, handing me a cup of tea.

It's hot and I embrace the slight burn, a reminder that I'm awake. That the horrific scene that played through my head was *just a dream*. I drain the cup and strong arms pull me into his side. A hand rubs my hair, a kiss dots to the crown of my head.

Exhausted, I relax into his warmth, letting my eyes drift shut for a moment.

*****

Ringing jerks me from Harry's side. It pierces the quiet.

The phone.

"Sweet Jesus, who rings at this hour?" he grumbles, pushing to his feet and heading toward the office. I follow on tender steps.

Ring. Ring.

He clears his throat.

Ring.

The clack of the plastic handset rustling from the phone base sounds so loud.

"Harry Rawlins speakin'."

The silence of the early morning crashes in. The faint trill of the sun-woke birds filters through the windows.

I press my hands over my mouth, not daring to breathe. Somehow, I make it halfway down the hall and lean on the wall.

"Hold on," Harry says, knowing I'm by the door. He hits a button on the phone. Static and breathing pour from the receiver. I listen, eyes closed and arms hugging my body tight.

"Mr. Rawlins, this is CNO Sergeant Miller. I'm ringing in regard to your son Mackinlay. Sir, I'm sorry to inform you . . ."

Chapter One

GRACE

THREE MONTHS LATER . . .

The morning paper slaps down beside my coffee cup, and I flinch. Protesting, the worn wooden dining seat creaks with the sudden movement. I wish . . . I was invisible.

"How long does it take to have a cup of coffee, Grace?" Joel snaps. He drops into the seat opposite me at the small round dining table, the morning sun beaming in through crystal clear windows behind him. A thrift store find, the old table looks how I feel. Scarred, weathered, and all the while standing on wobbly legs, one of my feet sometimes not touching the floor. "You have errands today. And we need more toilet paper, don't forget it *again.*"

I nod and sip my coffee. It burns my throat. But I like the pain, it reminds me this isn't some passing nightmare. These here are my waking hours. Between mouthfuls, I fidget with the charm on my bracelet. The one Mama gave me, before she cut me from her life. My fingers rub the smooth shine from the tiny silver painter's palette.

"You need to write that down or something?" He swipes the newspaper, the *Clarion-Ledger*, up from where he dropped it. The malice that's lined his eyes for the past eighteen months is strong today, darkening them. It isn't going to be a good day for me. Who in Mississippi reads the newspaper anymore? Apparently, the people of Raymond do. At least this Raymond-dweller. I stare at Joel and his paper, letting my hate sear into the back of the creased ink and pressed pulp between us.

I should have left the first time.

I have nothing. Literally. Not a cent to my name. If eighteen-year-old me could see me now, she would be horrified. I thought I was making a smart decision, getting the chance to paint and not have to work. We'd had a plan. I paint. He works. Then in a few years, I could start selling the art I create. And things were fine for a while. While Joel had a job. But like everything else this monster of a man does, he ruined that, too.

Lost his temper at work. Never saw a paycheck from then on. Benefits aren't conducive to a happy life. Or a happy relationship. We have been living on them for almost eighteen months to the day. I begged and pleaded for him to let me get a job. Every time, he took that to mean he was less in my eyes, weak, and I wore those bruises for a week. As if that would show me how strong a man he is.

Today, on my birthday, if I had a candle to blow out, freedom would be what I'd wish for.

Nothing else.

"Pick up a carton on the way home. Timmy's gonna be over tonight for cards."

"But—"

"Just fucking do it. God, no wonder your parents disowned you."

He turns the page on the paper. Pretty sure he can't even read. Big man in a small town. I tamp down the smile that threatens to push up on my lips. Thinks he's smart. What I wouldn't do to tell him otherwise. But I don't want to start another fight, one I know I won't come out on top of. So, I down the last of my coffee and take the plates to the sink.

"You better be out of whatever this female mood is of yours when Timmy rocks up, Grace."

I look over my shoulder. His eyes hover above the paper.

I nod.

Swallowing, I run the water in the sink and add the dish soap. The bubbles grow as I swirl a hand around the burning liquid. Washing up, I stack the plates, mugs, and cutlery on the rack to dry. As the water drains, I wipe down the counter and every bubble from the stainless-steel sink. "No bubbles, Grace. No mess." Joel doesn't do mess or *out of place*.

I would spend days once, before him, doing just that. Making a mess, painting. Creating. Being who I am. Happy.

Before Joel.

A clump of bubbles refuses to slide down the drain. I swipe them up. They sit on the side of my hand the way a ladybug would. Or one of those fluffy things that you make a wish on. Glancing over to Joel, who's still face-deep in the sports section of the paper, I blow on the bubbles. Closing my eyes, I make a wish.

A sliver of hope.

If only fleeting.

Please.

"What are you doing?" The harsh words snap me from my quiet state.

"Nothing, just thinking."

His hard stare doesn't waver. "Fix it, Grace."

Yes, drill sergeant, I want to banter back. Be a brat.

I won't. Being sassy hurts.

So, I clear my throat and wipe down the sink for a second time. When no trace of the frothy detergent remains and the kitchen is spotless, I make my way to the porch. The flag is up on the mailbox. A whisper of joy slides my veins. It doesn't last long. Hope, always hiding just out of sight as it waits for the chance to be part of my life, fades. Probably bills.

I take my time to travel down the four stairs and along the path. The neat, fresh-cut grass glistens under the morning dew. Post is early today.

Reaching the mailbox, I pull down the back and slide the letters out. Junk mail from a realtor. Phew. I flip it to the back. A bill for electricity. Heart in my throat, I slip a finger under the flap and rip it open. Less than last time. A tiny glimmer of relief curls in my chest. The cold showers and trying not to use appliances paid off this month, at least. The last letter is not commercial. I flip it over and gasp.

The return address is my parents'.

This is the first letter, first communication, I've received from them since the day I left with Joel. My breaths turn shallow as I run my bottom lip through my teeth. Did they remember my birthday? Is it a letter or an olive branch?

I slide a shaking finger under the wide flap and pry the envelope open.

A pink, glittery card sits inside. I double-check Joel hasn't come outside then pull it out. It's beautiful. Under glittery embellishment sits an easel, a girl facing it, hand raised, her back to me. Her long dark hair hangs loosely in a ponytail down her back. *Happy 21st Birthday, my favorite work of art!* the inscription reads. I slap a hand to my mouth. Mama used to call me her little work of art when I was small. I was her constant companion, even as a teenager. Until Joel.

Opening the card, fifty-dollar notes flutter from the center to the ground, surrounding my feet.

Shit!

I scramble to gather them up, gaze locked on the front door. Praying Joel doesn't choose this moment to come out. Or the money is gone. He will drink it away with his buddies. The thought sends my gut plummeting. I don't think I could take that.

My bubble wish came true. A two-faceted silver lining. A connection with my mama. Some money to squirrel away for something, someday.

"Grace! Where's my wallet?" The muffled words tell me he is in the front room. His wallet is always in the drawer in the kitchen. Was he watching this whole time? I stuff the notes into my underwear behind my belt at my back and cover it with my shirt. I leave the card and envelope out. That can't hurt.

I jog back inside.

"What's in the mail?" Joel says, leaning on the door. His belt runs through his hand. I force my gaze to meet his and not linger on the leather and buckle.

"Electricity, junk mail, you know . . ." I say, letting the last few words fade.

"Where's my wallet? I have to meet the guys at the bar to talk strategy."

"The guys?"

"Last time I checked, Graceless, I didn't need to tell

you who I'm hanging out with." He pushes off the jamb and stalks toward the bedroom.

"Your wallet's in the kitchen," I offer.

He turns back, threading his belt into the loops on his ripped jeans. I release a breath; thankful it's on its way to secure around his waist. "Don't forget those errands. And clean up while you're doing nothing all day. Can't have Timmy thinking we live like pigs."

"I'll need some money for the store."

I wait, holding my breath.

He grunts and tosses a twenty at my feet.

"I don't think that'll be enough, Joel."

"Well, I guess whatever that doesn't cover will be free."

He wants me to steal. Again. I swore I would never—not after last time.

"Keys?" I whisper.

He slides my car keys from his pocket where they live and throws them into the air. I catch them in one hand, heart in my throat, tears on the verge. I refuse to let them fall.

Not for him.

He slaps my ass as he walks past, wallet in the other hand. Snatching up the keys to his old, busted white Volvo from the small front table with one too-short leg, he's on his phone, tapping out a text before he disappears through the front door.

I slump against the wall and blow out the air in my

lungs. The cash digs into my spine, sticking to my skin. The early morning heat is catching up with me already.

Happy to be left alone, I tidy the already neat living room and vacuum the entire house. Dreaming of all the ways I could spend the money from my mama. Dreaming about throwing caution into the wind and calling her up. Wondering what I would say. What would she say to me?

What would be the point?

I lost all respect from my parents when I chose this pathetic existence over finishing my college degree and taking the internship at the art gallery in Pennsylvania that I'd been guaranteed as part of my scholarship.

I can't blame them.

I hate myself for that decision on a daily basis these days.

Once finished with the chores, I grab my keys and push my hair into a ponytail. The singlet top I have on is smeared with dirt from cleaning. I rush to the bedroom and find a button-down shirt. Tossing the singlet into the hamper, I pull on the shirt and button it up.

The short denim shorts I have on accentuate my toned legs. My long light brown hair sways as I turn on my heel and check my ass for stains. Light blue eyes stare back at me in the long mirror behind the door. Plump lips and dark eyebrows that seem to always be pulled down these days are the only parts of me I recognize now.

The driven, exuberant girl that was full of life is nowhere to be seen. That girl who was happiest when covered in paint and elbows-deep in a new project. Zoned into her creative mind, and hard to reach.

Now, the most beautiful thing I work with is watching bubbles die a slow death as they slip out of existence with water's demanding force. A little yoga when Joel's not around or passed out. I used to go to classes when we first arrived. I was competent at it, too. Thought about teaching it a few times.

My phone pings.

Joel.

Toilet paper. Ciggies.

Ugh. Alright, already. Men and their butts. Seriously.

I lock up and jog to the car. My 1960s Beetle sits in the sun, light blue paint blistering. It breaks my heart to see her in this condition. She should be taken care of. Have a proper home, like a carport or maybe a garage. She's a classic, after all. Precious.

I slide on the black velvet seat and pump the gas a few times before turning the key in the ignition. She splutters a little but purrs to life. I run a hand over the steering wheel. "Attagirl, Blue."

Backing out of the drive, I let her idle for a little before tweaking the radio. When I hit a catchy song, I shift her to drive, and we head to the store.

The parking lot is busy, and I grab one of the last spots. Locking Blue, I head toward the store. People pass me with a nod and smile in that guarded way they do when they don't want to talk to you. In the small town of Raymond, gossip travels fast. Questionable gossip, much faster.

The looks of pity started around a year ago. It was the first big fight Joel and I had. The first time I ended up on the wrong end of his temper. Judging by the sympathetic stolen glances that followed in the days after, what goes on behind closed doors is nobody's secret.

The sliding doors give way as I enter the cool shop. The wash of the air-conditioning is like heaven on my skin. This heat has the most even-tempered folk on edge. I stand in the doorway and bask in its bliss for a moment. I head straight to the toilet paper. No need for another fight. Wandering, I find a sign—whole chickens, half off. I close in and place one in the cart, then head for the fruit and vegetable section.

I miss my mama's Sunday roasts. Her food was delicious, but her company was the greatest comfort. Hindsight is funny like that . . . You never see what you're giving up until it's in your review mirror. What I wouldn't give to put our makeshift house in my rearview mirror for the last time.

I reach the checkout with a handful of items in my cart. The realization that I forgot to count the cost as I went hits me. The checkout girl grabs the items, scanning them as she goes.

"Oh and, Marlboro Reds, please."

She twists and grabs the pack, scanning it with the rest.

"That'll be twenty-two fifty." Her face is pushed up with another pitying smile.

Shit.

Heat crawls up my neck as the space caves in around me. I'm short.

"Oh, I forgot. You can use a second coupon today," she says quietly as she taps on the screen in front of her. "So, that comes back to nineteen ten."

I huff a strangled breath and hand over the twenty. "Thank you."

She gives me a sad smile.

Hey, at least I didn't have to steal it this time. I'll take humiliation over theft any day of the week. I leave the store like it's burst into flames and make my way home.

When everything is squared away, I start on supper. Roast chicken and a few veggies with a twist, herbs and lemon marinade. Extra butter under the skin for delicious crispiness. I rub the raw chicken like a trained masseuse, taking the quiet time for myself before the guys get home.

The front door slams. Two slurring voices bounce down the hallway and into the kitchen.

Oh great.

With the oven preheated, I pop the chicken in with the tray of vegetables and wash up.

"Hey, there she is!" Joel holds his hands in the air. A cocky smile lights up his face, as if he's happy to see me.

Timmy rounds the table and dumps himself into a chair, not bothering to look at me. "Grace."

"Timmy." The guy gives me the creeps. Too calm, like he's set to explode any second. Dark eyes that just follow every move I make. I suppress a shudder.

Beer breath and clammy hands invade my space. "Something smells half-edible in here." Joel's all over me, his lips hunting mine. The alcohol on his breath hits my face. I wince, trying to break free. A sloppy kiss lands on the side of my lips before he swats my ass, hard.

"See"—he turns to Timmy—"always so fucking frigid."

Timmy laughs, sucking back another mouthful of his beer. "We can fix that." Malice lines his hooded eyes. From the alcohol or something else, I'm not sure.

Joel walks into my space, and I back up against the oven.

Bracing my shoulders back, I hold my chin up. "I'm going to go have a shower. Supper will be ready in an hour or so." I hold each word like a weapon, hellbent on not letting either of them sense my fear. The second they do, I'm prey.

"Wash up so we can get dirty after supper." Joel runs a hand through his hair. The tattoos on his bicep move over the muscle. His arms aren't overly bulky, but if they're set on hurting something, I won't stand a chance. I rush to the bedroom and shut the door. Leaning on it, I flick the lock. Chest plummeting, I shake my head.

He wouldn't . . .

Something in the kitchen crashes. Glass smashes.

Fuck.

Fear snakes its way through my limbs.

Double-checking the lock, I dive to the floor by the bed and pluck out my overnight bag. Heart flinging against my ribs, I stuff clothes, underwear, and anything else I can find from my side of the dresser into a duffle. I grab the envelope with the money I stashed away earlier today and toss it in, too.

A fist thunders on the door.

"Fuck."

"Grace! Get out here!"

He's pissed.

If I leave this room, it's going to hurt. A fresh surge of fear prickles over my skin. My breaths, choppy and short, turn raspy. The door rattles under a new siege of anger and knuckles. I grab up the bag.

The door busts open.

Eyes catching on the half-packed bag, Joel stalks into my space. "What the fuck?"

I drop it to the bed and close my eyes, hands pressed into my chest, fingers tight around the charm Mama gave me.

Dear God, if you can hear me . . .

Chapter Two

MACK

I can't move.

Traction holds my body motionless. My mind, however, is not as blessed. Almost two weeks to the day, and the last thing I said to my spotter still runs on repeat through my head.

"Calm down, Daisy, it's probably backup comin'."

Liam Arnold Butler—Butters, we call him.

Called him.

My last words to him cost him time and, ultimately, his life.

I grind my jaw shut, pressing the thought—no, the memory—down. Happy smiles and cheeky pranks on base are what I will remember. Not the limp, lifeless version of him rescue pulled from the rubble of three stories' worth of stone.

A sigh drifts up from the visitor's chair by my bed.

The early morning sunlight splinters through the white blinds covering the wide windows of my very pale, very clinical hospital room. Ma moves in her sleep. Her hair mussed, her shirt crinkled.

"You're awake. Mornin'."

Pa waltzes in with two coffees like he's walking into a party. I'm pretty sure my family has a rotation. I haven't had a day to myself since being admitted to this place. They take it in three-day stints. This is my folks' last day. Huddo and Adds will most likely be here by noon to take the next allotment of days.

I love my family, I really do. But right now, all this fussin' and pity is sending me crazy. And I'm the last guy on the planet to deserve it.

"What's with the scowl, Mackie-boy?"

My gaze darts to the door at the sound of my big brother's voice.

Lawson.

"Hey, Laws."

"Well." He wanders to my bedside, coffee in hand like the parentals. "You most definitely put some effort into getting outta the chores, didn't you."

"Fuck off, Laws."

"Language, Mackinlay," Ma mutters. A sad smile stretches her lips.

"You seen Reed yet?" Laws asks.

"The first face I saw."

Laws chuckles and Ma stands, stretching her back.

"I'm going to grab some fresh air. Come for a walk, my love?" Ma says to Harry.

"Absolutely, this place is depressing." He winks as they pad from the room.

Laws sinks into Ma's chair. "How you really holding up, Mack?"

"I can't move an inch, and you have no idea how itchy all this shit is."

"Mack . . ."

"I'm fine. I'm alive, ain't I?"

"True, but sometimes that feels worse. Especially whe—"

"I know what you're goin' to say. I'm aware of the survivor's guilt, stages of grief, all that shit. I'm fine. Countin' my blessings, one rigid limb at a time."

"Well, at least you won't be alone." He sips his coffee and crosses a leg over his opposite knee, ankle resting on it. "How long 'til you get out?"

"Casts are off in two weeks, then I have to wear supports and such. Mobility will be an issue, they tell me. Will need to have an assessment by the physio before I'm discharged."

"Sounds like you have it all worked out."

"Yeah, this is totally on my life plan, Laws." I stare at the window.

Honorable medical discharge.

Which means my only option now is ranching. If I can even get back on a horse. As well as cope with the physical demands of ranch work. For now, everything is up in the air, along with my damn feet.

A soft knock raps on the door. Last night's doctor stands over the threshold. "How are we feeling this morning?"

"Same as last time I saw you, doc. Hanging around, tryin' to ignore the pain."

She makes her way to my bed. If I wasn't strung up like an invalid and hopped up on painkillers, I would have asked her out. She's my type. Brunette with a kind face. A gentle disposition and eyes that tell you there is way more to this girl than you get from her with just a conversation. Lawson stands, and I jerk at the movement.

For a second, I forgot I'm not alone. At this rate, my family is never going to let me out of their sight ever again.

Fuckin' fantastic.

She runs her hands over my torso, checking each bandage for seepage. "How's the pain today?"

"Manageable."

"No, not manageable, Mackinlay, we want as little as possible to aid with recovery. The less pain you have, the more your body can focus on healing."

"Sure. If you say so."

"I do." She offers a soft smile.

Lawson's gaze swings between me and her. *Forget it, brother, not happening.*

"When do you think we can take our patched-up soldier home?" Lawson asks.

"Well, if all goes to plan, and he can weight bear when the traction comes off, and makes it through his physio assessment . . . I think about three weeks, give or take a day or two."

"What will physio be looking for?" I ask.

"They will assess your muscle and motor capacity, and then give you exercises and figure out how long your support devices will be in use."

"Like a brace or something?" Laws asks.

"Yes, exactly. He will have a brace for the shoulder injury, a moon boot for the lower leg and ankle. I will be suggesting to them that you also have a support for your left hip and lower back. That should take care of keeping you aligned while you heal and regain muscle strength."

"Oh, that all." I close my eyes. So, I'm about to be bundled up like an Eskimo. Fuckin' awesome.

As if he reads my mind, Lawson shoves my shoulder—the good one—and says, "Still alive, little bro, focus on that."

"Yeah, how could I not?"

The minuscule sliver of joy I found having Laws here drains away as I remember I'm still breathing, still here.

Butters is not.

"Goddamn it, Laws, shit!" I stagger to the side. The foot of my crutch is stuck in a gap in the boards of my front porch. Fire streaks through my hip, and I slam my molars together to stifle the groan that rises with it. Lawson's hand squeezes around my bicep, holding me steady as I find my feet. I wasn't this useless at the rehab center of the hospital, but a four-hour flight and two-hour drive has all but seized up my body.

Porch – 1

Mack – 0

Jesus, I hate this.

Reed and Ruby walk inside, carrying the load of bags from the hospital and the one from base that the Sarge sent stateside after everything went to shit. Ruby chatters away, taking to tidying up the already spotless house. If I didn't know better, I'd think she's stress cleaning.

I do, and she is.

Gotta love her for that.

Adds has Huddo fixing a railing on the internal stairs. The parentals are stocking the fridge as we make our slow entrance into the ranch house I've called home for over a year now. The huge farmhouse always felt too big for one person. Right now, it's full and loud.

All I want is to be left to my misery.

I wish they would let me wallow in peace.

"You're stocked up with hot dishes and fruit, snacks, and some frozen meals, including soup," Ma says as Laws guides me onto my own sofa like a carer does for their elderly patient.

"Your live-in nurse will be here tomorrow. That's the earliest we could arrange one. They are hard to find in these parts. So, I'm afraid you're stuck with me tonight, Mackie-boy." Lawson's face is all kindness and understanding, but I hate it when he calls me that.

I suppress a grunt as I bend and meet the soft seat. Reed appears in front of me and squats like you would to talk to a little kid with a scraped knee. "Anything you need?"

"Nah, I'm good, gunny."

His face wrecks before me briefly, and he schools it back. "Sure, holler if that changes, okay?"

Swallowing, he rises and stands. I breathe through the burn behind my eyes and tighten my grip on the crutches I still cling to. Ruby melts into his side, sliding her hand into his. Reads that man like a book, she does. He swallows, pushing a small smile up for her.

"Help me with the linen, will you, Reedsy?" she says.

When she drags him from my orbit, I release a heavy sigh. I could cope a lot better with all this if I could nix all the pity company. They mean well, and I love them for it. Except, I can't breathe with the smothering gestures and sympathetic looks. Hell, the look on my little brother's face almost brought me to tears.

There's been enough fuckin' crying.

Ma crying that I got hurt.

Then again when I was discharged.

Adds and Rubes held it together, mostly. I know they were upset. And Reed. The thought that I could have caused one of his anxiety attacks twists my own gut into knots.

Laying my head on the back of the sofa, I listen to the puttering of the well-meaning people in my house. Harry is talking in hushed words to Ma in the kitchen, something about meals and burning my hands.

". . . you know he can't . . ." Ma trails off.

Light steps.

"There is spare linen in both bedrooms, if anything needs changing during the night," Ruby says to Ma.

Boots march through the house. The front door opens and closes, and Huddo's muffled curse words settle over the patio outside. With a crack and some hammering, I can tell the old board is up and a new one is in its place.

A castle fit for a cripple.

Grinding my molars for the umpteenth time today, I pinch the bridge of my nose as Addy explains to Laws my physio and medication regimes for the third time.

Tension coils low in my gut. *For fuck's sake, he was there when the medical staff ran the entire family through it, Adds. We got it, already.* Laws is only here for one night. The information is in the discharge summary for the nurse. Why is everyone acting like overbearing helicopter parents?

"Don't forget the pain meds, twenty minutes before he starts, to minimize the pain and maximize his workout-slash-physio sessions, okay?" she insists.

Fire tightens my chest, and I push up too fast on wobbly feet. The crutches clatter as I try to pull them to my sides. "Enough!"

The room falls silent.

Ma's shock-widened eyes find mine. I slide my heated stare to Addy. "We get it, Adds. But you're done." I wave my hands at my family, whose faces are a mix of hurt and empathy. "You're all done! I can manage by myself. I don't need a goddamn daycare routine." I shift my gaze to Laws. "Or a fuckin' babysitter."

Adjusting the crutches with a harsh grip, I hobble through the front door to find a fuming Hudson. Yelling at his wife wasn't my finest hour. Hell, I don't think I've ever had one of those. He crosses his arms over his chest, his hot gaze and drawn brows following me as I stagger over the porch and down the stairs. My knuckles turn white on the rail as I make a dubious descent.

"Mackinlay, come back . . . please." Ma's voice is all beg.

I don't want to respond.

A stone explodes in my throat, lodging tight.

I can't respond.

I hit solid ground with both feet, somewhat steady,

and head for the barn. Dizziness creeps in around me like an unwelcome blanket. Like hell I'm goin' back inside. Not until the welcome home wagon leaves this ranch in the dust.

Harry's soft words to Ma fade as I stalk awkwardly into the barn. The large space is one side of stalls, the other, rows and rows of hay. A small tack room sits in the back corner, and I head for it, like a man desperate for refuge in the worst storm.

Out of breath and hating every fiber of my being, I slump against the wall inside the darkened room. Groaning, I slide down the old wood and onto a pile of saddle blankets. The musty scent of horse and hay folds in around me.

Quiet seeps into my ears at an alarming rate. The sounds of the last few moments on that roof burst through the white noise.

It's then I realize, I made it home.

But I never made it out.

Chapter Three

GRACE

Hot tears roll across the broken skin of my cheek and set it stinging. Hands firm around the wheel, I squint through puffy eyes and unshed tears into the dark night. Blue's tiny headlights are all but useless. But I can't stop now. I refuse.

The constant rattle of the VW engine soothes the hurt in my chest and drives me forward. With only the bag I packed and half of the cash from my mom, I head for the county line. Praying Joel and Timmy are too drunk to follow. If they do, my next prayer is that the cops find them before they find me.

Northbound, I hold up my phone and reread the job post for a cleaner somewhere on a Montana ranch. That should be enough distance to keep Joel from looking for me. Or being bothered to come find me, at any rate. With only half the money Mama sent, I will have to use it all for gas. Luckily, Blue travels light in that department.

Should I run short, I will have to either splash and dash or earn some more money to fund the rest of the trip. I guess the best place to stop would be somewhere closer to Montana, but math has never been my strong suit. So, I'll drive until I can't, then figure it out.

When I'm a little past Little Rock, I pull over into a rest stop and lock the doors. It's well past two in the morning and my eyes struggle to stay open. Killing the engine, I twist the flared seat knob and lean back, following the seat back as it reclines. Just an hour or so and I can keep going . . .

Something hits the window in rapid succession.

I jolt up on the seat, eyes wide as I stare up into the face of an older man. His police uniform is immaculate, his hand still a fist by the window. The sun glares through the smudged glass of Blue's windshield, halfway up the pale sky already.

Shit.

Clearing my throat and fixing my hair, I roll down the window. Blue's old mechanism sticks, and I have to push the glass down as it retracts. "Sorry, Officer, did I do something wrong?"

His focus shifts to the damage on my face.

Heat soars up my neck and flushes through my cheeks.

"You heading somewhere, hon? Or you need help?"

"I—" Breaking his gaze, I drop my eyes to the steering wheel. "I'm fine, just got tired and needed to pull over, that's all."

"Well, you can't sleep here."

"I know. Won't happen again, I'm sorry."

"Don't be sorry, be safe." He digs a hand into his hip pocket. "Here's my card if you decide you need my help." With a not-so-subtle nod to my face, he forces a smile and returns to his police vehicle. I curl my hand around the card. Any luck, I won't ever need help with Joel again. Too scared to have called the cops the last few times, I suck in a lungful of air, reminding myself I got out.

I left.

Maybe eighteen months later than I should have. But I did.

Better late than never, right?

There is a sliver of me that hurts for the relationship I lost. The one I was still fighting for, even up until the last moment. For the guy I fell for at almost nineteen. The sweet, charismatic, and spontaneous man. Now, his words that turned vile when he found the money Mama sent for my birthday hook into my mind, talons sharp and deep, over and over.

"The fuck, Grace? You had this? You hiding money from me now?"

"No! I—Mama, she sent it to me. I swear." I hate the weakness stealing my voice.

"Your mom?" Incredulous words twist his face into a facade of utter disbelief. "That bitch wouldn't send you anthrax tied up in lit fuse. Don't lie to me!"

His roar scares me, more so than ever before. Terror snakes down my spine as his hands turn to fists at his sides. I scramble backward, heading for the en suite door. My back slams into the door and I snap around as it opens and weave through it, turning the lock as the air in my lungs turns to ragged sobs. I try to calm my racing heart.

He'll cool down.

It's fine.

I'll show him the card and—

The door rattles at my back under his thundering fists.

FUCK.

Fear turns to fire racing up my spine. A tremble starts in my hands and spreads through my body. I hunt for something to defend myself with. A disposable razor, a toothbrush. The sum total of the available weapons.

Fuck, fuck, fuck.

"Grace! Open this fucking door. NOW!"

Don't open the door, Grace.

Do not open that door.

My hand reaches for the knob as doubt creeps in. And my stupid emotional brain overrides my fear. The second the door leaves the jamb, Joel is in my space. Hands clamp down on my wrists with an iron grip. "Half of the money is mine. Don't care where you got it."

"But—I told you . . ."

His sarcastic laugh bounces off the tile in the small space. Forced backward, I hit the vanity with my hip.

"Joel, please. Stop."

"Why? You lie and steal and make me out to be the bad guy, hey?"

"No, I didn't—"

"Stop lying!"

"I'm sorry, please!" I lean in, curling into myself, torn between the need to run and my freeze-induced reaction.

His hands snap from my wrists, dragging my bracelet with them. The chain snaps and charms clink onto the tiles. All I can do is hug myself. With nowhere to go to put space between us, I wait, not daring to breathe.

He turns and walks to the bed and snatches up the wad of cash. All of it.

"For lying, this all belongs to me now. And you can stay in this room and wait until Timmy and me are ready for you."

God, no . . .

I struggle to tamp down the sob clawing up my throat. A mangled whimper slips past my lips. He stalks back to the bathroom, eyes dark and mouth twisted into something cruel. Some-

thing I've seen on him before. His knuckles smash over my cheekbone a heartbeat later.

I teeter and slam into the vanity. His back is all I see as I slide to the floor. Shock steals the air from my lungs, the burn and ache swelling on my left cheek and eye sending ugly sobs through my chest. I glance around at the shining silver charms and links of broken chain and release a whimper as I scrape them together.

"No. No. No."

The sun burns through my windshield and sweat trickles over my brow, sinking to my busted face. It stings. I wipe the salty sweat from my face with the hem of my tank top and pull in a ragged breath.

I got out.

Slamming my eyes closed, I force down the fear that's been repeating on me since his hand met my face. Somehow, I managed to wait him and Timmy out. Once they passed out, I grabbed what I could, the money he'd left on the kitchen table that was littered with bottles.

I got the money back. Well over half, at least. Stole my keys from his front pocket. That act alone almost cost me an aneurysm from the nerves racking my body as I slid a shaking hand into his jeans. Finally, I fired up Blue and got the hell outta dodge.

Not a moment too soon.

That part of my life is done. Boxed up and stored away. Destined to grow moldy and forgotten in some dank, dark attic. Maybe a rat-riddled basement. Never to be bothered with again. After fixing my seat, I lean forward and turn the keys in the ignition. The police vehicle is still behind me. Most likely waiting until I drive away. Evidence there are some good ones out in the world. I pull onto the highway and adjust my seat a little more, pulling the belt over my chest and clicking it in.

Next stop, Kansas.

Time to get my ducks in a row.

My gun-shy, frazzled, and battered ducks.

Leave.

Find work.

Sleep in Blue until I can find a place to rent.

The job posting I found in Montana sounds perfect. If there's one thing I can do, it's clean. I just pray Blue makes it to the mountains. I pray I make it.

I will.

I have to.

Going home to my parents isn't an option. Even now. Especially now. Going home with my tail between my legs after they tried to get me to see I was making a huge mistake isn't something I can bring myself to do. No, if this is rock bottom, I'm making the most of it.

Fresh start.

New life.

New possibilities.

As far away from Mississippi as possible.

I wince as the smile that tugs on my lips with the

glimmer of hope aches the left side of my face. With a heavy heart and shredded soul, I put all my focus into making it across the county line and into the next state. Then the one after that.

A large wooden arch towers over the entrance of the ranch.

R & R Ranch
R & R Rawlins

The place was easy enough to find. And the further down the drive I get, the more impressive the property is. Blue rattles along the gravel driveway. She's low on fuel and running hot. I can tell by the heated engine oil fragrance she's sporting.

"Almost made it, girl. Hold on." I pat the wheel and look for a place to park. Decided on beside the homestead gate, I let her idle for a moment before killing the engine.

A woman waves from just inside the yard and wipes her brow before making her way to the gate. Six white cabins with red trim sit along a winding stream behind the main homestead. Two barns—one that looks like stables, and a larger one to the east. The doors are closed, but it's enormous. Must be the event venue mentioned in the ad. Four of the cabins have guests, judging by the cars parked in the small driveways in front of each.

The gate squeaks, and I wipe my hands on my shorts. They feel too short. Since beggars can't be choosers when fleeing one's home, this is what I have. I plaster on a bright smile and hope it's enough to distract her from my inadequate clothes and bruised face. No amount of concealer was enough to hide the damage. Even after twenty minutes of trying my best to cover the impact of Joel's hand on my face, a shadow is still noticeable.

"Hi, I'm Grace. I'm here about the cleaner position." I offer her my hand.

She smiles, and the happiest green eyes framed by dark blonde hair light up. She frowns for a moment, and I am one hundred percent certain she is staring at my broken face. I swallow and make a point of looking around the ranch. "It's an amazing place you have here."

"I'm sorry, hon," the older lady says with a sad smile. "The position is already filled."

My gut sinks.

My hopes have been rising with every mile I drove down this dirt road. "Oh, okay. Sorry to have wasted your time, Mrs. Rawlins."

"Did you come far?" Her face is wrinkled with concern now.

"A little, but not to worry, I can find something back in town." I wring my hands together in front of me.

"Before you go, come in for some tea. You look like you could use something sweet."

The air in my lungs rises, only to lodge in my throat. She's definitely figured it out, then.

"That's not necessary. Thank you anyway, Mrs. Rawlins."

"Goodness, y'all call me Louisa. Mrs. Rawlins was my mother-in-law."

The ad was placed by a Ruby Rawlins. Who is this lady, then?

"So, you're not Ruby?" I ask.

She gestures for me to follow her into the house. I follow, looking around at the old trees in the front yard, the fairy lights draped from every single branch. I bet that's stunning at nighttime. I'm sad I won't get to see them now.

We walk inside, and Louisa calls out for Ruby. Footsteps rush down the stairs in the center of the front room. A blonde woman, around ten years older than me, skips down them. Her brown eyes land on me and a smile stretches her face.

"Ruby, this is Grace. She drove all the way here for the cleanin' job." Louisa waves a hand toward me as she walks to the fridge and pulls out a jug of what I assume is sweet tea.

"Oh wow. I hope you didn't come too far." Ruby shakes my hand.

I can't respond. I feel out of place. Underdressed. Out

of my element and altogether stupid for not checking the posting's updates.

"Where did you say you drove from?" Louisa says, prompting me as we sit at the round dining table off from the kitchen counter.

"I, ah—" My gaze swings between them.

Ruby glances at Louisa before sipping her tea.

"Mississippi, actually."

Louisa's eyes widen and she returns her tea to the table with a thump. "Well now, that is an *awful* long way for a job, young lady."

Ruby studies me for a moment. I fight the heat that rises under her perusal. So much for nobody noticing my bruises.

"Lou, don't you have that other position over at Mackinlay's that needs filling?"

The two women share a look before Louisa sits up and gives me a warm smile. "You know, I almost forgot, we have been needin' a carer, live-in housekeeper type, for the other ranch. You would be perfect for the job. The last three employees didn't suit. The manager, he is . . . well, he's particular."

A grin bursts over Ruby's face.

"Why? What's wrong with him?" I ask, eyes darting between the two women.

Ruby tamps down a smile before squeezing my hand. "He's just a bit of a grump after his accident. His mobility is a problem right now, hence the live-in position. I'm sure you can handle him."

I've come this far. No turning back now. Besides, after Joel, I'm certain this manager couldn't be worse. By the sounds of it, his injuries debilitate him. Safe enough, I guess. And much better than sleeping in Blue.

"Sure, when can I start?"

Louisa's face lights up. "How does tomorrow sound?"

Chapter Four

MACK

No more nannies. Nada. None. I'm fuckin' done. The last one actually wanted to cut up my goddamn meat like I'm some two-year-old. Besides, I can do this on my own. I do *not* need a babysitter.

As if on cue, the front door opens and closes. Ma's back.

I grip the washing basket with one hand and prop myself against the bench with my good hip, tossing dirty laundry out of the basket and into the machine with the other. The side of it digs into my bare chest, the base propped up precariously on my hip.

My left crutch slips outward, and I teeter on one foot as it, too, leaves my grasp. It clatters to the floor a meter from where I stand.

Fuck me.

Dropping the empty basket to the floor beside the traitorous crutch, I lean over and grab for the laundry detergent. The heavy box slips through my hand and crashes to the floor. White powder floods the small space, covering the wooden floor.

Sweet Jesus.

I brace against the counter and try to pick my way clear of the powder on the remaining crutch. On the second step, the crutch slips. I flail, arms flinging outward as I crash to the floor and onto my bad hip.

"Ah . . . Fuck you six ways to Sunday. Motherfucker!"

The pungent tang of detergent burns my nose, and the powder sticks to my now-clammy hands. It clings to my legs and covers my navy jogging shorts in its ghostly dust. Pretty sure the stuff will taint my skin for days. I may as well have rolled in the shit. I groan and close my eyes, hanging my head.

"You need a hand?" an unfamiliar soft voice fills the room.

Snapping my eyes open, I look up. A woman, young and looking as startled as I feel, stares down at me. She eyes the powder, the basket, and the crutches. It's then I notice she is holding an armful of linen.

The new nanny.

I thought by ignoring that last text from Ma, it would mean she would drop the whole idea of the live-in babysitter. But since a stranger, albeit a beautiful one, is standing in the doorway to my laundry room, I'm guessing ignoring Ma did not, in fact, translate to the word no.

The woman's pale blue eyes skate over my body, stalling momentarily on the braces on my leg and hip before snagging on my bare chest. Her hair is pulled up into a messy bun and her plump lips shine with some kind of gloss. Her sneakers look worn. Toned legs and lightly tanned skin consume me at eye-level. Tiny frayed denim shorts are topped with a pale blue checked button-down shirt. I clear my throat.

"I'm sorry, I was just wanting to put these—"

"Did you find it, Grace?" Ma calls from the kitchen.

Great, just great.

Here we go again.

Grace glances behind her and hovers for a second. "Yep, all good."

Her gaze meets mine and she offers a small smile, leaning in to pop the linen on the counter. But she doesn't turn and leave. Instead, she drops to her knees and starts sweeping the powder away from where I sit with her hands.

"It's fine, I'll clean it up." My words are harsh.

She stills for a heartbeat before sitting back on her heels. "Alright."

"I take it you're the new babysitter."

It's not a question. She simply nods and says, "Your mom said you needed some help around here. I needed a job. Guess it worked out."

"No." I lean forward and rise to my hands and knees. The stabbing pain in my hip turns to fire. "It didn't. I'm not interested in having a carer. Didn't work out the last three times, won't this time, either."

She pushes to her feet. I clamber through the acidic snow and haul myself up the doorjamb. She stares, folding her arms over her chest. Pushing up to my full height, I lean on the doorframe. I still tower over her by a head. She looks up. Her left eye and cheekbone have a purple-green bruise. Probably got into some catfight over something fuckin' stupid. Most likely over a guy. Like I said, don't need another carer. Let alone one who has drama following her around.

"You done staring?" Grace mutters.

"'Bout as done as you are here, I reckon." I drag my gaze from hers. "Ma!"

Footsteps hurry down the corridor and Ma appears, a smile brightening her face. "I see you've met Grace. Show her to one of the spare rooms, will you, my boy."

My face turns to stone, body ratcheting up the tension in every damn muscle. "She's not stayin'. We are done with the carer, babysitter, hand-holding bullshit. I'm fine."

Ma leans and glances to the floor behind me. "It looks anything but fine, Mackinlay. Now, show Grace where her room is, or I'll have your father come over and do it."

Jesus fuckin' Christ.

"Whatever."

I sound like a petulant child. Not feeling much more than one, either. I hate it. I hate this whole situation. But when Ma's steely gaze doesn't break from mine, I relent. Nudging one of the crutches with my foot, I try to slide it toward me. It flings further away. "Dammit."

Neither of the women move to help me. Ma folds her arms now, imitating Grace's stance.

"You want me to get that?" Grace asks, raising an eyebrow.

"Nope. I'm fine."

I try again. Bending at the hip, I grip the doorframe with one hand and swipe at the crutch with the other. My fingers curl around the side of it. I yank it toward me and use it to drag the second crutch to where I stand. With both crutches in action, I thunder down the hall, not waiting for them to catch up.

The bedroom at the back of the house faces the east. Its huge bay windows give it a ton of natural light. I stop and move to turn back, finding myself in Grace's space. Her scent, vanilla and peaches, crashes into me. I falter back a step as she peers into the room.

I take another step back away from the doorway and gesture for her to enter. "Have at it."

She wanders into the room, eyes taking in the queen-size bed. The attached en suite. The oak dresser and the window and seat by it. She spins back and opens her mouth, but she must have thought better of it, as she closes it and walks from the room and back to the kitchen. I push out the back screen door and wander into the backyard.

With difficulty, I lower myself onto one of the outdoor chairs by the firepit. The heat of the day is already rolling in, and I focus on the light breeze and the inhale and exhale from my lungs. Maybe it won't be so bad if she stays. She's much prettier than the last three nurses. And a *lot* younger. She must be around twenty-five or something. Knowing Ma, she never bothered to ask.

After twenty minutes of back-and-forth in my mind about the latest recruit to join team "fuck over Mackinlay's wishes," I push from the chair, stiff and sore, and head back inside. The washing machine is whirring away by the sounds coming down the hallway. I pass the laundry room. The powder is cleaned up, and is that coffee?

The distinct aroma of coffee percolating wafts toward me. I reach the kitchen, and Ma is nowhere to be found. Outside, her truck is gone.

"Coffee?" Grace asks from the kitchen.

"Fine." I slump into a chair at the kitchen table. A steaming mug appears in front of me. She comes to sit on the other side of the table with her own mug wrapped in fine, elegant hands. I narrow my gaze and take a sip. The black gold is delicious.

"I get it, you don't want me here. And I—"

I hold up a hand. "Let's set a few things straight before you dive into telling me your entire life story. You can stay for the short term. The second I am capable of doing my own laundry, you're done. There will be no drama here. Whatever happened to your face," I say, waving a hand at her, "none of that follows you home. I mean, here. It doesn't step foot onto this ranch. Got it?"

Her face is a mixture of shock and pure hurt. She swallows and rests the mug on the table, and I fold my arms over my chest. I've already been fucked over. I'm not buying into her shit as well. I open my mouth to explain as much, but she says, "Fine. I'll stay out of your way."

She rises and pads to the kitchen and pours her almost full cup of coffee down the drain. Moving toward the front door, she plucks up a small overnight bag and a phone, its screen so smashed, I can see it from here. With quickened strides, she disappears through the hallway, heading for her room, I assume. The door closes with a soft click.

I down the rest of the coffee and head out to the front porch, collecting my phone on the way. Two messages from Ma.

Please treat Grace with the respect you were raised with, Mackinlay.

I know you're hurting my boy, but I have a feeling about this time around. Be nice.

Jesus, Ma. Always with the cryptic bullshit.

She's right, though. I've been in a mood since the day that rooftop collapsed. I mean, who could blame me? The chopper crashed, the old building crumbled and took me down with it. In more ways than one. I was by no means a career soldier, that was never the plan. But I was good at my job, dammit. Leavin' the military was supposed to be *my* choice. The when and how. Not this.

I leave Ma's messages on read and toss the phone onto the seat. I close my eyes and lay my head back on the side of the house behind me. The second I do, it's too quiet. My brain too unoccupied. And the shouting starts. The radio on my shoulder squawks. The swoosh of rotors sinks overhead. Rounds fire off below me—

"Steak okay for supper? I just want to start organizing," a small voice interrupts the chaos.

I open my eyes and dart a glance to the door where she stands. Her eyes are rimmed red, her arms wrapped around her like that will protect her from whatever she fears.

I grunt in response and shift my focus to the pasture behind the barn.

"Hope you like salad," she utters, walking back inside.

After hours of watching Grace putter around, tidying up and prepping supper, I make a start on my exercises and physio treatments on the living room floor. Every movement the medical staff set out for me hurts. I am gaining strength, but too slowly. My body is shaking and covered in sweat, so I head for the shower to clean up before supper.

"Your meal will be ready in twenty," Grace throws over her shoulder.

Not bothering to reply, I wander to the shower. The plastic seat that accommodates my banged-up body stares at me with its mocking shape. Hole in the seat for water flow. Like my ass is suspended over a goddamn sieve. I strip down, not caring enough to close the door, and turn on the water. As steam curls around the white chair, I go about removing the braces. One at a time.

Each brace comes away easy enough, but without them, each movement is too sloppy, too painful. Like my body is made from rubber, and I have almost no control over it. I grit my teeth as the hip brace hits the floor and I clamber onto the plastic seat. The sound of Grace moving about the house has me wishing I'd shut the door now. I'm in the master bedroom en suite, but still. I should close the door. Noted.

Making quick work of my hygiene routine, habit from years in the military, I towel off. I rise to towel my back half, and the plastic chair slips. My unstable musculature jerks to brace from slipping onto the tiled floor, sending agonizing pain through my hip, lower back, and leg.

"Fuck!"

I groan through the pain as heat rushes my body, my hands scrambling for a hold. My fingers snap around the chrome handle Huddo installed. I groan through the fire lancing every single inch of my body.

"Mackinlay? Are you okay?"

Shit.

Should have closed the fuckin' door.

"Fine!" I snap out.

Her footsteps fade and I steady my breathing. Hurrying to reapply the braces, I dress and towel off my hair. Mostly healed shrapnel wounds dot my skin on my chest and shoulders. My short dark hair is getting longer by the week, and even I can see the lackluster in my dark blue eyes that used to carry joy and a zest for life. For *my* life.

Now, dull blue orbs stare back over a drawn face. All I feel is anger, regret—but most of all, guilt. Pushing Butters's face from my mind, I hobble to the kitchen on one crutch. My armpits ache from being propped up on crutches all day, and just one is a relief.

The table in the kitchen is set for supper.

One place setting, not two.

The second Grace realizes I'm here, she brings over the plate of food. Steak, as she planned earlier. Salad and potatoes. A glass of juice sits on the table already. I sit, wary of her attention following me. She sets the plate down, followed by my evening painkillers, and takes a step back. "Anything else you need?"

"Nope."

"Okay, well, I'm going to call it a day. Try not to choke on your steak."

I look up into those light blue eyes. Sadness is the only thing that I find there.

Grunting out an acknowledgment, I pick up the knife and fork and cut the steak. At least she left me to my own supper and didn't mutilate my meat in the name of "proper home care".

Grace – 1

The last three nannies – 0

With a full belly, I settle onto the sofa and flick on the TV to avoid the quiet. Lulling me into its soft haven, I doze off as the night wears on. A noise startles me awake, and I glance at the clock in the kitchen. Almost midnight.

I turn off the TV and push down the hallway on one crutch. Grace's door is closed. Her light is out. The floor creaks under my feet. I turn into my room.

A sniffle splits the air.

I wander to my bed and rest the crutch against the bedside table. Tugging my shirt over my head, I sit on the bed. Swallowing painkillers with a mouthful of water, I start the agonizing process of lying with a bed stick, poking up on my side of the bed. No handles dangling from the ceiling here. With my body on the bed and my legs straight and as comfortable as I can make them, I reach for my phone and AirPods.

A sob echoes through the quiet house.

Then another.

With a sigh, I shove the AirPods into my ears and scroll through my playlists. The last thing I need is to be surrounded by silence. I select a playlist, determined not to let the nightmares scream throughout the night.

More sobs, and I slam my eyes shut. Maybe I shouldn't be such an ass. Maybe she should harden up. Life sucks. The sooner she realizes that at her young age, the better off she'll be.

The sobs continue and I crank up the volume on the Nickelback playlist Reed sent me.

Suck it up, buttercup.

Chapter Five

GRACE

When Louisa told me everything Mackinlay went through, I was in shock. He's lucky to have come home at all. But even those thoughts are not helping me curb my temper right now as we stare each other down in the doorway to the laundry.

"I told you I can do it, Grace."

"And I told *you*, this is my job. I'll be damned if you are gonna take this away from me, Rawlins, just because you got out of bed on the wrong side since *whenever!*"

"The wrong side—" He scrubs his hand over the light stubble on his jaw as his eyes track to the ceiling, the other hand gripping the crutch like his life depends on it. By the way his gait wobbles today, it's possible it does.

"Focus on your recovery and let me handle the rest."

His fiery gaze meets mine again, and it only hardens. "If you say so."

He moves from the doorway where he's been blocking me from entering, and I step through with his hamper.

"I forgot to tell you, Addy is coming over later to run me through your regime in case I can help."

"Of course she is," he mutters, breaking eye contact. "Like I want your fuckin' help."

A knock on the front door has him drag his focus from our conversation toward the sound. I go about loading the washing machine and add the detergent, anger lighting up my veins. After getting the machine running, I head to the kitchen to load the dishwasher like a woman on a mission.

A guy a little younger than Mackinlay stands inside, leaning on the kitchen counter. He pushes off and extends a hand when he sees me.

"Hi. Reed, Mack's younger brother. You must be Grace. Ruby told me all about you."

"Oh, hi. Yes, I met your wife last week. Thank her again for helping me out with this job, will you?" I give Mackinlay the side-eye.

He also glances at Mackinlay, who rolls his eyes. Reed turns to me and smiles, the biggest megawatt smile I have ever seen. His green eyes are identical to his mother's. He seems nice.

"Don't let this surly prick give you any shit, Gracie. If he does, give it back, and more some."

Gracie. Nobody ever calls me that.

It's so casual, just running out of his mouth. The

charisma on this guy . . . makes Mr. Rattlesnake here seem downright mean. I tamp down the amusement that rises with that thought and give Reed a nod. He smiles at me again and turns to Mackinlay.

"I'll finish that fencing and shift the eastern mob of weaners today. Come back tomorrow to check the water, okay, buddy?"

"Sure, gunny, whatever you say."

Reed shakes his head and slaps his shoulder before offering one last smile in my direction. I decide I like Reed. And Ruby. I can see they make a stellar couple. Even from the small part of R & R Ranch that I saw, they have built something incredible.

"I'm going to duck into Lewistown and pick up some groceries. Do you need anything? Or want to tag along?" I offer Mackinlay. He waves a hand over his shoulder as he heads for the sofa for the umpteenth time since I've been here. He is the embodiment of wallowing. I know recovery is slow and his pain gets the better of him at times, but all this moping surely isn't helping. My annoyance fades out, letting empathy in for a moment.

"You know, I still get lost in town, believe it or not. Could you tag along?"

He stills, halfway to sitting, and shoots me a look I can't read.

"It would be quicker if you came. Please?" I worry my bottom lip through my teeth.

His nostrils flare as he straightens up. "Fine, but next time, get a ride with Harry or Ma."

"Thanks," I say softly, not able to help the smile that is itching to stretch my face.

Now I only need to fake being lost in a town the size of a postage stamp. It will be worth it to get Mackinlay out of this house. Lord knows how long he's been inside these four walls.

"Come on, we can take Blue." I swipe up my keys and phone.

"Blue?" He pulls on a cap, leaning on one crutch. His indigo eyes drill into me. Even with the attitude, and the moods he runs through, I can tell the real Mackinlay is in there somewhere. I would bet my last dollar he's more like his younger brother than the cranky, stubborn ass he is right now.

"My car. I'm not driving yours."

"What's wrong with my truck?" He straightens. Apparently, everything I do and say is an affront.

"Too big." I wave a hand at him.

We make our way to the tree Blue is parked under, and I open the passenger door for Mackinlay as he makes it a moment later.

"I'm not folding myself into three to fit into that tiny-ass car, Grace."

I snatch one of his crutches. I don't even care if he can't fit. Serves him damn right.

He shakes his head at me.

"You'll fit." I give him a sardonic smile.

He sighs and lowers himself onto the passenger seat, gripping the door with white knuckles. With a groan, he's in the VW. When his bad leg is securely inside and clear of the door, I shut it and walk to the driver's side. Dropping into the seat, I grab my purse from the back seat and toss my phone into it.

"What on earth possessed you to buy a tiny blue tin can for a vehicle?" Mackinlay's frown is almost comical as he sits cramped up in the passenger's seat.

"Blue is *not* a tin can. She's sweet. She's a classic. Size isn't everything."

His face is flat.

The second the words register, heat flushes my face.

After Joel, the last thing I want is another man. Let alone be considering size. Or talking to this ass about anything related to that . . .

Good Lord. "I, um—"

A half smile cracks over his face.

I brush a stray strand of hair from my face. That's the first time I've seen anything but a scowl or hard concentration on this man's face. Much less an almost smile.

I narrow my eyes at him, and he snaps his gaze toward the windshield.

Right. Time to go, Grace.

My smile grows exponentially as I start Blue up and roll down the driveway. He stares out the window, turned away from me.

"It's okay, you know," I offer.

After a beat, he says, without turning back, "What is?"

"To have happiness after everything."

He scoffs and stares out his window. The tension that now hangs between us ratchets up in his shoulders as he whispers, "No, it's not."

He can't honestly believe that. Every night I cry into my pillow until sleep drags me under. For the things I lost back in Mississippi, for the life I threw away before I ever reached Raymond. I have come to peace with the decisions I made. I can't take them back, and punishing myself for them, or feeling sorry for myself, won't improve things. I can only go from here. Am I still grieving what I went through? Still trying to wrap my head around how I got so far down that dark, sordid rabbit hole? You betcha. But I'm not in that makeshift house anymore. I'm clinging to that particular fact, every minute of every day that passes.

"Keep to the right," Mackinlay says harshly, breaking my train of thought.

I move Blue over a little. I'm not used to driving on unmarked gravel roads. Guess he's right, we'd drifted to the center. Not exactly safe.

"You never answered me before," I say, looking ahead at the road.

"About what?"

"Did you need anything in town?"

"Nope."

"Fine."

I turn onto the highway that leads to town. Blue rattles up to a good speed and we make it in under an hour. By the time I pull over on Main Street, I can see the unease written all over Mackinlay's face. He's been in one position too long. Cramped in the small seat space. It's possible this is a bad idea.

Maybe he shouldn't be such an ass.

I kill the engine and move to his door. He has it open and is leaning forward before I have a chance to help. "Got it!" he snaps.

"I need to grab my purse," I say with a huff.

I shift to the right and lean past his shoulder and pluck my bag from behind the seat. It's when warmth presses against my arm that I still. He didn't move.

I'm pressed into his shoulder. I glance back. His jaw is tense. His hands gripping the door and off his crutches. Dark blue eyes swing up to mine. Shit.

"I, ah—" I swipe up the bag and scramble backward away from the car. Without hesitation, Mackinlay pushes up out of Blue and steps clear of the door, slamming it behind him. I step around him and lock the door with the key. I push on my sunglasses and tug out my hair band, letting my long hair fall around my shoulders in soft waves.

"Where did you need to go?" he asks, gaze shifting over me. For the first time, his words aren't harsh. No order or a rebuttal.

It catches me off guard a little and I chew my bottom lip, glancing up and down the street. I need the grocery store. The pharmacy. Maybe the craft shop . . .

"Groceries first."

He waves a hand to my left, and we walk down the street, past the shops of Lewistown. Past an Italian restaurant, Mama's Place. A gift and craft shop sits across the street, and a convenience store one block down. As we walk, people smile, some say hello. A guy around Mackinlay's age in scrubs walks past, blond hair and pale blue eyes that widen as he forces a smile. "Rawlins, you back already?"

"Morley," Mackinlay grunts, not slowing down.

What the hell was that about?

We cross the street, and an older lady walks up to us, arms open, her smile topped with tearful eyes. "Mackinlay! Your mama told us you were back. Thank heavens you came home to us in one piece, sweet boy." She pats his face. It goes from pleasant to devastation. His jaw feathers and I steal the older lady's attention to let him catch a breath.

"Hi! I'm Grace." I hold out my hand.

"Oh, hon, are you his girlfriend?" Her eyes widen some more but delight floods in a second later.

I laugh and shake my head. "No, I'm the help."

She pats my hand now and glances to Mackinlay. "Well, young man, you make sure your help is looked after, you hear."

He nods, and I can tell he wants to roll his eyes at her. I tamp down a smile and say goodbyes for the both of us and take off toward the store.

"Thanks," he mutters.

"Sure," I breathe. He stares at me as we amble down the sidewalk. I can see the war in his eyes over his visceral reaction to this whole situation and the man that exists under all the hurt. I know what it looks like. It stared back at me in the rearview mirror for days. It still does, when my guard comes down.

We do a quick round collecting groceries and leave with half a cart of fruit, veggies, and meat. A few snacks for me. On the way back down the street, we pass the craft shop. I peer through the window, hands holding the cart as I push it in front of me. My companion is getting tired, I can tell by his now sloppy gait. Time to go home.

"You want to go in?" he asks, nodding to the craft shop.

"No, we should get back."

He walks on without a word, leaving me behind. Guess my quota of reasonable Mackinlay just ran out. Back at the car, he leans on Blue as I unlock the car and load the groceries. When passenger and purchases are all secure, I start up Blue and head for the town limits. Halfway down the highway, and thirty minutes into our drive home, he turns to me with a scowl. "Didn't wind up lost once."

"Surprising, did last time," I lie.

"No, you didn't. Next time you want company, phone a friend."

I glance at him with annoyance twisting my face, mouth gaping. *Ass!*

"Couldn't be any worse than spending hours with you."

And like that, we are back to square one. Him, angry and taking it out on me. Me, giving it back, when it's the last thing I want to do. It's not what either of us need right now. But I can't seem to override the mean bone he brings out in me.

My phone pings. I ignore it.

Forty minutes and a trillion annoyed thoughts that I keep to myself later, we pull into the driveway of the ranch, and he's out of the car like it's on fire. He wobbles his way back inside on the crutches. I sigh, letting my forehead meet the steering wheel. It's going to be a long few months.

Despite all that lies between us—the ocean of hurt and trauma, and the eggshells I constantly dance on—I feel safe here. I feel grounded. For the first time in my life, I have purpose and money of my own. Nope, he can throw whatever he needs to at me. I'm not going to give in and break. Not going to throw the towel in and leave. I need this job, as much as he needs an attitude adjustment.

My phone rings, vibrating in my bag. I pull it out and answer.

"Grace, how's things going?" Louisa asks.

"Hi, Mrs. Rawlins. Things are going, ah . . . well, they're—"

Her laugh cuts me off. "Oh, hon, I am fully aware of the moods my son goes through. He will come out the other side of this, I promise you. Hang in there. He needs you. Stubborn ass will never admit it. But his dark needs your light, if you catch my drift?"

How does this woman put so much stock and trust into someone she barely knows? A little of my annoyance fades. Partially afraid of another round of someone else's darkness. Mostly grateful I have a roof over my head and a wage. But my gut sinks, clogging my throat, as my eyes burn.

"Grace? Are you still there?"

I suck in a breath, wiping away unshed tears from my eyes. "Yes, still here."

"Lawson, Mack's older brother, is coming home for a few days to stay with him. He'll help you if you need a comrade in arms, so to speak."

"Backup. That sounds great," I say, too quietly.

"Sweetheart, I know you have been through it, too. A mother notices those things. We have your back, please know that."

Now the tears stream down my face freely. "Thank you," I choke out.

"And when you're ready to talk about it, any one of us is more than willin' to listen."

"Uh huh." I can't manage more words.

"Now, deep breath, hon, and get my boy off that damn sofa. He needs sunshine, you hear?"

"I'll see what I can do."

So, prying the sofa king from his kingdom is going to be a regular occurrence. Yay for me.

"And Grace"—she pulls in a breath—"thank you."

"Yep." My words are nowhere to be found.

The line goes dead. I haul air into my lungs like I've been drowning and just broke through the water's surface. It burns and replenishes at the same time. After a moment to fix my hair and dry my face, I cart the groceries inside. Dumping the bags on the counter, I start packing everything away. The TV blares as Mackinlay sits on the sofa, mindlessly flicking through channels.

After all is packed away, I drop on the seat beside him. He startles before giving me another scowl. I do nothing but return the stare, and his brows lower. "What?"

"Lawson is coming to stay. Where do you want him?"

He turns back to the TV, snapping a finger over the remote. The TV goes black. "In New York, where he belongs." He rises to wobbly feet and stalks down the hall as fast as those crutches can go.

Well, that went well.

Chapter Six

MACK

Addy relays the physio routine to Grace. "He needs to do these exercises three times a day."

With every word, my babysitter's face falls. "Are you sure? Because that hasn't been happening," she says, worry lining her voice.

Like she fucking cares.

She's too young to be bothered with me. Too much life to live to be saddled with this shit job. Man-baby sitter. Pay is shit. Patient is an ass. Nope, Grace should make better choices. In another time, another life, where I don't end up an invalid, she's damn near perfect. It's getting harder and harder not to notice.

Those eyes.

Her smile, smell, hair.

Peaches and vanilla.

Long fuckin' legs for days that get me hard every time

I close my eyes. Thinking about those tits is downright improper. Sends me to the brink every time I get close to her. The small noises she makes when she's concentrating. Like driving into town the other day.

Took everything I had. Every horrible thought I could muster to keep my cock from becoming a raging hard-on, sitting right next to her in her tiny tin can car. I tried to make nice, at the car before we ventured into town and again at the gift shop. But everything comes out shit. Everything I touch turns to shit. She should make tracks before she's sucked into my black hole of existence.

"Mack, you haven't been keeping up with your physio?" Addy's hands are on her hips. Her face is pulled down with knitted brows, and those big brown eyes that stole my brother's heart are full of concern.

"I do them enough."

"Bullshit, Mackinlay, you barely do them." Grace comes to a stop beside Adds.

Well fuck. Goddamn snitch.

Getting ganged up on by the girls. This is what my miserable existence has come to.

"They just make my body hurt, Adds." I refuse to look at the little snitch.

"Well, what about something more gentle, like yoga?" the snitch says.

"Not happening."

Still not lookin' at her.

"We'll see if your answer changes in twenty minutes." Adds narrows her eyes at me.

"Why?" Now my brows sink. "What happens in twenty minutes?"

Addy full-on winks at me. I eye her with the narrowed suspicion she deserves, and she pecks a kiss to my cheek. "Stop being so damn stubborn, or I'll have to send in reinforcements, Mack."

Grace snaps her gaze from the two of us and returns to the kitchen as Addy leans in for a hug. A sarcastic laugh slips through my lips, and I shake my head at her. We all know who runs the ship in this family. Our family wouldn't be the success it is without the matriarch we all love and cherish. So, I grunt and nod. There's never been a day go by where Ma's word hasn't benefited us all.

Addy is Huddo's captain and Ruby is Reed's.

You would be hard pressed to find better people than those two girls. I'm grateful for all they have done for my brothers. That kind of happiness is special.

Something smashes to the floor.

I jerk where I sit on the sofa.

Fear snakes through my veins, heating up my skin and swallowing me whole. My breathing crashes and the last of the air in my lungs bottoms out. I grip the crutch with one hand. The other turns to a fist on the sofa beside me.

"Shit," Grace mutters.

The tinkle of porcelain being swept up fills the space

between the ringing in my ears as I sit, too rigid to move. A strangled groan fills my throat.

"Oh, god, Mackinlay." Grace is in front of me a heartbeat later.

Quick footsteps rush toward the two of us.

"What happened?" Addy's in my space, hands on my face. She lifts my gaze to hers. "Mack, breathe, buddy."

Another groan escapes, and I choke on the small amount of air that follows. My body starts to shake. Ruby appears by Grace's side.

Where the hell did she come from?

Recognition spreads over her pretty features and she's in motion before I can tell her to stop. A tight hug braces me against whatever triggered the panic that's rising in my body.

"Tell me what you can hear," Ruby whispers, rubbing my back with her hand in circles.

"My breathing, ringing in my ears—" I choke on a breath. Dammit, I thought I was past all this trauma bullshit.

"What can you feel?" she continues.

"You wrapped around me, Rubes."

She holds me at arm's length and tilts her head, her lips pressed together. "Tell me three things you can see."

"I'm okay, it worked."

"Three things you can see, Mackinlay Rawlins."

I sigh. "Adds pacin'." I turn toward the kitchen. "A mess . . . and . . ." My gaze catches on Grace. She's wringing her hands through the hem of her shirt, her breathing shallow, her face twisted with something like worry. She steps toward us, tentatively. "Grace, I see Grace."

"Do you?" Adds mutters, glancing at me, her face pulled into a frown.

Okay . . .

Silence floods in, followed by white noise. Addy doesn't say anything else. Rubes drops her gaze to the floor. Grace presses a hand over her mouth and turns back, heading for the kitchen. I push from the sofa. All of a sudden, it's the last place I wanna be.

My body aches from minutes of rigidity, and I stretch my legs and hobble down the hallway on one crutch. I'm out the back door and in the middle of the yard in no time. Hip and leg aching, I lower myself to the log seat by the firepit that's currently all cold ash and half-burnt logs.

Ruby walks from the back door and comes to stand in front of me. "You have five minutes to feel sorry for yourself, then we're doing yoga."

"Not likely, Rubes."

"I wasn't askin', Mackinlay." She even fucking winks at me.

Sweet Jesus.

I rub my hands over my face.

Fine. Whatever.

Five minutes.

I finally drag my sorry ass back inside. Four yoga

mats are laid out on the floor of the living room. The girls have changed into fitted exercise clothes, and Grace appears from her room in something that is obviously Ruby's. A pair of fitted dark grey activewear bike shorts and a sky-blue singlet flowing over a navy sports bra.

An arm drapes over my shoulders. Strawberries close in around me. Rubes.

"See, told you yoga is a good idea." Rubes dots a kiss to my cheek. Grace stares at the two of us, and heat floods my cheeks. *God dammit, Ruby.* I bat her away and she chuckles, lowering herself onto a mat, patting the one beside her. Addy takes the one on the other side. The only one that's left is one in front of where I now stand awkwardly.

Grace walks over and sits, cross-legged. She drags her hair to one side of her neck and runs her fingers through it as she works it into a plait. Is she leading the group or something?

"Okay, so the best positions for flexibility and gaining strength are the following." Grace flexes, her gaze alternating between me and the girls. By the crimson flushing over her neck and chest, she is about as comfortable with this as I am. And when she tangles herself into a pretzel, legs crossed over each other and arm over her head, I shake my head.

"Did you want to try, Mackinlay?" she asks. "Just try this side stretch." She stands and puts one foot in front of the other and bends down like a chicken pecking seed from the ground.

"Go on." Ruby prods my side with a finger.

I roll my eyes at her and scramble onto all fours and push to my feet precariously. Adds offers up a hand and I take it on my right. Ruby's hand appears to my left, and I slap mine over hers. I wobble on my feet as I push one forward and try to lean down. Fire rips through my hip. I hiss at the pain that follows.

"Only hold it for as long as you can." Grace watches me. Her breaths have quickened. I drag my eyes from her to the ground, trying not to breathe her in. Not wanting to fuel the need that already sparked seeing her in those clothes. Those poses. This damn close.

"Great, that's enough," she says. Her hand rests on my shoulder as she shuffles closer on her knees. Her scent, the vanilla and peaches I have been trying to block out from the day she arrived here, swallows me whole. I lose my balance and slump to the ground.

"Fuck," I grunt and settle myself on my seat, not daring to meet her gaze.

"That's okay, you did great," Grace says, offering me a shy smile.

"No, I fuckin' didn't. Don't bother tryin' to placate me. Lying doesn't suit you."

"Mack, you know I love you, right?" Ruby says. Her face is stone. "But you talk to her like that again, and I will add more hurt to your long list of injuries."

Adds scoffs, hiding a smile.

"Fine," I grunt.

Ruby raises an eyebrow, shifting into the pose I just did.

"Sorry, Grace," I mutter.

"You say somethin'?" Adds leans in.

"Fuck off, Rawlins."

"Back at ya." She beams at me.

Of course she does. Little miss sunshine. Brown eyes, curly brown hair, and actual rays of goddamn sunlight for a personality. Huddo is one lucky mother-fucker. I sigh and turn to Grace. "Show me the other ones."

She shuffles on her seat before standing like a star. With one arm up, she leans to the side and slides her hand down her leg. Another hip stretch. She bends her leg at the knee and raises her hand to the ceiling and turns her face upward. I take in the fine lines of Grace Weston. Her elegant cheekbones, her pert nose, lush lips, the dip at her collarbone before her neck, the curves of her chest, hip and . . .

"You want to try this one?" Upside-down blue eyes meet my gaze.

Vanilla.

Peaches.

Blood floods to my cock. Surrounded by three beau-tiful women, who could blame a guy? But two of those are my sisters. And I love them the same way I love my brothers. Sibling love. It's only the girl right in front of me who is affecting me like no one before. Ever.

She shouldn't. Not at all.

I'm pissed off at her for it.

Shut it down, Mack.

"Yeah, I'm done, this isn't for me." I push up to my feet, swiping up the crutch on the way up.

"Mack!" Ruby snaps.

I wave a hand over my shoulder, dismissing her.

"I'm sorry, Grace." Addy is consoling her. *Way to get your priorities in order, Adds.*

Fuck, I'm a mess. Terrified of loud noises. A nasty piece of shit who can't be around other people without snapping some poor prick's head off.

"We can continue without him," Ruby says as I wander into my room and slam the door. *Do it somewhere else, Rubes.*

I don't know whether to be embarrassed or flat-out annoyed at this point. Either way, it comes out as angry and inhospitable. Grace should move on. Find herself another job. Another loser to baby. I bend to sit on the edge of the bed and miscalculate. My ass hits the floor a second later. My breathing turns to shit, and the telltale burn behind my eyes floods in. I pinch the bridge of my nose.

I can't stop the sobs wringing from my chest, clawing up my throat, and pushing past my lips. I send my hands through my hair, fisting the tufty mess. Groaning between sobs, I try to suck in air and fail. Clutching my arms, I rock on the floor.

I'm half a man.

I'm no good to anyone.

I'm a waste of space, and a liability to this family now.

How Harry hasn't come and taken back the ranch, I don't know.

Why the girls bother is beyond me. They shouldn't.

Why Grace keeps trying every day . . .

I groan into my hands, letting the sobs steal the last of the useful air in my lungs.

Grace.

God dammit.

The thought that I will always be this way. Never whole again.

Fuck this bullshit six ways to Sunday.

Fuck everything.

Hours later, when I pry myself from the floor, the house is quiet and dark. The girls are long gone, and Grace is sound asleep in her room. Tonight, her door is open as if she's listening out for me. I hesitate as I pass her door. The fume-filled tang of something like turpentine wafts around.

Ignoring the malodor, I wander to the kitchen on one crutch and grab a glass of water. Back in my room, I scramble in the dark for my AirPods, shoving them in my ears when I find them. The house is all shadows and darkness. I swear as I lift my arms over my head and sink into the mattress with a sigh. Something appears in my doorway before retreating.

I turn up the volume to drown out those rooftop sounds still haunting me. The last thing I see as I close my eyes is Grace. Her fingers in her hair sitting in front of me plaiting deftly, her soft blue eyes stuck on mine.

Sweet Jesus.

I roll over, hissing as the ache in my hip intensifies. Cock hard as a rock from the slightest thought of her, I rub the heels of my hands into my eye sockets. Stars burst into my blacked-out vision, and I try to push her from my mind.

Harry's tax papers.

Ma's disappointed face.

Nothing works . . .

Then Butters's grin hits me like a ton of bricks and the buzz that Grace brought fades.

A stone wedges in my throat, and I try to remind myself—like I have a thousand times before—it wasn't my fault.

Tell that to my broken heart.

Chapter Seven

GRACE

The text on my phone buzzes again. I'm too scared to touch it.

Where the fuck are you, Grace?

Joel.

Who else?

I have been ignoring his texts. But this is the first time he's wanted to know where I am. The previous ones were him yelling at me, in all caps, about taking off with my own money. Come back to do my chores. He needs to get laid.

Blah blah blah.

Not my problem.

Until now.

Now, he wants to know where I am.

Shit.

What part of *disappeared without contact* does he not understand?

I hold the coffee cup in my shaking hands, sipping cautiously, like it's the hot brown liquid's fault.

A knock rattles the door. I freeze, swallowing down the last mouthful.

No.

That was way too fast.

Another knock. "Mackie-boy? Anyone home?"

Relief floods my body and I all but drop the mug onto the counter. Rushing to the door, I fling it open. A guy, older than Mackinlay and dressed like he just stepped off the city subway, stands on the other side of the threshold.

"You must be Lawson?" I ask.

"Yes, ma'am." His grin is almost as charismatic as Reed's.

I chuckle and step back as heat floods my cheeks. I will never get used to this cowboy etiquette. The kindness bundled up with happiness, smothered in politeness. It's overwhelming for someone who's been living with the literal devil for almost three years.

"You must be Grace. I'm Mackie-boy's older brother. One of them, at least."

"Mackie-boy?" My face is twisted in disbelief that Mackinlay could have a lovable nickname like that.

"Oh yeah, he *hates* it when I call him that." Lawson's grin grows wider.

I hold a hand out to take one of his bags. He shakes his head and steps inside. "I know where I'm going, Gracie, but thanks."

"Oh, okay." I shut the door as he drops his bags and runs a hand through his brown hair. He's stunning. "How was your trip?"

"Long. But I don't have the chance to come home as much as I would like. So, any excuse is a good one, if you ask me. Plus, the county fair is soon. Can't miss that."

"Oh, I've never been to one of those."

A voice clears at the start of the hallway. Mackinlay leans on his crutches, eyes boring into his brother's. "Should have stayed in the city, Laws."

"How's those exercises coming along, Mackie-boy?"

"Fuck off." He pivots and stumbles before stalking away from us as fast as he can go. I move to go after him, but Lawson rests a hand on my arm. "I got it, Grace."

I force a smile, but I feel like this is my fault. I pushed him with the yoga. Pretty sure I caused that panic attack he had with the plate that slipped through my fingers and smashed to the floor. I can't seem to get it right. I feel safe here. But I'm not sure I belong. Or that my presence is benefiting Mackinlay.

If I have caused a setback for him, I will never forgive myself. After all his family has done for me.

I crack the window as Lawson wipes the sweat from his brow. The machines are heavy lifting. I'm helping, but who am I kidding—he is doing the bulk of the grunt work. I have a layout sketched in my book, setting out the room in the order of the physio program Mackinlay is supposed to do. We are setting it up to suit.

"You think he needs another fan in here?" I ask.

Lawson glances up from the ground where he's sitting, legs spread in his running shorts and t-shirt. He pauses, his hands mid-hex-key turn on the back of the weight machine. "I guess he will be exerting himself in here. Yeah, put it on the list. I'll grab one in town tomorrow."

The idea of Mackinlay exerting himself in any sense sends my blood thundering through my veins in a way it absolutely shouldn't. Lawson interrupts the thoughts I can't rein in.

"You should take a room for yourself, Grace. This house is huge. Make a craft room or a library or some-place for yourself. Hell, I bet he wouldn't even notice."

"I can't do that."

I pluck a towel from the linen hamper and fold it in half. Folding it in half again, I roll it up. Placing it on the small table in the center of the wall by the door, I bend down to pluck up the next one.

"Sure you can. Since you'll be the one making him do this routine three times a day, you're going to need somewhere to hide out." The grin that breaks across his face sends a chuckle up my throat. I toss a towel at him, and he catches it with one hand before throwing it back. I fumble the catch and fold the towel in half twice. Rolling it up, I glance to Lawson. "You really think he wouldn't mind?"

"Nah, what did you have in mind?"

"Well, apart from a space for yoga, I—" I turn back and place the towel next to the first on the table.

"You what?" I can hear the curiosity in his voice.

"Paint. I paint. It's kind of messy, though."

"That's what drop cloths are for. You need a hand to set something like that up?" He pushes from the floor and moves to the next machine, setting the adjustments.

"I can do it."

"I have no doubt. Yell out if you want a hand, okay?"

"Thanks, I will."

There is a comfortable silence between us as we go about our tasks. I roll the remaining towels and head to the kitchen for a jug and glass to add to the table. Mackinlay is at his doctor's appointment with Reed, so we have a few hours to get his new space done. When I walk back into the room, Lawson is standing in the center, studying the layout against my sketched one.

"Looks good, Grace. He'll like it, *eventually*."

I scoff. "I highly doubt that."

His blue eyes find mine. "He's not like this, Grace. Nothing like it. I don't know how long it is going to take for our Mack to find his way back. But this angry version of him is the complete opposite of the man who left six months ago for tour."

A stone lodges in my throat. I've seen a handful of glimpses of the man Lawson is talking about. Little moments. Some I caught when Mackinlay thought I wasn't watching. "I hope you get your brother back, I do. But I'm not sure I will be here to see it."

"This arrangement is—" He shakes his head.

"What? Am I not doing what you all wanted?"

He squares his shoulders and rests his hands on mine. "You need to be here just as much as my brother needs you here."

"I don't understand, did your mom—"

"She told us nothing. When Ma decides something is important, we listen. Ruby already tried to get her to spill, and she won't. Not her story to tell."

His hands fall from my shoulders. Louisa must have figured it out. Why a twenty-something woman would travel halfway across the country for a low-paying job with nothing but an overnight bag and a shiner on one-half of her face. Guess I wasn't exactly subtle in my actions. The tug to leave and head to Montana over-whelmed everything else.

Now that I'm here? There is no way in hell I would ever go back to Raymond.

Not ever.

It's like night—a very dark and long one—and day.

"I have an idea. How about I clear out that spare room beside your bedroom, and you run into town to pick up some supplies to create your space."

"Are you sure? I mean, is there more to do here?"

He studies the room, a smile blooming on his face. "Think we're done. Take off and have some free time before Sergeant Grump comes home."

"Okay," I say with a chuckle. I head for the door but hesitate, one hand on the doorframe. "Lawson?"

"Yeah?" He spins back and looks up to face me from checking his phone.

"Thank you."

"Anytime, Gracie."

I can't help the warm feeling that washes over me. It feels like safety, and a semblance of belonging. Lawson is a blessing. He's like the universal big brother. If I'm honest, having a buffer between me and Mackinlay for the past few days has been a relief. I don't know what's been happening, but every night is getting harder for me. I'm so tired. Every interaction Mackinlay and I have grates more than it used to. Joel's texts have been messing with my head. The long stretches between them also make me anxious.

Surely, he wouldn't bother to track me down this far

from home. I am desperate to move on from that disaster of a relationship. But the last message sent me spiraling for hours. I am thankful for the workload of cooking and cleaning, medications and the physio routine. Busy hands, calm mind.

I'm clinging to that tactic for now.

I grab my bag and head outside to Blue. An hour later, I pull up in a free parking spot by the gift and craft shop. As I walk inside, the bell chimes and an older lady wanders toward me. "Well, hello there! What can I do for you today, lovely?"

"Ah, I am needing to pick up some painting supplies."

"Wonderful, follow me. Which medium are you wanting?"

"What do you have?"

She stops in front of the painting section. Shelves of brushes, pots, all sizes of canvas, and a large easel. The bell on the front door chimes again. "You holler if you want a hand, okay?"

"Sure, thanks." I run a hand over the smooth fabric of a canvas, not looking back as she moves to help another customer. I slide out a medium-size one and flip it over, hunting for the price.

My eyes widen.

It's obviously been a few years since I paid for supplies. I slide it back in and move along the shelf to an A3 sketch pad. The paper is thick enough for oil-based paints. I pluck one out and track down a brush set and a packet of twenty-four oil-based paints. Basic colors. Since I want to save most of what I earn at the moment, it's enough.

I daydream all the way back to the ranch about the setup I can make. I don't have any furniture. Maybe I can find something from a charity store and upcycle it. That would make another fun painting project. My mind wanders to what I could create. As I drive into the ranch, I look up to the mountains. What I would give to have the chance to paint them, or to be up high in them looking down and painting the landscape below.

Maybe one day.

If I stay that long.

If Mackinlay still needs me.

I kill the engine and haul my new stuff up to the porch. The front door bursts open, slamming against the wall. Mackinlay stands leaning on one crutch, face stone, brows down, and hand gripping the doorframe. "Where have you been?"

His hard tone stops me in my tracks.

"I was just in town." I nod to the items in my arms.

Where is Lawson? Why didn't he tell him where I went?

"When did you get back from your doctor's appointment?"

His jaw feathers. "An hour ago. The house was empty."

"Sorry, I didn't realize you needed to keep track of me."

He waves something around in his hand. "You left this behind. What if something had happened?"

My phone.

Shit. I forgot it, I was so excited at the prospect of painting again I literally ran out the door without it.

"I'm sorry," I say, walking up onto the porch. "I forgot it, is all. Where's Lawson?"

"Ma's."

He shoves my phone into the bag I'm holding and spins on the spot. He winces as he moves inside. When I get to my room, I drop the bags on the bed with a sigh. I can't tell if he's worried about me or pissed I wasn't here when he got home. Giving him the benefit of the doubt, I walk back to the kitchen. He isn't there. Sitting on the sofa, his head is in his hands, his elbows planted on his knees.

Something in my chest twangs. Its sharpness drives me to where he sits.

"I'm sorry, I should have been here when you got home." I stop a few feet from him.

"Who's Joel?" he says from behind his hands.

"What?"

"Your phone. You have three messages from Joel."

My breath stops.

More texts.

The notifications that Mackinlay saw must be on the

lock screen. Fear heats low in my spine and my hands clam up. Mackinlay lifts his head, and his eyes meet mine. His face is unreadable.

"If you need to be somewhere else, Grace, say so."

All I can do is shake my head.

He pushes to his feet, and for the first time since I have been here, it's without his crutches. "Go home, wherever that is. I can manage on my own." He raises a hand, moving closer. But his hand falls. His chest cycles through deep breaths.

I move closer, glancing him up and down, taking in the fact that he has no crutch. That he's a solid head taller than me. He tucks a stray strand of hair behind my ear, eyes searching mine. I open my mouth to tell him I'm not going anywhere.

He steps back abruptly. "Go home. Leave and have a life. There's nothing good for you here."

"I can't leave until you've recovered," I say breathlessly. The absence of him from my space hits acutely. "You're not getting rid of me until then."

His face tilts back a little, his shoulders square, mood changing in an instant. "If you say so."

He leans down and snatches up the crutch and hobbles away, the toll of standing without it evident. This man is always walking away from me. We are always fighting. Over everything. Maybe he's right, I should go. But I promised Louisa to help him. To do what she couldn't.

And deep down, I don't want to leave until I meet the real Mackinlay. The man his family is so desperate to get back. Because I'm invested now. I need to see for myself the man so incredible that he has each one of their hearts in a stranglehold, on tenterhooks as they patiently wait for him to find his way home.

Chapter Eight
MACK

"With a face like that, little brother, I'd need an escape room, too." Lawson drops on the sofa beside me. I know Grace getting another room was his idea. Always the good brother, Lawson.

"Fuck off, Laws."

"Can't, Ma needs you to stop harassing the help."

"Whatever, you all just can't help yourselves, can you."

I snap the remote toward the TV. Sports bursts to life on the screen. Another reminder of something I can no longer do.

"Get over yourself, Mackie-boy, not everything is about you."

"Yeah, right. That's why every single member of this family is bending over backwards for this invalid."

He sits up, face stone, and twists on his seat to face me. Grace is in the kitchen going over the pain meds and what I assume is the paperwork for the physio routine.

"Mack, you've got this backward, buddy. We're not accommodating you, we love you. This is where we want to be. You're not an inconvenience, you're our *priority*."

I can't respond. Instead, I shift my focus to Grace. She leans against the counter on one hip, her hands crossed over her chest, hair falling around her shoulders, eyes focused on the papers on the counter. Her gaze drifts from the counter and finds mine, as if she's thinking about me or something. She smiles, and my gut flips into my throat.

Fuck.

I snap my eyes to my brother. Whose eyebrow is raised now, a shit-eating grin blooming across his damn face. "Stop with the bad attitude, Mack. The hole you dug is deep enough. Time to claw your way out. Or I'm coming down after you to drag your sorry ass out."

"Fine, I'll try. But I don't need a babysitter."

"Like I said, not everything is about you, little brother."

What the hell's that supposed to mean?

"Whatever," I grunt.

"Stop fighting, Mack."

We fall silent and watch the TV. The men run around chasing a ball to entertain the masses. I zone out.

You got this backward.

Not everything is about you.

Grace is here, even though I asked them not to find another carer. Does she *need* to be here?

The fleeting moment of empathy fades.

What the hell does that have to do with me? She can find her refuge someplace else. The last thing I need is temptation I have to squash every time she walks past, or when we're caught in the same space as each other. She's too young. She must be at least ten years younger than me. She should leave and find herself someone who can give her everything. That Joel guy. He keeps texting.

Not stay here and end up anchored to half a man.

The bitter thoughts send a sardonic laugh up my throat. Laws glances at me before returning to the game in front of us. Here I am, assuming she would be into me. I highly doubt it—she barely tolerates me. Pretty sure if the paycheck dried up, she'd hightail it out of here on the next wind change.

On that note, I slump further into the chair, letting the pity party I'm throwing myself pull out all the stops.

When the cake is cut and the clowns are sent in, I let the fire consuming my chest take me down.

Fuck my miserable life.

The delight on Grace's face drains as the words I spat at her sink in.

"Addy said—"

"Don't care. Not doing it. And *definitely* not with you."

Her eyes widen, mouth gaping, brows snapping down. I take in the spare room she's spent hours turning into a home gym, all set up to accommodate my exercises and physio routine.

I'm an asshole. I'm aware.

"Mackinlay. You *have* to do this. The doctors—"

I hold a hand up. "Stop, Grace. I'm not doing it."

I don't dare raise my voice, lest the cavalry—in the form of my older brother—hears and falls in to help defend her position.

"You are a stubborn ass, you know that, right?"

"Not very quick on the uptake, are you, young'un."

She scrunches her face with a head tilt. "Did you just call me young'un? What are you, ninety? For your information, I'm not as young as I look."

"Okay, Miss Sorority."

"Fine, if you won't do it for yourself or even your family, do it to get rid of me." The hurt flashing through her eyes sends the stone that lodged in my throat with her last words sinking to my gut.

I open my mouth to respond, but Laws appears in the hallway, leaning on the opening, still in his running clothes, arms folded over his chest, eyebrow raised.

"Fine, out of my damn way." I wave a hand toward the door.

Grace retreats, and I swear a glint of moisture lines her eyes. She's halfway down the hall before I have the chance to repair the damage I did. I walk into the gym space. The posters from the physio are up on the wall. Towels sit rolled up on a small table. A water station. A radio. The equipment is set out in the exact order I need to use it. A new fan in one corner.

Guilt washes over me like a bucket of ice water dumped over my head.

Fuck me.

Might have to dial back the asshole. I run a hand over the closest machine and walk to the small table to check the exercises I have to do and in what order. A note is written in the margin of the page.

Mackinlay,
The sooner you can get your strength back, the sooner I'm gone.
Grace.

There it is, in black and white, hard evidence of my behavior. Laws is right—hell, they all were—this isn't me. It's like I lost who I was on that rooftop. This other version of me has taken over. I would like to say it's purely survival mode, but I know deep down, that's not an excuse. Never was.

"You should be grateful, and you should also make nice with Grace before I hand you your ass on a platter, Mackie-boy. Don't think I'm above beating up a crippled man." His brows are lowered but he winks at me. The sentiment rings true.

"Yeah, I know." I can't meet his gaze.

"If you stop feeling sorry for yourself for just a moment, Mack, you might see she is hurting as much as you are."

I stare at him, mouth agape.

Is that it? What everyone has alluded to, but never voiced? Grace is here because she's hurting? Never before in history of mankind has a man fallen so far, so fast. Propelled to a deep guilt by way of selfish ignorance and self-absorption.

Sweet Jesus, I am a first-class heartless asshole.

Running a hand through my hair, I close my eyes and exhale.

"Maybe if you're nicer to her, she'll show you what she's been up to in the spare room?" Laws knows that's been bugging me since the day she set it up and closed the door. I could tell myself I'm not interested in what's in there, but that would be a lie.

I've been smelling fumes and shit for days.

I'm guessing paints, or something. Maybe she's taking

apart the Beetle's engine. It hasn't moved in days. Not since I railed her about not being here when I got home from my appointment. It could be oil I'm smelling . . .

A hand waves in front of my face. I jerk up and meet Lawson's amused face.

"You need a hand to get through these exercises?" He nods to the first piece of equipment.

"Spot in for me?"

"Sure," he says, sitting on the bench portion of the abdominal machine, his AirPods in his hands. I sink to the machine that runs my legs through their paces. I start off on the lowest weight and grunt through the first few reps.

Laws studies my form. "I mean, come on. Life's not all bad if your workout partner is *that* pretty."

I scoff a laugh, and he beams at me, the handsome motherfucker.

Nicely played, Laws. Somehow, I doubt Grace is going to want to be my partner in anything after the last few weeks of living with me.

I continue the reps on the chart, but the burn in my legs forces me to stop. The fitness I gained as a soldier is nowhere to be seen. My body is weak and the tremble that rose with the last few reps only serves as a reminder of how far backward I've slipped. It's my own fault. I knew the routine I was supposed to uphold to regain my strength. I didn't do it.

I've had this equipment since the week I came home, thanks to my brothers. I never used it, just left it stored away. Shut the door and ignored it most of the time. Serves me damn right if I never recover. Maybe I don't deserve to.

I feed Laws something about a suggested rest period between body parts and move to the machine for my upper half. I have a little more luck. Most likely from using crutches and hauling my half-useless body around for the last three months.

"How are you feeling?" a soft voice asks from the doorway.

Laws gives her a half-assed salute as he leaves the room. This time when I meet her gaze and find a response, it's more honest than before.

"Feelin' useless . . . and stupid."

I slump against the back rest and wipe the sweat from my brow. Grace hands me one of the towels, and I dry my arms and the back of my neck. Only fifteen minutes of real exercise, and I'm exhausted.

"You should feel proud, not stupid. You turned your one day into day one." Her smile is genuine. Kind. Nothing I've seen from Grace until this moment.

Now I feel guilty on top of stupid.

Own it, Mackinlay. I can hear Ruby's words. Thank heavens Ruby is not the one running my recovery, or I'd be outside halfway through a ten-mile run right now. I love my sister-in-law to bits, but that girl has bigger balls than Harry.

Life wouldn't be the same without her. She will always have my love and respect for how she turned my brother's life around. Period.

"You're doing an awful lot of thinking." Grace's smile is still as beautiful as it was moments ago when it appeared, only now it has a hint of cheek to it.

"I don't—"

I shift on the seat and clear my throat.

The apology I rustled up before she walked in is stuck, wedged behind my Adam's apple like a damn stone. She tilts her head and drops to the seat of the abdominal machine. Now her smile slips, and she presses her hands over her denim shorts, chasing away non-existent creases.

"Grace, I don't want you to go. I'm sorry about what I said. How I said it."

She looks up from staring at her hands, now clasped in her lap. "Okay. Are you still going to fight me on every single thing? The housework, your recovery?"

"Well, not *every* single thing . . ." I smile at her.

Her eyes soften and she runs a hand through her hair by her ear, tucking it away. It's thick and slips back around as she dips her head. "I should make a start on lunch." She stands and walks toward the door.

"Grace?"

She turns back, a hand on the doorframe. Her tank top rides up, and between her short denim shorts and the soft material of her top, a small sliver of her stomach shows. I force my gaze to stay on hers.

"Mackinlay?"

"It's just Mack."

Her face bursts with a grin, lighting up her eyes. A second later, the air that was inflating my lungs is nowhere to be found. My heart rate elevates like it's mid-rep on the leg press and every ounce of blood sinks south.

Sweet Jesus.

No, Mackinlay, she's ten years younger than you.

An employee.

Don't even go there.

I rub my hand over my face, and when I look back up, the doorway is empty. Me and Grace, being nice to each other, is a dangerous place to be.

For her.

I start on the leg machine, aiming for maximum discomfort. Anything to tamp down the hard-on that's fighting its way to life from a single interaction with her.

No, if anything, we can be friends. Nothing else would be fair to her. How can half a man be anything a woman like Grace would ever want, let alone need?

I push up and let the burn swallow my muscles whole.

Thankful for the punishment to replace the thoughts running my body into a frenzy like I've never experienced over a woman before.

One Mississippi.

I groan against the weight as the muscles in my thighs bulge to life.

Two Mississippi.

I exhale, trying to shake those blue eyes and that beaming smile from my mind.

Three Mississippi.

They don't budge.

Fuck.

Chapter Nine

GRACE

I stand in front of the biggest animal I've ever been up close to. He rubs his muzzle into my palm, plucking the sugar cube up with his teeth. With Lawson gone, I make sure to get out of the house a few times a day and out of Mack's way. He may have apologized, but he is still awkward and short when we are in close quarters.

I'm well aware I'm in his space, in his home. If the shoe were on the other foot, I'm sure I would be surly about a stranger being holed up in my place, too. I rub a hand up the gelding's face.

"He likes you," a low voice says from behind me.

I spin back to find Mack in jeans and a polo, leaning on his crutch.

"I was getting some air—thought he might like a treat."

He walks to his horse and places his hand on his cheek. "Hey there, buddy."

"What's his name?" I ask.

"Trigger."

I chuckle. "Of course it is."

The horse nickers and nods his head up and down, as if responding. Mack is gentle and sweet with the gelding. Another glimpse of the real Mackinlay. A smile tugs over his lips as he rubs the horse and chats away to him.

I stand, one hand on the stall door, the other raised up to the gelding's neck. The butterflies taking flight with Mack's soft words have me stunned. The horse nudges his hand, and he chuckles. My mouth gapes, sending my heart into my throat.

I stagger back, shoving my hands in my back pockets. "Excuse me."

I march over the hay-littered ground toward the doorway. Outside, sunshine hits me, and I suck much-needed air into my burning lungs. The too familiar burn behind my eyes starts. The kindness, the effect he has on me when we are too close . . .

Joel never elicited any such physical reaction. I was head over heels for him purely on his charisma. His too-casual, freedom-chasing personality was a breath of fresh air after my strict parents. Maybe I was desperate for change. But that change had me just as desperate in the end.

Shaking my head at my stupid choices since the day I

met Joel, I walk over the gravel driveway toward the house.

"Grace, wait up!"

I stop and stare at the gate to the front yard, bottom lip worrying through my teeth. The hurried scuffle of his lone crutch closes in behind me. A hand touches my shoulder, and I turn back. His worried face is still gorgeous under a week's worth of stubble.

"What do you need?" I ask.

He stands taller on the crutch and swallows. "Nothin'—I just . . ."

I turn back and walk toward the house.

"Dammit, Grace, slow down."

"Why?" I say, not slowing one iota.

"I wanted to ask you something." His voice is soft, vulnerable.

That's a first.

I sigh and walk back to where he stands, folding my arms across my chest.

He huffs a strangled laugh and swallows. "I guess I deserve that."

"Yep, you do."

He dips his head, muttering something that sounds like "Sweet Jesus."

"Well?"

His dark blue eyes meet mine, and his Adam's apple bobs. "The county fair is on. Thought you might like to go."

"Sure, I'll make a point to ask my ass of a boss for the night off."

He tilts his head, and for a second, I think he's going to stalk off. But he leans on the crutch and studies my face. "We can take my truck."

"I told you, Mackinlay, I'm not driving that thing."

"I know." He smiles and walks around me, his strides lighter than before.

With my best clothes on—the best of slim pickings, that is—I sit in the white Chevy pickup and wait for Mack to climb into the driver's seat. He leans over the driver's seat and hands me his lone crutch. Our fingers brush as I lean over and take it from his hold. He hauls himself into the seat and closes the door. Within a heartbeat, his cologne fills the cab.

He shaved.

Wow.

I shake my head and snap my gaze forward, waiting for the Chevy to start. The loud engine roars to life, and I swear he moans. Running his hands over the steering wheel, he takes a look around, as if it's been a lifetime since he was last here. Emotion floods his face.

"Been a while, Mackie-boy?" I can't help myself.

The second the words register on his face, I wish like hell I'd kept my mouth shut. Or chosen my words more wisely. I open my mouth to take them back but his gaze flicks down the driveway, and his jaw feathers.

He growls at me and slams the pickup into drive. I squeal as he floors it, and we thunder down the driveway. Hot and cold, this man. Or maybe we haven't had the chance to get to know each other well enough yet. The first month or so of being here, it was him wishing I wasn't. Me avoiding him and praying he didn't get his way and have me shipped off like the last three carers.

He says not a word on the hour drive into town, and I busy myself with looking out the window. Bag and phone in my lap, I'm comfortable sitting here in silence. Like being in Mack's orbit is some sort of safety net. I haven't had that since I lived at home with my parents.

The sun is setting when we reach Lewistown and Mack pulls into the fairgrounds. His parking is a little uncontrolled, and I'm guessing he's not supposed to be driving yet. Unlike an hour ago, I keep my thoughts to myself. In front of us, the fair is in full swing. Rides lit up with rainbow lights, more pickup trucks than I have ever seen in my life, and gazebos, stalls, and so many people.

"Ready?" Mack asks.

I nod, and he pushes his door open as I hand him his crutch. I turn to push my door open and the end of the crutch lands on my forearm. "Wait."

I can't take my eyes off him as he walks around

the front of the vehicle and pulls my door open. Chuckles bubble up my throat, blush filling my cheeks. "You don't—don't need to do that, Mackinlay."

"It wouldn't be taking you to the fair if I didn't. Let me be useful this once, please."

That does it. My face falls. All he wants to do is get back his normal.

I can do that for him.

"Sure, go for it," I say softly.

He doesn't move from the doorway, and I study his face. He holds out a hand and I rest mine inside it. Warmth folds around my hand as I step down from the truck. Emotion clogs my throat when I clear the door, and he closes it for me.

"Thanks," I whisper.

"Where do you want to go first?"

I look around the fair. It's overwhelming, there is so much to look at and do. "I don't know, what's your favorite part?"

He thinks for a moment, scanning the fair. "Shootin' ducks."

I stiffen. "Oh . . . I can't. I'll just watch."

He grabs my hand and pulls me toward the noisy crowds. "You'll manage, just wait."

We weave through lines of people, groups chatting and laughing. Children run about, delighted, squealing and giggling. We reach the stall with yellow tin ducks lined up, and I huff an embarrassed snort. Not actual live ducks. *Thank heavens.*

Mack's hand is still around mine. "You wanna go first, Grace?"

"Um, okay. I've never done this before."

He drops my hand and pays the man working the booth. "Two, please."

A small rifle is placed in my hands, and I watch Mack check his over before raising mine to the ducks. Pointing, holding with both hands, I shoot. The rubber bullet hits the wall behind the slow-moving yellow birds. Shit.

"God, I'm hopeless at this," I say, lowering the rifle. "Show me what you've got, Mackinlay."

He grins, and holy shit, I'm almost boneless at the sight. Mesmerized, I gawk as he raises his weapon and aims. Four seconds later, six ducks are down. He's so quick, his movements hardly registered.

"Damn, poor ducks," I quip.

He chuckles. "Had a bit of practice."

"Oh yeah, right. The whole sniper thing. How did I forget that?"

"You win, buddy. Pick a prize," the man standing to the side says with a frown, as if aware he's been played. I tamp down a smile and suppress the laugh that's rising in my throat. The prize bin is overflowing with stuffed toys and cheap plastic odds and ends.

"You want to pick something?" Mack asks me.

"Ah, no, I'm good. You won, you should pick."

With a few steps, he hovers over the bin, hunting for god knows what. A minute later, he hands the prize to the man, and he cuts the tag off it. Waiting, I look around at the happy people, fun written all over their faces. Mack's cologne folds in around me, and I look over my shoulder. He stands at my back, dangling something on a chain beside my head.

I spin back. "What is that?" I raise my palm to catch it where it swings from his fingertips. A drop crystal is suspended, clear, a little bigger than my thumb. Smaller crystals dot the chain it hangs on. It's beautiful. "For your truck's rearview mirror?"

"Nope, for Blue's."

"Oh."

I swallow. The amber light of the sunset hits the crystal and its light splits across my face. I raise a hand to the rainbow and chuckle as it dances across my palm. "Thank you."

"Sure, consider this my wholesome and very large apology for the last three months."

"A cheap-ass crystal?" I raise an eyebrow.

He adjusts his stance on his crutch, and his gaze drops to the ground. "Not the crystal. The outing, I guess."

"Oh, alright. Well, in that case, I really, really want to go on the Ferris wheel."

Mack looks up at the enormous wheel rising into the sky. Its circumference is lit with rainbow lights, and the line isn't too long, as most folks are making their way to the bar and large building where supper is being served.

Running a hand across the back of his neck, he glances between me and the large ride. "Come on, then."

We walk past bumper cars, kids' rides, and a hammer and bell game. People wave and smile at Mack, and a few stop to say quick hellos. Mack buys two tickets, and we join the line.

"Sure you're up for the Ferris wheel, Rawlins?" a voice says from behind.

We turn back in unison, and it's the same guy we met in the street the other day. Morgan? Manning?

"Morley. Sure you're old enough to ride the wheel by yourself?" Mack snaps.

Morley, that's right.

"I can always be *your* third wheel." His gaze tracks up and down my body, real slow. My heart clambers through the next beat. I move into Mack's side, trying to ignore the thump rattling up my airways. The last time I saw that look on a man's face, Joel and Jimmy had just decided I was prey.

"Tickets!" the woman on the gate calls.

I stumble backward and rush for the gate, grabbing Mack's hand. He all but topples over, trying to catch up to me on his lone crutch and one good leg. I force air in and out of my lungs, gripping his hand too tight. He hands the lady the tickets and follows behind as we pad down the walkway to the first free carriage. Safely inside, I turn back and lock the gate.

Mack is on the seat beside me in a heartbeat. He leans his crutch by the half door.

My chest is rising and plummeting so fast, stars fade into my peripherals. A hand folds over mine on my leg. "Hey, you alright?"

I can't respond.

I think I shake my head. I can't tell.

"Morley has that effect on people." He chuckles, but it dies out when my rigid body doesn't move. I don't look at him and my chin wobbles.

Dammit.

"Grace, look at me." His hand is on my face. My breathing shatters. He turns my chin so I face him.

His hand drops away.

"Fuck, Gracie. You need to get off the ride?"

A moan slips through my lips, turning to a whimper as he folds me into his side, his arm around my shoulders. He holds me there until the ride starts up and we are high in the sky. The cool night air washes in, brushing over my heated cheeks, cooling the salty tears covering my face. I wipe them off and suck in a breath.

"You need me to listen?" he offers. His voice is soft, like with Trigger.

I want to say something. To have the courage to open my mouth and tell him. But it's my burden. He has enough of his own.

"Grace, nobody has a reaction like that and can hold it in without it eatin' them alive."

Now I look up at him. Worry claims his face—his eyes are tight with it. I dry my palms on my jeans and sit up taller. He removes his arm and nudges me with his shoulder. "You're safe, okay."

I nod.

If anyone understands feeling afraid, it's him. My fear pales in comparison to the things he's seen and been through. With that thought, I push past the self-conscious part of me that wants to bottle up my life and toss it to sea to be washed away.

"If I can, I want to tell you where I was before the ranch. Only, after all you've been through, it feels stupid. I mean, most of it was my own fault."

His face hardens. "I doubt that."

I huff a strangled breath.

"I know we're not exactly friends, so I'll keep it to the abridged version."

"Unabridged, please." His voice is gravel.

"Okay, fine. I'll start with the moment everything changed for me."

I tell him about the day I met Joel. My studies, my art, and how painting was my life. My scholarship. My guaranteed internship. My parents and their lofty expectations and strict rules. The moment I thought I was in love with Joel.

Mack shifts on his seat, as if uncomfortable with being

holed up in the small carriage. He prompts me to keep going. I tell him about the day I left home and how my parents turned their backs on me. The freedom I felt living my own life and just painting day in and day out. The week all that was taken away, when Joel lost his job. The hard, long months that followed.

Lastly, I tell him about the first time I ever felt real fear. On my twenty-first birthday, the night I left. With the threat of being raped by the man who was supposed to love me and his junkie friend. The fist that met my face.

My words run out.

His face is strung out. His chest plunging. My hands are numb, wrapped around the hem of my shirt. My jaw is clamped shut, tight. Tears stream down my cheeks, but this time, ironically, they are not tears of sadness. They are for the gratitude I feel for my freedom.

The Ferris wheel whines to a stop and every person gets off. We don't move, and the lady walks to our carriage and gestures for us to move.

"Send it around again," Mack bites out.

When she starts to object, he swipes out his wallet and hands her a bunch of cash. "Again!"

A moment later, we jerk upward, and the wheel goes around.

This time, it's just for us.

Chapter Ten

MACK

We've been home for hours. Grace made tea and we went our separate ways, to sleep. Or not, in my case. The vision of her terrified at the hands of that fuckin' asshole runs on repeat in my head. There're no war scenes in my head tonight, only played out versions of what she told me on the Ferris wheel.

The house is quiet.

I toss and turn. The tea's not doing anything tonight.

I push out of bed and hobble to the kitchen on my own two feet. Somehow, being on crutches doesn't make sense to me now. My hip screams in retaliation at my independence. I ignore it. I pull the fridge open and bend to find something to take my mind off every-fuckin-thing.

"There's a plate of chopped veggies and cheese on the second shelf," a soft voice says behind me. Seeing it, I pluck it up and close the fridge. Grace stands two feet from me, her cotton dressing gown wrapped around her pajamas, her hair up in a messy bun that's more mess than bun. Looks like I'm not the only one who's been tossing and turning.

"You wanna share with me?" I offer.

"If you don't mind the company?"

"Nope, prefer it, actually." I pad to the sofa.

"Mack!"

I freeze. Shit, did I forget my boxers or something? I glance down. No, they're on. And she's used to my bare chest by now. *What the?*

Her hand rests on my forearm as her face lights up. "You're not using your crutch."

"Oh, yeah. Sweet Jesus, Grace. Thought I'd forgot I was naked or something."

She laughs, loud and hearty. More hair slips from her bun and around her shoulders. She folds over with hysterics as she drops onto the sofa and tucks her legs under herself. She takes the plate from me as I lower myself onto the sofa.

I swear she blushes as she studies my face. "You know, you seem even taller without it. Bigger, or something."

In the dimly lit living room, all I can focus on is Grace backlit by the moonlight outside from the almost full moon. The angles of her face, the softness of her brown hair. Those light blue eyes that are a contrast to her other features. All I want to do is take her beautiful face in my hands and kiss her.

As comfortable as we are around each other, I'm one hundred percent certain we are nothing else but boss and employee. After everything she told me tonight, her heart has been through enough. I won't be another person to hurt her.

She moves closer to share the plate, and our shoulders touch. "Out here with you is so much better than alone in my room with the same old nightmares."

Her voice is too soft, and it's like someone slapped me in the face.

"Nightmares?" I manage to ask.

"Same one, every time. A repeat of the last night in Raymond, but I never leave. I don't make it that far. Then it changes, they are taking what they want, my vision turns red, my body jerks with every move they make. After, it's as if the red darkens until it's black, and I'm suffocating."

Holy fuck. That's damn horrific.

"Do you feel safe here, Grace?"

She snaps a carrot stick between her teeth and chews. Swallowing, she nods. "I do. I know I'm safe with you."

The air rushes from my lungs.

I brush the stray strands of hair behind her ear, and she lifts her gaze up at me, her blue eyes darkened by the night. "You did get out. Look around, Gracie, you're safe. And I'm glad you're here."

"Me too, but . . ." A sad smile grows on her face before she looks away. "I was in denial, I guess. I thought I was okay. Turns out, I was just tucked away here, busy and with good people." She scoffs breathlessly. "Not even a full hour in the real world, and I was a mess." She pulls her hair to the side and twists it in her hands. "God, I'm so angry." The words teeter on a sob. "Angry for all the promises Joel broke. That he stole the last bit of trust I had in people after my parents. But most of all, I'm angry at myself for the *stupid* choices I made. For giving up my career. For staying . . . as long as I did."

"Not every choice you made was bad. You chose to leave. Great choice. You chose to work here. Brilliant choice." Eyes burning into hers, my heart thunders in my chest.

A soft sigh falls from her lips as she takes a celery stick along with a cube of cheese. "Maybe." Slumping into the sofa, she stares into the unlit fireplace. "I miss them."

Brows dropping, I take a piece of cheese and a cherry tomato. "Who?"

"My parents. I understand why they did what they did. I threw everything away. We worked so hard to get a spot and the scholarship. I'm their only child. I know they felt betrayed. Probably still do."

"That's a possibility, but you're their daughter. You do for family, Grace. No matter how hard it gets."

Sweet Jesus, now I sound like Harry. And I realize, turning out like my old man isn't such a bad thing. He's spent his whole life protecting, loving, and helping his family. Even when it didn't match his plans, meet his expectations, or if it was hard on him and Ma. My military career being the first example I can think of.

"I wish I could see Mama. I miss her the most." The wobble in her voice has me shuffling closer. She leans her head on my shoulder. I can't take my eyes from her beautiful face. Even broken with regret like it is now, she's the most incredible woman I have ever met.

Determined—has to be, to put up with me.

Smart—abso-fuckin-lutely, look at everything she's accomplished in her short life and the way she runs my life and home.

Tough—more than she will ever know.

"Anyway, thanks for letting me get stuff off my chest. It helps." She swallows. "I know you suffered much worse, so I'll shut up now."

She dries her face, and I feel like that's all she's done in the past few hours. I plan to correct that the second the sun comes up. She thinks I'm tougher than her because my body was banged up worse. Physical wounds heal. A mindfuck like she's lived through? Much harder to bounce back from.

"Soldiers are trained to cope with worst case. You didn't sign up for the shit that went down in that house. If anyone on this sofa is the tough one, it's you."

She huffs a laugh and turns to face me. "Maybe we can be the tough ones together."

God, my body reacts to those words like she just rose to her knees, crawled over the cushions, and sunk onto my lap. With every ounce of blood now racing south, my cock is rock-hard before the next breath.

Fuck, that is not what Grace needs.

I rein in the effect she has on me, being this close, this open, softening before me with her blue eyes now studying mine. A flash of her in the cinder block dump in a makeshift trailer park with him, scared and hurting, sees the wind in my sails disappear in an instant.

"What are you thinking, Mack?"

I brush a hand over my jaw. Her gaze follows the action, like she's cataloging the shape of my face. "Just thinkin' I should turn in."

"With a face like that, you need all the beauty sleep you can get." She stands and darts away from the sofa as I toss a cushion at her. With a giggle, she rounds the sofa and readjusts her dressing gown around her chest. "Night, Mack."

"Night, Gracie."

She walks down the hallway to her room. The door closes. I lay my head back on the back of the seat and blow out a breath, eyes closing. The fire in my core hasn't lessened a bit seeing her walk away. The ghost of her softness pressed against my side, the weight of her head on my shoulder. The feel of her hand in mine . . . Every sensation blooms back to life as if she is right in front of me.

I'm impossibly hard.

And in need of a damn cold shower.

Pushing off the sofa, I pad to my bedroom. My hip is more settled than when I tried this an hour before. I lean on the counter and brush my teeth before flipping the shower on. Stripping on wobbly feet, I step into the water. The icy cold hits my skin, and I grunt. But unlike in the past, I'm still hard and strung out.

Hands against the tile, I hang my head. The water cools my body, not able to tame the heat I'm holding for the woman across the hall. I knew if I eliminated the space between us, this would happen. Knew it from the day I met her gaze, surrounded by laundry detergent. When those blue eyes found me. She looked at me—she *saw* me. Saw me as whole. Not like every other person who's laid eyes on me since on tour.

She's never once felt sorry for me or treated me like an invalid. She gives it as good as I give it to her. Maybe it was her anger with what happened to her bouncing off my own. Whatever it was—*is*—we are in this mess together. If a man ever needed a reason to dig his way out of a hole, this would be it.

She would be it. I'll be fucked if I'm going to be unable to protect her if she ever needs it.

The giggles and small noises she makes wander into my mind. I grip my cock. Slamming my eyes shut, I see her take my hand, that gorgeous body as she walks away. I imagine she pads from the kitchen and sinks onto my lap, wearing one of my old T-shirts. I take her face in my hands. Her light meets my dark. Her soft to my hardness. Vanilla and peaches all around me. I come hard and slump against the tile. My legs tremble. My heart flings against my ribs.

She needs a friend now, not another man to shatter her to pieces.

This stays between me and the shower.

Pants and little moans travel from the yoga room to where I lay in bed. Morning wood at full mast, those little noises are not helping my case. I roll over, hoping that will douse the fire the woman in this house sparked weeks ago. With the conversation on the sofa last night, all raw and close, I'm tumbling head over fucking heels into her more and more.

Technically I'm her boss, so there's that.

She needs space and time. Not another raging asshole with an agenda.

I sit up and run a hand through my hair. I'm not using the crutch today. Three rounds of physio like I'm supposed to do from now on. I should have started out that way. But sometimes you need something bigger than your own well-being to pull you forward.

"Morning." Grace walks past in her activewear that highlights her shape, water bottle in hand. Her neck glistens with sweat. Breasts pushed up in a sports bra that sees two perfect-as-fuck mounds pushed up over the top. Her hair is tied up in her usual messy bun, damp around the edges from her yoga session.

"Morning," I reply, but it's almost a rasp.

Her face tweaks, but she flattens it. "Want some coffee?"

"Sure, but—" I push from the bed.

"You okay?" Her brows drop, and she steps forward, stilling when she realizes she's in my bedroom.

"I'm good. I was just gonna say I'll make breakfast."

"Wonderful! I'm going to grab a shower, then."

She takes off toward her room, hips swaying. The door doesn't close this time. I hear the shower start up. Shaking my head to dislodge the thought of Grace showering, I wander to the kitchen and start the coffee grinder. The beans whiz, smashing around until they're nothing more than powder. I fill the top of the coffee maker with the grounds and pull out the receptacle and fill it with water. With the coffee brewing away, I start on some eggs and toast. I glance outside. Dark clouds hang to the west, far enough away not to affect the day yet.

Vanilla and peaches have me fenced into the kitchen as Grace walks in. She's in shorts and a navy T-shirt that makes her blue eyes pop. She winds her damp hair up into a messy bun. I crack three eggs into the pan. What I wouldn't do to run my hands through those gorgeous long brown locks. Run a thumb over her bottom lip, press kisses to her jawline, cheekbones, nose, and forehead.

Heat stings my hand. "Shit!" I snap my hand away from the burner.

"What's got you all distracted today, Mackinlay?"

She sits at the table and scrolls through her phone. I return my focus to the eggs and flip them over. The toaster pops, and I find two plates and toss the toast onto them before slathering butter over each slice. When the eggs are done, I place two on my plate and one on Grace's. Carefully, I tote the plates to the table and rest hers in front of her.

"Thanks, Mack," she says brightly, looking up at me.

"I'm starving," I say, dropping into the seat. Fuck, forgot cutlery. I rise to stand.

Her hand covers mine. "It's okay, I got it. Think the coffee's ready, too."

Pouring two mugs of coffee, she adds cream to both and sugar to hers. Cutlery appears at my side, and I take it from her hands. She swings back into the kitchen. Two steaming mugs of coffee are in her hands when she stands by my side a second later. I shovel a mouthful of eggs in.

Anything to distract me from her peaches-and-vanilla scent. Which is impossible when she leans over and places the coffee by my plate. Her hair falls from its precarious makeshift bun, spilling over her shoulders. Her shampoo, spice and something sweet, floods over me. I grunt, gripping the cutlery, determined to focus on the food.

"What are you going to do today?" Her voice cuts through my veil of concentration.

Swallowing, I glance over to her. "Exercise. Maybe visit Trigger."

"You gonna ride him?" Her hands hover over her plate, cutlery gripped in her fine fingers.

I want to. Whether or not my body will let me is another thing.

"You ride?" I ask.

"I never have. Always wanted to learn."

"If you're going to work and live here, you should. Adds is a great teacher, she'll have you loping along in no time."

She stares at me before saying, "Sure, yeah, okay. I'll text her later."

She doesn't want to.

Doesn't want to learn to ride? Or doesn't want Addy to teach her?

"No pressure. If you're not a horse person, it's fine."

She pushes her eggs around the plate, her thinking face in place. "Can you teach me?"

I sip my coffee and hold her gaze as she waits for an answer. My mind is spinning with what that would look like.

"Never mind, it was stupid. I'll ask Addy," she says quickly.

Standing, I clear the plates away, taking hers with her uneaten breakfast. I dump them by the sink and head for the front door.

"Hey, I wasn't finished." Her hands are up in protest.

"Let's go." I grab my cap from the hook by the entrance. "Trigger's waitin'."

Chapter Eleven

GRACE

I don't know much about riding, but I'm pretty sure denim shorts aren't what you wear. I sprint to my room and lose the shorts, pulling on my old jeans. Tight with holes at the knees, they feel much better, considering what I'm hopefully about to do.

Moments later, I reach the barn to find Mack leading Trigger from his stall. Faltering on the hay-covered ground, he steadies himself with one hand on the horse. I step in his space and take the lead rope from his hand.

"Show me what to do," I breathe, almost against his chest.

He stills, so close. The wind picks up outside. The clouds that hung low on the horizon are now closing in. The air temperature has dropped, sending a chill over my skin that was flushed with heat only an hour ago. Trigger waits patiently, seemingly unaware of the barometric changes in his surroundings. Or the rapid increase of my blood through my veins.

Thunder rolls in a soft echo. The weather is turning.

Mack studies the sky. "Maybe just saddle him up. That's enough to learn for one lesson, at any rate."

"Sure, where are his things?"

He nods to a small room with an open door at the back of the barn. "Tack room."

"Can I lead him over?"

Mack steps back, his face unreadable. "Of course." He waves a hand toward the small room.

I cluck my tongue like I've seen in movies and give a small tug on the lead. Trigger walks by my side instantly. I huff a disbelieving laugh. Wow, he understands me. I mean, obviously, he's well-trained. This is my first time, and it's surreal that an animal this magnificent will follow the smallest of commands.

The gelding stops before the door, prompting me to halt, too. Good lord, the horse is smarter than the rider. Nerves skitter along my veins. My heart picks up pace with the realization that maybe learning how to ride is more than I imagined it to be.

Mack catches up and walks past into the dimly lit room. He tugs a rope, and a light bulb zaps and flickers to life. One side is covered in tack and equipment, the other, feed and buckets and what not. He takes a bridle from a hook and walks out, handing it to me. I study the soft leather in my hand.

Returning, he eyes a large looking western saddle sitting on a round rack, a thick pad underneath. Setting his shoulders back, he moves in and shoulders it with a grunt. The weight must be too much. His face strains. A soft curse falls from his lips, but he takes long, confident strides out to us and hauls the saddle onto Trigger's back.

Sweat breaks over his brow and his chest heaves from the exertion. He steps back, leaving what I assume is the girth dangling. I open my mouth to call it quits. This is too much for him. He shakes his head, face tight in warning. He wants to do this.

"Mack," I plead. "It's okay, we can try another day."

He leans over, hands planted on his knees. With every long breath he sucks in, his back muscles move under his T-shirt. His biceps, carrying a light sheen, flex in his sleeves as he pushes to stand tall, homing his gaze to mine. "Saddle." He points toward Trigger's back. "Seat, pommel, and fenders." His hand moves over the tack as he explains. "Stirrup iron."

I nod.

"I'll show you how to put his bridle on. Then you can take it all down and redo it yourself, okay?"

"Okay," I say. Still in awe of this man's grit and determination, I find myself staring. He moves closer but stalls with a wince. Oh no.

"Mackinlay?"

"It's okay, I'm fine." But a flush has claimed his neck and face, his breathing quickening.

"You're not. I can put Trigger back in his stall."

"If it doesn't hurt, you're not making progress, Grace. I'm fine. I'll rest later."

I shake my head at him and move aside as he files in closer to Trigger and explains the bridle. He slides it up Trigger's face, waits while he takes the bit into his mouth, then gently slips the band over the horse's ears. Mack's eyes are tight with something I can't place. My mouth dries up and my stomach turns into a fluttering mess.

". . . and then you lift the reins over his head. Let them rest on his neck while you fix the girth."

The bay gelding moves, shifting his feet, and Mack teeters on the spot. He grabs a handful of mane and steadies himself. I grab his arm, hoping to help, and move into his space. The last thing I want is him hurting himself because he's entertaining me. His gaze drops to where my hands are wrapped around his bicep.

Thunder crackles overhead.

I retract my hands like I've been burned, and Mack's eyes snap back to the horse. "Should probably get inside before the storm gets a go up."

I reach up and pull the saddle from Trigger's back. Shit, it's so heavy and awkward. Bulky to hold. I walk it back inside and try to haul it onto the high rack. Halfway up, my arms falter—and it's all I can do to keep from dropping it. Warmth folds in around me. Long arms slide around my arms, hands griping the wide seat. We lift it up onto the rack in one movement.

Four hands, two beating hearts. One movement.

Wow, where the hell did that come from?

The warmth disappears along with the very distinct, heady scent of Mackinlay, and I stand dazed. Still. Listening to my heart rattle through my head. Soft clip-clops see me turn away from the wall to find Trigger walking back to his stall. Mack leads him, talking away as they go. I wonder if not riding, not being physically able to ride, bothers him.

After chasing any type of romantic thoughts about my boss from my head, I cross the hay-littered floor to the barn doors to find Mack leaning against the frame. Rain is falling in light, misty waves. Shit, now the driveway is slick with it.

"Do we wait it out?" I ask.

A grin splits his face, mirth lining his eyes. "Hell no." He grabs my hand and hauls me into the rain. With an awkward gait, he turns a circle, arms out, head tilted back, eyes closed, and mouth open. I laugh at him. Guess rain means something else entirely to ranchers. Up until now, it has always been an inconvenience. Something to duck out of, something to dampen spirits.

The joy on Mack's face is changing the way I see rain. Lightning hits miles away. The thunder that follows echoes in, quicker than the last clap. We should go inside.

The wind moans. The rain gets heavier and heavier. I stand, getting soaked. His spinning slows and his laughter fades as he steps up to where I stand.

His dark hair is soaked. Drops run over his jaw, down his neck. Veiny forearms hang by his side as he studies my face. "Smile, Gracie. It's rainin'."

My lips part.

I don't want to smile.

I want to smash my mouth to his. Send my fingers into his hair. Rest my palms on his chest and let the fire that bloomed in my core minutes ago rage to life and take me down. Every short, quick breath burns.

"Mac—"

Thunder drowns out his name. He takes my hand, lacing his fingers through mine.

Oh god.

Moving into my space, he dips his head, closing his eyes. "You have no idea how much I needed you."

Needed.

Past tense.

Is this a thank you for helping him back onto his feet?

"You're welcome," I choke out.

Rain falls even harder. He straightens, standing tall. "Come on, we should get inside before lightning finds us."

Right now, that doesn't sound so bad. For a second, I thought something else was going to happen. To my surprise, I wanted it to. I *want* it to.

I follow behind, picking my way around the more slippery looking parts of the driveway. The driveway is turning muddier by the second. I hold my arms out to steady myself on cautious steps. My sneakers are slipping. Mack's more sturdy footwear is proving to be a better choice. I glance up at his back. The tight shirt, now soaked, highlights his muscles moving to steady his own footwork.

My foot slips and I gasp as my ass hits the ground with a splash. "Ah shit!"

I scramble to get back up, feet slipping. Mack is over to me a second later, laughter spilling from his stupid, handsome face.

"Not funny, Mackinlay, these are my only other jeans."

I tug on his arm. He winces.

Fuck. I slap a hand over my mouth. God no. Why did I do that? "I'm so sor—"

He swipes up my hand playfully, trying to haul me to my feet. His grip on the muddy earth slips. He flails, arms windmilling. Mack hits the ground beside me. He groans and lies flat out. Muddy water seeps into his hair. Splashes cover his shirt. I sit beside him, waiting for some sign I didn't cause any more damage.

The smile blooming over his face is followed by those dark blue eyes narrowing in on me. He grabs my waist and pulls me down to the muddy ground. "Down here with me, Gracie."

We lie in the driveway, looking up into the falling rain. The cool water soaks my shirt, jeans, and underwear. The sky sways with falling droplets. I lie, mesmerized as much by the leaking sky as by the man lying in the mud beside me.

"Are you alright?" I finally breathe.

"Better than alright. I'm alive."

"Have been for a while."

His hand slips around mine by my side. I turn my head, and he's staring at me. "I have you to thank for that."

Not really true, but I get what he's trying to say. I turn my face back to the sky. "Just doing my job."

"Right." His voice is sharper than a heartbeat ago. A million tiny droplets fall around us. Looking up into them as they fall is nothing short of tranquility. The grey clouds cover every inch of the sky, pelting drops down over us. It's humbling.

We lie in the pouring rain until lightning chases us onto the porch. Dripping with muddy water, we stand, both hesitating.

"I don't want to drip mud through the house," I say, looking at the front door, still closed.

"Same." His chest heaves where he stands, and he runs a hand through his wet hair. "Or I can clean it up, if you wanna go inside." His gaze dips to my mouth.

I don't want to move from this spot. I'm sure the desperate, strung-out look that just claimed his face is not because he's scared of the lightning or staving off pain. I step up to him and tilt my head up. He studies my face before running the ends of my hair between his fingers by my arm. I wrap my own hand around his wrist, not wanting him to leave when he realizes how close we are.

"There's mud in your hair." His voice is gravel.

"I know. I need a shower. And so do you."

His hand drops away. He turns and opens the door, gesturing for me to go on in. With a shallow nod, I do. Every step toward my room, I have the heat of his stare on my back. As if something just shifted and we're both stunned. Spectators blinded by headlights.

I tiptoe into my room, like that will minimize the mud that hits the floor. Not bothering to shut my door, I pad to the en suite and turn on the shower. I rip my T-shirt off my body, the sucking noise it makes sending a giggle up my throat. It's ridiculous.

Today is the most alive I've felt in a long time, and the best fun I have had in years. I release the button on my waistband and tug my pants down. Wet jeans. They don't budge. Shit. Managing to get them over my panties, I lean on the vanity counter and struggle. Both hands tighten to white knuckles as I try to pry one leg of denim away from my skin. I may as well be Velcroed into the jeans.

"Dammit."

I try again, arms tense, palms cramping from using the cold muscles. "For the love of—" I fall against the vanity with a thud.

"You okay in there, Grace?"

Crap. I hop on one foot and suck in a breath. "Yup!"

My foot slips, and I slam into the open door. It bangs into the wall.

Heavens above.

Footsteps close in on the wooden floor of my room. Before I have a chance to close the door or grab a towel, Mack fills the doorway. My hands tighten on the opening of my jeans. "They're stuck."

It's then I remember I'm shirtless, a black lace bra the only thing covering my now hard nipples. I'm not a hundred percent sure if my body is reacting to the cold or his gaze. He steps back, dragging his gaze up to my face. "Sorry, I—"

Fuck it.

Leaving any inhibitions on the floor, I close the space between us and wrap my hands over his jawline. I pull his mouth down to mine. He stiffens in my hold, and I realize I've made a mistake.

I pull back so fast, he teeters forward.

"I really shouldn't have don—"

Mack's stunned face turns desperate in a heartbeat, his eyes searching, brows down, lips parted. Before the next beat, his hands are in my hair, his mouth over mine. Pressing his body against me, he claims my mouth. He's hungry but gentle. I palm his wet shirt, and he wants in with his tongue.

I open.

He grabs me under the butt and his arms flex as my feet lift from the floor. His strength gives out, and I'm dropped awkwardly to the floor. He breaks the kiss, having to steady himself on the doorjamb. Devastation has now replaced hunger.

"What is it?" I say on ragged breath.

"I can't." He hobbles a tight turn and pads for the door. Fingers gripping his wrist, I stop him mid-step.

"You will, okay?"

He turns back, and the heartbreak is eating him alive. The part that makes him feel less than. So I offer, "Help a girl out of her jeans?"

He hangs his head for a moment, and I am sure he's about to deny me the help. But he closes in and tugs them down as he kneels. I wriggle my hips, and under his strong grip, they fall to my feet. I can't help myself when my hands sink into his hair.

He looks up, those dark blue eyes searching my face.

"You'll be okay, Mack. You'll get everything you lost back. I'm not leaving until you do."

The brief interlude of softness hardens as he pushes to his feet. Before I can inhale enough air viable for life, he's out the door.

His slams a few seconds later.

Chapter Twelve

MACK

Of all the consequences of being injured, not being able to hold Grace hurts the most.

Mack – 0

Explosion – 1

I can rattle off a ton of things I've lost, some more permanent than others. But never did I ever think not being able to be with the woman I want would be on that fuckin' list. It's twofold, and it's my own stupid damn fault.

One, because I was an utter asshole when she first arrived. I'm pretty sure she doesn't have plans to stay.

Two, I will never be the whole man she wants and needs.

We sit in silence at the doctor's office, waiting for my checkup appointment. We haven't spoken a word since yesterday. I'm too much of a coward to ask. Not wanting

143

to know if it's because I crossed the *you're my employer* line. Or whether it's our age difference. Or the worst option. She's not into me.

That would fit, I guess. I'm no Great Reed Rawlins. No stoic, chip off the old block Hudson Andrew Rawlins. Just another middle child with a grudge big enough to see him enlist in the military to prove a point.

Look where it got me.

"Mackinlay?" the nurse says at the end of the hall, file in hand. I stand and Grace follows.

"You want me to come in with you?" she asks, worry lining her face.

"I'm good, won't be long."

She pushes up a soft smile and wanders back to the chair she's been sitting in for the last hour.

The nurse fills the silence along the long stretch of hallway with mindless chatter. Something about the weather. I tune it out.

"Here we are, doctor won't be too much longer." She waves a hand, and I walk into the room and lower myself onto the chair on the opposite side of the desk.

Five minutes and about five hundred knee jumps later, the doctor enters and shuts the door. His white overcoat is crumpled. He looks tired. His dark hair is peppered with grey, but he beams a genuine smile as he sits in his chair. "How have you been, Mack?"

"Good, making progress."

"Wonderful. Do you have some help around the

house? I think the last time I saw you, you were in between housekeepers?"

"Yep, have help."

The words burn my tongue. Grace is so much more than the help. She's my constant companion. My sounding board. My biggest cheerleader. The only person who's managed to get my ass into gear and stop the ongoing pity party that held me captive before she came along.

"I'm glad to hear it. However, we have the results of your last scans. And I'm afraid it's not the best news. Preliminary tests were inconclusive, but the damage to your lower back and hip may mean you never recover the full range of motion, not without extensive physio."

"Will I be able to ride again? It's kind of an occupational requirement."

"A fall could be disastrous for your mobility now. So it's a maybe, at best."

"Fine."

"Let's take a look at your range of motion." He stands and gestures to the small bed. "Hop up for me, will you?"

I slide up onto the bed and lay my head on the plastic-covered pillow. His hands grip my ankle, pushing my leg up, bending it at the knee before laying it out to one side. My hip clunks. But there is no pain like there was weeks ago.

Progress is progress.

He tests the other side. When he is satisfied with what he finds, I slide off the bed to my feet.

"This is your last visit with me. You can see your GP for pain meds. But *only* use them if needed. Your recovery will only stall if you become reliant on them."

Not likely.

I haven't taken anything since the Ferris wheel. Didn't feel like a necessity after that point. My focus has shifted. My goals, loftier. My routine, stricter.

That angry man who hated the world and barely tolerated his loving family was left somewhere on the second go round on the wheel lit up with rainbow lights. When the only thing that hurt was seeing Grace broken. It was as if someone slapped me awake.

My eyes are wide open now.

And she is all I see.

I will bend into whatever she needs.

Friend.

Great boss.

Platonic companion.

Her heart is safe with me.

If that fucker Joel ever sets foot on my ranch, he's a dead man.

Grace pulls her phone from her back pocket as it vibrates. With nothing more than a frown, she returns it to her pocket as she leans against Ma's kitchen counter.

Ma putters around, cooking her Sunday favorites. Addy is by the fridge with Rubes, explaining the plans for Ma's next birthday party. If anyone deserves a birthday celebration, it's Grace.

After what happened on her twenty-first birthday.

Harry sits at the table with me, newspaper in hand. Reed waltzes through the front door, making tracks for his wife. Wrapping her in his arms, he folds himself around her from behind. She melts into him.

Lucky bastard.

Adds chuckles and pads to the table. "What you workin' on, Mack?"

I clear my throat and drop my eyes to the tax papers I'm supposed to be giving the once-over before Sunday lunch. "Ah, the usual, Harry's dirty work."

The newspaper rustles, and my old man's gaze turns into an incredulous expression over his reading glasses. "Son, you never been anywhere near my dirty work."

"Damn straight," Huddo says, walking through the front door as he tosses his Stetson onto the hook and toes his boots off. He's covered in dirt and sweating up a storm. "Hey, sweet girl." He drops a kiss onto Addy's cheek, and she screws up her face, scrunching up her pert nose.

"Don't you dare hug me in those filthy clothes, Huddy," she squeals.

Huddo chases her down the hallway with his arms out like a monster. Huffing a laugh at my ridiculous brother and the way those two are insufferably happy, I turn back to the papers.

Assets.

Liabilities.

Depreciation.

Yada yada yada.

I zone out.

Ma's arm slides over my shoulder as she bends over. "Can you give me a hand with the table?"

"Sure, Ma."

I follow her to the counter, and she loads me up with warm dishes. They all smell amazing, the savory fragrances tangling together. We push through the back screen door, and Charlie, Huddo's dog, growls at me.

I growl back. A giggle hits me from behind. Snapping my head back, I find Grace, also with a stack of lunch stuff. *Nice one, Ma.*

I head to the weeping willow we have every Sunday lunch under and unload onto the long wooden bench seat. Addy appears with a cloth and flings it open, letting it settle over the long table. Without a word, she heads back inside.

Grace stands, cradling her load. "Ah, where do you want these?"

Shit. I move in and take the top two dishes covered in foil, setting them on the table. She pops the last one beside them. Turning back, she slams into my chest. With a breathy laugh, she steps out of my space, tucking a long strand of hair behind her ear. "So, Sunday lunch is kind of a big deal for your family?"

"Yup, every Sunday."

Her eyes widen as her brows lower. "Then why is this the first one we've been to?"

I run a hand behind my neck. *Because I'm a selfish ass who couldn't be bothered to show up for my family.*

"I told Ma I wasn't up to them. Honest to god, the last thing I felt like was being around all this happiness when I couldn't get out of my own angry way."

She slaps my arm. "Mackinlay!"

"Hey, we're here, aren't we?"

"I could have come without you, if I'd known."

"Guess you could've. Ma would have liked that . . ." I sway on my feet a little. "But—"

"What?" She tilts her head, brown hair slipping over her shoulders. The V-neck shirt she has on over her jeans has my head utterly messed up.

"I like our bubble, Grace. At home. Where there's no expectation, and it's comfortable. Safe."

She bites her bottom lip and moves closer. Peaches and vanilla shroud me. "Oh, I have expectations of you, Mack."

Her gaze wanders over my face, settling on my mouth

before she snaps her eyes back up. I swallow as the blood pumps faster through my veins, heart thundering behind my rib cage as her hand comes to rest over it.

"I do have expectations. I expect you to do your physio three times a day. To eat every last mouthful of the healthy food I make you. To let the sunshine touch your skin at least once a day. And I expect you to make a *full* recovery."

She pushes up on her tiptoes and plants a soft kiss to my stubbled cheek. Stunned, I move on my feet and turn to watch her as she walks back to the house, her long hair bouncing around her shoulders and down her back. On long legs that have my cock harder than humanly possible, she sways, the tilt carrying on her hips and ass like temptation personified.

When she reaches the screen door and glances back, there's something in her eyes I haven't seen before.

Fire.

My heart crawls into my throat, and my cock twitches. My head is spinning.

Four hours and three whiskeys later, Grace is behind the wheel of my Chevy as we head for home along the gravel road. She hasn't said a word since we climbed up into the truck. Despite the effects of being around my family and the vibrant conversation, merriment, and alcohol, my mind is stuck in a loop.

Grace's hand on my chest.

Her words, hope and confidence in me rolled into one.

The way my body responds to being in the same space as her. That look in her eyes before she went inside at lunch. This thing in my head, the chemistry that has had me on edge for weeks, isn't just me. It's not one-sided.

Grace glances at me with a shy smile. "You're quiet."

"Pot, kettle, Gracie."

She scoffs a laugh and slows the truck as we turn into the ranch driveway. She's good at driving it. I don't know why she thought she couldn't do it.

"I don't think I could eat another thing after today. I can make you a coffee or some tea, if you like."

Her words are a reminder she's still my employee. I'm still her boss. She is still waiting on me. I should let the chemistry fizzle out.

"I'm okay, thanks. Gonna do some physio and some weights and take a shower."

Something like hurt flashes through her eyes as she sends her gaze out the windshield.

"Sure." She parks the Chevy inside the barn and kills the engine. Hopping out, she wanders to my door and leans on the open window. "I'm going to go for a walk, then. Mind taking my stuff in?"

"Okay. Keep an eye out for snakes."

"Yes, Dad." She smiles, but it fades, and she pushes off the door and walks toward the fields. The afternoon heat is mild, and I haul ass out of the truck and head inside with her bag and phone. Skin warming under the sunshine, sweat sheens over my forearms, neck, and face. Inside, the cool air of a closed-up house with an air conditioner that's been running for hours greets me.

Bliss.

I set Grace's things on the kitchen counter and grab a glass from the drying rack, filling it in the sink. The cool liquid sinks all the way to my stomach, cooling me down as it goes. Vibrating from under the handbag makes me still. I flip the bag off to find Grace's phone ringing.

The name flashes on the screen.

Joel.

What the fuck?

Why the hell is he still calling her?

I swipe up the phone and answer it, pressing the speaker icon. Nothing comes through the line. Faint puffs of breath buffet against the speaker. I slam a finger onto the red icon and hang up. I oughta block his number.

Not my place.

Not my phone.

Not my girl.

Fuck me.

Instead, I slide it into the bag and take it to her bedroom, depositing it onto her bed. Five minutes later, I'm taking out my anger over a man who doesn't deserve the air he breathes on the home gym. The heavy weight clunks with a vicious snap on every rep. I push the bar up again, biceps screaming at me to stop.

Arms akin to jelly, I make a start on my legs. The muscles in my thighs bulge and flex as I lift the bar with my ankles, toes pointing up. Sweat covers every inch of me. It trickles down my back and through the valleys in my chest, and my palms are too slick to grip much of anything. Focus homed on the poster on the wall by the door, I jerk back to reality when Grace appears in the doorway.

"Anything interesting happen while I was walking?"

"Nope."

I swing the bar up as my thighs start to burn. The weight slams back to its cradle with the next down movement.

"What did the machine ever do to you, Mack?" She raises an eyebrow and folds her arms over her chest.

I grunt and swing the bar up again. This time my legs fail, and it pushes my ankles down with weighted force. Fuck.

"How was your physio?"

"Didn't do it."

"Mackinlay Rawlins," she scolds, walking to my side, arms still crossed over those perfect fucking tits. I force my eyes anywhere else. The floor. The wall. The rolled-up towels.

"You wanna talk about it?" she asks, wry words slipping through curved lips.

"Nope."

Her hand grips my jaw, turning my head to face her. "Well, I do."

"Nothin' to talk about, Grace."

"Is that what you think? That nothing exists here?" She gestures between the two of us.

Of course I don't.

But she's too young.

I'm too fucked up.

I won't—I refuse—to be someone else who hurts her in the long run.

"It—" I start. I run my hands through my damp hair before letting my head fall back on the padded headrest behind me. I close my eyes. How the hell do I confess what I want, when it's unfair to her?

I don't.

She moves beside me. My eyes are still closed. The vision of her walking away from me earlier hums to life. My chest tightens. A weight settles onto my lap, and I open my eyes.

Grace sits on my lap, her hands flat on my T-shirt over my pecs. Her focus is on her hands, her breaths fast and shallow. "Have you ever really wanted something, but things that happened before ruined it for you? Or at least, you thought they would?" she whispers.

My nostrils flare. My cock is at full mast, and I'm sure

it's digging into her ass. "Kind of," I say, not sure where she's going with this.

"I thought after Joel, romantic relationships would be out of the question for me. That love and sex and everything that goes with it could never appeal to me again."

Hearing the word sex from her lips as she sits on my rigid-as-fuck cock steals the last of my air.

"Gracie," I choke out.

"Mack, I know you would never hurt me. So, if you don't want me, please tell me."

She closes her eyes.

As if that will save her from what she doesn't want to hear.

Chapter Thirteen
GRACE

Mack's hard length underneath me has me breathless as I wait for him to tell me to hop up. Get off him. Because rejection and conditional love are the only two things I have felt from a man. Joel was only ever interested in his own release. The only way I have ever reached that point was a few times in the shower when he was not home. At least, I think I did? It wasn't anything worth committing to memory.

Deep blue eyes study my face as Mack stands and shifts me onto his hips. It's all I can do to hang on to his shoulders and wait for him to dump me on my bed. His gait is steady but slow. The extra workouts have paid off exponentially.

"Where are you taking me?"

"I need a shower."

"And you need me, because . . ."

"You're now also covered in sweat; ergo, you require one, too."

"Mack. My room is the other way."

"I know."

"You need me to undress you and give you a sponge bath?"

"The only person who deserves pampering in this house is you."

I scoff. "Yeah, right."

He stops mid-stride. "I'm serious."

I stare at him, heart flinging against my ribs. I let my hands wander up his neck, one into his hair, the other cupping his jaw as I search his gaze. "You do, too."

Heat coils deep in my belly. I'm wet simply touching his face. It's the first time I've held onto him that hasn't been to help or platonic. It's all-consuming. Overwhelming. If he doesn't kiss me, I may implode from the intensity.

I want him to touch me. I want his warmth around me.

But even his free hand rests softly against my back as if he's holding something fragile.

"You can touch me, Mack. I won't break."

"It's your choice, Grace. It will always be."

Relief unfurls in my rapidly moving chest. I nod. I knew this about him already. The day I saw him with Trigger, I discovered the shape of his heart. He continues down the hall, and when we walk into his bedroom, I can't hold back a second longer. Hands around his face, I sink my lips over his. He opens for me, and I take everything I can until we're a tangle of tongue, teeth, and breath.

Breaking away, he groans, "Fuck, Gracie."

Eyes darkened, he lets me down to my feet. I stand, waiting for the blow. He's changed his mind. Realized who he's kissing.

Holding my face, he walks forward, sending me backward. The back of my legs hit his bed. "I'm going to have a shower," he rasps. "When I'm clean, we can—"

I press a finger to his lips.

He stays silent, so I drop my hand and grab the hem of my shirt, lifting it over my head. His throat works.

I release the button on my jeans and push the zipper down.

"Gorgeous girl, you don't have to do anything you don't wanna. Not for me," he rasps.

My hands still on the waistband of my jeans. "Maybe you're right. I need a shower, too."

"You don't need a damn thing, you're fuckin' perfect."

A blush floods my neck and face, and I can't look at him. An iron fist grips my heart with his words, fighting the disbelief that's too quick to spring to mind.

His hand lifts my chin, turning my head until I'm forced to meet his gaze. "I would ask who did this to you, but we both know. So now, I'm going to show you exactly what you're worth. How fuckin' incredible you are. That okay with you?"

All I can do is swallow, ignoring the tears burning behind my eyes, as I give him a shallow nod. He tugs his shirt off and tosses it onto the bed. A second later, I'm being hauled into the en suite, his hand wrapped around mine. In only shorts, he leans into the shower and turns on the water.

Seconds later, steam curls through the small space and out the en suite door. Filling the room, but not doing a thing to settle the blood thundering through my head. Or the rattle my heart is making watching him. His forearms flex as he pushes my jeans from my hips, and he throws them out the door and to the bedroom floor. He turns back to find me breathless. Tilting his head, he shutters his eyes closed ever so briefly.

I fight back embarrassment and the whimper wanting out of my throat. Desperate to fixate on anything but my insecurities, I let my eyes wander over his muscled body. The fire in my core that sparked with the touch of his hands on my skin a second ago sinks. Now I'm glad the lacy navy lingerie I splurged on last month is what covers my skin.

Mack raises a hand. "Can I touch you?"

"Me first?" I utter on threadbare breath.

He smiles and steps forward. I lift a hand to his sculpted chest, running my fingers over the peaks and valleys of his shoulders and pecs, and letting them drift lower. Small shrapnel wounds dot his skin. Their coarseness files against my fingertips. "Did these hurt?"

Stupid question, Grace. God, I am ridiculous right now.

"A little," he rasps.

I follow the defined V past his hips. But the scar from his surgeries snags my fingers. And all I can see as I trace the raised line is Mack laying on some foreign street in some crappy country, banged up so bad he can't save himself. Emotion clogs my throat as I whisper, "Shit."

Warm hands cup my face. "It doesn't hurt anymore, Gracie."

I don't understand why I'm on the verge of tears. We're only a little more than friends. We didn't even know each other when this all happened. But stripped down to the bare necessities, it's like my first chance to heal. After months of survival. Mack seeing me vulnerable and raw is a growing pain I desperately need.

"Shower's ready, gorgeous girl."

I'm swept into his arms and against his chest a heartbeat later. A second passes and my feet meet warm tile. The steaming water courses down my body and soaks my lingerie. Why am I still wearing it? "Take it off, please."

He swallows, hesitating. "We can take our time, if you need to."

"Sure."

That little voice pops into my head, screaming, *See? He's not into you, Graceless.*

"Okay if I shower?" he asks.

"Sure." *Ugh, know any other words, Grace?* I'm so hot and bothered, and he still has his shorts on. He's not touching me. He simply stands beside me in the water and squeezes shampoo into his palm. The rejection burns. My neck and face are on fire. I push out of the shower, plucking a towel on the way past the rack. "Excuse me," I choke.

I leave my jeans where they lay on his floor, opting for a quick exit over retrieving them. I fly from his bedroom and into mine in a few strides.

Shit.

Shit.

Shit.

I scrub my hands over my face, refusing to let the tears lighting up the bridge of my nose with a hot prickle fall. I wrap the towel around my shoulders and sink onto the end of the bed. I scream, low and quiet, into the towel bunched in my hands. God, what is wrong with me? I want him, I don't want him. I don't want to be wanted. I can't take not being wanted.

Lord above.

Water drips onto my feet. I drag the towel down from my face.

Large feet are planted on either side of mine. Water continues to drip to the floor, running down his legs. I don't want to see his face right now. *Please don't make me look up.*

Knees bend.

Dark blue eyes appear below me as he crouches down, and warm hands rest on my knees. "Need to talk about it?"

I scoff quietly and glance out the window, not wanting to see his handsome damn face. *That's rubbing salt in the wound, Mackinlay.*

"Gorgeous, what happened?"

"Don't call me that."

"Why not?"

"I don't like it."

I see his brow raise in my peripheral.

"What do you want me to call you?"

"Grace."

"Okay, gorgeous Grace," he says as the corner of his mouth lifts.

I sigh and snap my gaze to his. "Really, Mack, you don't owe me anything."

"That's debatable, but okay . . ."

"Stop treating me like I'm something you want."

He pushes up and stands tall. "Right." He walks out the door. A moment later, he returns.

"Give me the towel," he barks.

I jerk and stiffen on the bed. He tugs at the towel, and I let it go.

"You want to know how much I *don't* want you, Grace?"

I lower my brows. He's dried off, his shorts tented. His jaw clenched. His chest heaving.

"Answer the question," he prompts.

"How much?"

He takes my hand and tugs me to my feet, pressing my fingers to his throat. His pulse bounds, hard. Fast.

Lowering my hand, he rests it over his chest. His heart slams into my palm. His breaths are quick, shallow.

I force my eyes up to him and this time I send my hand downward by itself. The hard ridge in his shorts jerks when I brush my knuckles over it.

His breathing shatters as he rasps, "I want you about as much as I want oxygen. But I'm not taking anything from you. I'm not him. I'm giving instead. My turn to take care of you."

I open my mouth to say something. I don't even know what.

He dips his head. "Do you want this?"

I know he means this thing between us. The tension. The chemistry. The bond we've made, living and recovering in this house together. I know Mack like I've never known another man before. Another person. I trust him.

"Yes," I breathe out.

He crowds me now, his hot breath hitting my face. Nipples hard, panties soaked, I can't get close enough. His hands cup my jaw, his mouth dropping to cover mine. Pliant, I lean into him, opening as he sweeps in. My fingers are in his hair. His trail down my neck and over my shoulders.

He breaks away, pressing kisses to my throat, tracking

lower across my collarbone, one side and then the other. I pass the point of no return, my insides melting further with every carefully placed kiss. He takes his time, checking back in every now and then. And when his lips brush over the soft flesh of my breast, I can't help the whimper that falls out.

"You want me to stop, gorgeous?" His voice is deep, gravel.

"Please," I pant, "please don't."

He pops his head up, eyebrows raised as if needing clarification. I shake my head and push his head back down with both hands. His hearty chuckle vibrates through my chest. Resting my palms on his broad shoulders, it takes all I have to stay upright as Mack continues his work of taking care of me.

Each kiss brings electricity to the surface.

With every press of his lips to my body, it's as if I'm waking up from a numbness so constant, I forgot it was there. He's more overwhelming—in the best way possible —than I imagined.

I need more.

I need his touch, everywhere.

So, when a hand slides over my hip and tugs me closer, I huff a moan in assent.

"I could do this all day, gorgeous."

"I would let you . . ." My words are almost inaudible.

He rises and sweeps me off my feet, one strong arm under my butt, the other wrapped around my shoulder. I can't take my eyes off his face. I'm the one getting loved on, but it's his face that's strung out. I touch his jaw with my hand absentmindedly. He turns, kissing my palm. Like it's the most natural thing in the world.

He falters a little as he places me on the bed. I can tell all this carrying and lifting me is taking its toll on his hip and leg. So I shuffle backward. He crawls over my almost naked body, eyes roving my curves. "Sweet Jesus, gorgeous."

I fight the urge to cover up.

My hands drift toward my chest, and he bats them away. He slides his under my back, dipping his head between my breasts. His teeth skate over my hard nipples. I arch off the bed. The clasp on my bra snaps apart.

"Very clever, Mackinlay," I gasp through a smile.

A soft chuckle slips past his lips. "I thought so."

The cheekiest grin lights up his face. I all but melt into a puddle on the duvet. Dark blue eyes tighten as his breathing kicks up. His hands slide the straps over my shoulders. Material still covering me, he nods to it. "Take it off for me, Grace."

I know what he's doing.

He wants me to own this.

To feel confident.

An equal party in this, not the doormat I was. Lying down for three minutes to be a good girlfriend and carrying out my obligations.

My eyes shutter closed briefly before I meet his hooded gaze. I want to be that woman. For myself. For him.

I slide a finger under the lacy fabric. The short breaths failing to fill my lungs burn. My throat thickens. The pad of my finger brushes over one sensitive, hard bud and my lips part.

His nostrils flare. His strung-out face is all but wrecked.

"Now, gorgeous," he rasps.

I slide the lace down, letting my breast pop out and spill over the bunched-up cup.

I swear he stops breathing as he growls, "Fuckin' hell."

I do the same with the other, tossing the bra to the floor. He sits back on his heels, fisting the duvet by his sides. With a jerk toward my panties, he grunts, "Those go next."

Shit.

I worry my bottom lip through my teeth.

"Gracie, you're killing me. Please . . ." No man has ever begged for me—or asked, for that matter. It was always just an expectation.

I wedge my fingers under the band at each hip and lift off the bed. As they slide down to my knees, he grabs the thin fabric in one big hand and tugs it off my legs, and the panties join the bra.

My heart flings against my rib cage.

Partly from being self-conscious. Partly from being this wound up.

Mack opens his mouth to speak, but shallow rasps steal his words. Working his way up my legs with kisses, he dots one on each hip. One just above the aching throb in my center. He crowds me against the bed, hands on either side of my head. He drops his mouth to mine. I open instantly, needing him more than ever.

A hand cups my breast, his thumb flicking over the nipple. A whimper rushes from my mouth, and he devours every small sound I make. My body is shaking by the time his hand brushes over my stomach and his fingers circle my clit. I'm on fire. I swear I could combust from him touching me there.

"Can I kiss you there, Grace?" he says, forehead pressed to mine.

"Um, you don't have to."

"What if I want to?" He pushes up on one corded arm, hand planted by my head.

My brows shoot down. "Nobody's really ever—" I shift on the bed. His erection digs into my center. It feels huge. "I never saw the point, I guess."

"The point?" Now *his* brows fall. "Grace, have you ever had an orgasm?"

Blush fills my face faster than air can pour into my lungs. "Um, I'm not sure . . ."

"You would know if you did, gorgeous, trust me."

"Then I guess not."

"Fuck," he mutters. He leans back on his heels again. This time, he studies my face. "Hold onto the bed, Gracie."

I grab the duvet like my life depends on it. I close my eyes as his head lowers and his hands slide under my thighs.

Oh my god.

Hot kisses dust over my belly before he starts to trail them lower. And lower. I can barely breathe when his hands move, shifting my thighs wider.

His tongue runs through my wet center. I arch off the bed so fast, I'm sure I break vertebrae.

His hand splays over my stomach, holding me down. The other trails featherlight touches up and down my inner thigh.

Another long languid stroke through my center, and this time I swear he groans. *He likes it?* The pad of his finger dances over my entrance. I almost choke on an inhale. Warm lips close around my clit.

"Ma—Holy. Shit!"

He suckles it before his hot tongue strokes over it again and again. Warmth pools fast, sending wet need to my core. My knuckles whiten around the bunched-up duvet I cling to.

"Mack . . ."

"Mhmmm?"

"Oh. What th—"

Again through the center, and two fingers sink into me

as he sucks on my clit with long, hard pulls. Lightning floods my veins as I shatter at the core.

"Mackinlay!"

Arched off the bed, my body convulses more with every wave he coaxes from me, each languid pump of his fingers, every move his mouth makes. My hands are in his hair, and I grip tight. He smiles against my pussy. I can't breathe.

I don't want to.

Settling, I plummet back to the bed, arms by my head on my pillow, eyes slammed shut. My chest caves with every deep breath. He crawls over me, his warmth covering me again. His scent folds around me. A soft kiss presses to my forehead. I close my mouth and open my eyes. He pecks each temple before landing a kiss on my lips.

When he pushes off the bed and disappears through the door, I stare after him in awe.

Chapter Fourteen

MACK

Seeing Grace come undone snapped something in my chest I'm sure was supposed to be whole. She's quiet when she comes out to make supper. But finding me already halfway through making our evening meal, she hovers by the counter, like she doesn't know if she should stay or leave.

"Wanna help?" I ask, scraping diced chicken into a hot pan. It sizzles and the aroma from the spice blend I coated it with bursts to life, filling the kitchen.

She walks around the counter and comes to my side. "Sure, what do you need?"

I turn and pull her into my chest, dipping my head into her hair by her neck. "Just this."

"You'll starve if you only need this."

I push up tall and hold her at arm's length. "I would

never go hungry or alone if you were here. You've proven that to me time and time again."

She rolls her eyes at me.

"You need me to show you how you satiate me again?" I ask, raising a brow.

Her cheeks blush, but she holds my gaze this time. "Thank you for the orgasm." She turns to head to the fridge.

I grab her wrist. "Grace, it's not tit for tat. There's no your pleasure in exchange for mine."

"Only because you haven't had yours."

I shake my head. She's not getting it. "That's not how it works. There is no score sheet for this shit."

"Noted." But her face is pulled into a frown.

"You don't owe me because I made you come. I got as much out of it as you did."

She scoffs. "I highly doubt that."

"I mean, I know I'm good, Gracie, but still, the fact remains."

She slaps my arm and plucks the juice from the fridge, setting it on the counter. Moving beside me again, she starts cutting up the salad ingredients I have laid out. I dot a kiss to the crown of her head. I wasn't lying—taking care of this girl is my pleasure. Seeing her come almost made me lose my load in my shorts.

Those blue eyes glance my way, and she clears her throat.

"What?" I ask, shunting the chicken in the pan around with a wooden spoon.

"Scorecard or not. I want you to have what you gave me, too."

The spoon slips from my hand, clunking onto the side of the pan. "Lunch first?" I manage to rasp.

The vision of those pretty pink lips wrapped around my cock hijacks the functioning part of my brain. She leans a hip against the counter, her tattered short denim shorts sitting over her fitted pale blue V-neck shirt. The cleavage I had my head buried in half an hour ago heaves. Apparently, I have the same effect on her as she does on me.

But she says, "Lunch first."

An hour and two full bellies later, we curl up on the sofa. Grace flicks through the channels. I'm not paying the big rectangle any attention, with my gaze fixed on her. Her long hair is pulled around to one side. We bask in the AC like lounging lizards. She turns on her seat and drapes her long legs over my lap.

"Can you give me a riding lesson later, when it's cooler?"

I can't help the grin bursting over my face. I chuckle and rub my stubbled jaw.

She pulls the cushion from under her head and tosses it at mine. I lean down and dot kisses up her leg.

"Stop," she says between breathy giggles. "Stop it, I'll pee my pants."

"You want me to get you wet, gorgeous?"

"No, I want a riding lesson on a *horse*. Thank you very much, Mr. Rawlins."

"Mr. Rawlins?!" Both eyebrows shoot into my hairline. I scoff at her. "Gracie, I am *not* that old."

"Sure, you are."

"One orgasm and you turn into a brat." I toss the cushion back to her and it smacks her in the face. I freeze.

Shit, I didn't think before I threw it.

A fit of giggles bursts from her lips as she throws her head back. Her legs disappear from my lap, and a heartbeat later, she is straddling me, her hands gripping my face. Soft lips press to mine. I open for her, like she has for me.

She can take anything she finds in this man's heart.

Gracie's a natural. She rises with every other footfall Trigger makes around the round yard. In her old jeans and a yellow checked button-down shirt rolled up at the sleeves she found at the charity shop, she grips the pommel with one hand, the other holding the reins. The wind is up this afternoon, but the gelding is sound, head down, ears forward. It's as if he knows he's responsible for precious cargo.

"How about a lope?" I call to her.

"What?" She glances at me, gripping the pommel tighter.

"Push him into a lope. Squeeze him with your legs and sit back as he rocks into the faster gait."

Her face twists, and she reins the gelding to a stop.

I walk to where they stand. Grace's breaths are quick in what I'm sure is excitement and a little fear. I mean, who wouldn't be a little scared on a horse the first time?

"You want me to hop up there with you?"

"Can you do that? It won't be too heavy for him?"

I slide her sneaker-clad foot out of the stirrup, and it hangs by Trigger's side. I make a mental note to get her real boots. And a hat, for that matter. Sliding my left boot into the stirrup, I push off the ground and haul myself up onto the horse behind her. I remove myself from the stirrup, wrapping my arms around Grace. She glances back, happiness radiating over those elegant features, concentrated in her blue eyes.

I cluck my tongue and Trigger walks on. "The trick to lopin' is to relax into the rocking motion."

I push Trigger from the walk into a lope and Grace tenses, grabbing onto my hands. I twist my cap backward and hold her closer. We sway with the gelding's long gait. The wind pushes her hair around us. I sink my face into her neck and breathe her in.

"Mack," she breathes, leaning her head back on my shoulder.

I catch a glimpse of her face. Her eyes are closed.

In this very moment, I realize heaven is right here.

And I'm getting used to this beautiful view.

I drop the reins to Trigger's neck. "Open your eyes, gorgeous girl."

She does, and I open our arms out wide like wings to fly, our fingers laced together. Like the Titanic moment, but on horseback. Her laughter reverberates through my chest. Her head rests on my shoulders again, the smile over her face stealing the air from my lungs.

We lope the round yard, rocking with Trigger's sturdy footfalls, another three times before her face turns serious. "Mackinlay."

I rein the horse in, and he slows down to a walk. She tugs on the reins in front of my hands. Trigger halts.

"You okay?" I ask.

She twists in the saddle, pressing her palms to my chest. "Thank you."

"You're so welcome." I search her eyes, hoping I haven't triggered some horrible memory for her.

"Can I teach you something?" she asks.

"As long it's not yoga."

She laughs. "Definitely not. Can't have you going to yoga class and checking out all those Lycra-clad girls."

I brush the hair from her face. "I only know one Lycra-clad girl worth lookin' at."

Her gaze drops.

She still doesn't believe the words. If she could see what I see . . .

What we *all* see.

Unfolding myself from our spot on the horse, I dismount and hold up my hands to help her down.

"I got it." She swings her leg over the back of the saddle and slides to the ground.

A natural.

"Pretty soon, you'll be out riding with Adds."

"Really? Gosh, I would love to do that. She was a show jumper, wasn't she? Maybe I could learn to jump?"

"Absolutely. But Trigger here is more of a reining cowpoke. Sure Huddo'll have a horse for you, though."

"Imagine! Grace Weston, horse owner." Her hand waves in front of her like she's reading some city billboard. I chuckle at her enthusiasm and lead Trigger through the yard and back into the barn. Grace lags behind, looking up at the mountains.

I unbuckle the girth, and Grace tugs the saddle from Trigger's back, walking it into the tack room. I swap his bridle out for a halter and run the hose over him, washing away the sweat that accumulated in our one-hour lesson. Grace talks to him at his head, rubbing his muzzle. It's the most female attention Trigger's ever had. Poor old man probably doesn't know what to do with himself.

With a nicker, he rubs his forehead into her hand, pushing it up to her chest. "Love you too, sweet man," she says softly.

My gut flips.

After the two lovebirds have had their fill, I rise from the bale of hay I sat myself down on and walk with them as Grace puts Trigger back in his stall. She unbuckles the halter, and he stands rooted to the spot as she says her goodbyes. Poor guy is lovestruck.

"Come on, gorgeous, leave him to his new crush."

She smiles and kisses his forehead, rubbing a hand between his ears before walking out and closing the stall door behind her. She hangs the halter on the hook by his door, and I wrap an arm around her shoulders. "I think you're Trig's first love, Gracie."

She beams up at me.

I kiss her forehead.

The gelding can take a number. This girl is mine.

Sweet Jesus . . .

Jealous of a damn horse. I drag a hand through my hair as we walk from the barn, and Grace stops abruptly. I falter to a standstill as she gives me an incredulous look.

"What?"

She huffs a laugh. "Nothing."

"Not nothin'."

"Never mind, I'm going for a shower before supper." She glances at the house. "Would you . . ."

"Spit it out."

She hovers on the spot, worrying her bottom lip through her teeth. "Can you—I mean, did you wanna join me?"

"Are you inviting me into your shower?"

She blinks, as if she can't believe she said those words. With a sliver of hesitation, she steps into my space, tilts her head up, and looks me in the eyes. "Yes, Mackinlay, I want you in my shower."

"Well, sure, if you ask nicely." I grin at her.

Annoyance lines her scrunched-up face before she huffs, "Mack, will you please have a shower with me?"

"Nah, I'm good. Not dirty."

Her mouth drops open, and she slaps my arm playfully.

I compose myself, tamping the smile trying to tug my lips up, and stand taller. "Okay, ask me again."

"Hmmm." Her eyes narrow. Then, as if something flipped in that beautiful brain of hers, her eyes turn from frustrated to fire. She undoes the top button of her shirt, then the next. Shirt fully open, a lacy cream bra with a sweet bow in the center covers her perfect skin. Those dusky rose nipples are hard and my mouth waters, wanting to be over them *yesterday*. I all but groan at the sight.

I know she has read the change in my composure and is going to exploit it. Because I want her to. Because I have been helping her own what she wants and take what she needs.

A sly smile blooms over her lips. She sweeps her hair around one shoulder and turns on her heel and walks away from me. Her shirt, still stuck between two fingers, flings over her shoulder and rests at her back. The world's best *follow me* eyes home onto mine. "You coming, Mackinlay?"

"Yes, ma'am."

Chapter Fifteen

GRACE

He's big and so damn hard. The soft, velvety tip is heaven under my fingertips. I brush my thumb over it again, and the aching in my apex intensifies taking him in naked. Raw. The way I am, bare and on my knees for him.

"Fuck, Gracie."

His legs tremble. The tile bites my knees as I take him into my mouth. I've never enjoyed doing this. But it's completely different when you want to do something versus having to do it. The head is warm and soft and hard at the same time. It's a literal oxymoron, hard and soft. Gentle and tough. So many ways to describe this man.

I slide him into my mouth. His hands snap from flat on the tiles, where they were for the past five minutes, to straight into my wet hair. The shower is warm. The drops caress my skin as I stroke him, one hand tight around his base, the other bracing against his thigh. His muscles move, bulky under my splayed-out fingers.

Swirling my tongue over the tip, I pull up, sucking hard.

"Gracie. Gorgeous girl, you're gonna have to stop."

I lose him from my mouth with a pop. His hooded eyes drop to my face. Chest heaving, every muscle in his beautiful body strained tight, he looks like a god from my place below him on the shower floor. If it wasn't for the large scar on his hip and the smaller ones dotted over his torso, you'd think he's Zeus. Or maybe he's Zeus *because* of them.

"It's just fooling around, Mack."

He huffs a strangled laugh. "Yeah."

I used to think about this kind of thing, once. Dropping to my knees for a guy. But the shine wears off when you're at someone's beck and call with nothing ever received in return. I push the memories from my mind and focus on the man standing in front of me. The good one.

"Can I keep going?" I ask.

"Are you asking for my permission or yours?"

A bit of both.

"Yours."

"No, Grace, tell me what you want."

He means this has to be what I desire. Something I get a rush out of as much as he does.

Gathering up a whole lot of bravado and a little sass, I reply, "Come in my mouth, Mackinlay."

His guttural groan is followed by his hands in my hair. I sink over his cock, taking him in as far as I can. Throbbing blooms to life in my clit. I absolutely get something out of this.

With the last scrap of bravery I have, fueled by the fire that's now licking my core, I sink my free hand between my legs. I'm soaked. Slick. And not from the warm water pelting down around us. Looking up, I find Mack's gaze roving my body, snagging on the hand at my center. I take a long, languid pull on his cock, sucking my way over every hard inch and swirling my tongue around the tip before plunging back down. My grip on his base is firm.

Brushing my fingertips over my aching center, I moan around his length.

"Sweet Jesus, Grace."

I have never been so turned on in my entire life.

I pick up the pace, sucking his shaft, teasing the tip. His legs tremble. One hand slaps back onto the tile to brace against the overwhelming pleasure that looks like it could take him down with any given stroke of my lips.

I sink two fingers into my wet core, moving them in time to the pulls of my mouth. Heat pools in my belly like it did on the bed when his face was buried in my pussy. The next sweep of my thumb over my clit, I explode around my fingers, whimpers cascading from my mouth.

"Fuck . . . Good girl."

As the sensation flooding my body settles, I lick a long stroke up the length of his cock. His breathing shatters. He's so close. I pump hard and suck with slow, coaxing movements. His hands, still in my hair, tighten. Salty warmth streams into my mouth. "Fuck, gorgeous girl."

His eyes are closed, his head tilted back.

Every inch of Mackinlay trembles.

I swallow every last drop he gives me. His legs falter. I grab his hands as he slides down the shower wall to his seat, only somewhat in control of his motions. Dark blue eyes meet mine. Strong arms reach for me. "Come here."

I crawl onto his lap, and he folds me into his chest.

He drops a kiss into my hair, another to my temple. My heart all but explodes. We sit on the tiled floor, soaking up all the warmth the water and steam allow. His heartbeat drums against my cheek. Mine races along. How is being intimate with Mack so easy? So satisfying?

So . . . *addictive.*

I glance back up, and his eyes are closed. His breathing slow and even. He's asleep. Or at least, almost.

"Mack?"

He grumbles something incoherent and cracks one eye open.

"If you fall asleep here, I'll never be able to shift you."

Brushing the hair matted to the side of my face behind my ear, he nods. I move to stand, but he holds me in place. With a swift motion, he's on his feet, the tremble in his legs from before nowhere to be seen. Padding into the bedroom, he walks us straight past my bed and into his room.

A moment later, I'm in his bed. He spoons me and pulls me into his hold.

"I should get supper organized," I mutter. Not sure if me being in his bed is the best idea. What would his family think if they knew?

We're only fooling around. *Right?*

"A few minutes, then we can go back to the real world."

"A few minutes." I wriggle further into his hold, my back flush against his warm chest. My ass bunted up to his groin.

He slides an arm around me and buries his head in my hair. "I'm proud of you, Grace, for taking what you want."

I huff a laugh. "Wait until I put *that* on my resume."

A hearty laugh huffs through my hair.

A handful of heartbeats later, my eyes flutter shut.

Clink.

Clink.

Clink.

I sit up, only a sheet over my body. It falls away. Confusion sets in for a second. The room is different.

Mack's room. And . . . I'm naked.

The last hour before we snuggled into bed floods back in. Heat instantly fills my belly, low. I glance at the clock on his bedside table.

5:00 p.m.

Crap! I have to start supper.

I fly out of bed and tiptoe to my bedroom. I pass the gym on the way, slowing as I do. I watch as Mack pushes out another rep of his shoulder and arm exercises. Holy hell, he is definitely putting on muscle. His sweat-covered arms rise, pushing the weights up again. I hold my breath.

Corded forearms and bulging biceps.

Pretty sure my ovaries just did somersaults.

He meets my gaze as he lets the machine back down. Jaw clenched tight, legs bracing his body, he finishes the set and shakes out his arms.

"You alright?" he asks, raising an eyebrow.

My face must look ridiculous, if the expression on his is anything to go by. Dammit.

"I—I was—" I clear my throat. "Nope, I'm going to make supper." I'm naked and blushing like an absolute idiot. I have one arm wrapped over my breasts, and a hand covering my now very wet center. *Damn you, Mackinlay Rawlins. I have chores.*

He simply smiles and nods to the hallway. As if telling me to get on with it. *Ugh, fine, two can play that game, Mackie-boy.* I cringe at the stupid nickname Lawson calls him. I can see why he hates it. It's childish and corny.

And my best weapon.

Pulling on short denim shorts and a T-shirt, I forgo the bra since it's just the two of us and I'll be going to bed in a few hours. My phone buzzes on the dresser. A text.

I pad to where it sits and swipe it up.

Opening the screen, I tap on a number I don't recognize. The message is empty. Like someone tapped out a bunch of spaces and hit send.

My gut sinks.

I haven't heard from Joel for weeks. The last text he sent—which I ignored—was during Sunday lunch at Louisa's. Nothing since.

Same old thing every time.

Where are you?

Why did you leave?

None of your goddamn business. Should have left sooner.

I will never respond. I can't. I won't.

The phone vibrates in my hand again. It almost slips from my hand when I realize it's ringing.

Joel.

All I can do is stare at it.

Too angry and shocked to answer, I let the call go to voicemail. I toss the phone onto the bed like it's on fire.

"Everything okay, gorgeous?" The low rumble comes from the doorway.

I spin back, my heart in my throat. It's as if somehow Mack knew Joel is still contacting me. My place here is over. He grips the top of the doorframe with both hands and swings forward on his feet. His focus drifts to the center of the bed. Fire consumes my cheeks. I shove my hands in my back pockets and swallow, dropping my eyes to stare at the floor.

The phone rings again.

"You gonna get that?" Mack says, nodding toward the buzzing.

I lift my head to meet his gaze and shake my head.

"You should. Tell them what's what, Grace."

The air lodges in my windpipe. Releasing his grip, his arms fall, and he steps over to where I stand. "Do it for your own peace of mind."

I should.

I should be brave enough to tell Joel to take a hike. To never contact me again.

A firestorm of wasps in my chest have stolen the last of the useful oxygenated blood from my brain, leaving my neurons to short-circuit. "I'll just let it go to voicemail . . ."

Mack raises an eyebrow at me for the second time this afternoon. "You know, ignoring a problem doesn't make it go away. This really smart, beautiful girl I know taught me that."

I roll my eyes at him.

He's talking about me, right?

I lean over the bed and pick up the phone. My hands shake. The missed call notification sits on the screen. I tap it and hit the messages icon. The unknown number and Joel's last text still show in the recent tab. Opening Joel's messages, I tap out a message.

> Do not contact me. Ever again, Joel.

I hit send and Mack folds me into his chest, his chin on my head. The breath he releases is long and his body relaxes around mine. But I can't help but feel that responding, even telling Joel to leave me alone, will only make him more persistent. Because now he has confirmation that I'm alive and well. Choosing to be anywhere he's not.

"See, that wasn't so bad, was it?" Mack dots a kiss on my cheek before unfurling his hold on me. The chill that falls in as he moves away is part his absence and part my unease. If I know Joel, he won't heed anything I tell him. He never has.

Shaking it off, I wander to the kitchen, sliding my phone into my back pocket. Mack is pulling items from the fridge. "I'm cooking tonight. Pick a movie on Netflix, will ya?"

I hover by the kitchen counter a moment. I would rather be busy. My mind doesn't need a second's leeway to dwell on the threat from Mississippi. So, I try to help, and he bats me away. "Ah! My turn. You do enough around here."

The sofa gives way like an old friend when I sink into it and hunt through the cushions for the remote. With the telltale echoing sound of Netflix bursting onto the TV, I lean into the softness. Like I'm searching for refuge, and its cotton filling is my sanctuary where none shall find me. I toss my phone onto the small side table and flick through categories trying to find something we will both like.

Romance movies – no.

Thriller – hell no.

Military flicks – ah, probably not.

Comedy – sold!

I chose a popular standup gig that's a good hour and a half long. Enough time to eat and cuddle up. A man and two bowls appear as I shuffle the cushions around to make our spot in the center. I take the bowl from his hand and toss the salad and chicken with ranch dressing using the fork already dug into the mix.

Mack is planted by my side a second later. I press play and a British guy starts up. He's like a life-size version of a ventriloquist doll. But hell, he is funny. Inappropriately so, most of the time. I shovel my delicious meal into my mouth between bouts of laughter. Mack is doubled over by midway through.

It's so wonderful to see his face lit up with pure joy. Tears leak from his eyes as he clutches his stomach. When his hysterics finally die out, he shakes his head. "Jesus, Grace. I'm gonna choke on my chicken."

The mouthful I was chewing lodges in my airway. Choked out gasps compete with the laughter I can't stifle at Mackinlay's ridiculous face. He pats my back, and I manage to swallow the food, coming up for air like a diver on their last run, all out of oxygen.

"Fuck, sorry, gorgeous."

His face is twisted, fighting hysterics. I push from the sofa and pull out two glasses, filling them with water from the fridge. On my return, Mack's face has fallen, his gaze set on my phone. Like moving through molasses, I turn to find what has his attention.

Another text.

Joel.

I pass the glasses to him and grab the phone. Not hesitating this time, I open the message.

Bile claws its way up my insides, burning like a house fire in June. I can't pry my eyes from the screen.

So few words.

Impact—unfathomable.

> You don't walk away from me, Graceless.
> I WILL FIND YOU.

The air in my lungs stalls out. My chest burns. My heart flings against my ribs, sending a burning flurry of ash down my limbs.

"The asshole agree to leave you alone?"

I snap my head up. Hopeful blue eyes study my face. The happy man I'm falling for from just moments ago flashes through my mind. Everything he has gone through after his tour . . . I will solve my own problems. Fight my own battles.

Mack pats the cushion beside him. On wobbly legs, I walk between his and drop onto his lap, burying my head into his neck and letting my hair fall around his shoulder and arm. Right here, I'm safe. So here is where I intend to stay. He turns away and chugs down water. I delete the message and toss the phone onto the sofa.

"Yep," I say, but even the word burns my tongue. I already regret my first and last lie to Mackinlay Rawlins.

"You want to see what else the funny man has to say?" he whispers into my ear, sending goosebumps over my body.

"Sure." I ignore the stone forming in my throat.

Chapter Sixteen

MACK

The woman on the horse beside me isn't the same one who arrived here months ago. The girl who was broken, reserved, and always sad has grown into a confident, sassy, and smart woman. A woman who, right now, has Trigger wrapped around her little finger. I mean, who can blame a man for falling for Grace Weston?

"Trig sure likes your company these days," I drawl, chewing on the dried stem of grass I found before mounting one of Huddo's new yearlings he hasn't had time to work.

Saw right through that one fast. My family may be a lot of things, but subtle ain't one of them.

"Why are we riding out here instead of the usual field behind the house?" Grace asks. Her suspicion is alive and well.

Good girl.

"No reason, just sick of the same damn circuit. Besides, Trig was asking for a change of pace."

"Will you need him back for real cowboy stuff soon?" Hope fills her eyes, as if daring me to say no.

"I will, actually."

Her face falls. *Sweet Jesus, don't do that, Gracie.* A thought flies into my head—I'll have to fix her horseless situation. While I'm at it, I'm willing to bet Ma would help me put together a birthday party for her. Something small. Nobody should have to miss a milestone like turning twenty-one. But having a day straight outta the pits of hell for your twenty-first birthday, that's fuckin' unacceptable.

I'll be fixin' that.

"What are you thinking about, Mackinlay?" Grace is squinting at me like she's trying to read my mind. Hell, I'm not sure she can't sometimes.

"Ready for a lope, cowgirl?"

"When you are." She beams at me. What I wouldn't do to keep that gorgeous smile on her face. Before I have a chance to push the young'un into a lope, Trigger shoots forward. Grace's laughter as she glances back over her shoulder carries on the wind. The sound is like the air I breathe. Life-sustaining.

I send the young horse after them. We catch up and I press the gelding sideways, moving in beside Trigger. I pluck the hat from Grace's head.

"Hey!" She squeals as I rein my horse to the right.

"Winner takes it all!" I send the mount into a gallop. I call back at her. Now the cat-and-mouse begins. Like a horseback capture the flag. With the "all" for us being each other.

Hooves thunder, closing in on my line as I head toward the mountains. The summer grass sways like waves on the ocean as we fly through it. The blue mountains fade to ridges and trees as we get closer. I push the gelding harder, and we clamber up the side of the incline. I duck the few low-hanging branches and wind him through the rough-bark trunks.

The sound of running water carries on the breeze. My mood changes instantly. I slow the horse to a walk and turn him around. Grace and Trigger lope toward us. Their pace has slowed, her gaze fixated on the mountains in front of her. Wonder evident all over her gorgeous face. The playfulness drains from me, replaced with an overwhelming need for her.

Heart in my throat, I dismount and tie the gelding to a branch and walk toward Grace as she trots up the slope. Trigger stops just shy of me.

"What's that look for?" Grace breathes.

Coming to her side, I look up at the woman in the saddle. She holds out a hand. "Hat?"

I glance down. It's still in my grip.

"Course," I choke, handing the hat to her.

She leans down, bending in the saddle until her face is

in front of me. Her breath hits my face a second before her lips are on mine. I step closer, taking her face in my hands, like it fuckin' belongs there. Always will.

She opens and I taste her. Trigger leans, lifting one foot from the ground, lazy old man. I sway with her as she moves with the horse. She nips my bottom lip and sits back up.

"Grace, I—"

Trigger jerks to the right, ears pointing forward. I snap my gaze ahead. My gelding, no longer tied to the tree branch, gallops past us, heading for home. "Ah, dammit. Stupid fool. Better not hurt himself, or Huddo'll skin me alive."

"Looks like you ride with me, cowboy." Grace's face is lit up with cheek.

"Looks like it, gorgeous."

She slips her foot from the stirrup, and I shove mine in, springing up onto Trigger, behind the saddle. Grace leans into me. Despite the warm weather and the runaway horse, this is as good as it gets.

"Any excuse to wrap your arms around me, Mackie-boy?"

I stiffen at the ridiculous nickname Laws insists on using. With the next breath, I dig my fingers into her ribs.

"I'm sorry!" She squeals with delight, twisting in the seat, trying to flee my tickles. "Please, stop."

I splay my hands around her sides, letting my fingers

brush under her breasts. "Repeat after me, Grace Weston."

She nods, wrangling her breaths back to something less hectic.

"I will never ever use a nickname for Mackinlay again," I command.

She repeats the phrase, mimicking every syllable in my Montana drawl. I nip her earlobe, and she turns and grabs my face with both hands. "As long as we both shall live."

With a wink, she twists back and picks up the reins. We lope in the direction of home. I wrap myself around her, sending a prayer to the heavens. Hoping somewhere up there Butters is doin' okay. Finally letting go of the guilt I have hauled along with me since that day.

Vanilla and peaches shroud me as Grace sends Trigger faster.

She is my peace.

The one element of my life that grounds me.

Sometimes because I can't see a day in the future without her. Sometimes because she needs me to be strong. Sometimes both.

I will never be able to repay her for bringing me back to life.

She's my home.

And I will use every last breath I have to be hers.

The reins swing, loose in her grip as we walk for home. Trigger, lathered in sweat, was sanctioned a breather by his ever-adoring crush. Those two really are made for each other. Poor old fella's gonna be heartbroken when she gets her own mount and he is stuck with me again.

"You never wanted to do anything else, live anywhere else?" she asks, eyes following the horizon as the sun sets behind us, setting the whispering grass to a shimmering gold. We walk through the sea of glimmering grass. When I take too long to answer, her eyes search me out.

"Not really. Army was my plan B."

"Oh. I'm sorry."

I mull it over for a while. It was never the long game. But I always wanted to be the one to decide when to call it quits. I tell her as much.

"I get it. Being able to have the choice is important."

"Yeah."

I pluck a long, thin golden strand and put it between my teeth. She chuckles and rubs Trigger's neck. Home comes into view a moment later, and we fall silent for a while.

Reaching down and grabbing a handful of stalks, she lets them loose to the wind, watching them fly in every direction. "Freedom is, too."

The words are quiet. I know they run deep for Grace.

"What makes you happy, Gracie?"

She rests a hand on Trigger's neck as he plods along, as if he's her comfy blanket. A half-a-ton bay, fury, sweaty comfort animal. "Colors."

"Yeah?" I perk up.

"Painting. Sketching, although that's not colors, but the line, shape, angles, marks. It all makes me happy."

"How long since you painted for real? Not the small stuff in the yoga room."

"The yoga room." She chuckles, but it fades out and she sighs. "A while."

"You should paint."

"It doesn't pay the bills, Mack."

"Maybe not yet."

"How would that even work? I'm guessing the day you don't need me is coming soon. You're functioning fine, from what I can see. Besides, it feels wrong to take your money when you could be doing all these things yourself."

"Technically, it's Harry's money. But I agree, you need to find something better."

She stops.

Trigger grinds to a halt beside her, swaying into her. Protective old man.

"So that day is today?" Her voice is strained. "You want me to go?"

"Want?" I pluck my hat from my head and run my

hand through my hair. Shoving it back on, I step into her space. "No, I don't want you to go, Grace. I want you to be happy. Free. Doing something you find meaningful. Not this."

"Oh." She studies my face. "Like what?"

"Something in the arts? We could see if there is anything in town you could apply for."

"Like a course or something."

"Or a job. I mean, you already have eighteen months of an arts degree under your belt, not too many folks around here can claim that. And art or yoga, god forbid, would fill your cup better than keeping house ever will. I want more for you." I rest my palm on her cheek, and her fine fingers wrap around my wrist. Tears line her eyes and her breathing shallows out.

Dammit.

"You don't want that?" I ask.

Her mouth twists somewhere between a smile and a broken cry. "Of course I do. I—" Her voice breaks. Trigger nickers, and I swear the old shit glares at me for makin' his girl cry.

I dip my head to capture her gaze. "You can do this. I'm right there with you. All the way."

She huffs a tangled whimper and pushes her face into my chest. I rub a hand around her back, wanting so badly to erase every last piece of hurt that fuckin' asshole caused her. If the day ever comes when he stands in front of me, a reckoning will be in store.

She finally leans out of my hold, and her blue eyes glitter with tears. Ones I pray are the happy kind. I want her to have that.

Happiness.

She gave me mine back.

After so long.

"You sure you want me to stick around, Mackinlay?"

"Woman, you are my oxygen. Without you, there is no breathin' for this man."

She rolls her eyes at me, and the unshed tears spill over, running down her cheeks. "Corny, but I'll take it."

I can't help the smile cracking my face. I kiss every last tear from her face until she is giggling in my arms again. That sound will never get old to me.

"Come on, Trig's gonna miss his old-man bedtime if we're not careful."

"Can't have my favorite boy worn out," she coos to the gelding, planting a kiss to his dark brown jawline.

We wander home, making it to the barn as the first star pops in the dark sky overhead. I've never felt so revived, so exhausted from walking miles on my aching hip, and so alive all at once.

With Trigger tucked up in his stall and thoroughly loved up on, I lead Grace back to the house. With a quick shower, we crawl into bed, and sleep takes her under before I have a chance to tell her what today meant to me.

What *she* means to me.

I guess I will have to show her at Ma's in a few days' time.

I have plans for her twenty-first birthday do-over. To see her smile, I would do just about anything. So, I roped in the cavalry.

Chapter Seventeen

GRACE

Mack is acting strangely. He's been distracted all day. Checking his phone every hour. What is with this man? Said device now lies on the kitchen counter in front of me as I rub seasoning into the skin of a whole chicken. I was instructed to make it for Sunday lunch that turned into early supper because of Harry's workload this week. Buzzing, the phone vibrates over the hard surface. I dare a peek at the sender.

Ruby.

Curious.

"That my phone or yours?" He flies down the hallway and snatches his phone up from the countertop. Sliding the message open, a smile splits his handsome face. I fold my arms over my chest and raise an eyebrow.

"Something you wanna share with the class, Mackinlay?"

"Hey, what—" He's furiously tapping out a reply, not looking up. He finally snaps his gaze up. "Huh, you say something?"

"Spill, Rawlins."

He pecks my cheek. "Sorry, gorgeous girl. Can't." He practically bounces on his feet. The worn-out Wranglers and light blue T-shirt he's wearing show off his shape that's becoming more defined by the day. On long, determined strides, he's out of sight before I have the chance to form a rebuttal. Shaking my head, I return my attention to the chicken. I plan on roasting it for an hour at Louisa's.

It's the first time I have made my favorite dish since Mississippi. Making this always makes me homesick. Parent-sick? Mama-sick, to be more specific. We used to make this together. I guess that's why it became a staple when I lived in Mississippi, my way of clinging to the one person I desperately needed and missed. Miss.

I still miss Mama so bad.

Sometimes, I wonder if I shouldn't anymore. I mean, I'm not a child anymore. Or a frustrated teen. But her warm cuddles. The sounds of her chuckle. The way she would hug me, one arm around my waist, the other behind my neck, drawing her forehead to mine . . .

Today is exactly six months since my twenty-first birthday. Another thing I lost, not having Mama there for that particular milestone. Wetness splashes the counter between the roasting tray and the marble edge. Thickness coats my airways, and a burn blooms at the bridge of my nose.

I never thought there would come a day when my mom wasn't a part of my life. Then I blinked, and she wasn't. Now, I'm miles away from her. It may as well be an entire continent. I chug a sob, rubbing the seasoning in some more. *Sorry, chicken, but this hurt's got to go somewhere.* I rub the shoulder of my sleeve over one eye, then do the same with the other.

Losing her is the thing I regret most. The one thing I would change if I could.

The rest taught me about myself.

Mothers and daughters aren't built to be separated.

Not this daughter, at least.

Warm arms fold around me. "Be ready to go in an hour?" His stubbled chin drops to my shoulder, his jaw scratching the hollow where my neck meets my shoulder. I giggle a sob-laugh. "Must be one depressing bird to have this girl all choked up," he says.

"Must be . . ." I rest my cheek on his head and breathe him in. After the sadness has dissipated, I dot a kiss to his temple and stand tall. "Me and Cheryl here will be dressed and set to supper in no time."

"Cheryl?"

"That's this delicious girl's name."

"Grace, baby, you can't name the bird you're eatin'."

"Why not? She deserves respect, too. Just because we are higher up the food chain doesn't mean we have to behave like animals, Mackinlay."

He chuckles. "You are too sweet for your own good, you know that, right?"

"Painfully aware."

I think back to all the stupid second, third, tenth chances I gave Joel. Too naive, more like it. Mack shifts on his feet, glancing at the time. Shifty is an excellent word to describe this man today. He has me intrigued, to say the least.

He claps his hands. "I'm gonna go change. Wear somethin' nice, okay?"

"Sure." I place the cut veggies I prepped earlier around the bird in the roasting pan and cover it with plastic wrap before sliding Cheryl into her spot in the fridge until we go. Passing the yoga room, I hesitate, running an eye over my painting set up. It's lame. I need to get organized. I would love to paint and maybe one day sell some.

Grabbing a quick shower, I wash my hair and towel it off before slipping on the blue dress I found last week at the charity store. It's pale blue with small peach floral clusters. It starts with a deep V-neck silhouette that's centered with a waist band, and three-quarter sleeves that end in a gathered trim. A full A-line skirt that ends at my knees and sways when I move. This dress makes me feel pretty. I decide on light makeup this time. I blow out my hair and leave it to hang around my shoulders in light waves. A small, silent celebration of my own.

Twenty-one-and-a-half years old.

I feel younger, sometimes. On the bad days.

It hits me as I stare at my reflection—aged since the day I arrived here—that it's been a long while since a bad day has found me. Emotion flares again, and I blink the tears back, not wanting to spoil my face, no matter how simple it is.

After I'm dressed and done up, I wander toward Mack's room. I can smell his cologne. The scent flips my gut over in an instant. He appears, clean-shaven, wearing a navy dress shirt with the sleeves rolled up and a pair of dark jeans. Something like nerves roots me to the spot. My mouth gapes.

He leans sideways, his top half disappearing for a moment. Reappearing, he wears a black cowboy hat. My heart is wedged tight in my throat a second later.

Holy hurling heavens.

"Mackinlay . . ." The word is more like a breathy moan. Heat flushes my face.

"You look stunning, gorgeous girl." He dots a kiss to the crown of my head and grabs my hand, pulling me down the hallway. His shiny boots clack on the wood floor. My silver flats scuff behind, and I am grateful I chose to do my makeup and hair after seeing him all dressed up.

I grab my bag and phone from the small front table as

Mack collects Cheryl and two six-packs of beer. I hold the door for him, and we head for the barn. I grab the back driver's side door, pulling it open as he places the chicken and beer in safely.

The passenger door opens from the inside. Mack is leaning over, corded arms flexing as he waits for me to open it further and climb on up into the truck. I slide into my seat. But I don't put my seat belt on; instead I turn to face him as he starts the engine. I can't take my eyes from his jaw, those dark blue eyes, the goddamn hat. My breaths shallow out in no time.

The Chevy rumbles to life.

Mack slides his chair back before rubbing a hand over his clean-shaven face. "Come here, Gracie."

"Okay . . ." I don't move.

"I'm not askin', gorgeous." His eyes burn. He plucks the hat from his head and plants it onto mine. "Here, now."

Bunching up my skirt, I maneuver over the center console and sink onto his lap. He's hard already. The second I'm settled in place, his hands are on my face. "You're killin' me in that dress."

A smile grows over my face. "Can't have that." I pull one side of the top aside. One of the perks of the design—at least, I thought so when I found it in the shop.

The light yellow lace bra pops out and Mack drops his head back onto the headrest, slamming his eyes shut. "Sweet Jesus."

"They are all yours, Mackinlay."

"Fuck, Grace. We won't even make it to Rosewood at this rate."

"Maybe we don't have to—"

"Nope, we're going alright. Just have one thing to do before we go."

"Oh?" I ask, breathless.

"I wanna see your beautiful face fall apart as you come on mine."

If I had words, which I don't, I would scream *yes please* to the heavens. But they're stuck somewhere deep, because nothing comes when I open my mouth to respond. Mack grabs the hold bar above us and flips us over, depositing me on the driver's seat. I can't help the giggle that huffs from my lips. He shuffles backward, sliding one leg out the door and planting his foot on the ground.

"You sure this is okay with your hip?" I protest with breathy words.

He's disappeared under my blue skirt a heartbeat later. His tongue runs over the already soaked panties, from start to finish. My hands grip the sides of the seat, chest heaving as he taps my inner thigh. I lift up and my panties are on the dash before I drop back down.

"Wait," I breathe.

He pops out from under the fabric. "You okay, gorgeous?"

I shake my head.

His brows lower.

"Please, kiss me."

He crawls up the seat, a hand pushing him up on the console with the other cupping my face. His lips meet mine, and I open so fast. Drowning. Falling. As his tongue sweeps and caresses, I soak him in, gripping his face like he's my lifeline. After a long, slow day and thoughts of all I have lost, I want him close.

I turn my head when I have to come up for air and he nudges my chin with his nose. "Never be afraid to ask for the things you need, Gracie." His words rumble against my chest. I run my hands through his hair. His drift to my stomach.

"I won't."

"Promise me, whatever you need, you'll ask for it. There's nothing you could do or say that would—"

I grab his head and raise it so his eyes are on me. "I promise. I will. But it goes both ways, okay?"

He nods. Cheek floods his face a moment later and he swings under my dress again. I lie on the seat and let the man I adore wake me up.

In the best way possible.

He runs his tongue through my center.

Slow.

I arch from the seat and whimper.

"Fuck *me*, Mackinlay."

His hearty chuckle against my soaked center sends me higher.

We are going to be *so late . . .*

Louisa meets us at the white gate to her homestead yard. We are absolutely late. The fairy lights hung throughout the old trees are lit up, turning the space around us into a wonderland. Ruby's influence, so I have been told. It's stunning. She did good.

"You're here!" Louisa pulls me in for a hug.

"I'm so sorry we're late," I say softly.

Mack files in behind me with Cheryl and the beers, and Louisa steps away and pins him with her best mom glare. "I'm guessin' that's your fault?"

"Guilty," he says with a wry smile before his gaze slips to me. "Where you want Cheryl, Gracie?"

"She needs an hour at least. Can I heat up the oven, Louisa?"

"Oh, hon, it's already on. Moderate heat. Ready to go. Who's Cheryl, and why are we cookin' her?" Her face pulls with confusion.

"Long story, Ma," Mack says as he heads inside with the roasting tray and armful of drinks. Addy and Ruby hustle out the door in a hurry and sweep me away from Louisa. We head inside. Harry sits at the kitchen table. He's in his good clothes, too.

Okay, what gives? I thought he had a huge workday . . .

I run an eye over Ruby. She wears a floaty white dress with pink-topped boots. Addy is in a yellow summer dress and flats. Both women have their makeup done, wearing dangly earrings. And they both smell divine!

"I love your perfume," I offer Ruby as she plants me on the sofa by the hearth.

"Thanks. It's Coach."

She sure does like nice things.

"You like perfume, Grace?" Addy asks.

"Um, yes. I guess. I've never bought it for myself before, but—"

"Great!" Ruby squeaks. "We, ah, need to grab the entrée. Give me a hand, Adds?"

Addy smiles at me and pats my hand like a child. "Be right back. You want some wine?"

"Sure, white?"

She springs from the sofa and glides into the kitchen. Now I'm sure something is amiss. They're always sweet to me, but their overeagerness is unnerving. My gut flips. I wring my hands in the paisley fabric and stare into the hearth, racking my brain as to why everyone, except maybe Louisa, is acting odd.

A glass of wine appears in front of me, and I pluck it from Ruby's hand. Her elegant fingers finish in baby pink nails. Her hair is wavy, her brown eyes lit up as she drops to the sofa beside me. "Okay, I can't keep a secret to save myself, so here goes. We wanted to do something for your birthday."

What?

The air leaves my lungs and doesn't return. My mouth opens. Nothing comes.

Ruby raises a hand. "We realize it was a little while ago. We also know it was a big milestone birthday. And the Rawlinses are not ones to let a significant date go by without celebrating it. So this, Grace Weston, is your twenty-first birthday soiree!"

I'm literally speechless.

"You and I are going to go out back, where the boys have put together a little party. It's not much, just us, but we all wanted to do something for you."

I clear my throat and suck in a breath. "Well, that explains Mackinlay."

Ruby laughs and sips her wine. "I bet it does. He's fond of you, Grace."

I choke on the sweet liquid in my mouth. Somewhat recovered, I mutter, "That's one way to put it."

"Ready when you two are," Reed calls from the back door.

Watching Ruby's face bloom at the sound of his voice makes my heart ache. Gosh, those two are so incredible. Ruby stands and extends a hand. "Come on, birthday girl."

I take her hand, and we pad down the hall. Nerves spring to life, like any minute now, the entire family is going to realize they made a mistake. I'm not worth their time. Too young for their son. That I am taking their hard-earned money while I'm fooling around with Mack. I sip the drink, letting it burn my throat.

I stall, stopping in the hallway shy of the door.

"It's okay, Grace. Only people who love you are here."

Her brown eyes find mine, and I understand.

This kind of love is unconditional.

Chapter Eighteen

GRACE

More fairy lights and lit up faces.

Addy is snuggled into Hudson's side.

The soft sounds of the night insects buzzing between the crackles of the flames of two firepits. One by the back door, one just shy of the weeping green of the willow.

Reed, patiently waiting for his wife as we walk across the grass to the old tree where the long family table is covered in a blue tablecloth that sways from each end of the weathered planks.

With dishes atop and more candles than I can count, the table looks set for royalty.

Louisa and Harry stand in front of the table.

Then I see him.

Mack.

Standing by one of the long bench seats. Hand clasped behind his back, like he's standing to attention in a morning lineup. But his face is soft, happy, and a smile pushes his lips up as my eyes find his. Butterflies take flight in one big swarm, and I cling to Ruby's arm.

She leans in. "Happy birthday, Gracie."

I stare at her, scrunching my nose up to stifle the tears that threaten again. Oh boy, it's going to be a long night.

Something tells me it's turning out to be one of my best.

The tree moves, and Lawson appears with a large chair, placing it at the head of the table.

"Hi!" I gasp. He came all the way from New York for me? My chest tightens. He winks at me and moves to stand by Reed. Now Mack steps forward, gesturing for me to sit.

This is too much.

He pulls the chair out for me, and I release Ruby's arm and take his hand. His eyes never leave my face as I sink into it, and he tucks me in. A moment later, everyone is seated at the long table. Me at one end, Harry at the other. Hudson, Addy, and Lawson on my left. Louisa, Reed, and Ruby to my right. Mack pulls out another chair and sits beside me.

I open my mouth to thank them all. They most certainly didn't have to do all this for me. Harry stands, tapping a fork on his glass tumbler. The amber liquid at the bottom swishes and he clears his throat.

"Now, around here, we believe that family is the most important part of life. It builds a good life. Makes the hard days a little easier." He pauses, glass in hand. "It wasn't long ago, our family was shook to the core." His gaze settles on Mackinlay. I find his hand under the table, and he laces his fingers through mine. I squeeze his hand, hoping the rest of the table doesn't notice the expression he's giving me right now. Because there's nothing employee and employer about it. At all.

Harry smiles. "However, with every storm, a rainbow follows, almost always guaranteed."

Reed shakes his head. "Jesus, Harry, that's damn corny."

Harry's crooked smile is aimed at his youngest son. "Maybe, but sometimes the right words don't matter. It's actions that matter."

"Sure." Reed grins.

Louisa pats his face like he's a little boy. Ruby plants a kiss to the other side. The whole table cracks up. "There's your actions, Reedsy," Ruby says, leaning into him.

He plucks his whiskey from the table and takes a sip.

"Yeah, Reedsy, where would we all be without Rubes's actions?" Hudson winks at him.

Reed chokes on his mouthful. Louisa slaps his back and more laughter spills over.

"Now, the preschoolers have had their say." Harry dips his head, eyeing his two sons. "I'll continue." His attention drifts back to me. I hold my breath.

"Gracie, we consider you our rainbow after the storm. You will always be part of this family, no matter where you decide to go next. Or where your dreams lead you. I think that about sums it up. Happy birthday, darlin'. Let's eat!"

"Finally," Reed drawls.

Ruby slaps his shoulder. It's playful. He's always the joker. He's kind and funny. I see so much of him in Mack. More and more each day, I discover the incredible man he was before and is coming back to. From the moment I saw him stranded amidst the floor covered in laundry detergent, unable to move and so damn angry, to now, strong and healthy, but most of all, happier.

"Mackinlay, did you want to say something for Grace?" Louisa asks.

The table quiets instantly.

His jaw feathers but he stands, and all eyes are on him. All but Ruby's, whose stay on me, her smile soft. It's as if she can read my mind, or maybe Mack's.

Mack picks up his glass of whiskey and drops his gaze to me. "Grace—Gracie." He hesitates, but when he glances at Harry, it's as if every person holds their breath. "If anyone at this table deserves happiness and a life well-lived, it's you. You literally scraped me off the floor and gave me the kick in the ass I needed. You put me back together, one mangy piece at a time. You're part of me now, Gracie. Here's to being your first mate."

He sinks to his seat and swallows his drink down like a man dying of thirst. Everyone stares at him, some faces confused, a few with goofy smiles. Reed's, mostly.

First mate?

I don't get it. What'd I miss?

"To Mack's saving grace!" Reed quips. "Pun *absolutely* intended." A megawatt smile stretches his face. Ruby side-hugs his arm, her face strained to stem emotion.

Louisa stares at me, wonder claiming her face.

Harry smiles over his drink with an all-knowing look before he picks up the dish in front of him and passes it to Ruby. When nobody speaks, Reed salutes me and plucks the next dish before piling food onto his plate. Dishes circulate, food covers each plate, and Ruby swipes up a small remote, pointing it to the back porch.

Country music begins to play, and chatter starts up.

I take up my cutlery, my mouth watering at the amazing looking meal. Cheryl sits in the center of the table, already half gone. Poor girl. I guess it was always her fate. There's a bowl of pasta with some kind of red marinara sauce that Ruby is devouring. A salad that Addy brought and Hudson is shoveling onto his fork.

I load up a forkful of the potato dish and some salad. Flavor explodes in my mouth, and I stifle a groan. Wow. This family really knows their food. Oh my . . . This is divine.

Woodsy caramel closes in. I open my eyes and Mack is

leaning close. "Happy birthday, Gracie," he whispers. I smile at him, letting the warmth that floods my chest with his gorgeous smile take me under. I don't even care if everyone can see whatever it is that hangs between Mack and me.

We finish the mains and Hudson and Reed collect the plates and head inside to grab more drinks. Louisa follows.

I push to stand.

"Stay put, Grace—there's dessert," Addy says.

"Oh, how am I supposed to fit another bite in?"

Lawson leans forward. "Trust me, you'll manage when you taste Ma's—"

Addy slaps him, hard.

"Jesus, Adds. A *shush* would have done. Vicious woman."

"Not our Addy." Harry laughs.

"Pretty sure you're thinking of me, Laws." Ruby gives him a sly expression followed by raised brows. Lawson holds his hands up in a *don't shoot* pose.

This family is incredible. Sometimes I can't believe I got so lucky as to end up here. It makes me wonder if I will ever find this again. If I move on, what would I find? I'm guessing my odds of finding a man like Mack and a family like his would be slim to none.

"Hap-py bir-th-day," Harry starts singing in a low melody, "to you." The rest of the table joins in as Hudson and Reed return. Reed is holding bowls and spoons, and Hudson holds the tallest, most decadent layered chocolate cake I have ever seen with sparklers blazing. The song continues and Mack stands and moves behind me. Hudson sets the cake in front of me. A 21.5 is piped onto the top with hearts of white chocolate adorning the circumference. I slap a hand over my mouth.

Mack leans down and whispers against my ear. "Make a wish, gorgeous girl."

"I don't think I can blow out sparklers."

He raises a brow, so close. Every set of eyes is homed onto us. My face flushes.

"Grace, ask for what you want. I promise I'll do my best to make it happen."

I turn to face the sparklers. Their glittering bursts fill my vision, and it blurs a little. Warm hands rest on my shoulders. I grip them both with mine and close my eyes. I make my wish. One I would do anything to have come true.

After the last six months, it's all I want.

Opening my eyes, I tilt my gaze up at Mackinlay. "Done."

Louisa hands me a large knife.

"You hit the bottom, you kiss the nearest boy," Reed hollers, hands cupping his mouth.

Lawson shakes his head. "You talking about yourself there, little brother?"

Hudson tosses his head back with a hearty laugh. Ruby tosses a scrunched-up napkin at Lawson's head.

I make the first cut, and the knife hits the bottom.

"Pretty sure that's the bottom," Reed mutters, nodding to Mack with wide eyes.

"Damn straight it was." Mack bends down, taking my face in his hands, planting his mouth to mine. Cheers explode around the table. Mack's slow, gentle kiss pulls me in, and I don't want it to end. I open for him, and he deepens. Eventually, both of us breathless, we part.

The surprised and ecstatic faces that I find around the table send a stone into my throat. I wasn't sure of the reception I would get if his family found out about Mack and me. *Thrilled* is the last thing I expected. But that's what they seem to be.

"Would you like me to serve the cake for you, hon?" Louisa says, beaming.

"Sure, I have no clue how to do it without messing it up."

She slides the cake plate toward her over the table and plunges the knife into the tower of chocolate layers over and over, until everyone has dessert at their place.

I fork a bite from the plate to my mouth.

Oh . . .

I swear to god.

This is like chocolate velvet. Rich and exquisite.

"Louisa! This is incredible!" I mumble with my mouth full, one hand covering my lips.

Lawson laughs. "No turning back now, Gracie."

I swallow. "Nope. You've ruined all other chocolate cake for me from this bite on."

"I'm glad you like it. It's my birthday gift to you, sweetheart."

"Thank you." Tears threaten again. Knew it was going to be a long night.

"Oh! Speaking of gifts, it must be present time." Reed springs from his seat and shuffles past Ruby. We finish our cake and, one by one, each member of the Rawlins family disappears until only Louisa and I are left. I run the fork over the plate. This is the best birthday I can remember in a long time.

"We have all put together something for your special day, hon. Hope that's okay?"

"You shouldn't have. This is too much."

She shuffles closer. "It's just the right amount." The smile that lights up her face is pure love.

A voice clears behind me. I turn in my seat to find Reed with an envelope in his hand. He holds it out to me, and I stand to take it. "Reed, thank you."

"You might take that back when you see what it is," he says with a chuckle.

"Um, okay?"

Ruby walks up behind him, as do the others. I open the envelope. A receipt sits in my hand. For the craft shop in town.

"$599.00. What? No, Reed!"

"Well, when I ordered your supplies, Doris kind of hit too many zeros. So, you are now the proud owner of a *pallet* of canvases. Like a huge freight, wooden palette, not the type you hold in your hand. About one hundred and fifty of them blank cloth-framed rectangles." He gives me a cringy, sorry-I-messed-up smile. "Paint your heart out, Gracie."

"Holy hell!"

"It's nothin', happy birthday."

I hug him and he bows out to let his wife through as I place the slip of paper back into the envelope and lay it on the table. Ruby hands me a blue box with silver ribbon, about the size of a shoebox. I pull the ribbon and slip it over the side. Lifting the lid, blue tissue paper lines the inside. I lift it and find a smaller box. Perfume and . . . A brush set, with wooden handles, rose gold metal crimping holding luxury bristles. "Oh wow, Ruby . . ."

"The perfume is Versace. Since a little birdie told us your favorite color is blue." She dots a kiss on my cheek and moves aside to let Lawson through.

He hands me a long parcel wrapped in blue polka dot paper. I guess everyone got the memo about blue. He hugs me and says, "Happy birthday, Grace." I rip the paper off to find a new yoga mat and block. Also blue.

"Lawson, thank you." I chuckle, beaming at him.

With a grin, he messes up my hair with one hand and takes his seat at the table.

Hudson is next. And by the size of the enormous,

almost-wrapped gift he is lugging toward me, I'm getting an easel. I bounce on the balls of my feet. He hands it to me with an enormous grin. "Happy birthday. If it ever needs fixin', send it back to its maker."

My eyes widen. "You made this?"

"Yes ma'am."

I hug him awkwardly, not wanting to let the easel fall.

"Open it, Grace."

I pull the paper from it and run a hand over the smooth wood. It's perfect.

"It's oak, so it should see you out, I reckon."

I fight back the tears. God, I am a mess. A blubbering, stinking mess. *How to tear Grace Weston apart: just add kindness.* "Thank you!" I kiss his cheek, and he nods with a smile and drops down beside Lawson.

Harry steps up and pulls me into a hug before holding me at arm's length. "You're a strong soul, Grace. You are in the right place." He hands me an envelope. "So, make sure you use the return ticket."

My mouth hangs open. He nods to the envelope. I slip a finger under the edge and rip it open. Tickets to Pennsylvania. Home. To my parents.

My hands shake around the paper. My chest tightens.

"Oh, there's something else." Harry turns me by the shoulders to face the side of the house. The faint clip-clop of hooves closes in, drifting toward me through the dark.

No . . .

Addy appears with a bay gelding. Saddled up and walking, head swaying, ever so relaxed.

His muzzle meets my palm, and I return my focus to Addy. She beams. "He's all yours while you're here. Grace, meet Sergeant."

He nickers as I run a hand up his face and into his forelock. An arm wraps around my shoulders. "Now, I know you and Trig have a thing. But give old Sergeant a go, hey. He's his older brother." Mack kisses my cheek and winks at me.

"I can't . . ." I choke. "This is all too much."

I turn to face the family seated around the table, shaking my head. "I don't—"

Tears stream, hot and fast, down my face. I try and fail to hold them back, pressing a hand over my mouth. Louisa comes to where I stand and takes my hands in hers. "It's just the right amount." She's nodding, tears lining her eyes. I look to Mack. His jaw is clenched, like he's fighting a sob back, the same as I am.

Harry comes to my other side and drops his head. "If you can take one more hit, darlin' . . . we have one last surprise."

Headlights swing past the house, lighting up the driveway, as a car pulls up beside the white gate. Hudson is up and walking for the newcomers a second later.

"Hold my hands, gorgeous girl. This one's from me." Mack folds himself around me, his chest at my back, and crosses our arms over my chest. I slam my eyes shut. Bracing myself.

Grass crunches.

"Breathe, Gracie," Mack whispers. "Just keep breathin', okay . . ."

A whimper comes from whoever the new arrival is.

"Grace?"

I would know that voice *anywhere*.

Chapter Nineteen

MACK

The woman, the exact likeness of her daughter, falls apart where she stands. Her husband stands, hand behind his back, face unreadable. Grace goes limp against my chest as she hauls in a lungful of air. My heart is crushed between two boulders.

"Mama," she sobs.

Grace looks up to me, her face wrecked. Eyes red rimmed. Breathing shattered. Face contorted. I release my hold on her. She flies into her mother's arms. Both women sink to the ground. Raspy breaths of my own slip past my lips. Happiness never hurt so bad before. Laws wraps an arm around my shoulders. "Excellent work, little bro."

I can't respond.

He grips my neck and pulls me in for a side hug. I

wasn't prepared for Grace's wrecked face when she saw her mom. I've never lived through not having mine. Not one day. I suck in a breath and shake my brother's arm loose. "They all but abandoned her once. But she's been missing them so much. I couldn't let her go another month without her mom. We'll see, Laws."

"She'll work through it. She's strong. Already proven that. And you're forgetting the most important part." He slaps my back proudly, despite me putting distance between us. "She has you."

I huff a strangled laugh. "Not so sure I'm much of an asset."

"Maybe not before. But now? Buddy, you have come a long, *long* way."

"I couldn't have done it without her."

"Sure you would have. Grace's way was quicker, though."

I slam a fist into his shoulder, and he chuckles before striding over to introduce himself to Grace's father who stands watching still. He still hasn't engaged his daughter. Laws offers a hand, and he shakes it. I can't hear what they're saying. They glance over at me in unison, and my ears turn to cinders.

Grace's dad steps around the two women, who are fiercely hugging, now en-route to me. Whispers and sobs exchanging back and forth. I brace myself. Whatever he has to say, his argument better be a fuckin' stellar one, after leaving Grace to fend for herself. What kind of parent does that? It was Ma who finally made the call to the Westons, with me being in two minds about it. But I trust her judgment, and with my permission, she picked up the phone and worked her mother-knows-best magic.

"Mackinlay?" He squares up with me, and I set my shoulders back.

"Sir." I offer a hand.

"Brian." He shakes it. Firm and brief.

"I take it this is your initiative?" He lets his focus wander around the lit-up yard. But the smile on his face doesn't reach his eyes, and I study his reactions.

I glance to Grace. She's somewhat recovered and is drying her face with a tissue. The shock of seeing her mom must be wearing off, because she is closing up as the seconds tick past. I force myself to stay rooted to the spot and let her fight her own battles. Even though I would be her human shield, any day of the week. I shift my attention back to Mr. Weston. "Yes, sir. You three have a lot to talk about. But not all of it is going to be easy to hear."

His face slackens and he turns to look at his only daughter. "She—"

I raise a hand. "Your daughter deserves the explanations. Not me."

I wave a hand in her direction, and he gives a shallow nod before walking to where his wife and daughter stand.

I need to give them space. But I don't want her to think I abandoned her to them.

"Gracie?" I call out.

She excuses herself and pads to where I stand. Her face is blotchy, her eyes red. "You okay?" she whispers.

I shake my head. "Gorgeous girl, I'm not the one I'm worried about. I'm goin' to head inside and give you guys some time and space. I'll be right inside. If you need me, just say, and I'll be right back here."

She huffs a small laugh and lays a hand over my heart. "How are you this wonderful to me?"

My throat closes over. How is being loved such a foreign concept to this beautiful woman? She pats my chest lightly and forces a smile before turning back to her parents.

"We can sit at the table. There are some things I need to tell you."

"Sure, sweetie," her mom says, glancing at Brian.

I wait until they are seated before heading inside to find my own family seated around the kitchen table, a mug of coffee or tea warming every set of hands. They all stare at me, expectantly.

"Well?" Ma says.

"They're talking."

"Good, that's good. Right?" Addy says.

"I sure hope so. The poor girl has been through so much," Ma says, gaze directed into her mug.

Harry leans over and grips her wrist. "Our Gracie is a strong one. She will be fine."

Our Gracie. Like we get to keep her. Like she's not going to go off and have a big, wonderful life and leave all this behind. I mean, her housekeeping job is a front as it is now. Without another job, she's going to need to move on.

Reed pulls a chair out by his and I sink into it, dropping my head into my hands, fingers wedging into my hair.

"You alright there, gunny?" Reed asks.

I can't face them. All this effort, and she may not even stay. I don't want her to stay and have nothing. I want more for Grace.

Eventually, I look up. Hudson leans back on his seat and drains his coffee. "Well, you want my two cents, Mack?"

"Sure, Huddo, go for it."

"It is better to have loved and lost than never to have loved at all." He smirks at me.

"Ha ha," I huff.

"If you wanted it, then you shoulda put a ring on it," Rubes sings.

"Not funny, Robbins."

"Ha, it's Rawlins, remember? *He's* smart, he put a ring on it."

My family cracks up with laughter. Despite their overzealous romantic notions, my family will always have my back. And Grace's. Maybe they're right. Still, we're not there yet. Nowhere close. I would marry that girl in a heartbeat. But she deserves better. Deserves the time to fall. The time to recover from the last asshole who broke her to pieces.

"Leave him alone, you lot. One kiss does not equal a marriage proposal." Ma gives everyone her well-worn warning glare. Harry smiles as if knowing something the rest of us don't and folds his hand over Ma's.

The sound of raised voices has everyone stilling in their places. I'm out of my chair faster than a bolting horse, out the back door and rushing toward Grace a few seconds later. She is standing by her chair, bent forward and arms hugging her body. Her folks stand, trapped between the bench seat and the table.

Fuck.

"Gracie!" I growl, putting myself between her and them. My ire is directed at her lousy parents. "What the hell did you do?"

Fine hands grip my right wrist. Grace huddles into my side. She's shaking.

Heat plummets through my core and twists in my veins like barbed wire.

"I asked you a question." I'm looking directly at her father.

He has the audacity to wave two hands in the air like we are the ones overreacting. "Now, we should all calm down. We're simply stating Grace's choices were her own."

My jaw grinds shut. I turn to face Grace. "Go inside."

"I tried to tell them . . ."

"Now, gorgeous girl. I'm not askin'."

She nods and I plant a kiss to her forehead, holding her to my chest briefly before turning her on her feet and ushering her toward the back door. As she clears the door, I spin back.

Her mother is staring at the ground. Her face is almost as distraught as her daughter's.

So, I fire at the patriarch—what a fuckin' joke—of their messed up little family.

"Do you have any idea what it cost your daughter when you washed your hands of her?"

He tilts his chin up. "Like I explained to *our* daughter, those were her choices, son."

I step forward. "I am *not* your son. And you are grossly out of line. Instead of protecting your only daughter, your *only child*, and swallowing your fuckin' pride, you chose to let her fend for herself in a world she was *not* prepared for. Hold up, there's a choice. You chose to abandon her when she needed her parents the most. News flash, asshole, you never stop needing your parents. The roles may change over time, but they still exist. She went through hell and had *no one*. Not a single fuckin' soul. Not one miserable person to help her. So, you can take your pride and your ridiculous standards and get the hell outta dodge. You ain't welcome here. Not now. Not ever. Get back in your car, and fuc—"

A firm hand clamps down on my shoulder.

Harry.

"Your son needs to watch his language and learn some respect," Brian hisses.

"Like you watched over your daughter? Respected your daughter?" Harry growls. "You heard the man." His gaze drifts to me and back to the worst parents on the goddamn planet. "Leave."

Helena speaks up now. "I'm sorry, Mackinlay. I really thought we could move past this." She glances at her husband, but then her eyes drop. It occurs to me *he's* the roadblock here. He's the reason Grace could never see her mother and was disowned. Rage flares in my core. My hands turn to fists.

"I don't see anyone movin'." Harry sets his shoulders back.

It takes everything I have not to slam my fist into Brian's snotty face.

"Well, this was a colossal waste of a trip," Brian says, grabbing up his wife's hand. She falters, struggling to keep up with his long gait as he stalks back to the car. When the car starts up and drives away, Harry turns to me.

"Not too bad for a first mate, son."

I can't help the strangled chuckle pushing up my throat. God, I was so close to decking the asshole. He can take a damn number. Along with anyone else who ever puts a foot wrong around Grace.

Line the fuck up.

No fucker is going to make it past this wall. She's mine to protect and love. And I don't plan on wasting another second doing anything else.

Grace is quiet on the ride home. The truck is loaded up with her gifts and leftovers that are gonna feed us for weeks. But it's hard to say no to Ma. Harder tonight, after the gigantic clusterfuck with Grace's parents.

I know my mother, and she will be housing guilt somethin' fierce over this. The copious amount of leftovers is her way of trying to make things better. It was all Ma could do. I'm not sure what will happen now, but until the Westons take the time to listen to Grace, they are not welcome. She has gone too long without someone lookin' out for her.

"Do you think they'll get a flight straight away?" she says softly, looking out the window into the darkness flying by.

"Reed and Ruby put them up." I wish they hadn't, but Laws insisted burning bridges is not going to help anyone. A trace of the anger I felt standing in front of her douchebag of a father remains. I tamp it down. My focus can't waiver from drivin'.

"Oh." Her hands wring in her lap.

"You did nothing wrong, Grace. Not a damn thing."

The Chevy hits a pothole and the rig shakes. A flash of green and grey whips through my mind. Frowning, I grip the wheel tighter. That hasn't happened for a few weeks. I thought I was making progress. I can only put it down to getting riled up over this whole shitshow. Like hell I'm lettin' that two-bit hack of a man make his daughter cry—again.

"What are you thinking about, Mackinlay?" Her face is tight with concern.

"Ah, nothin' much." I give her my best smile.

She gives me an incredulous face and cants her head. "Sure, *nothin' much* has you white knuckling the wheel there."

I glance down at my hands that are indeed strangling the wheel, and my grin slips. I loosen my grip and force the smile back onto my face. After all, it's the girl's birthday. *Don't screw it up, Mack.*

Just don't.

"You wanna head to bed when we get home?"

"I am a little tired," she says, directing her gaze straight ahead.

A smile pulls up on her lips. Her breaths quicken.

"I can organize this stuff and then we can sit on the porch and unwind if you want?" I offer.

"You're not carting this all in by yourself. Don't be chivalrous on my account." She gives me a playful sideways look with the prettiest smile, but her face flattens a moment later.

"It's not chivalry I've caught, gorgeous girl."

Her mouth gapes and her gaze sticks to mine. I swear she stops breathing.

"It's okay, Grace. I don't expect anything in return." I return my focus to the road. Half not wanting to see her final decision about what's alternating over her face. Half out of self-preservation—okay, just preservation, an accident with her in the vehicle is not in the cards. Not if I have anything to do with it.

Silence hangs between us for the remainder of the drive. When we finally turn into the drive for the ranch, I pull up close to the house to unload. Grace is out her door before I can kill the engine.

Damn.

Too far, Mack. Should have kept my mouth shut. I all but declared my undying love for her. It's one thing to fool around and make each other feel good. Another thing entirely to fall for someone this deep.

Sweet Jesus, I'm an idiot.

I'll be lucky if she hasn't already packed her shit by the time I make it inside. I shut off the truck and grab up my hat and wander toward the house. Unloading the leftovers is the last thing on my mind now. I jog up the few steps onto the porch and fly through the door. The house is quiet. The kitchen light on. Grace's light is on, but her door is closed.

"Fuck," I breathe, running a hand over my face.

I dump my hat on the hook over the front table, toe off my boots, and shut the front door. I'm going to have to bring in the leftovers at least. Unable to ignore the pull propelling me down the hall to her door on socked feet, it's all I can care about. I stop at her door, trying to find something to say to undo what I did in the truck.

No. Hell no. I meant every damn word.

She doesn't have to feel the same way. But it sure as hell doesn't make what's consuming me go away.

The door opens and she stands on bare feet, makeup smudged. Her breaths are too shallow. Her hand is still on the doorknob, the other one sitting on her hip. Her face is stone.

Jesus.

I dip my head. "I—"

Two fingers press over my lips, hard. She closes her eyes and sucks in a breath. "Let me say this before I don't have the nerve."

It's all I can do to nod.

She studies my face for a heartbeat before letting her fingers fall away. "I'm not indifferent to you either, Mackinlay." She sighs. "I haven't done this before. A functional, loving relationship. And the last thing I want to do is hurt you. That would kill me."

My heart flings against my ribs like shrapnel fired from a canon.

She worries her lip through her teeth. "There's something else . . ."

I grip the doorframe above my head and shutter my eyes. "Just say it, Grace," I rasp.

A wobbly breath huffs.

She sniffs, but her warmth closes in. A hand rests on my chest, over my heart. Then the other beside it. The blood thundering in my head is too loud. I open my eyes to drown it out. Her face is broken.

"I don't know *how* to love you," she sobs. "Not the way Addy loves Hudson, or Ruby loves Reed. I've never had that. After . . ." Her face twists. "I think I'm broken. Apart from acting on every whim I have when you're around, and sometimes when you're not, I don't know the rules. Where to even start." She swallows. "I—I want you to have that kind of love . . . so much it hurts."

I stare at her.

The stalled-out air in my lungs burns. I swallow past the rock wedged in my throat. My hands fall from the doorframe and around her face. I open my mouth to say something, no sound comes. She's all heart, this girl, but right now she's letting her head lead. It's steering her off course something fierce.

"Gracie," I choke out. "Follow your gut. Your heart. It hasn't put you wrong lately."

"What if it doesn't work out? What then? You go back

to sitting on the floor in the middle of a laundry detergent storm?"

She thinks she's responsible for my actions?

Fucking hell.

"Beautiful, the only thing I am going to do if you leave is be grateful you were ever here. That I had the chance to live my life with you in it, even for a little while."

She sobs, screwing up her face, desperately trying to stem the tears.

I press my forehead to hers. "I'm not gonna lie, not having you around would suck."

She huffs a strangled laugh.

"Gorgeous girl, my heart is all yours. For however long you want it."

Her trembling fingers trace my jaw, and I lean away a little as those blue eyes follow where they go. I fight back my own emotions as they clog up the rest of the words I want to say to her. But tonight has already been enough.

"Come on, let's bring your cake inside. We can't leave that to spoil."

"Never, but . . ." She takes a quick deep breath and grips the opening of my shirt. "Come here, first."

I move into her space. Her arms slide around my neck. "I think I have what you caught, too. So, I'm going with my whims from now on."

I smash my mouth to hers. She opens, soft but hungry. This time, the tug between us is so much more intense. As if changed somehow. My hands capture her face. Hers work into a tangle in the opening of my shirt. My cock is hard instantaneously. The effect this girl has on me is something otherworldly.

Her fine features.

Her laughter.

Her tears.

Her strong and determined ways.

Her heart . . .

She's all heart, my Grace.

Chapter Twenty

GRACE

I pull Mack forward as I pad backward to my bed. Every part of my body tingles, lit up and waiting for his touch. This feels much different to our fooling around. We both know our relationship, or whatever it is that hangs between us, has changed. It's deeper. More all-consuming.

My heart rattles in its cage.

I can't get close enough.

The back of my legs hit the bed, and I break from the kiss, breathless.

He's stunning. All angles and jawline. Dark hair, messed up. Blue eyes, darker still. His chest heaves.

He's hard.

He's strung out.

He swallows.

"Mackinlay . . ."

He closes his eyes and cants his head a little, as if his name on my breath is heaven. "Yeah, gorgeous girl?"

"I don't want to have to ask for you every single time. Not anymore."

Opening his eyes, he meets my gaze, his thumb brushing over my lips. "This will *always* be your choice, Grace. Every single damn time."

"I know. It is. From this moment on."

He nods and dots a kiss to my forehead.

"I trust you, Mack," I breathe. Those words have been impossible for me to say, up until a short while ago. But with Mackinlay, they have never been truer. The mileage we have on our time together is more than most experience in one lifetime. We were both broken. Hell, he could barely tolerate me when I first arrived. Then he bent, and I saw a glimpse of who he really was. It was beautiful.

And now . . .

His jaw feathers. "Good. Because I have wanted to love you the way you deserve for weeks."

I laugh and kiss his lips.

His forehead drops to mine. "Let me love you, Grace."

"As long as it goes both ways."

"See, you're all heart, Gracie."

"You love it." I sink my mouth to his neck, kissing and nipping as I rise on my tiptoes and track a line to just under his ear.

Strong arms sweep me up and I squeal as his mouth covers mine. A heartbeat later, I'm dumped on the bed, and he rushes out the door. A ruckus echoes down the hallway.

"What on earth are you doing, Mackinlay Rawlins?" I call out, propped up on my elbows where I lay.

He returns, arms loaded, and flicks the light off on the way past.

"Close your eyes, gorgeous."

"What for?"

"Just do it." He chuckles.

I lie back, cover my eyes with my hands, and my breathing settles. Small thuds. Shuffling feet. A match strikes, and sulfur lances the air.

Oh...

A scent of rose fills the room. Something light and soft hits the bed. The bed dips by my hip. Warm hands pry the fingers from my face. I sit up and look around, my mouth agape and eyes wide. Candles on every surface. Pale pink rose petals are scattered over the bed, and across the floor.

"It's the best I can do with"—he glances at the bedside clock—"four minutes notice."

"It's perfect."

I move from the bed and stand. Mack does the same. I meet his gaze and slip one finger under the shoulder of my dress. Pushing it down, I slow my hand as his breath deepens. I bare the other shoulder and nudge the dress down my chest. Wriggling it over my hips, I let it drop to the floor. The yellow bra and panties are all that cover my trembling body now.

"Sweet Jesus, you're beautiful."

I wave my hands in an *up* gesture and his arms raise. I lift the hem of his shirt past his hard abs, and he tugs it over his head. I trace a finger over his collarbone. Then the other. Palming his neck before dropping my hand to his abs and reducing it to one finger again. I love the feel of him. He's hard, warm. Sturdy. Grounding.

Home.

I slide my finger behind the button clasp on his jeans, and his jaw tenses. Eyes hooded, he studies my face. As if this is more about me than it is about him. I undo the button and lower the zipper. It's not like I've never seen him naked. But, just like everything about tonight, it hits different. Like this matters so much more than it did before.

I pull the jeans down and he steps out. His boxers are tented. His legs are as tense as the rest of his body.

My panties are beyond soaked. The heat that's been growing in my core has my clit throbbing. I need his hands on me.

"Please touch me. You don't have to ask. Or be gentle. You won't break me."

He shakes his head.

He doesn't want to touch me?

"I don't understand."

"I'm pacing myself, Gracie."

"You want to go slow?" I wind an arm behind my back and work the clasp on my bra.

"I want it to *last*. I want you—"

The clasp releases, and the bra falls to the floor.

"Fuck," he growls.

The sound pulls a whimper through my lips. Taking the waistband of his boxers, I shove them to the floor. Slow is overrated.

This man in front of me is not.

Reining himself in to protect me.

Always, I'm at front of mind with him.

"My turn to give." I make quick work of my panties and lower to my knees.

"Sweet Jesus . . ."

I grip the base of his thick, hard length and slide the tip into my mouth—my eyes trained on his face. I want to see it wrecked. To know I make him this way. He gathers my hair up into his hands as he cradles the back of my head. I take him in as far as I can, pulling back up, cheeks hollowed out. A deep growl rumbles from his chest.

Holy hell.

I send my tongue around the tip and sink back down. Mack tenses, hands turning to fists in my hair. There it is —the face he pulls. The one that takes my breath away. I repeat the action, and his head drops back, the veins in his neck pulsing. Good.

I release him with a pop and push to my feet. His head dips, eyes opening. "On the bed."

I like it when he orders me, too. Like I'm strong and he doesn't have to hold back. Like his control over this overwhelming pull between us is threadbare. Just like mine. Wanting him badly, I've soaked up every close contact. Every time his hands, lips have been on my body.

I'm done having to ask.

"Take what you want, Mackinlay. Because I will."

I lie on the bed with slow movements. He rounds the foot of the mattress and wraps his hands around my ankles. With one quick tug, he slides me down until my legs drape over the edge and he's wedged between them. Hot kisses dot up my inner thigh, and he skips over my hip bone and across to my belly. They continue until wet kisses are planted between my breasts. Over my collarbones. I push my hands into his hair with a giggle, as he trails soft pecks that litter my neck.

It tickles a little. Goosebumps flood my skin.

He nips my ear. "Come on my face, my girl." Warm lips wrap around my nipple next, and I arch off the bed. He flicks his tongue around one and then the other. His teeth graze one breast with the lightest touch, one hand caressing the other. Planted on the other hand, his arm flexes with his weight as it shifts.

I can't form a coherent response.

My heart is literally in my throat.

How have people not suffocated from this much love and affection?

With quick, brief kisses trailing their way back down

to my belly and then further still, his hands grip my thighs as his knees hit the floor. I cling to the bed, desperate to anchor myself before I'm so high I can't find my way back down.

His tongue circles my clit. Whimpers fall from my lips with every stroke he takes. He runs two fingers through my center.

"So wet for me, Gracie."

"Always."

One long, earth-shattering stroke of his tongue through my pussy that ends with him sucking my clit steals my last breath. I shoot up off the bed, sinking my hands into his hair. "Mack!"

He stops and lifts his head up, raising an eyebrow.

I fall back onto the bed. Hands desperate for contact, I fondle my breasts. Heat roils in my core. Growing like it did last time his mouth worked me over.

"Goddamn, Grace."

I track his gaze. It's on my chest, following my hands as they move. I roll my nipple through my fingertips and can't help the moan that follows.

He groans, sinking two fingers into my center.

I moan again, my ragged breaths burning with every pass now. But I don't care. His knuckles bend as they pump in and out of my wet core, and he bites down on my clit playfully.

"Come for me, Gracie."

I arch from the bed again as he tugs at my clit with his teeth and lightning floods my body.

"Ah . . . Mackinlay."

My hips rock with each wave he pulls from my body with his tongue, his lips, teeth, fingers.

I'm empty.

I want more of him.

I'm so damn desperate for him to fill me up. To wake me up.

I tumble back to earth as the orgasm fades, and I sit up. Mack is still on his knees, my release all over his five o'clock shadow. His hand a mess with it. I take his hand and pop two of his fingers into my mouth. Eyes closed, I suck them clean. Evidence that I'm putting the pieces back together every time we do this. Every time he loves me.

This good man fixes what one before him obliterated.

When he absolutely didn't have to.

The candles flicker as the soft night breeze slips past the curtains. The angles of Mackinlay's face are ethereal in this light, his body something akin to a man carved of marble. I know how hard he worked to get back to this place. From a broken soldier to this incredible cowboy.

Mack stands, pulling me onto his hips and stepping around the bed. I cover his neck, jaw, and shoulders with kisses as we travel. He sits at the head of the bed and swings his legs over, abs flexing.

I cup his face. "I can't get close enough," I whisper.

He reaches for the drawer.

"Do we have to? I had a checkup when I arrived in Montana."

He draws my face to his with both hands. I sink into the kiss, raising on my knees. His tip brushes my entrance. Velvety soft and so warm. I am desperate to sink onto it.

"Mackinlay, I can't wait a second longer."

"Slow, gorgeous."

I pull away a little, hands on his face as I sink an inch. "Ah, oh my—"

The air in my lungs burns, disappearing, leaving my chest in cinders.

Lord above, he feels so incredible. So big.

The stretch is delicious. My body vibrates, limbs trembling and hands shaking from the contact. And he's only given me the tip.

"You alright, Gracie?" He brushes a strand of rogue hair from my cheek, tucking it behind my ear.

"Uh huh, I want more."

"All of it?" he rasps, eyes burning into mine. Hunger has captured those dark blues whole now.

"Please . . ."

Gripping my hips, he slams up into me with a raw growl. His chest plunges, deep cycles swallowing each inhale.

"Ah, Ma—" I whimper. My mouth waters. It's bliss. I can't breathe.

My forehead drops to his. "Again."

Body trembling too much to have any control over it, he lifts me from his lap and slams me back down.

A whimper mewls through my parted lips, long and breathy.

His hard stomach brushes over my clit with every pass. He picks up the pace and our breaths smash into each other's—waves over a rocky shoreline in the darkest storm.

My body is electric.

With every move he makes, it wakes up a little further.

My heart and soul were dormant.

Until this moment.

This man.

Chapter Twenty-One

MACK

My heart is set to burst from my chest. This woman, who patched me back up and refused to take my bullshit, takes me higher and higher with every sweet sound that tumbles from her pretty pink lips. The curve of her body over mine. Those gorgeous tits in my face. My mouth waters for them.

Sweet Jesus.

Nothin' on earth compares to my girl. Never fuckin' will.

I clamp my teeth around a nipple and run a hand up her spine, drawing her closer to me. I want to feel her around me. Everywhere, until she's the only world I see. God, this beautiful woman has me. By the balls. By the heart.

Seen my soul? Probably tucked away inside hers somewhere.

She takes up the rhythm between us and I slam my hands on her hips as heat coils in my spine.

Fucked if I'm ruinin' this for her.

"Slow, Gracie. Slow."

Her hands are on my face, mouth covering mine a second later. I open for her like she could just crack me wide.

Who am I kidding? She already did that.

Cracked this broken man to smithereens and meticulously put each piece back where it belonged, one after another. 'Til the man she recreated was better than the original. Every day that follows this one is goin' to be one I use to make her feel as loved as she makes me feel.

"Mackinlay . . ."

She's close.

I take over, raising her and thrusting into her as I allow her to fall back to my lap. She slams her eyes shut.

"Eyes on me, my girl."

Her eyes open, strung out with a silent plea. Lifting her again, I thrust up and slam her down. She tightens around me before exploding in a cascade of pulses milking my cock. I breathe hard, tamping down the urge to follow her over that same edge. Not yet. Not until she's had her fill.

"Mack, Mackinlay . . ."

Best fuckin' sound in the world. Every hard day, every

bit of pain, every setback was worth it to get to this moment. Grace stills on my lap, her chest heaving. I push off the bed and hold her with one arm. I lay her on the bed and pull out.

Flipping her over, I grip her hips and drag them toward me.

She moves backward, pushing against my throbbing cock.

I tilt my head back in an effort to slow my body down. Dipping my head back down, blue eyes meet mine. She wriggles those hips again, cheek pulling at her face.

"Like that, is it, Gracie girl?"

She laughs and spreads her legs. Her hand slips to her center, and she rubs her clit. "Come on, Mack. Don't make me wait."

Fuck me.

You don't have to ask. Or be gentle. You won't break me.

She doesn't want me to see her as fragile. I get it.

So, I won't.

I slap her ass and drag her closer still. I run the tip of my cock through her wet center, and she moans into the duvet.

"Mackinlay Samuel Rawlins, fuck me already."

I slam into her, and the mewl she makes strangles my balls and sends an ache into my chest. I pull out so slow, her legs begin to tremble. The flare of her ribs tells me she's sucking in a deep lungful. Her hair is scattered over her back and shoulders. And all I can think of is the messy bun she wears that I love.

I brush my hands around her shoulders, sweeping her hair in one hand, and twist my wrist until I'm wound into her tangled locks bunched in my fist. Her head tilts back, and soft pants turn her moans erratic. This, this is what turns her on.

"Fuck, gorgeous," I growl.

She grabs my wrist with her fine fingers and cants her ass up further, wanting more. I trail my other hand up her spine and dot kisses to the small of her back and rise with a thrust so deep it's impossible to tell where I end and she starts. She clenches around me.

She's so fuckin' close already.

Sweet Jesus, this damn girl.

"You're gonna come on my cock for me. But I want to see your face when it happens this time, Grace. Not yet, gorgeous."

She whimpers.

I'm cruel. I know.

I'm selfish when it comes to her.

I want to watch her unravel.

I want her for myself.

I want her. Period.

I slow the rhythm and coax a few more whimpers from her before releasing her hair and pulling out. She turns and is climbing me like a tree before I have a second to move further than resting back onto my heels.

"You can see me. Fill me up, Mack." She sinks onto my cock.

I'm not even mad about it. What man on earth could deny this girl a thing? She rises on her knees, until the tip rims her entrance and sinks again. Her breasts bounce with every move she takes. I drag a nipple through my teeth before suckling it to replace the gentle sting I created.

"Mack, I love that. Don't stop, please."

"Ain't stoppin', gorgeous."

"I am so close. I can't breathe. You—"

I would tell her she does the same to me, but my heart has blocked my airways. Jaw clenched, I drag in what little air I can and force my body under some resemblance of control. Her mouth covers mine as I pull a parcel of air into my lungs.

I splay my hands over her ribs as she picks up the pace and breaks the kiss.

Fuck, I barely have a say in what's happening right now. She works me over like nobody has before. I'm desperate for her. I'm a wreck for her. I want to give her everything she wants. I dip my head to her chest and play her hard velvet peaks like a fine instrument with my tongue. One, then the other.

Her hands find my jaw as she raises my head.

Her face twists. Her blue eyes hold mine as she tightens around me and explodes, milking my cock in heavenly waves. I follow.

"Good girl," I rasp.

The growl that leaves my lips as hot ropes shoot deep inside her rattles my chest. She tilts her hips again and takes me higher still.

After the last wave between us fades out, I kiss her forehead. Each eyelid, her nose and then a brief kiss to her lips before meeting her gaze. Emotion takes over her face. I pull her into me and breathe her all the way in.

"Mackinlay . . ." she says on a wobbly breath.

"I know, Gracie. I know."

I hold her for as long as she'll let me. Our hearts have steadied and the trembling in our bodies has subsided when I lift her from my lap and move from the bed.

"Come on, let's get you cleaned up."

She shuffles to the side of the bed. I scoop her up and carry her to her en suite. She wants down, and I lower her to her feet. Flipping the water on, I test it with a hand before taking her hands behind me and walking us both into the warm water.

A loofah and a sponge on a stick are placed neatly on the shower rack. I reach for the loofah and plaster it with her body wash.

Vanilla and peaches.

Who knew?

"You don't have to wash me. I can do it." She grabs for the loofah. I hold it out of her reach.

"I know you can. I want to. Just let me love you, gorgeous girl. This is part of it."

"Okay, but you're getting the sponge stick."

I laugh as I lift one of her arms and lather the soap up and down the elegant limb. After I've done both arms, I drop to my knees and gently wash each leg before running circles around her belly. Soapy trails run over her hips, her pussy, down those long legs I love. She studies every move I make. Amazement tangled with adoration claims her face.

I grow hard again.

I ignore my cock, opting to love up on this woman who deserves every ounce of affection I can give her.

I rise and track the loofah around each perfect breast. She takes a sharp inhale as the fine material grazes over her right nipple and her eyes flutter shut.

"Jesus, Gracie. What have we started?"

"You have no idea how addictive you are, Mackinlay Rawlins."

I huff a laugh and pass the loofah over her collarbones and around her neck before spinning her on her feet to cover her back and ass.

One look at her curves from behind and I go from hard to fuckin' stone.

"You alright back there, Mack?" The amusement in her voice tells me everything I need to know.

I finish up, and she smells like a peach. With a playful slap to her ass, I tug the shower head from the cradle and wash her off.

"Now, your turn."

In a few minutes, her deft hands have my entire body lathered. She takes her time with my aching cock, her hand caressing the tip and the long vein up the center. I slap a hand to the tile, and she releases me.

I swear to god, Grace Weston.

Studying my face, she frowns and pulls the shower head down to wash me off. I sag into the heat of the water, letting my eyes drift shut. The water stops. Fingertips brush my brow, and I open my eyes. Grace's frown is still intact when she says, "You're exhausted. Let's go to bed."

"My bed. You're not sleeping alone anymore."

A smile tugs up on one side until a full, beautiful upward curve covers her face. "You scared of the dark, Mack?"

"The only thing I'm afraid of is not waking up next to you tomorrow morning, Little Miss Sass." I step out of the shower and pluck a towel from the rack and hand it to her.

Dripping water over the hardwood floors, I blow out the candles and walk to my own bathroom to dry off. Running a hand through my hair, I sit on the bed and wait for her. When she doesn't appear, I make my way back to find her still drying her hair.

There's no way I'm spending another minute without this girl. So, like a Neanderthal, I drag her to my bedroom.

A heartbeat later, she hesitates in my doorway. "It smells like you in here. I love it."

I pull back the covers, and she climbs in. I'm beside her before she has time to roll over, and I wrap my body around hers.

"Me big spoon. You little spoon." I tickle her belly with my fingertips.

She giggles and her ass pushes into my groin.

I groan into her hair. "No fair, gorgeous."

"I'm sorry, we should sleep."

"We should."

She wriggles from my hold and rolls over to face me. "Did you just have candles and rose petals lying around?" She cocks an eyebrow at me, the covers slipping down her body. Still naked. Still perfect.

"Nope, they're R & R stuff. Rubes had to store some things here to prevent the heat from damaging them. Ran outta room in their little house, apparently."

"Can I sleep here tomorrow night?" she says sleepily.

"You better."

She chuckles, but it fades out as her eyes close briefly.

"Well, I mean, we won't always be *sleeping* in this bed . . ."

She rolls over and bites my earlobe. I grab her with one arm and hug her to my chest. She squeals but nuzzles my neck. A moment later, resting her palm over my heart, she traces the angle of my jaw.

"Sleep, gorgeous, it's past midnight. We need rest."

A gentle kiss presses to my lips. "Goodnight, Mackinlay."

I wait and watch as she falls asleep. Her breathing steadies to a soft and slow rate. Shallow, almost. Her face slackens a little. Her fingers curl against my chest. I tuck a strand of hair behind her ear, letting the pad of my fingertip glide over her jaw.

"There's nothing I wouldn't do for you, my girl."

Eyelids heavy, I fold her in closer. My chin resting on the crown of her head, my heart wraps around hers.

The overwhelming need to keep this girl safe and loved sends a burn behind my eyes.

Who woulda knew a man could need a woman this much.

So damn much.

Chapter Twenty-Two

GRACE

Two weeks after my birthday party, I'm standing outside the Lewistown Arts Center. Despite the printout of my resume Ruby helped me write up, I'm nervous as hell. She's good at this stuff and makes everything sound so easy. I wish I had her confidence. Instead, I cling to my portfolio with one hand, my bag with the other as I lock up Blue and cross the sidewalk to the large building in front of me.

I have no intention of leaving this small town now that I have finally found somewhere safe and stable. But I refuse to be deadweight. Hence, the job hunting. And when an opening for the arts program teacher came up, I knew I'd be kicking myself if I didn't apply.

Getting to spend my days putting my half of a Fine Arts degree to use is a win in my opinion. But I never finished it, and that makes me nervous. The first question they're going to ask is why. It's for the stupidest reason under the sun. My parents were right about that part, at least. I just never thought that it would be all it took for them to drop me from their lives.

I push on the glass door and walk into the spacious front showroom. The woman sitting at the small counter stands with a smile. "Can I help you?"

"Um, hi. I'm Grace Weston. I'm here for an interview about the arts teaching position?"

Did that sound like a question? Ugh, I can even fake an ounce of Ruby's confidence. Heat flushes my neck, and I grip my portfolio to my chest like a complete idiot. She moves out from behind the desk and gestures for me to follow.

We walk through the showroom, its walls covered in art of all types. My gaze snags on an oil painting of a landscape. I stall my pace, taking in the fine detail of the green hills, the thin, winding stream that flows between craggy rocks and tall piney trees. It's mesmerizing . . .

Maybe I could paint the mountains one day? Camp out under the night sky, and when the sun finally cracks over the horizon the next morning, I would be set up. Easel. Brushes. Blues and whites. Browns and gold—

"Miss Weston?" The small brunette lady's eyes volley between me and the landscape painting. "I can't blame you for your fascination, it's a stunning piece. A local artist, to boot!"

"Are you serious?" I ask, face lit up.

"Oh yes, she doesn't paint much anymore. Once she was a bit of a local legend. I'll introduce you the next time she comes in."

Assuming I get the job, I guess she means.

"That would be amazing. Thank you."

She continues to the back of the room and pushes through the door labeled *staff only*. Down a short hall, we arrive at a door on the left. "Well, this is you." She knocks before pushing the door open. "Your interview is here, Don."

"Come in, come in," the voice of an older man says.

The woman steps aside, and I step into the small office. An elderly man stands at his desk, hand offered over the desk in a welcome. I take it and shake it firmly, hoping I appear more confident than the complete mess I feel right now.

"Don Anderson. You must be Grace?" He smiles and drops into his chair before waving at the one on my side of the desk.

"Yes, thank you for seeing me."

"Of course. We were hoping to find someone to fill the arts program teacher last month. With all the talent in this old town retired, we had no luck. What have you brought with you there?"

I hand over the portfolio that has my resume tucked into the first clear slip pocket. "It's my resume and my art portfolio, from when I was practicing. Not everything I've ever done is in there, only the better pieces . . ."

I twist my hands in my lap, hiding them beneath the desk, as he flips through the oversized pages in the black folder. "I'm used to working in most mediums, but oils are my favorite."

He holds up a hand. "You don't need to explain yourself to me, lass."

Shit.

Damn, trust me to mess this up. A lump rises, obscuring my airways. My button-down shirt, slacks, and jacket are suddenly far too tight. Too hot. Every second drags as he starts from the beginning and goes over each page again. Slowly. Painfully slow.

I don't know what to do with myself. Sitting across from the man who is charge of whether I land a job in a place I have wanted my entire life. Granted, it's not the MET, but it's still art, and it's close to Mackinlay. And his family.

"Hmmm." Don closes the portfolio and clasps his hands, elbows resting on the arm rests of his chair. "I'm afraid—"

The air in my lungs burns.

Calm down, Grace, it's simply the start of the process.

But this job was *perfect.*

Spots filter into my peripheral, and I grip the seat of the chair. Hanging on like I'm at the bow of the Titanic. That moment before Jack tells Rose to breathe in and hold her breath.

"Miss Weston, are you alright? You needin' a glass of

water or some air?" Don's voice slips through the ringing in my ears that I don't remember starting.

I force myself to relax. Noting the things around the room, like Mack had when he had the episode the day I dropped the plate in the kitchen. Ruby's words filter through. *Three things you can see, Mack; three things you can hear.*

A heavy hand presses to my shoulder. I glance up to the worried and weathered face of Don.

Oh god.

If the floor could open up and swallow me now, that would be fantastic. He sits on the edge of the desk and grips the edge with a soft smile, and my breaths come a little easier.

"Now, I know you didn't just have a conniption about gettin' this job."

"Maybe a little. I need this. I will work hard and I'm a fast learner. Art is my dream, my life—"

"Grace, you have the job. And if you had let me finish, I was going to say, I'm afraid you're far too qualified for this small town and this hack of a job. But it's a start. And we would be thrilled to have you as part of the Lewistown Arts Center team."

My jaw hangs slack.

"Honey, it has been a long time since this old place has seen new blood. Can you start Monday? I'd love to revamp both the kids' and adults' classes and, if you're up for it, a daily gallery tour—pending numbers of course—and staff the shop front during business hours?"

"I would love to!"

"Great! Any other ideas you can come up with to generate interest in this relic of a community center are appreciated."

He leans and collects my portfolio up and hands it back to me. "Impressive, Grace. Somewhere down the track, you could paint something to hang here. Gauging by the response it gets, a commission spot on the wall could be yours."

I'm speechless, again.

"Shall we?" He heads for the door. Stunned, I follow him out and shake his hand as we say our goodbyes. Don walks back the way we came as I follow. With a brief goodbye, I push through the doors and spill onto the street. The first thing I see is the black hat. The cowboy leaning on Blue. The bouquet of pink flowers that dangle from his hand.

Deep blue eyes track me as I close the distance, his grin matches the fireworks currently flying around my body. I got the job! I actually landed an art job.

"You got it, didn't you?" He rests the flowers on Blue's roof and picks me up the second I'm close enough. My feet swing as he twirls me around. I squeal and his hearty chuckle sends the warmth that rose in my chest moments ago spilling over. My feet hit the ground, and his hands are on my face. "I knew you'd get it, gorgeous girl. Your work is brilliant. Now to celebrate, name it, it's yours."

"You been sneaking into my yoga room, Mackinlay Rawlins?" I chuckle and brush a kiss over his lips. "Anything I want?"

His hand lifts my chin a little higher. "Absolutely anything."

"Hmmm, I might take you up on that, Mack. But first, take me somewhere to eat. Now the nerves have worn off, I am starving."

"How about Italian?"

I scan the street up and down. His truck isn't here. "Pasta and you? Sign me up! Hey, how did you get here?"

"Reed dropped me off."

He swipes the flowers from the roof and places them in my hands and folds me into a warm hug, soft words caressing the shell of my ear. "Congratulations, my girl."

I turn my head and catch his mouth with mine. Dragging his bottom lip through my teeth, a hand pressed to his chest. "We could skip the entrée, have a quick bite and grab dessert at home . . ."

"You read my mind."

The pasta at Mama's Place was almost as good as Louisa's. Her cooking is outstanding. I wonder if she would show me how to make that chocolate cake . . .

"What you thinkin' about?" Mack says, mischief in his eyes as we drive the long dirt road home. His black hat sits on the back seat. He can't fit in the Beetle with it on. It was hilarious to watch him try.

"Your mom's chocolate cake, actually," I say with a laugh.

"Yeah, that one makes my top three. So damn fine."

"Agreed. You know what would make it even better?"

"No, what?"

"If I could smear it all over you and lick it off."

He veers to the side of the road, pulling the car back to the center a second later. "Sweet Jesus, Grace. Make a man go cross-eyed with that talk, why don't ya?"

I let out a laugh so hearty, so life-affirming, it kind of hits me as the sound falls from my lips. How free, how happy I am. I know I did the hardest part by myself, but this man in front of me brought me the last mile. "Mack, pull over." The words are breathy, strained.

"What, what is it?" He slows Blue and pulls over on the side of the gravel road.

I undo my seatbelt and crawl over onto his lap. It's cramped, but I don't care. "I need to tell you something . . ."

My heart bangs against my sternum. *It's now or never, Weston.*

His eyes search my face. "Whatever it is, Gracie, you can tell me." Warm hands hug my face.

And the feeling is cemented.

"Mackinlay, I—I think I'm falling. I mean, for you."

His face slackens. His chest caves like it took a hit. "Gorgeo—"

He slams his eyes shut, breaths coming too quick. His hands grip my hips. I plant kisses over his jaw. Tracing the angles of his cheekbones with my fingertips. My favorite thing to do with Mackinlay Rawlins. Touch. Kiss. Hold. Drown in.

Possibly . . .

Love.

Swallowing hard, his Adam's apple bobs. "I have—I'm fond of you too, Grace." Face twisting for a second, his eyes light and the biggest grin erupts. I laugh at him, and he frowns as he leans in and nips my earlobe.

"Mack, Hallmark called. You're fired. You're going to have to do better than that."

He growls, low and soft. "Gorgeous girl." Dark eyes find mine. "I already fell."

He pushes me back and forth on his lap. Grinding me over his erection. We oscillate from amused to aroused. It seems to be our constant cycle the past week or so. Right now, I'm not amused. Nipples hard and warmth pooling in my belly at an alarming rate, I cup his jaw and kiss his lips briefly. "I wonder how fast Blue can go . . ."

"No way, we are not speeding home. Besides, the wait could be considered foreplay."

I climb back to my seat as he shifts the Beetle into gear.

I can't take my eyes from him as he puts the VW through her paces. Never speeding, but he's not slacking off by any means. In the side mirror, I catch the wake of dust flying up behind us. Mack looks ridiculous driving little old Blue, his bulky frame folded into the driver's seat. Hands gripping the wheel, making it appear smaller than it is. I chuckle at him. Amusement returns.

"Care to share, Miss Weston?"

"Just the sight of you crammed behind the wheel. You're like a cartoon character, bouncing down a bumpy road in a tiny matchbox car."

"Pretty sure the first time you ordered me into this tin can, I told you that . . ."

"You did." He absolutely did.

He glances at me, a shit-eating grin on his face.

"Why did you let me get away with that, you obviously don't fit." I chuckle again as he flaps his elbows like a bird trying to fly. When he looks at me with those deep blues and says, "You have no idea the lengths I would go for you, Gracie."

The laughter dies out and I sit quietly, taking him in. His gaze drifts back to the road. His face has fallen to something akin to mine. Serious. Contemplating. Like we both knew, but only now realized who we are to each other.

"Mackinlay," I whisper.

He stares ahead for a beat before turning his gaze to me. "Yeah, gorgeous." His voice is raw. The emotion I feel is evident in his words, too.

I swallow back the other confession that wants out, schooling my face to something lighter. "Are we there yet?"

The hearty rumble that breathes from his chest spreads warmth through mine.

"Almost."

"Don't you dare be gentle," Grace breathes. My teeth graze her neck as one hand cups a breast. I wind a hand around her back and release the clasp on her bra. The sky-blue lacy underwear joins the rest of our clothes on my bedroom floor. With an erection that could drive through titanium steel, I am beyond desperate for her. She kneels at the edge of the bed. Bare. Breathless.

Fuckin' beautiful.

"You sure?" I rasp.

"Yes, Mackinlay. I am very sure. And I am not having sex in this bed. Neither of us is that boring."

I loose a choppy moan as she grips my cock, her thumb brushing over the tip. This girl. This fuckin' girl. I lower my mouth to clamp my lips around her nipple, and she arches into me. Using her now-curved posture, I scoop her up off the bed and onto my hips.

The washing machine whirs away as we enter the laundry room.

"Hmmm, I like your thinking," Grace whispers.

The puffs of every word hit the shell of my ear, sending goosebumps over my skin. I deposit her on the machine as it clicks over to spin cycle. She spreads for me. Her wet, glistening pussy so damn ready.

So *mine*.

I hook my hands behind her knees and tug her forward. Spreading her further, I run my tongue through her center.

"Fuck, Gracie. You taste incredible."

My balls tighten with every move my tongue makes through her soaked center. She moans, leaning back and bracing herself with her hands on the sides of the washing machine. The hum of the spin cycle grows louder. I suckle her clit and circle my fingertips over her entrance.

She wriggles.

Desperate for more.

The machine picks up speed, vibrating. I thrust two fingers into her tight, hot core and she arches again. "Mackinlay . . . Oh. My god."

Pre-cum leaks from the head of my cock. With every suckle, lick, and sweet sound Grace makes, I spiral higher and higher.

"I need to come, please."

I lean back and retract my fingers. "I'm not done with you yet."

Her eyes find mine. Mouth agape, breaths so choppy I imagine they're useless. And we've barely started. I guess the drive home was foreplay done too well.

"Fuck me, Mack. Hard. Fast. Don't hold back."

I stand tall and lean over her with a growl. "Beg for it, Grace."

Excitement flashes through her eyes. She shoves me backward with a hand and slides off the machine, onto her knees.

A second later, her hand is wrapped around my leaking cock. "Please, Mackinlay. Fuck me. Hard. Rough. Break me . . . Let me fall apart."

My peripheral vision folds in, the lump in my throat having shut off all air supply. The pure trust in her eyes undoes me. She trembles where she kneels.

"Suck," I bark. Needing her focus to be on something other than being submissive before I goddamn snap. Her soft, lush pink lips close over my aching cock instantly. I slap a hand to the machine. Every muscle in my legs coiled to hold me rooted to this spot. To not let my damn knees give away with the way she drives me insane in the best way possible.

She takes me in. All the way. Her eyes water and she pulls up, sucking and swirling her tongue over my engorged tip.

"Fuck . . ."

"Mhmmm." The syllable vibrates along my cock. I grab up her hair, bundling it up to hold it in one fist. Her eyes flutter shut, and I groan as she increases the suction and slows the rhythm.

Sweet. Fuckin'. Jesus. Grace.

Her hand closes around my balls, a finger rubbing the line between them and my ass. My gut bottoms out. Heat tingles up my spine.

"Hell, Gracie. Stop."

She releases me with a pop, my pre-cum smeared over her lips. Her mouth agape. I want nothing more than to see her pretty mouth dripping with my cum.

Not this time. This time, Grace gets what she wants.

I slam a hand around her throat and yank her to her feet. Her gaze burning into mine, she grabs her tits, pinching her nipple. How far this gorgeous girl has come. From being used as some fucker's plaything and shut down, to so strong. So trusting, that rough is something she not only handles, but is loving. She's come full circle.

An overwhelming, heart-wrenching realization hits me. Just how trusting she is of me. How comfortable we are with each other. How comfortable she is here with me. It's not only lust and adoration lying between us. It's heartbreak. Recovery. Redemption. Friendship.

It's *everything*.

I give her neck a squeeze and back her into the wall. Smashing my mouth to hers, I take what's mine. Whatever she is giving up. Tongues tangled, I swallow down every small, breathy moan she makes. They are like my fuel. My guideposts.

I slip a hand to her pussy, thumbing her clit over, and her moans turn to whimpers. I take those, too. I'd take anything this woman had to give me. The good, the bad. Anything. I slide two fingers into her center. Her legs tremble, her hips bucking as I curl them forward and find that spot that floods her with need.

Breaking away from the kiss, I remove my hand from her neck and slam it onto the wall. "Kitchen counter."

I pull my fingers from her pussy and slide them into her mouth. She homes her gaze to mine as she sucks them clean, licking each finger and diving them back into her mouth, sucking hard. I grind against her. My hard to her soft.

I need to be inside her. Yesterday.

I pull her from the wall and lead her to the kitchen. Her thighs are wet with need. And when she leans over the counter and cants her ass for me, I lose the last of my restraint.

Hands gripping her hard and fast, I thrust into her sweet, wet pussy. Balls deep.

"Ah, ah. Mackinlay." My name is a panted plea.

I wind her hair around my fist again and slap her ass with my free hand. She jerks and the movement is heaven, sending my cock throbbing. Her hands are splayed against the marble top, cheek pressed to it as she looks back at me.

So fuckin' gorgeous.

So damn mine.

She slides her hands behind her, pushing her wrists together at the small of her back. I capture them in one of mine. A slight tug, and I pull her head back a little. Each little moan comes out of a shallow breath, her ribs flaring as she holds my gaze with her desperate blues.

"Fuckin' hell, Grace."

I slam into her and pull out with a lazy pace. She bucks against the counter in protest.

"Chasing my cock, gorgeous girl?"

"More, Mack. More, now." Her words are the closest thing to a growl that's ever passed through those sassy damn lips. I thunder into her. Hard. She cries out, her moans turning raspy.

To remind her who's in control, who she trusts, I pull out excruciatingly slow. My head spins as the fat tip of my cock rims her entrance.

Unable to hold back a second more, I thrust in.

Deep.

Hard.

I do it over and over again, until the only word leaving Grace is my name.

Each breath she takes is studded with it.

Her body shakes under me.

My legs tremble.

The intensity of this thing between us fuels the lightning that's tearing the skin from my bones with every thrust. Every burning breath. Deep in my gut, a coil of tingling heat roars to life.

No way am I falling over this precipice without my Grace.

I tug her head backward and loose my grip on her wrists, sliding my hand around to her belly and straight to her throbbing clit. The moment my fingers find her swollen bundle of nerves, she snaps up in an arch over the counter that would put most yogis to shame.

"Ma—" she whimpers, and it blooms into a cry.

"Sweet Jesus, gorgeous girl. You take my cock so damn good. Look at you. Look at us. So fuckin' perfect." I thrust harder as I feel her constrict around me, swirling my fingers over her clit.

"Mack." Her eyes find mine, holding them as she milks my cock. My cum spilling into her hot and fast, she breathes, "I want it all . . ."

"Then it's yours, Gracie."

I give her every single part of me I can. She eases off the counter to her feet and leans her back against my chest, turning to capture my mouth with hers, her hand gripping my jawline. And my heart. It's all hers.

I pull out and spin her on her feet to face me. Hauling her onto my hips as she persistently kisses my mouth, cheekbones, neck, anything she can cover, I walk us to the bathroom. With the water warm and steam flooding the en suite, I step into the shower. Grace hugs me, her head resting on my shoulder. This moment, right here, is everything.

More than the sex.

More than all the fun we have foolin' around.

More than daily routines, even though I get to spend them with her.

The trust. The raw, bared version of herself she lets me see. That is the greatest gift I'll ever receive. I push the hair off her face and behind her ear to find her eyes. See for myself she is okay. That I didn't take too much. Didn't take something she didn't want me to. Only sleepy, satiated eyes stare back at me.

"Gorgeous girl, we should clean up before you get cold."

"Mhmmm."

I set her to her feet, and she steps back and into the warm stream of water. The bar of soap in my shower is gliding over her body as my focus returns. I've never been this caught up in my head about a woman. Ever. My heart rate picks up, sending blood thundering through my head.

What if something happens to Grace?

What if she realizes small-town life isn't what she wants? I mean, I have no idea what kind of size Raymond, Mississippi is, probably not a metropolis, but Lewistown is *really* small.

She'll get bored with the art teaching gig and . . .

Tingling starts in my fingers.

Grace replaces the soap and reaches for the shampoo. It slips through her fingers and falls.

Bang!

I flinch. Ringing starts up in my ears.

I shake my head. But it sticks.

My hands curl to fists. The water hitting the tiles hisses to gunfire. The sound of someone calling my name is drowned out by the swoosh of rotors.

I cling to the air in my lungs, terrified to exhale, not knowing if the next breath belongs to me. Something closes around my face. Tight. Warm.

Memories, no reality. No, they have to be memories . . . Flip through my mind.

Butters walks away from me.

I shout at him to stay put.

That never happened.

This is not my reality.

I can't find my way back.

". . . Mackinlay . . . plea—"

I smack both palms up the side of my head violently, trying to knock the sound out, and drop to my knees.

A gasp penetrates the swoosh of the rotors. I force air into my lungs.

Out.

In.

Out.

In.

Out.

Something stings my face. I snap my eyes open, hunting for the source. Blue eyes close in. Tight with worry, they search my face in erratic passes.

"Oh my god, Mackinlay . . . where did you go?" Her voice shakes, her reddened palm shaking by her side where she kneels on the hard tile in front of me.

"I—"

I haven't had an episode like that since before Grace arrived. Sure, I had that small thing with the plate. But nothing like this since the hospital. I was doing great. I thought I was okay. Thought I'd moved past it. I got caught up in my head. About Grace. More specifically, the absence of her. And it's the most helpless I have felt since the explosion. It was the sensation of absolute desperation my brain must have linked to the only other similar experience it could.

A sob claws its way up my throat.

No way in hell do I want to associate Grace with any of it. She is the reason I made it this far.

Fuck.

Tears fall, hot and fast, down my burning cheeks.

No, fuck.

"I don't want to lose yo—" The words fall apart with my face.

Her hands close around my face before the next heartbeat. Her face twists with devastation. "Hey, you're okay. I'm right here. You're home. You're safe. Mack." Her forehead drops onto mine. "I am not going anywhere. You're stuck with me, sweet man."

"What if I can't get past this, Grace?"

"You will. You have—it's only a relapse. I read that can happen. With time, they get further and further apart. I *promise* this will get easier."

"You read up on PTSD?"

"Of course, came with the job description. Louisa sent me some light reading." With a soft smile, she snuggles into me, wrapping her arms around my neck.

"Course she did."

Ma is always taking care of her family. Where the hell would any of us be without her?

When I've relaxed enough to drop my head on her shoulder, Grace raises to her feet and drops a hand down. "Come on, shower and bed. I want you wrapped around me. That comes with *your* job description, Mack."

Grace is always pulling me up and along with her. Not letting me wallow. Making me do the hard yards. She sees me. She raises me one up and expects me to do it for myself. And I do. But deep down, I do it for her. There will never be a time when I will be able to deny this girl the things she asks for.

Not one moment in time.

Chapter Twenty-Four

GRACE

It's a good thing I'm not taking the Rawlinses' hard-earned money anymore. Because my *caring* for Mackinlay is as dodgy as it gets. Heavens above, it seems every time he has an episode, it revolves around something I do. At this point, I think time to himself at the ranch is the last remaining piece of the puzzle to let him heal. He doesn't need me holding his hand. Not anymore.

Not sure if he ever did . . .

I'm sitting in Blue, parked by the curb in front of the Lewistown Arts Center. Day one of my new job. Currently, I'm trying desperately not to be swallowed whole by the swarm of whatever invaded my stomach. My hands tremble a little. I keep thinking any minute now Don is going to figure out he made a mistake. That I'm a fraud. No talent. No experience in the art department.

Sweet Jesus.

Huh. The phrase pulls a smile over my lips.

Thank you, Mack.

I am happy to have a new direction. This direction. It's a huge step in the right direction for me. Career-wise and independence-wise. Don pulls in driving an old Mercedes that's from before Jesus and I push out the driver's side door of Blue and grab my purse. I shove her key into the door and lock it, turning back to find Don holding two coffees in a tray with a huge smile on his face.

He's definitely a morning person.

"Morning," I say, shouldering my bag as he lifts a paper cup from the tray and hands it to me. "Oh, you didn't have to . . ."

"The way we start our day is everything. I figure that goes for first days as well. So, here's to a good start." He tips his cup in cheers toward mine. I reciprocate, pleasantly surprised. I mean, living and working with Mack and his family has almost rewired my brain to expect the best in people. This is above and beyond for a first day, boss-employee moment, I'm sure.

"Right, let's get this day rollin'." Don takes a sip before unlocking the double glass doors that mark the front entrance of the Arts Center. I take a tentative sip myself. It's hot but not burning, and I take another. Cappuccino. Lovely.

He holds the door for me before punching the security

code into the panel by the doors. I steal a moment to let it all soak in.

I work here.

I really work in a place surrounded by art.

With people who are as inspired and as obsessed with the industry as I am. Was, I guess. It's been a minute. I'm so damn thrilled to be back amongst it.

"Alright. So, I will give you a more in-depth tour than last time," Don says, waving me in further. "We'll cover the amenities and schedule first. Then, you can wander and explore for a bit while I man the front. But at ten I have meetings, so you'll be on reception and sales. Judy, our last teacher, used to use the computer at the desk to do up her lesson plans for classes."

"Of course. Point me to where you need me. I'm keen to dive into the content. Do you offer all mediums?"

"Mostly. Pottery is out, though. No budget for a kiln. Most artistic processes we can handle. We try to fill most of the classes with skills that are attainable to folks in a few lessons, or thereabouts. Watercolors, oils, collage with mixed medium, etc. You'll find the old lesson content on the computer. Aim for something similar, and you shouldn't go wrong."

"I can do that. And differing skill levels for the kids and adult sessions, I assume. Is there anything that you don't offer the kids?"

"Ah, glitter. The last time we supplied that, we were still cleaning it from obscure places months later. Also, bit of hazard with some of the younger kids, they put everything in their mouths." He chuckles.

I can well imagine.

After a tour of the amenities, he shows me how to log in to the computer, sets my login details up, and hands me a folder of the previous lessons and schedules. A list of resources is also laminated in the last clear slip pocket. Old school. But easy to use.

"Thank you, Don, this looks wonderful."

I slide onto the tall swivel stool at the front reception desk as he excuses himself for his meeting. I meander through the computer, looking through vendors, suppliers, the contact database for local and regional artists, before I come to the lesson template.

"Bingo."

I open the master and save a fresh one under a new name. Fingers hovering over the keyboard, I imagine all the wonderful projects I could set up for the classes. With three adult classes and two kid-focused sessions a week, there is so much potential.

I decide on my favorite to start out.

Oils.

Classes start in January after the holiday break. So, I have six weeks to organize my lesson plans, order supplies, make up the flyers, etc. Excitement bubbles up. It's been a long time since I've had something to dive into with my whole mind and heart. Something that's mine to bring to fruition.

The doorbell chimes. I look up from the screen.

"Happy first day!" the newcomers chime in chorus. Grins all around. Three of the happiest faces beaming at me. Louisa, Ruby, and Addy walk to the counter.

"Hi! What are you all doing here?" I slide off the stool and round the counter.

Louisa has me in her arms a second later. "We are so stinkin' proud of you, sweetheart."

I blush at her words.

Ruby wanders down one side of the gallery. "Wow, these are lovely."

"How are you feelin', Grace?" Addy says, her coat hiding her scrubs. She must have taken a break from her rounds to join the surprise visit.

"Great. Excited. A little nervous."

"You will do great. Plus, maybe you could sell some of your artwork here when you have a chance to wear that easel in."

Now heat flushes my face. I haven't even had a chance to paint a thing since my birthday party. I have been otherwise occupied with Mack. Not that I would trade that time for anything else. Not even painting. But her words have me contemplating.

"I would lov—"

"Nope!" Ruby raises a hand and walks to where we stand. "Grace, before you hang anything here, I have a proposition for you. Can you squeeze in a visit to R & R after work?"

"Sure. What do you need?" She could tell me now.

She taps her lips with a finger. "Later, babe."

"Okay," I say with a smile.

Ruby walks over to where Louisa is eyeing a hand-woven basket, and Addy leans in. "Wonder what that's all about?"

"Guess I will find out this afternoon?"

"Knowing our Rubes, it's something awesome."

Those two are like sisters. I envy them. They are so close. For a tiny moment, I wonder if I will ever be considered a sister to them. If things go the way I want them to, at least. And like it has been all morning before Don filled my head with dreams, Mack fills my mind. It's odd not seeing him all day. He will be doing his first workout around this time.

Ranch work after lunch. He's still easing into it. But I know he's itching to get back to everything he did before.

"Grace, you'll be just what this town needs," Louisa says, walking toward me with the basket.

"I hope so."

"No hoping, Gracie. You're gonna smash this." Ruby steps in beside Louisa, a small handblown glass vase in one hand, a red crocheted scarf hanging from the other. Addy appears at her side with a book on flower arranging.

"You don't have to buy things because I'm here," I say softly.

Addy tilts her head and glances at her best friend and

mother-in-law. "I've been meaning to come in here for ages. I want to set those wildflowers right. So, yes, I do."

"Same goes for us," Louisa says, nudging Ruby with her shoulder.

I ring the items up for each of them and place them in brown paper bags before handing them over.

"See you later, Grace," Ruby calls as they head through the doors.

"See you then." I wave and watch as they walk down the sidewalk, chatting, laughing. They disappear from view, and I sink back onto the stool and start my work rewriting the lessons.

First up, oils.

An hour later, Don finds me, head down and tail up, rearranging the handmade goods on the front stand.

"Grace, would you be okay with a small write up in the local rag?"

"Oh, sure, anything to help raise interest in the classes."

"Great, Billy from the paper will be around in ten. An article will go up tomorrow. Online and in the weekend gazette. You okay if we use your name, etc.? Locals like to know the folks who front places like ours."

"Of course. Consider me part of the town."

"Wonderful."

Billy floats through the entrance doors not even five minutes later. I pose for a photo by the wall of art that caught my attention on my first visit here. Don and I smile and a flash snaps, our picture immortalized, ready for print.

"This is going to be something good. I can feel it," Don says before walking Billy to the door, thanking him for making the effort.

Now it feels like the next chapter of my life.

Pride swells alongside the excitement I've been carrying for the entire day.

R & R Ranch will never cease to impress me. I drive under the overarching sign inscribed with Reed's & Ruby's names. The mountains around me remind me how magnificent this land is. How small we are in comparison to Mother Nature out here. It's humbling. Grounding. Fulfilling, just taking it in.

Nothing could take this day down.

I pull in by the house and kill Blue's engine. Reed and Ruby are on the front porch swing. Reed's arm is wrapped around Ruby's shoulders and his head is buried in her hair. A low rumble comes from his chest as I walk toward the house. Ruby's laughter as she throws her head back echoes through the trees. Heavens above, these two are something else.

"You two look cozy." I step up onto the front porch.

"Hey, Gracie. How's that brother of mine?" Reed asks, his green eyes shining with love and happiness.

"Mack is good. Ready for ranch work like yesterday."

"I know. I don't want him to overdo it too early, you know."

"Yeah, I know. But he's working his butt off to get back what he had."

"I have no doubt." He stands, dotting a kiss to Ruby's forehead as he does. "You two girls have fun. I have horses to feed up."

He slips his hat on and tips it to us as he walks out the yard, heading for the stables. Ruby's gaze doesn't leave him until he's out of sight. *Oh my gosh, my heart.*

"Right!" she says, startling me. She chuckles. "Follow me, Miss Gracie."

"Sure."

Moments later, we are pushing through the front door of the first cabin. The red door and crisp white paint are such a wonderful contrast. I love everything about this place. Ruby stops and stands in the middle of the front room. "You notice something missing in this tiny house?" She waves her hands about.

I scan the space, trying to catch her drift. "Um, sorry, I'm not great at interior design."

She steps to where I stand and rests a hand on my shoulder. "Imagine this," she says, her other hand moving through the air like she's waving at a billboard. "Original artwork, by local painter, of the very mountains that people spend evenings staring at mesmerized in this very cabin, on that very front deck."

"They would pop against the white. I could send you the contact list from the gallery for local artists to paint them."

She drops her hand from my shoulder and shakes her head. "No, Grace. We want *you* to paint them. You're our artist, babes."

I open my mouth, but nothing comes. "I, ah—"

"Before you decide already and turn me down. I'm sure, after a little research I did, you can sell a medium-size original for a nice sum. Also, we don't require commission."

"Ruby, I couldn't . . ."

"Don't make me bring out the Harry, Grace."

"The what?"

"I ain't askin', darlin'." Ruby raises an eyebrow, pulling a ridiculous face.

I laugh at her. "Fine, I'll do something up for you to take a look at."

"The Harry always works." She beams at me. "Now, let's grab some wine."

Not too keen on the wine but ready for another turn in my favor, I follow. We head to the house and into the kitchen where she pours a glass of white for me then red for herself. Footsteps trudge up the steps outside, and she grabs out a tumbler and drops a nip of whiskey into it.

"Stayin' for a little while?" Reed asks, pushing

through the door, plucking the hat from his head and toeing off his boots.

"Sure, how's the horses?" I ask.

"Fed and happy. How's the first day?"

"Amazing." I smile at him.

He takes his whiskey from Ruby with a peck to her cheek. The affection between them is constant. Swoon-worthy, even. It makes me miss Mack with a sudden fierceness. I swallow down the wine and hand Ruby the glass. "Actually, I should head home and start supper."

"You sure? Mack can wait a beat." Reed grins.

"He could. But I'm wiped. Today's been huge."

"Oh sure, no problem." Ruby walks with me to the porch.

"Later, Gracie," Reed calls out from inside.

"Yup, see you later."

"Thanks for coming over, and take your time with the painting. No rush. I have been told art takes as long as it takes."

"Reed?"

"Who else? My plans sometimes lack the finer detail of realistic timelines. Especially when I'm so enthusiastic for them."

"Can relate. I will do my best to have something ready in a few weeks."

"Yay!" She folds me into a hug. It's warm and tight and genuine.

"Thank you, Ruby."

She releases me. "Of course! This is only the beginning, Grace."

"I sure hope so."

She waves me off as I slip into Blue and fire her up. My bag is buzzing. Crap, I forgot to tell Mackinlay I was going here on the way home. He's probably freaking out. I hunt through my bag until my fingers brush over the smooth, flat surface of my phone. I snatch it out.

And freeze.

Not Mack.

Not anyone I want to exchange words with.

But call it habit, or the part of myself that refuses to accept any sort of self-worth. I slide to answer.

"Hello?"

Static is the only reply.

A breath.

"Say something," I say quietly.

The line drops out.

I huff and drop my forehead on the steering wheel. Fear snakes up my spine like it hasn't done since Mississippi. Tears burn my eyes, but I sniff them back. I'm not that girl anymore.

Not ever again.

Tossing the phone onto the passenger's seat, I slide Blue into gear. She rattles down the driveway.

Don't give him airtime, Grace.

Not a single second.

Don't you dare.

Chapter Twenty-Five

MACK

I pull on my work shirt and Wranglers and slide my old, worn belt into the loops. The fit is tighter than last time I wore these. More muscle in my legs. Shoulders and arms are bigger, too. How is it possible my physique improved from being nearly blown to pieces? I guess I put it down to months of recovery, physio, and Grace.

Lastly, I grab my old, battered work hat from the wall by the bedroom door. I don't know what it is about my hats, but I like them in my room. Not hanging by the front door, if I can help it. I slide it onto my head. Dark cream with an old thin leather band wrapped around where the brim and the crown meet. I've had this hat since I was twenty-one. It's like coming home. The familiar. This hat symbolizes who I am more than anything else. More than the military training or the shooting skills

I garnered from my time in the army. Running my fingers up the shirt, I slip the buttons closed as I walk out into the hall.

"Gracie?"

She appears, spatula in hand, in faded denim overalls and a t-shirt, a too-big sweater hanging from one shoulder, hair up in a messy bun. The moment her eyes take in my old work clothes, her lips part and she goes still. Her gaze roves from the hat on my head to my socked feet.

"Mackinlay . . ." Her eyebrows raise over a smile that grows. "Wow. Hello, cowboy!"

I chuckle and do up the last button, closing the distance between us and dotting a kiss to her forehead. Before I have a chance to move back, the spatula hits the floor, and her hand curls around the opening of the old shirt.

"I was wondering how long I had to wait until I saw the *real* Mack."

Her eyes study my face as her fingers brush over my jaw. Her grip tightens and she pulls my mouth down to hers. I pluck the hat from my head and let it fall to the floor, hands cupping her face as hers climb into my hair. I open for her.

I'm all hers.

She claims it all.

I pull her onto my hips. Her hunger grows. Legs wrap around my waist. I turn and plant her against the wall. A little moan slips from her to me. My cock is so hard, I swear I'm going to have blue balls all day after this. I break away, putting space between us before pressing my forehead to hers.

"It's goin' to be one hell of a long day without you," I breathe.

"Toughen up, cowboy. You can handle it." The prettiest little smirk pulls over her lips.

An entire day with Huddo and his horses. After that, my least favorite ranchin' task—and Harry's fuckin' favorite—fencing. I swear it's his way to test the strength of will of a man—how many miles of fencing-related tasks he can pull off in one lifetime. Lord knows, every single one of us has earned a VIP place in heaven for the endless days we have spent on damn wire and posts.

"As long as you're here when I get home, I think I can." I groan and sink my face into her neck.

"I'll be here, and probably messy and needing a long, hot shower."

I pop my head up. "Oh?"

"Yeah, Ruby wants some mountain landscape oils for her cabins. I'm going to make a start on one today. So, I'll be painting, hopefully . . ."

Her gaze drifts away and her head turns a little, as if lost in her own self-doubt. I shift her back to face me with one finger.

"You will, gorgeous. And I will be home to help you get all cleaned up." I can't help the cheeky grin almost swallowing my face. "All day, while Huddo drones on about his horses, my mind is goin' to be cataloging every part of you I love most."

Emotion floods her gaze. Her hands tug my head down. I chuckle, sinking my lips over hers. I press her into the wall harder, showing her how much I need her. Her hips wiggle, and I know the message is received. Sweet Jesus, I could do this all day.

But ranch work waits for no man. Nor does my grump of an older brother. Or Harry, for that matter. Who will no doubt be checkin' in today. I break from the kiss and thumb her cheeks with both hands. "When I get back, we will pick up where we left off, okay?"

"Sure, cowboy." She smiles and snaps her lips around my earlobe.

"Jesus, Gracie, a man would never leave the house with you in it if he had the choice."

"Good to know," she whispers. I watch as realization washes over her face. The moment that the fact I see her worth, and he never did, solidifies from a mere hope to a permanent feature.

She drops from my hips. I slam my hands onto the wall on either side of her head. "Now, gorgeous girl. Go paint. Do it all damn day. And when I get home, I want to see every single brush stroke you've made." My words are raw. Her breath hitches. "You've got this, Gracie."

She nods, but her throat bobs.

"I gotta go." I lean down, swiping up my hat. It slips

from my fingers as she pulls it away and plants it on my head.

"Go get 'em, cowboy." Her words are soft. Heartfelt. We know this is a milestone we've both worked for. The day I get my world back. Normality closing in. With one very significant difference—Grace.

My *new* normal.

I head for the door. Making my feet follow the orders my brain is sending, ignoring the pull to turn right around and hide away with her in this house for the rest of my days. I reach the front door and hesitate. She's leaning on the corridor wall with one shoulder. Her head rests on it as she watches me leave. She waves, her face soft.

I tip my hat and grab the door handle.

It's not the gesture I wanted to leave her with.

When I turn back, she is walking away. My heart flings into my throat.

"Gracie?" My two favorite syllables are gravel as she looks back over her shoulder.

I raise my hand, two fingers tapping my forehead.

She smiles, so damn happy, and salutes me right back. Without a beat, she heads for her art room. I stand, planted to the floor in socked feet still, as I hunt for a breath to fill my lungs. I shake my head as the sounds of her puttering around the room, prepping pots and brushes, starts up. In a daze, I tug on my boots.

Tires over gravel let me know Huddo is here. Right on

time, too. The early morning sun splinters over the mountains as I trudge out to the porch and shrug on my coat. Flipping the collar up, I cross the front yard and push through the gate. Hudson's Chevy and gooseneck rolls in. He kills the engine as he climbs out.

"Mornin', Mack."

"Huddo."

"Gracie up?"

"Yep, gettin' stuck into her art."

"Good for her."

"Sure is. How's Adds?"

"Busy, never stops. You ready for this?"

"One way to find out, I guess."

He cracks a smile. "Let's go find out, then." He walks for the back of the gooseneck, unlatching it before he lets it fall to the ground. Three young horses are tied up inside. He brings the first two out. I take the lead of a grey gelding, and we walk to the round yard behind the barn.

"What's needin' with this one then?" I ask, eyeing the gelding over. He's not as tall as Trigger, but alert, his ears forward and head up as we close in on the yards.

"Daily workin'. Maybe some beast work. He's green, but he's got a good head on him."

"Right."

"This mare is up for auction in the new year, so I need her confident in the field and around cattle." Huddo tilts his head to the mare he's leading as we enter the round yard. I tie the gelding to the rail and head inside to grab tack. Hudson is behind me a heartbeat later.

"Reed says you and Grace are pretty serious." He hauls a saddle onto his shoulder and slides a bridle from the hook near the rack.

"Does he?"

"Is he wrong?" Hudson pushes his Stetson up, wiping at his hairline before pulling the brim back down.

"Not wrong." I handle a saddle, managing to rest it on my own shoulder, and toss a bridle on top. The bit slams into my back and I wince. Not my best idea. But, in my defense, I'm distracted. Anything that involves Grace turns me from a logical, intelligent, hard-working man to a puddle.

"So, she's stayin' put then?"

"Guess gettin' a job in town means she is."

"Good for you two."

He sounds like Harry now. He slaps me on the back with his free hand, almost dislodging the saddle. *Hell, Huddo, more and more like the old man every damn day.*

"Come on, lover boy. Day's waitin' for no man." Huddo calls out from outside.

With a scoff, I trudge after him.

Gonna be a great fuckin' day.

Each muscle screams in my wrecked body. It's been months since I've had to earn my keep on a green horse. Hell's hounds, I'm feeling every second now. My legs burn as I pad up the front steps and onto the porch. The sun is setting, blanketing the mountains in its golden hue as our day finally finishes up.

"You look exhausted," Grace says softly somewhere to my left.

I startle, turning to find her on the seat on the porch, a wine glass in her hand. Light blue overalls cover a white t-shirt, her cardigan hanging loose around her shoulders. Her hair is a mess, the semblance of a bun with wisp aways framing her face, some sporting various paint colors. She was so quiet, so still, I didn't even register her being there. "Jesus, Gracie. Kill a man."

She chuckles and scoots over on the seat before patting the space beside her. I pad to the seat and fall in beside her and say, "Dammit, I'm wrecked."

I groan as she lifts the hat from my head and pulls my head onto her shoulder. "You smell like horse and dirt."

A hearty rumble spills from my chest, a smile stretching my face, as I let my weight sink into her. "You smell like . . . paint."

"Got done a few minutes ago. Didn't get a chance to wash up yet."

I lift my head and lean back a little. Her face sports smudges of color over her chin. Blue is splattered in her hair. Her fingers are covered in splotches of blue and grey.

"I wanna see your painting. Only, I need a moment to relocate my legs."

She worries her bottom lip through her teeth.

I push my shoulders back and take hers in my hands. "Anything you do is bound to be amazing."

"Ha. Says the elite sniper turned pro cowboy."

"Nothing elite about this man, I promise you. Now, show me your work, gorgeous girl."

With a sigh, she stands and offers a hand. I take it and push to my feet. My muscles scream at me again, but I ignore them, determined to follow her as she leads me through the house and toward her yoga-turned-art room. I toss my hat onto the kitchen counter as we pass by. We round the door and walk into the room, and the pungent tang of paint and thinner hits me.

Jesus, she spent all day in here? I double-check the window is open. It is.

She turns back, placing her glass on the small table by the door, and rests a hand on my chest. "Before you look at this, please remember I haven't painted so much as a dot since I left Pennsylvania." Her brows lower. "But I want to show you."

"Grac—"

She presses a finger over my lips. "No speaking until you've looked at it. Fully. And please, please remember it's just the start."

I nod and she sucks in a breath, turning on the spot and grabbing my hands with hers behind her back. She pulls me toward the easel Huddo made. The large canvas sits on its side. I come to stand in front of it against the round stool she sits on. She drops my hands and hugs herself, stepping back.

Fuck me six ways to Sunday . . .

The mountains, as you see them from Reed's ranch entrance, are brushed to perfection on the canvas. The colors meld from one to the next, every detail so damn accurate. It's almost like nature's giants are alive. White caps each peak, the golden grass that sways in the fields below flanks the base, covering the bottom of the canvas.

She nailed it.

"I know it's not to proportion, size-wise, between the natural elements, but I thought the colors were pretty close," Grace breathes beside me. I sink onto the stool and swivel it to face her. Legs spread, I grab her arms and pull her into my space. "You did so good, gorgeous girl. This is —" My throat thickens. She thinks this is not good enough. I can tell by the worried expression she's nursing. The fact she hasn't let herself uncurl from the defensive position. As if that asshole is somehow still able to see this. Like she is waiting for me to realize it's crap and tell her as much. "Your painting is incredible, Grace. Ruby's goin' to be thrilled. For the record, art is most definitely your calling."

Her face breaks.

Fuck.

To prove what I'm saying, I swivel us back to the

canvas. "I like this part here," I point to the dark blue of the valley of the mountain to the left. "And, this bit, the contrast is epic." I have minimal knowledge about art, but I can sure as hell point out the elements I admire. And I do. "The grass . . . I can almost feel it swayin' against my legs just looking at it."

"You can?" she breathes.

I brush a paint-speckled strand of hair behind her ear and meet her eyes that are now silver lined. My heart all but cracks in two at the sight. She puts a little space between us.

"Abso-fuckin'-lutely," I rasp, hands held out to her, wanting her back in my arms.

She forces a smile. It's twisted between pride and sadness, and strung together with the happiness she wants so desperately, but is too afraid to let in. We have come so far. Some days, when our heads get the better of our hearts, we are both victims of old haunts. "Come here, let me show you all the parts I adore." I grip her hips and pull her closer.

I grab up a paint brush, a clean one from the pot sitting beside the easel. "Here." I swipe the bristles over her forehead. It's like I'm painting the most beautiful portrait. I am, because it's her.

It's Grace.

There isn't a thing on this earth I wouldn't do or go through for this girl. I trail the tip of the brush over her cheekbones, one and then the other. "These, so fuckin' pretty."

She huffs a laugh. But her posture relaxes, her shoulders lose tension, and she moves back into my space.

Good girl.

"And these"—I swipe the bristles over one eye as she lets them flutter shut—"do things to me I can't explain."

I drag it over her lips, slow. Her breath hitches, and she opens her eyes. "These sweet lips . . . covering mine, pressed against my skin, wrapped around my—"

Grace snatches the brush from my hand. She dips it into the dark blue paint I admired earlier, swirling the bristles through the satin liquid. Her gaze drifts back to me as she considers something. Delicately, she wipes the tip on the edges of the pot and lifts it out.

"These are my favorite parts of Mackinlay Rawlins . . ."

The brush floats over my eyebrows. I chuckle as her eyes follow the blue as it coats my forehead.

"Shhhh, I'm working." She gives me a mock-stern look. I clear my throat and adjust my seat on the stool, sitting up straighter. Her obedient subject. The brush dips, kissing my jawline, before the bristles cascade over the angles and onto my neck below my ear. Blood rushes south. More so, when her fingers trace the same path.

"And this." Swirls of cool liquid cover my Adam's apple. Her lips part slowly, eyes narrowing with concentration as the brush travels. Eyes dilating as I swallow. I hold her gaze. She puts the handle between her teeth, and my cock is rock-hard. Her fingers flip the buttons loose before she pushes the dirty shirt from my shoulders, and it hits the floor. The next breath I take nose-dives, crashing only to burn out. How many times have I been shirtless in front of this woman? Since day one. But now, it's as if everything has shifted. *We've* shifted.

Everything is a thousand times more raw.

More real.

"Gracie . . ."

The cold bristles press against my lips. "Shhhh, I'm not done. Going to mark every last place."

Gorgeous girl, I'm so far gone it hurts.

So completely gone for this girl.

Chapter Twenty-Six

GRACE

Blue looks good on Mackinlay. My favorite color on my absolute favorite person. I track the paintbrush over his collarbones, and he groans. Dark blue eyes follow my hand before flitting back to my face. I wonder if he's connected the color yet? His dark blues now the valleys of the mountains on my canvas. The depths had to be him. My reminder of how far he has come. Come back from. Just how deep he lives inside my heart these days.

"And this part, is what kept me here. I knew it was in there, all it needed was a little coaxing out." I run the bristles over his chest, right above his heart. I want it to be mine. So much. I'm desperate for this to be permanent. To not wake up one day to have him change his mind, realize I'm not enough, not what he wanted.

"Hey, and you did." His hand raises my chin. Those

dark blues reach my own eyes. I can't breathe. "Finders keepers, gorgeous girl."

Lord above, how does this man read my mind so easily? I huff a strangled laugh. It's as if he can see right through me. "I'm going to hold you to that, Mack."

"Good." Warm hands frame my face. "I can't promise it will be easy, not all the time, Grace. Nothing this strong ever is. Only worth it."

I slip the brush between my fingers, cupping his face, smashing my mouth to his. I open, wanting him in. Wanting him to claim me. Needing him to take what's been his for so long. Strong arms fold me in closer. The brush drops from my fingers to the floor. Hands work my ass before he hauls me onto his lap. He's hard beneath me, shoulders plummeting with every breath he takes in.

"I'm guessing this paint ain't edible?" he asks.

I laugh, my head tilting to one side. "Nope, it's not. But . . ." I lean back and pull open a drawer from my small desk. Fingers curling around a flat tin, I rock back toward him and hand over the watercolors. "These won't kill you."

Cheekiness pulls at his face, his shit-eating grin widening. "God help me, I've created a paint-eating monster," I say, pushing my palms together in mock prayer. Mack stands up from the stool and lowers me to my feet. Swiping up cushions from the small sofa I have against the wall for sketching, he drops them to the floor.

"What are we doing with those?" I ask.

He doesn't answer, simply sending his fingertips over my neck, down my sternum. My gaze follows his hands as they gently work my body. I stand, heart thumping against my ribs, breaths shallowing out. Snapping up a brush, he dips it into the water sitting in the jar by the easel and flips the lid of the watercolors open. "Which color, gorgeous?"

"You choose," I breathe.

He eyes the palette of dulled blues, greens, yellows, and reds, then swirls the bristles through the lightest blue. The brush hovers in front of my chest, like he's hesitating. A thought about my wellbeing no doubt holding his mind hostage. I snatch up the handle, claiming it back. "I need the rest of these clothes off, Mackinlay."

He studies my gaze for a moment before working the buckle of his belt and letting the Wranglers fall. Next the boxers go, freeing his hard length, making my mouth water. "I'm dirty, Gracie. Needin' a shower."

"Better make it worth your while then . . ." I trace the brush over his shoulder and down his biceps, into the crease of his elbow and down his ropey forearm. A flood of goosebumps trails over his skin as the brush moves. I can tell he's itching to touch me. But I'm going to take my time. Make the most of this moment and make certain it becomes a memory I'll never want to lose.

The bristles dry out and the light blue fades out with the next stroke. I replenish the paint and pick up where I left off. Blue trickles over Mack's chest as I move the tip of the brush over each angle, every plane of his body that does something to me. He stands still as ever as I let the tip trail downward.

The bristles bump over the ridges of his six-pack, above the defined V, and his body tenses, chest heaving, hooded dark blues homed in on my face. Beautifully wrecked. The words I would choose to describe Mackinlay Samuel Rawlins in this very second. I refresh the blue again and this time send the head of it over the V, slowly.

A strand of hair falls into my face as I lean down to capture the deep angle. I blow it away and run my bottom lip through my teeth. A growl from above my head sees me swinging my gaze upward.

Rough hands have my hips in a tight grip before I can read the emotions filing through those dark eyes, tugging at my hip. The side buttons of my overalls are released. Both sides. I fight back the smile trying to win over my face at the hungry desperation on his.

This.

This is what it feels like to be wanted.

Needed.

Desired.

Something I thought I would never have.

His hands close around the buckles at my breasts, and I slide my own over them.

"Mack," I whisper.

I'm crushed against him instantly. His forehead

presses above my brow, ragged breaths shattering over my face. "Yeah?"

"Take what you want. No gentle."

Lord, my words barely make sense.

He knows what I mean. He tugs the straps over my shoulders and shoves the denim to the floor and rips my ratty old t-shirt from my body. I stand in nothing but the yellow lingerie that has become our favorite as he draws me up onto his hips, smashing his mouth to mine. A few short strides and I'm on the table by the door, his tongue working me over in long, delicious strokes. I return them, hungry for this man who woke me up. Breathed life into my timid, beaten-down soul.

He pulls back, taking me in for a moment.

"Fuck, Gracie," he growls.

"Please, Mackinlay. Don't make me beg . . ."

I palm my breasts, knowing exactly what it will do to his control.

Rough hands snap around the backs of my knees, dragging me toward him. He dips his head and nips my nipple. The sting is followed by a long, slow, sensuous suck that lifts me, arching my body off the table with a heady moan. The clasp of my bra releases. The synthetic material burns my skin as he rips it away. The panties go next. Not caring to look, he tosses them away, and they land on the corner of the easel.

I pull him down to me, wanting his mouth on me, my lips, my skin. I don't care. His cock rubs into my already throbbing clit. Blood sinks, pooling delicious heat deep in my belly. I pinch a nipple and slide my hand down my stomach toward the ache. Needing to see him watch me touch myself. Wanting him to unravel even further as I do.

Nostrils flaring, he stands upright, making space for my hand. Lips parted, breaths too quick, he watches as I circle a finger over my clit. Lightning floods my limbs with the slightest touch to the oversensitive apex. I arch again, and a whimper slips out.

Something thuds on the floor. My hand is batted away. His warm tongue sweeps through my center. I'm fucking soaked. If I wasn't as wound up as Mackinlay right now, I might be embarrassed. The fact he does this to me. I do that to him. Nothing ever felt more right. His lips close around my clit, and I grip the edge of the table, trembling with every suckle, every movement he makes. The jars of water and mixed paints on the table wobble.

"So fucking wet for me, gorgeous girl. I'm not going to be able to control myself."

The elation flooding me at those words is overwhelming. "I don't want you to. Break me, Mackinlay. Don't you dare be gentle."

With a long stroke of his tongue, he pushes to his feet and grabs me up, his mouth crashing to mine. He tastes like me—it sends me higher. I grab his hand and shove it back to where I want it. His fingers sink inside me a heartbeat later. I moan, arching into him. Fuck.

"Jesus fuckin' Christ, so damn tight."

"Fuck me, Mackinlay. Now."

Pulling his fingers out, I send them straight to my mouth, sucking them clean. Sucking them so hard, my cheeks hollow out. His other hand slams down beside me, rattling the jars. His tip nudges my entrance. I hold his gaze. He pushes in. The stretch makes my mouth water. He gives me another inch. It's not enough. It's too slow. Too controlled. I sit up and let a hand wander between us, fondling his balls. "This is the last time I'm asking, soldier. Ruin me."

"Gracie, you sure?"

"Yes," I rasp. "I want it all. I trust you. Can you do that for me?"

He closes his eyes, still only just inside me. His hands rest at his sides for a few breaths. When his eyes open, the man standing before me is transformed. Hungry.

Wild.

Savage.

I know the second our eyes lock that this is the version of him I am going to want for the rest of my days. I lean back on the table, elbows propping me up. "Do it. I know you want to."

His hand wraps around my throat as he slams into me. So fucking deep. The other slaps my legs wider. He pulls out and slams in again. Sinking deeper. I'm impossibly wet. Every feral sound he makes driving me more and more insane, I meet him with every thrust. The table rocks, hitting the wall. He tilts his hips up and drives in again with a husky growl. I slump, back and head meeting the hard wooden surface. Feeling too much. I'm losing control a little more with every move he makes.

He leans over, slamming his hands beside my head. Eyes burning into mine, he mouths something I can't place before snapping his head down. Teeth sink into the side of my breast. I cry out. The sting. The pleasure building in my core. The contrast sends me spiraling. I claw at him as he picks up his unrelenting pace. The table hits the wall with savage force. Jars of paint and water pots scatter to the floor.

"Fuck me, Grace. The strongest fuckin' woman I've ever known. You've met me at every milestone. Braved the world in the worst way possible. And this is what you give me. Strong doesn't even begin to cover it."

His lips close over my nipple. This time, his tongue flicks around the hardened peak, and I whimper, sending my hands into his hair. Pulling at it as he thrusts harder. My body trembles all over with the current he's sending through me. I moan past his hand as it closes over my throat again. Straightening up, he thrusts deep. Beautiful agony builds, and I snag his gaze, my hand on his jaw. He knows what this means.

"Not yet, gorgeous."

I'm scooped up off the table, and he pivots and lowers me to the floor. Making space between us, he falls from my dripping center, leaving me empty. I fucking hate it.

Flipping me over, he pushes my head into the cushion. Snatching up my hands, he cuffs them with one of his behind my back. My ass is in the air. My pussy so wet that my need is leaking down my thighs.

I turn my head to find him fisting his cock for a moment. He shoves my legs wider and closes in between my legs. Leaning over, he gathers up my hair in a rough-fisted hold and sinks into me. The angle, the depth sees me cry out. "Fuck, Mackinlay."

He's so deep, it's impossible to tell where he ends and I start. Our souls fused together.

He pistons into me. Keeping me where he wants me, one hand holding my wrists at the small of my back, the other still tight in my hair. I'm putty in his hands. I'm his to control. And I fucking love it. Submissive to this man is not the same as to anyone else. Anything else. The willingness to give yourself over fully to another person. Heart and soul. It's an act of trust.

It's . . .

Love.

My breath leaves.

I gasp for more.

Finding none.

Love.

The last thing I thought I would ever find.

And to have found something this deep. This all-consuming and otherworldly . . . I realize in this moment, watching his face fall apart more and more with every strong thrust into me, my life can't go anywhere else but in this direction. I have arrived. Found the place I'm meant to be. The heart I am meant to protect.

His.

I swallow past my tightened throat. As if reading my mind, like he does in so many of our moments, he leans down. Releasing my hair and wrists, he pulls me up to my knees, my back to his chest. His hand trails down my stomach as he thunders into me. His breaths all but gone, his body trembling. I turn back and kiss his mouth. Needing to be closer. Wanting to show him this moment means *everything*.

He breaks away, dipping his head by my ear. "I love you more than you'll ever know, Gracie."

I suck in a ragged breath, and a sob tumbles out with the next exhale. Tears sting the back of my eyes.

Mack's hand squeezes my breast, reducing to two fingers as he pinches the nipple. I gasp, hardly able to catch a single breath.

He growls against my neck. "Now, come with me, gorgeous."

I lean my head on his shoulder, and his mouth covers mine. His tongue sweeps in, stroking. The fire in my belly he's been igniting since I landed on the paint table surges. Two warm fingers find my clit, pinching, swirling across it. I explode around his cock. Each wave tightens. "Mackin—" I jerk my hips against his hand, legs shaking.

Splintering release encapsulates every cell of my body. "Oh my god. Mack!"

"Good girl." He grunts. "Fuck!"

His pace turns erratic. He pushes me to the floor with one hand, slamming into me harder than before. He bends down, fingers sliding into my mouth. I suck them before they hook over my jaw. He slams in, faster still.

"Gracie!" My name is a roar. The slap of his body slamming into my own. Devine. Hot rope floods my center. A moment later, his thrusts die out, and he peels me from the floor. I'm pulled flush to him, sweat sticking us together. Gentle hands search my body quickly, as if checking me over for damage. When none is found, he pulls out. I am at a loss without him. Spinning on my knees, I take his face in my hands.

"Mackinlay . . ." He studies my face, as if waiting for me to tell him he hurt me, his face falling by the second. "It's okay. I'm good. Better than good. And . . ."

"What is it?" His breath hitches.

I kiss his jaw. His lips. Pulling his head down, I dot another to his forehead. Tilting his head up, I meet his gaze. "I love you, Mackinlay Samuel Rawlins."

I'm folded into his hold before the next heartbeat.

I haven't only found my place. I have found my home.

Chapter Twenty-Seven

MACK

Grace sleeps peacefully beside me. I haven't slept a wink all night. I glance over at the clock.

3:07 AM

Jesus, today is gonna be shit. I can just feel it.

Grace's phone vibrates on the nightstand on her side of the bed. What the fuck?

Who. The fuck . . .

I reach over and glance at the screen.

The name glaring back at me, burning out my retinas with the brightness turned way up, dumps a rock into the pit of my gut.

Joel.

Sweet fuckin' Christ. Doesn't this loser know when to give up?

As if on cue, Grace starts murmuring in her sleep.

Torn between letting her rest and moving across the bed to burn the fucker's existence out of her phone, I stay where I am and do nothing.

A small whimper slips through her lips.

I lean back, straining to gauge the expression on her face in the darkness. She's asleep, but her face wars with emotion. I lay back down and pull her into my arms, hoping that by being wrapped around her I will protect her from whatever is plaguing her dreams. I'm no stranger to nightmares I would rather escape. And I would walk into hers if I knew I could save her from that particular torture.

"No, please . . . sto—" A small sob keens from her throat.

Fuck.

I hold her tighter. Brushing the hair from her face. "You're okay, gorgeous. Just wake up."

She writhes in my hold, and I release her, leaving my arms wide to give her room to move. Her hand curls around my wrist. Her breathing is shallow and rapid. "Nooo. Don't."

She jerks and then stills.

A tear runs down her temple, soaking into the sheet beneath us.

That's it.

"Wake up, Gracie."

I grip her shoulders and gently shake her. But her eyes stay shut. Her face breaks. She's crying. Sobbing. I sit up and lift her into my chest. "Gracie. Wake up. Come on."

My voice is a harsh rasp.

Her hands move in front of her and shrink to fists. Like she's . . . protecting herself?

Goddammit, Grace.

I shake her again. "Gracie, open your eyes. Enough!"

The words snap in the quiet of the early morning. She jerks awake, a cry tumbling from her lips as she cowers away from me.

Sitting on the bed, the sight of her afraid of me twists my gut into knots and shreds my heart. *Sweet Jesus.* I open my mouth to say something. Nothing comes.

I extend a hand to her but retract it faster than I mean to.

She hugs her arms around her body and swallows. Tears flow, flooding down her face. Her hair, a tangled mess that spills over her shoulders, is stuck to the tears wetting the sides of her cheeks. She's dazed. As if she has no idea where she is.

"What happened?" I ask. The crack in my voice takes me by surprise.

"Mack?"

"Yeah, Gracie," I force out.

Her face twists with something like regret as she searches my face. "I'm—" A sob chokes her words out. I'm desperate to hold her. To know the look of terror on her face wasn't from me.

"Did I hurt you?" I rasp. My hands fist the sheet by my sides.

Her head shakes. She's still disoriented.

What the hell did she live out in that damn dream?

"You—you're okay?" She sobs, her hand lifting as if trying to touch me but not able to get there.

"Of course, gorgeous. I'm good. What's happening?"

She's scaring me now. I glance at the phone. Has that asshole been harassing her all this time? Is that what had her stuck in a goddamn nightmare with no way out?

"I need—" She tilts her head, her face breaks.

"Come here."

The flood gates open. She sobs, crawling into my lap and curling up against my chest like a little kid. *Fuck me.* I run a hand over her hair, brushing the wet, matted strands away from her face and smoothing out the chaos her tossing and turning created. Tears slide down my skin as she chugs through sobs. I wrap myself around her, like I can shield her from any fucking thing that could ever hurt her.

A muffled request finally reverberates over my pecs, and I loosen my hold. She sniffs, wiping her face before looking up at me with those stunning blue eyes, and sits on the mattress. Something like sadness and fear laces through her eyes. My gut sinks. Shaking my head, I ask, "What, Gracie?"

"He was . . ." She closes her eyes.

"Who?"

"Joel."

Motherfucker.

"He been harassing you?"

"I don't—I mean, I'm not sure. The dream, it felt so real."

"What happened?"

Jesus, I'm repeating myself, but *fuck* . . . I need to know.

"He was hurting you. You were . . ." She runs her bottom lip through her teeth, her eyes tightening with devastation.

"You're okay, we're both okay."

She sniffs again, setting her shoulders back. Tears start again, and she lets them fall. I have an idea of what is coming.

"We were here. But I went out to feed the horses. I came back and he had you tied down. And—" She chokes through a breath, but her eyes stay on mine. "He was hurting you, with a knife. As well as the poker from the hearth. Over and over again. I was helpless. I couldn't help you. Save you. I was watching him kill you slowly. An—all I could think of—" A sob cracks through her words, but she wrangles it back. "We never even had a chance at a life together."

"Fuckin' hell. Come here, gorgeous." She sinks into my lap, clawing at my neck, sobbing into my chest. "Shhhh. It's okay, we will have everything we want together, okay? I promise you. That fucker isn't taking a single damn thing from you ever again. I promise he won't ever hurt you again."

"I'm not worried about me, Mackinlay."

I huff a strangled chuckle into her hair. "Of course you're not. You're the sweetest, most caring woman who ever lived. And I will spend the rest of my life making sure you're never alone or scared again. You hear me?"

I cup her face with my hands and tilt her head back so she meets my gaze. She nods and I plant a kiss on her forehead. Her fingers trace patterns over my chest, and my cock swells. I ignore it, pulling her into a hug and laying her down on the pillow. She rolls over, pulling my arms around her. Her ass grinds into my hard cock and I moan her name into her neck before pulling her tighter still. "Get some sleep. I'll keep watch. Promise to wake you up sooner if it happens again."

"Always protecting me, Mackinlay."

"Where would I be without you, gorgeous?"

"Still sulking in a mountain of laundry detergent, probably," she says with a giggle.

Brat.

I dig my cock into her ass cheek and bite her neck playfully.

She laughs. "Hey!"

"Sweet dreams only this time, okay?"

"Keep up that boner, and I'll be having wet dreams."

"Sounds like an upgrade, if you ask me."

"Absolutely," she breathes.

I hold her until she relaxes and is sound asleep. Wide awake, I lay and watch the sun come up with the love of my life in my arms. I have never been so damn grateful I made it home than right now.

I toss Grace's phone onto the floor. My heel comes down on the cracked iPhone screen a second later. Her eyes grow wide in horror as I destroy the only way that asshole has to infiltrate her life from afar.

"Mackinlay," she whispers, brows knotted low. "Shit."

"Nope. He doesn't get the chance to make your life hell. You're done with the asshole, Grace."

"That's my phone. My only means of communication. With the world. With *you*." She runs a hand over her head. "With work!"

"I'll buy you another one. This one is trash." I bend down and swipe up the smashed phone and toss it in the kitchen bin to drive my point home. She stares at me, her bottom lip worrying through her teeth as she folds her arms over her chest.

"I'll drive you to town for work, grab you a new iPhone, okay?"

"Sure."

I can't read her expression. She's not mad. Not upset.

She's emotionless. Far too quiet. I usher her to the kitchen counter, and she settles on a stool. Pouring both of us coffee, I slide hers across the bench to where she sits. She can be angry at me as much as she likes. I will always do what it takes to keep her safe and loved.

"Need me to run any errands after I drop you off and pick up the phone?" I ask, sipping the hot, earthy brown liquid. She blows over her mug, cooling it before testing a sip.

"I'm not sorry for taking care of you, Grace. If anything, I'm annoyed you didn't tell me this was an ongoing thing. Could've smashed it sooner."

I can't help the small cheeky smile popping up one corner of my mouth.

Finally, her mug meets the counter, and she holds my gaze. "I wish you had let me figure this out for myself. I understand you're trying to look out for me, and I appreciate it. I do . . ." She glances away, sucking in a breath. "I was totally dependent on Joel. That's where I went wrong last time. I won't do that again, even if I know—which I do—you're a good man. It's something I have to do for myself."

Stunned, I grip the mug with both hands.

This girl will never cease to impress me. A lesser person would take the first chance to hand their problems over to someone else. Not our Gracie. Head on, she stares down the ugliest situations in the eye and learns from them. *Fuck me.*

Not even I have the right to say that much of myself.

"I get it. I'll butt out." I put the coffee down. "But—"

She cackles a laugh and turns the mug in her hands as it sits on the counter. "But?"

"If that waste of oxygen so much as lays a fingertip, says one word outta place. I will step in, gorgeous girl."

Now she stands and rounds the counter, placing her mug beside mine. "No. You will let me handle this, Mackinlay. Whatever the outcome. I'm done being dependent. Period."

"Yes ma'am." It's all I can say.

The fire in her eyes renders me appropriately subdued. *Good girl, Gracie.* Don't take anyone's shit, least of all mine. She walks toward the hallway, heading to ready herself for work, I assume. Her retreating back has me mesmerized. I have no doubt she will handle this just fine.

Now, to rein in my overprotectiveness of her.

Because the last thing I will ever do is make her feel less than.

That was his mistake.

Chapter Twenty-Eight

GRACE

I fire up Blue and stow the new blue travel cup Mack bought along with my new phone three days ago in the center cup holder. Coffee secure. The weather is getting colder. Mack, Hudson, Harry, and Louisa are busy on the ranch, herding the cows and calves closer to the barns before the wolves find them.

I rub my hands against the cold, pulling my coat tighter before checking my hair in the rearview mirror. If I make it home early enough, I might even have a chance to help feed up in the yards. The prospect of cuddling a sweet little calf is too much. Today is going to drag. All I want to do is return home and get my fill of baby cow cuteness. And Mack, of course.

Huddled up in their jackets, the Rawlins make a fierce posse as they trot away from me, rifles slung over their backs and hats pulled down against the icy winds that have been up for a few days now. Mackinlay taps two fingers to his forehead over the most gorgeous smile as he rides away. I wave at him, returning the smile. The second in time freezes, solidifying this exchange between us into a memory.

Louisa trails the line on her black horse. It's the first time I have seen her on horseback. She turns back as I pull away from the house and onto the driveway and tips her hat with a smile.

Pretty sure when I grow up, I want to be Louisa Rawlins. Or Ruby Rawlins. Gosh, those two women know exactly who they are. They own it. They have all their ducks in a row. Mine have absconded, died from the cold or ended up someone's supper, I swear. With only work and Mack in my life, I sometimes feel a little like I'm missing something.

Heavens knows what on earth that *something* is.

By the time I hit the gravel road, the Rawlinses are deep into the fields, loping away, heading for another herd. I focus on the road and make town in under an hour. Pulling up to the curb, I kill the engine and down the last of my coffee. The street is relatively quiet for a Thursday. Only a few cars parked outside businesses.

I step out of the car, grabbing up my bag and phone, and lock her up. The wind picks up, and I shiver. Flipping my collar up, I glance up and down the street. A somewhat familiar scent carries on the frigid air. I frown, but don't find anything amiss, or anything to place the scent.

Putting it down to my imagination, I cross the pavement and go inside.

The warm inside air thaws my frozen nose and ears. They burn as blood flow returns. Don meets me at the front desk. "Mornin', Grace. Cold out this early."

"Sure is. I hope it doesn't deter the attendees tonight."

"Doubt it. We mountain folk are used to whatever the weather decides to dish out. You'll have your first class full and humming along, mark my words."

I chuckle and put my bag under the counter. Flipping the power switch under the desk, the lights blink to life and the computer buzzes alive. I settle into the tall stool and double-check the list of students for tonight's first adult oils class. After having all but memorized their names, I walk out back to check I have everything I need, plus a little extra. It's always better to have too much than not enough.

Satisfied that I have everything I need, I return to the front showroom to find patrons filling in through the front doors. They rub their hands together, as I did, chatting away as they peruse the artwork.

"Morning," I offer.

"Good morning. Do you have any of those canvases that you paint on? My grandson fancies himself a painter this week. I promised to pick one up for him," an older lady asks.

"Actually, supplies can be bought at the craft and art

store. We only provide canvases to students in our mixed medium classes."

"Oh, shoot. Of course! Where's my head? Doris would have my guts for garters if she knew I forgot her shop. I'll pop in there next. Thanks for the reminder, lovely."

"Anytime. And if your grandson would like to sign up for classes, we have ones for the kids on Mondays and Thursdays."

She waves a hand and cackles. "Oh, bless your heart. He's thirty, but I'll be sure to tell him about them. What days are the adult classes?"

"Oh gosh, sorry, I assumed . . ." I straighten a pile of handmade cards, hoping the heated flush infiltrating my neck will disappear.

Her soft, wrinkled hand rests on my wrist. "Don't be. He's a grown man, should have come here himself." She winks.

The blush that crept up my neck sinks to guilty heat in my gut. I'm not interested in meeting guys. Now I fear I gave her the wrong idea entirely.

"Well, if you need anything, give me a shout." I hurry back to the front desk and update my new phone number, if only to give myself something else to focus on. I update it on the Art Center's website for the classes' contact number while I'm at it.

Is that the only reason people come in here? To check out the new girl in town? I knew small towns were tight, but this is next-level. I mean, everybody knows everybody, sure. They all know I've been living out at the ranch with Mackinlay. And if that's the case, shouldn't they also know that Mack and I are together?

I make a mental note to ask him about the small-town protocols where romantic relations come into play. Raymond is no metropolis, but Lewistown is literally a speck on the map in comparison. Quaint and appealing in some ways. Outdated and intrusive in others. I mill about until after lunch, when I set up the large back room with eight easels and canvases. Eight lots of paint, palettes, and water jars.

Six o'clock rolls around and the sun has made its retreat, leaving us in the cold darkness of winter's shadow. Don locks his office and wanders to the front doors.

"See you Monday, Grace. Don't forget the security panel before you lock up, hon."

"Of course, have a great weekend."

He's worried about me being here by myself. But I assured him that Lewistown is safe with regard to crime. I'll be fine.

He frowns but leaves with a small smile and heads for his car.

I turn the open sign to closed and have my supper while I wait for the first of my students to arrive for my first oils landscape session. I brought my mountain landscape in a few days ago as an example to show the class.

Remembering I never sent a picture to Ruby, I slide off

the stool and walk to the back room to snap a picture. As I'm rummaging in the room, the door rattles. I startle. Shit.

Maybe being here alone was not my brightest idea. I'll be a quivering mess before the cohort even arrives. I walk into the hallway and make a beeline for the adjoining room. Flipping on the light, I look around. Nothing. Only office supplies and out-of-date technology. The sounds echo overhead again. Scurrying.

I huff a wobbly laugh. Just something in the ceiling. A squirrel or the likes. I press a hand over my thundering heart and shake my head. *Grace, how on earth are you going to own this ship if you can't be left alone in a place that's your every-day? That's safe?*

"Stupid girl," I mutter to myself.

Returning to the back room, I finish setting up. The alarm on my phone rings.

Showtime.

My gut flips.

No, Grace. I haven't come this far to flake out now.

I push my shoulders back and decide to own this shit. Now and from this moment on. Channeling my inner Ruby Rawlins, I open the front door and greet the small crowd of excited folks. A range of ages, from my age to somewhere around the eighty mark, with the oldest man wobbling in on a walking stick. Good on him.

"Evening! My name is Grace. Come on in."

Every face beams back at me with wide smiles.

Of course they know who I am. I usher them to the back room and wait while everyone finds a place. Sucking in a long, grounding breath, I clap my hands together. "Welcome to your first painting class."

And we're off.

The next ninety minutes fly by. With me showing the class basic skills, we prep and dream up projects for the next ten weeks in which they will sketch out their piece and decide on technique and use of color. Then finally, in week five, we will put brush to canvas and make a start on their first oil piece.

Eight o'clock rolls around too fast, and I have an excited and motivated bunch of brand-new artists. We pack away our work for the night and study each other's brush strokes, the techniques learned tonight. "Well, that is all for tonight. Tuesday, our next class, we will start sketching out the project. So, over the weekend put some thought into what landscape you want to paint. You all have done amazing work this evening. Enjoy the rest of your night."

They collect their belongings and file out, chatting with fervor as they go. I switch off the lights, trailing behind. Once the last student finds their car and is safely away, I tap the code into the security panel and lock up. That familiar scent from earlier today lingers on the gentle night breeze. I scan the street, now convinced I have missed something I shouldn't have. But in the darkness, nothing is amiss. Again.

Unlocking Blue, I toss my bag and phone onto the passenger's seat and slide on in. It's when I close the door and turn over the VW engine that I see it. The car parked in front of mine. Stilling, I let my gaze roam the street. Every other car has left. Leaving Blue and the banged-up white Volvo in front of us.

I study the car, my gut sinking at a rapid rate.

Mississippi plates.

Chapter Twenty-Nine

GRACE

I open the driver's door and stalk down the sidewalk, eyes frantically searching the inside of the only car left on Main Street Lewistown besides Blue. Trash lines the back seat. Chip bags, empty cigarette packs, and the thing I wasn't wanting to find.

Joel's tattered cap.

Fuck.

Buzzing starts up in my pocket.

I slide the phone out.

Unknown number.

Double fuck.

I stare at it, rage burning its way up my core and flooding my limbs. This shit ends now.

"Who is this?" I snap into the phone the second my finger slips the answer bar across the screen.

"Hello, Graceless."

His voice sends fear skittering down my spine and bile surging up my throat.

"How did you get this number?" I hiss out.

"Oh, you know. Small towns and all." He's chewing something. Most likely gum. "Nice jacket, by the way."

I whip my head around, needing to see between the shadows. But the street is deserted. As I'm about to give up, something moves in the darkness mere feet from where I stand.

My throat closes over, stealing the air from my lungs. I smash a finger on the screen and shove the phone into my pocket, grappling with Blue's door handle. After what feels like an age, the door pops open and I throw myself into the seat.

I start her up and screech backward in reverse before throwing her into gear and taking off down Main Street. I fly through the gear changes, heading for the outskirts of town, only releasing a breath and sucking more into my burning lungs when I clear the last set of lights and turn onto the highway, no Volvo in sight.

"Fuck. Fuck. Fuck. Fuck. FUCK!"

I slam my palms onto the steering wheel, regretting that decision as the freezing hard plastic bites back.

"Sweet Jesus," I moan.

Why is he doing this? Why can't he leave me alone?

I send Blue into the darkness faster than I ever have

before. This is not happening. How on earth am I supposed to tell Mack that Joel is here? And his visit is far from friendly. I'm of half a mind to let Mackinlay deal with him. No . . . that's not what I wanted. Not what I asked for. Not the strong and independent woman type I'm wanting so badly to become.

What would Ruby do?

What would Louisa do? I've yet to witness her darker side. Anyone with eyes can tell she wears the pants. In a household of men, nonetheless. I get the feeling that when one of her own is threatened, she comes out swinging. Guns blazing. Much like her son. I see elements of Louisa in Mackinlay. The fierce loyalty. The protectiveness. The open heart.

I glance in the rearview mirror. Only darkness folds in behind me. No headlights. I release a choppy breath. As much as I want to face Joel, I don't want to be in a mindset of less than, or of fear. Not anymore. Never again with him or any other man.

The second I walk through the front door, Mack's arms wrap around me.

"How was your first class?" he says into my neck.

Something divine hits my senses. He cooked supper. He smells better than the food. I run a hand through his damp hair. I suck in a wobbly breath, composing myself. Mack cooked, showered, and is holding me close. Just what I need, after—

He breaks away, holding me at arm's length now. "What happened?"

His brows lower, mouth parted. Worry lines those deep blues.

"I—" I can't lie. Even aching for this to not be real, I won't lie to Mack. "Joel's here."

His face falls, slackening with a semblance of shock before setting hard. His jaw ticks as he pulls me back into his chest. I huff out a breath, body squeezed tight. Like if he holds me tight enough, nothing can hurt me.

"Please tell me he's only passing through?" he growls beside my head.

"I'm not sure." His presence was anything but innocent. He literally waited until I was alone on a dark street. Parked his car in front of mine. A mindfuck. Then the jump-scare of the century. His voice replays in my mind. *"Hello, Graceless."* Grating my nerves a second time.

The fear I had convinced myself was a knee-jerk reaction on the way home spikes again. Now, with a little retrospect, I realize he's taunting me. This is only his first play. I run through every sad memory I have still burned into my mind from our life in Raymond. The controlling. The anger. Each time his hands found my body, seeded by anger or lust. Sometimes both.

Staring at the wall over Mack's shoulder, I can't help the tears that burn and flood my eyes. I grip his shirt tight. "I got out," I utter. "I left." I'm reminding myself more than anyone else. Still, my heart racks up a swift pace with the terror of that part of my life coming back to haunt me. Coming back, period.

Mack groans, a guttural, emotional sound. A fresh flood of tears streams down my cheeks. I sob into his shoulder. His body shakes against my own. The pain I feel hurting him as much as it does me.

His hand runs over my hair. He whispers trembling words, his breath hitting the shell of my ear. "He can't hurt you anymore, Gracie. I promise you."

I asked Mack to let me handle this. To not swoop in and save me like I know he wants to. But I'm not strong enough.

I will always be broken.

My father's voice echoes in now. *"You made your own choices. This is what you chose, Grace."*

Like any woman would *ever* choose this.

I whimper as my knees give out. Mack lowers me to the ground, pulling me into his lap and cradling me. His hard shell around my vulnerable broken one. At least for this moment. I thought I was going to be able to hold it together. To do this for myself. For Mackinlay.

I can't.

I'm scared.

Hopelessly needing to be free of who I was before.

I was doing so well.

Sobs rack through my chest. My eyes burn. My lungs void of enough air, spots filter into my vision despite my eyes being closed. I slump against Mack's warmth, curling into myself. Clutching his shirt like it's the last lifeline I have. Somehow, I know he is.

Something drops onto my head. Then another something. Moisture sinks into my hair, hitting my skin. I quiet, stilling as I listen to his breathing.

A groan claws up his throat. His Adam's apple works fast. The veins in his neck pound quickly. Tears create a sheen over his stubble. I look up to his wrecked face. This stoic, kind, amazing man is falling apart with me. For me. I push up, fingers wrapping around his jaw, pulling his face down to meet my gaze. "Mack—"

I haul in a breath and whimper. "Mackinlay, I'm o—" I slump my forehead to his. "I'll be alright. I'll be alright."

He groans, staring at me. It's raw. Unrefined pain released in one single sound. His shattered, quick breaths have him distraught. I stroke his face with my trembling hands and sniff back the tears. Seeing him this way straightens my spine. I push down my own demons before they take him under, too.

No way.

I won't let them touch him.

"Breathe, Mackinlay," I whisper.

He pulls in a lungful, and his face softens. I don't let his dark blue gaze sway from mine, my palms planted on his face. I study him, taking in the strongest, bravest person I have ever met. And the way *my* suffering destroys him?

This is what real love is.

When *everything* is shared.

The good, the bad.

The pleasure, the pain.

"Gra—" He sucks in a lungful. "I'm sorry."

"You have nothing to be sorry for." I press a light kiss to his mouth. He tilts his head, allowing me more. My hands trail down his neck. I ground myself before looking back up at him. With a lone finger, I trace the curve of his bottom lip. His breathing settles, only to bottom out again with my touch. I plant my knees on either side of his lap. "Never be sorry for loving me this much, Mackinlay."

His face cracks a little and he schools it back. "Seein' you hurting is like having my insides ripped out. Worse than anything I've ever felt." His voice is no more than a rasp.

I have never loved another person the way I love this man right now. It's so strong, so beautiful between us that it downright hurts.

We love, we hurt.

We fight, we hurt.

We breathe, we hurt.

It's the agony of something otherworldly that I'm certain not many find. The kind of ache that lets you know you're alive. Comforted in the fact you're the most important person in the whole world to the other. Sweet, sweet agony.

I trace my fingertips over his jaw, his lips, his nose,

and across his forehead. He closes his eyes. His breathing settles, and I readjust myself on his lap, my distraught body now softened to his, with heat pooling low in my belly. The emotions concentrate to one point, pulling me closer to him. His hands grip my hips. I follow his gaze as it studies my face before dipping to my lips.

"Supper can wait," he rasps.

I chuckle softly. "Yes, it can."

He smashes his mouth to mine. I open for him instantly. I'm his. He is mine. With the baggage between us, the sentiment means so much. The hurts we have both overcome.

His hand slips under my button-down shirt, thumbs skittering over my ribs then find my aching nipples. Hands around his throat, I press closer. Somehow, no matter how intimate we are, I can never get close enough to Mack. I tug his shirt from his back, wanting more of him. Needing to love him. The overwhelming yearning to bring this man the soul-shattering exaltation he gives me drives my hunger.

"You wanna move, gorgeous?"

I shake my head, too desperate to care we are on the floor in the middle of the living room. Planting kisses down my neck, his hands work my clothes free, sinking down until his mouth closes over my hard peak now aching for the tug he brings. I arch into him as he gives me everything I want. He knows me so well. Plays every achingly sweet spot in my body with his fingers, his mouth . . .

His rigid length rubs into my wet, thrumming center. I grind on him, needing the pressure on my clit. Needing him inside me, I claw at his shoulders.

"Mackinlay, more. I need more."

Now.

Chapter Thirty

MACK

Grace's beautiful face is peaceful on the pillow beside mine. Last night was a combination of agony, realizations, and the best fuckin' sex of my life. Who knew the asshole showing up would drive us together in such a profound way. It's a blessing and a curse, all rolled into one.

The night turned out to be one I'll not soon forget. Apparently, all the wolves have come down from the mountains, literally and figuratively. With the actual wolves howling last night between the thunder and lightning strikes, the air was electric. And not in all the best ways.

I flicked Harry a quick text last night. Something about this situation has my hackles up. Small towns have a way of banding together when one of our own is in trouble, and I want the old man and my brothers in the loop, in case shit gets real.

I'll talk to Huddo more about it this morning. Maybe call Reed. We're working the green horses at the ass crack of dawn. Typical Hudson. More and more like the old man every damn day. Good for him. There are worse people to turn out like.

I ease from the bed, not wanting to wake Grace. Slipping into the bathroom, I wash up and dress in my work clothes. I lift my hat from the wall by the door as I tiptoe in socked feet from the bedroom. I set the kettle to boil on the stove and grab a mug, wanting to save the good coffee for Gracie.

The hot water steams as I pour it over the instant grounds. Dashing a little milk into it, I take my first sip as Huddo's truck pulls in near the house. His busted old truck looks worse for wear in the glint from the light dust of snow covering everything outside.

Sweet Jesus, he must have been up before the damn birds. He kills the engine and wanders for the barn. I grab up the coffee mug and find a bagel from the fridge, smothering it with cream cheese. I slide my boots on at the door and head out. I close the front door with a soft click and tear a portion of the bagel off with my teeth.

I've finished my breakfast when I reach the barn and chase it down with the last of the coffee, leaving the mug on the rail. The clip-clop of shod hooves along the cement wash-down bay by the barn lets me know where my brother is. I make my way to the stall of the young mare I'm riding today. After last night's storm and the howling wolves, I'm hoping she's not too skittish today.

My hopes are dashed the second I lay eyes on her. Her head is up as she weaves at the stall door. *Fuckin' awesome.* I lift the halter from the hook by her stall and slip inside. She steps back, shaking her head. "Yeah, I know, girl. The wolves have us all up in our heads."

She nickers as I wait for her to lower her head. I slide the halter over her head, securing the buckle, and lead her out. She hesitates but follows with a little coaxin'. I saddle her up in the barn; the less stimuli, the better right now. Soft clucking sounds come from outside—Huddo's already into it. I walk the mare to the round yard, finding my older brother holding the two long lines behind the gelding he's working with. Line training to increase the horse's receptiveness to commands.

Hudson always does things the most thorough way. It's what makes him a brilliant horseman. Which makes for sought-after mounts. All his effort and attention to detail pays off. Pride swells as I watch him talk to the gelding, reining him back to a walk. He drops the lines and walks to the horse's head, patting his neck as he praises him. With a brief rub between the gelding's ears, he wanders to the rail and leans on it.

"Mornin'." He grins at me as he eyes me over, readjusting the Stetson on his head, like there's something different about me from last night after the family text about the new Joel development. The wind picks up, its icy tendrils slipping beneath my coat. I zip it up and the mare shies away from me.

"Hey," I grunt. "You sure this one's ready? Little skittish."

"Basic gait change commands. A little groundwork. Take her slow. You know how to do that." He winks.

Fuck off, Huddo.

As if what lies between Grace and I is anything like training a goddamn horse. I swipe up a blade of golden grass poking through the rails. Sliding it between my teeth, I chew it, studying the mare. The snowfall from the early hours dusts the rails. The hard earth under my boots is probably half frozen. Not a place you wanna fall.

I decide it's now or never—for the both of us. Sometimes you gotta bite the bullet and charge ahead. I gather the reins up and slide a foot into the stirrup. She moves on her feet, and I sway with her, my foot still lodged in the stirrup. Pushing the hat on my head down tighter, I swing up into the saddle. Her head's up instantly.

Sweet Jesus.

I squeeze her forward with my legs, hoping to move past whatever wound her up. She walks on, and I send her around the circular yard a few times before urging her into a trot. She bursts forward. I take up the slack on the reins as her head pops up again, her gait too choppy.

"Woah up. Mack. She's not listening," Huddo calls out.

No shit.

I rein her in, but she rounds her back.

Dammit.

She hops before lowering her head. Ears flat back.

Fuck.

I wrap my legs around her tighter and grip the pommel, knowing what's coming next. She bucks. I ride her through it. My legs are tensing with the exertion of holding my seat to the saddle. Huddo leans on the rail now, studying me and then the horse. "Calm her down and try again."

He keeps watching as I walk her out until her head is low and swinging. Until she is relaxed. It takes a full five minutes to rein her attention back to my commands.

"Push her into a lope, keep her head down." Huddo waves a hand into the yard.

I sink my seat and squeeze her forward. She breaks into a faster gait. I let out a breath when we reach a full go round.

"Great!" Huddo says with a slap to the rail.

The mare shies. I falter and grip the pommel.

Jesus.

This girl is flighty as they come.

"Push her out," Huddo offers, knowing we need to get her mind back to listening to my signals. I squeeze her back into the steady lope. She does two full rounds before she settles and her head drops. I relax in the saddle.

Huddo is swapping out his long lines for reins. He

mounts the gelding and walks him through the large yard. I keep the mare loping around before reining her in and changing direction. From the walk, I send her to a lope as Huddo trots past on the gelding. The mare tosses her head.

She sinks her head and bucks.

"Ah!" I grunt out.

I fumble for the pommel. Gripping the reins, it's like I'm grabbing for thin air. She spins. My aching legs give way. I fly from the saddle and slam into the rails with my side. Shoulder hitting the cold ground, I groan when my back slams into the post behind me with a crack. Air is sucked from my lungs. I lay gasping. Burning fills my lungs. I roll over.

Something snaps in my back. Stabbing pain seizes my muscles. "Fu—swee—moth—a—Jesus . . ." I grip the rail, panting through the blinding pain.

"Hell! Mack."

Huddo's off his horse and climbing through the rail at my feet. His Stetson falls from his head and hits the dirt as he sinks by my side. "You okay, buddy?" Hudson's placating words grind my gears. I try to push to sit up.

I can't.

What the—

"Help me up, will ya?" I grunt.

He slaps a hand into mine and pulls me up. Pain screams through my side. I pull in a breath, and it burns like a motherfucker. I growl out a moan.

"I'll get Grace," Huddo breathes.

"No!"

I don't want her worrying about this, too. I push to sit up again. This time, I manage to make it halfway to upright before the pain blinds me again. I groan with the next breath. Dammit, must have busted a rib.

"For fuck's sake," I growl.

Now, of all times, I can't afford to be injured. With that asshole hovering around. A predator biding his time to close in on his damn prey. Grace needs me.

I slam a fist onto the icy ground.

"You wanna talk about it?" Huddo breathes.

"How the hell am I supposed to keep her safe if I'm fuckin' laid up?"

His brows lower. His bright blue eyes flood with concern. "You think she'll need protectin'?"

"I don't know. But I'm not leavin' it to chance." I clench my jaw and roll onto all fours. Hudson stands and gives me some room. I stand on wobbly feet. Huddo eyes me over, and I take a step.

Instantly faltering as my foot meets the ground, and my legs buckle. "I do—"

Huddo catches me before I hit the ground. My vision turns spotty, and the ringing in my ears all but drowns out his words when his tightened eyes find mine and he says, "*Now*. I'm gettin' Grace."

Grace stands over me. Fuzziness traps me like a bundle of heavy blankets. A heady buzz fills my chest. My body is mostly numb. My head is hollow and like a rock at the same time. I tilt it and the room spins.

The hospital bed is too hard and there is no way in hell I'm stayin' here. She shoulders her bag, running a hand through her messy bun. What I wouldn't give to let that gorgeous hair down and pull her onto my lap. Who cares if there's other people in the emergency department.

Maybe I've had too much green whistle . . .

Soft lips brush over my forehead before planting there. Lifting my head, I look up with moony eyes. The grin on my face is too wide and absolutely automatic. I breathe her in.

She stands back up, a smile warring on her face with something sadder until she schools it back and the smile wins out. "You're high, Mackinlay." She releases a strangled, small chuckle, and her smile slips again. "Better than in pain, though." The last few words are no more than a whisper.

Why is she whispering?

"Why're you—"

The curtain explodes.

No, it shifts sideways. A white glowing figure floats

toward the bed. I shake my head. The white glowing figure sharpens to a doctor in a lab coat. I clear my throat. That could've been awkward. I huff a laugh. He cocks a brow before flipping the paper in the chart. "I see the pain meds have kicked in. Good."

"What did the X-ray say?" Grace's voice sounds funny.

Not ha-ha funny either.

Just wobbly or something.

"It's not the best news. However, it could have been worse." He sounds mean.

Grace sits on the side of the bed. I feel like I'm going to slide right into her any second now. Like down a slippery slide. I wonder if they have one?

"How so?" she asks, softly.

"The old damage from the incident on tour has been agitated. Nothing major. I predict it will take a month or so before he regains full mobility. The lower back is, unfortunately, unforgiving when it comes to repeated injury. He will need a cane, for lateral support. A brace to help with the two hairline fractures in the lumbar area. Something like his previous recovery process will see him right."

"Who are you talkin' about, doc?" I say with a slow drawl.

Grace smiles at me sadly.

No, please don't be sad, my gorgeous Gracie girl. She drags her gaze from me, back up to the doctor.

Look at him! Lookin' at my girl. I push up off the pillow. I think I can take him . . .

"Mackinlay, it's okay. We will get through this. You did it once, with way worse odds. Baby, you can do it again. I won't let you fall, I promise." Her face is so close.

I love her so much.

"I love you, Gracie," I mumble.

She dots a kiss on my cheek. "I know you do."

The buzzing fades a little. I scrunch my face up. Something stabs my side. "Ugh, ouch." My hands curl to fists. But I can't feel the skin over my knuckles. That's odd.

I try to shift away from it.

"Try not to move until we have your brace on, Mackinlay," the white man says and disappears through the wavy green thing.

Arms wind around my head, the bed dips. Her vanilla and peaches surround me. I slam my eyes shut.

Her breathing gets faster, and something wet hits my shoulder as she starts to shake. I don't want to move. I want to keep her wrapped around me forever.

The fuzziness swallows me whole.

It's an impressive sight. The horseback duo. Hats. Winchester rifles and snow-dusted carts. Harry and Louisa trot past. Louisa waves as they head to the south fields today, bringing in the last of the cows and calves. Harry salutes me before they round the barn and slip out of sight.

I salute him back, leaning on the porch post, coffee in my hands. A chuckle sounds behind me. I turn back to find Mack in the doorway, cane in hand. The brace over his abdomen supporting his lower back. His dressing gown is open, and his winter PJs are crumpled. He had a better night last night. Still, this is a setback neither of us saw coming.

Work was understanding, giving me two weeks off to help him settle into a routine again. It breaks my heart seeing him like this after how hard he fought to return to his old self. His face sports a shadow of stubble, his hair messed up from sleep. The pain meds have him groggy and he wants to wean off them. I'm sure it's too soon. It's not even been a week.

Compared to the first time he went through this, he's a different man. Not the angry, sulky version who had given up when I met him. If anything, he's forging ahead too quickly. And I know why. He wants to protect me. It's the sweetest thing I've ever felt. I pray the absence of calls and texts since the scare after class two weeks ago means Joel has moved on. Deep down, I doubt he's done with me. His ego and malicious mind would never allow that.

"You're up!" I smile at him. Even disheveled, he sends my heart into a rapid beat, something akin to a humming-bird's. Maybe more so. I usher him inside before the cold finds him. He tucks me into his side as we amble for the sofa. With his arm around my shoulder, he steers me toward it. I help him sit before snuggling up beside him. "At least there's more time for cuddles," I whisper.

"Always a silver lining, Gracie." Mack hugs me tighter, dropping a kiss to the crown of my head. "You should do some painting while you have the time off."

"I want to take care of you. I want to be here for you."

"You are, but I don't need a babysitter, gorgeous. I do, however, need you to be happy."

I huff a small laugh at him. His hands cup my face, tilting my head up to his.

"I'm serious, Grace. You're it for me. My priority. You always will be."

The breath I took lodges in my throat. I can't pull in another. I open my mouth to say something, anything. Dumbfounded, I study his face. I knew he was in this for the long haul. But those words cement every feeling, every sliver of hope I have for the future I want for us.

When I haven't responded, he pulls me into his chest. It's one of my favorite places. Second only to having him wrapped around me while he's inside me. We are joined, so intimately, the rest of the world simply ceases to exist. "You're it for me, too." The words are muffled.

He chuckles and releases one breathy word. "Good."

My phone vibrates in my bag.

An alarm I set last night. I'm due over at R & R ranch to hand over six of my landscapes for Ruby to place in her cabins. Mack's hold loosens and I lean back, taking in his handsome face. Looking this man over never gets old. "I'll be back in a few hours. Need me to take anything to Reed? Bring anything back?"

"Nope. Just you." His smile cracks and I rise up on my knees to kiss his mouth. He grabs my face. I deepen the kiss, tasting morning coffee and the man I love. Perfect way to start the day, if you ask me.

"I'll be home for lunch, alright?" I say, pushing from the sofa reluctantly.

"Yes ma'am." He stands with the help of the cane and follows me. I swipe up my bag and keys from the kitchen counter and throw them over my shoulder. Walking to my art room, I hug the six canvases, individually wrapped in brown paper, close. They're large, more than an armful. Mack hobbles to the front door ahead of me, opening it for me. He walks out into the chilly air, robe still flapping, and holds Blue's door open as I slide the paintings onto the back seat.

I wrap my hands around his face, thanking him with a kiss. "I love you, Mackinlay Rawlins."

"Yeah, I know." He winks at me and runs a thumb over my jaw before stepping back cautiously to allow me to open the driver's door. I slide into Blue and start her up. She's cold and splutters a little before finding her rhythm. Clouds puff from her exhaust as I shift her into gear and head down the driveway.

R & R is the place I would go if I didn't have anywhere else in the world to be. It's stunning. Every time I drive under the oversized sign at the entrance, it hits me all over again. It should be one of the great wonders of the world. Truly.

Pulling over next to the small gate by the homestead, Ruby waves from the porch. Already bundled up, she holds a tablet. Always working. So damn inspiring. She meets me at the car, and I haul out the paintings. "Morning, Mrs. Rawlins."

I beam at her, knowing calling her that name is a double-edged sword.

She scoffs. "Morning, Gracie. I'm so stinking excited to see these. Are you excited to have your work out in the world?"

She is all but jumping out of her skin. The red scarf around her neck flings as she bounces on the balls of her feet, blonde hair dancing around her shoulders. Her warm coat is collar up. Skinny jeans and those tan-and-pink boots she's always wearing finish her outfit. Always so put together. Ugh. Changed my mind. I want to be Ruby Rawlins when I grow up. Honest to god.

"A little, I guess."

"Grace." She slaps my shoulder, jostling the pile of canvases. "This is only the beginning."

I chuckle. "Sure."

She relieves me of half the canvases. "Come on, let's hang these beauties on the walls."

We wander to the first cabin. I hold my breath when we step inside and she unwraps the first one. It's the view of the mountains from under the entrance sign. Big blue giants—snow-capped, of course—golden grass trimming the base. The rustic barns in the foreground.

"Oh wow!" Ruby holds one up. I worry my bottom lip through my teeth. She pivots on her heels to find the natural light, painting in her hands, eyes lit up. "Seriously, this is incredible. The detail, the colors. Just . . . wow."

The front door snaps open and Reed wanders in. "Hey,

our artist in residence!" He folds me into a hug. "Mornin', Gracie. How's that grump of a brother of mine today?"

I soak up the friendly hug for a heartbeat before breaking away. "He's doing good. I swear, he thinks his recovery is a sprint. Much different from last time."

"He has a better incentive this time." Reed's face is stretched by a megawatt grin.

Heat rises in my face. I guess it's true. I'm glad Mack has someone with him all the way this time. But I would rather he never had to repeat this process in the first place. He's gone through plenty. It's enough already.

Ruby hangs the artwork on the wall and bends down by the entrance table, writing something on a piece of white cardstock. After she's done, she slips it into a small black photo frame and walks to the wall by the painting, propping it up by my artwork on a shelf Reed must have made.

"Stellar work, Gracie." Reed studies the work. "Jesus, it's like standing by the front entrance."

Ruby nods, throwing him a knowing look with wide eyes.

I glance at the price on the card in the frame and my mouth drops open.

"Five hundred! No, that's far too expensive." I wring my hands together.

"Actually, it's not. I ran the comps. For the size. The technique and local talent element, it's midrange. We could ask more. However, this is a smart starting point, which allows you growth, artistically and financially."

For the second time today, I have no response. My breaths shorten as the bridge of my nose prickles. She's put so much thought and effort into this.

Reed slings an arm over my shoulders. "I would pay ten times the price to have a Gracie original on my wall. You're the talent around here, darlin'."

Ruby loses it over his old-man talk. They all do it. Imitate Harry. It's funny that he has such a unique way with people and words. They are so incredibly lucky to have a father like him.

"If you say so, Rawlins," I spout back.

"Sure do, sweetheart." Reed can't even keep a straight face. I slap his arm, and he squeezes my shoulders before releasing me to his wife. "Catch you later, captain." He tips his hat to me.

I am dying to know what the captain thing is all about. I make a mental note to ask Mack about it later. Ruby walks me back to Blue, offering a coffee, which I decline. I want to get home to Mack. Lunch and pain meds will be due when I do. I don't want his pain to break through because I was lazing around, sipping coffee with my idol.

"Thanks for everything. Thanks for helping me with the art." My words almost wobble. I am so grateful for everything Ruby has done for me. This whole family has done for me. I can't imagine where I would have ended up if Ruby and Louisa hadn't offered me a place and a job.

Just like that, the thought of not having Mack in my life steals the icy air from my lungs. Urgency thrums through my veins. All I want to do is get home. I give Ruby a rough hug, holding her as she chuckles and says, "You're so welcome, Grace. We're basically sisters at this point. You do for family. It's a Harry rule. One I fully support." She tightens the hug momentarily before pushing me to arm's length. "I'll let you know when your payload comes in."

I scoff a laugh and drop into the driver's seat.

All I want to do in this moment is bury myself in Mackinlay's embrace.

Melt into him and never ever leave.

The sun is high in the sky when I turn Blue into the ranch's driveway. The small tracks of my little VW Beetle have been marred by bigger ones. My brows drop. We weren't expecting company today, and Harry and Louisa aren't due back until after lunch. I can just see the front grill of their silver Chevy through the barn door.

Heart flinging in my chest, my gut sinks as I round the gravel drive and find the white Volvo sitting behind the trees before the house yard. Panic clawing up my spine and flooding my body, I scan the porch for Mack.

Passing the car, I see the last thing I want to lay eyes on ever again. Joel and Timmy. Boots on the dash, they sit in their car, smoking. Timmy drains a beer.

Jesus fucking Christ.

My heart jumps into my throat as Joel's gaze meets mine, and he turns his head to keep eye contact as I drive past. It's like the interaction happens in slow motion, sending my gut into a knot of sickness and splinters.

"No," I breathe. Not this time. Not on our ranch. Not in my home. I slam Blue to a halt and kill the engine. He wants to do this? *Bring it on, asshole.* I get out of the car and walk into the yard as if I hadn't seen him. I open the front door, and Mack is asleep on the sofa. He must not have answered the door.

Maybe I can have those two losers gone before he wakes up. He doesn't need this kind of stress.

I walk back through the front door, ready to set them straight. To tell them to leave and never look back. I close the door behind me with a soft click, and when I turn back to the yard, I find Joel gripping the stair rail with one hand. His strung-out eyes meet mine.

Dammit.

"Graceless. You know, this town put up a good fight, trying to hide you from me. But here's the thing, I'm smarter than them. Than *you*. You've got nowhere left to run. Time to go home."

"I'm not going anywhere with you. Leave, and don't bother coming back. Ever."

I square my shoulders back and set my jaw, like that will make my words pack more punch.

He takes a step moving onto the first tread. "Yeah, you realize you belong to *me*. You don't belong here." He waves a hand around and leans forward.

I step back.

Sliding my arms crossed, I think of Louisa, Ruby. Addy. Every woman in this wonderful family who owns their life. Doesn't take shit from anyone, least of all a pathetic excuse for a man like Joel. "Listen to these words because they're the last you're getting from me: We are over. Leave. Now." My words are a growl.

Something thumps inside.

Shit.

Please stay asleep, baby.

Joel closes the distance between us until he towers over me. The tang of stale cigarettes and old bourbon hits me. I recoil and put space between us. I grit my teeth, grinding my molars before tilting my head to meet his bloodshot gaze. "Get away from me. Get out of Montana. I'm not yours. I never will be, ever again."

He rubs a hand over his chin and scoffs a manic laugh.

The door opens behind me.

Sweet Jesus, no.

Joel backs up a step. His face splits with a smirk. "Oh, now I see how it is."

The guttural raw sound leaving Mack sends goosebumps over my skin. He hobbles over the threshold on his cane.

"The fuck off my property, asshole."

The vein in his neck thunders. His knuckles are white around the stick.

Something is clip-clopping toward the house, but the sound is drowned out by the blood now thundering through my head. Rage swells like wildfire in my core. I step in front of Mackinlay. I shove Joel with one hand, hard. "Leave."

He cackles. "After you." He waves an arm toward the car, his movement sloppy.

"Never."

His head snaps down as his lip curls up with a growl.

His hand slams around my throat.

"Fuck you, bitch. You come with us, or we torch this whole fucking joint, with your loser of a fuck buddy inside."

The loudest crack splits the air.

Every head swings toward the sound.

I smack his hand from my throat, breathless as fire flings into my veins with his cruel words. It's all I can do to keep my gaze on the source of the sound. Rifle. Horse.

Louisa sits on her black horse, her rifle still pointed at her target. The Volvo's trunk. Timmy flies out of the car in a tangle of limbs, curses tumbling from his mouth.

"She asked you to leave. I suggest you do as she says, son." Louisa trains the rifle on Joel and cocks the lever in one fluid motion. Her face is stone, black hat tilted so she can find her aim. Gaze homed in on Joel.

Harry sits on his horse, hands resting on the pommel, reins rolling through his fingertips. The epitome of calm. His gaze is set on me. One the protector, one the fighter. I huff an elated but surprised chuckle as emotion clogs my windpipe.

"What the fuck?!" Joel stumbles down the stairs.

Louisa jerks the rifle toward the car.

He turns back to me and points with a dirty finger. "This isn't over, Grace. Enjoy your damaged boyfriend while you can. Your days here are over." He pushes through the gate. Louisa's horse steps forward, closing in on him as he slips into the Volvo. He starts it up as Timmy clambers back inside, winding his window up, like it will help him. The idiot.

"Not over, Graceless!" Joel roars as the car spins out on the gravel and barrels along the driveway.

The first breath I take burns as I turn back to Mack. He's gripping the doorframe, his cane fallen to the floor. I didn't hear it fall. My hand flies up covering my mouth. I shake my head. He hobbles, eating up the distance between us.

Joel called him *damaged*.

The piece of my heart that tore with the comment sinks to the depths of my soul. Mack's hands have me safe against his chest before I take my next breath.

"Sweet Jesus, I'm so fuckin' proud of you, Grace."

I close my eyes, letting the fear, the anger, the wounded part of me over Mack having to bear any of this, fade away.

As soon as it's gone, the reality that this really isn't over hits. Joel isn't going to let this go.

And now, I have everything to lose.

Chapter Thirty-Two

MACK

"Are you sure you'll be okay?" I ask as I slip my coat over my shoulders, cane leaning by the front table, Reed waiting on the threshold. Grace tilts her head with an exasperated expression.

"I will be fine, Mackinlay. Go to your appointment. I'm safe here."

Reed shoves his Yankees cap onto his head. The thing is tattered and worn, but for some reason he won't give it up. "She'll be alright, Mack. We won't be long."

I shove my black hat on my head and close the space between Grace and me. Her hands rest on my coat, fingers fiddling with the collar as she studies my face. "Don't forget to fill your prescription, okay?" she whispers.

I cup her jaw with my hands, planting my mouth over hers. She leans against me.

Fuck, I don't wanna leave.

After yesterday, my nerves are up. As they should be. Despite the fact Joel left and hasn't been heard from since, my gut tells me the threat isn't over yet. My gut is usually right. Saved my ass more times than I can count on tour—I'm not about to ignore it now.

"Go. I'll be painting the morning away, anyhow." She pecks a final kiss to my jaw and slips out of my hold. Hesitating, I turn back to Reed. "Let's get this over and done with, gunny."

The trip to town is quiet. Me lost in thought, Reed glancing at me every few minutes as if he has something to say but hasn't found the balls to let it out yet.

"Spill it," I grunt.

He huffs a breath, running his hand behind his neck. "I dunno . . ."

"Don't know what, Reed?"

"Maybe you shouldn't be doin' so much ranchin' work?" His gaze flicks to me and then back to the road.

"I'm not sitting' around being a damn burden. That's a fresh hell I'm not signin' up for."

"Sure. But—"

"Stop." I hold a hand up. I know he's trying to look out for me. But I'm not having it. "It doesn't matter how long it takes, Reed, I will be earnin' my keep and workin' the ranch. I'm not letting Grace shoulder the weight. Or anyone else, for that matter." My gaze burns into his.

He nods, and I know the message sunk in.

"Just . . ." He sucks in a breath. "Don't push it and end up worse off. Grace deserves the whole Mack, not the shell of him."

He's insinuating I'll end up broken and leave her with less than a man. I punch his arm. *Fuckin' little shit.*

We pull in by the doctor's thirty minutes later, and three minutes late for my appointment. The doorbell chimes as I hobble through, making a halfhearted effort to hold the door open for my brother. He beams at the receptionist, and she perks up like a goddamn meerkat. Jesus, this guy will never lose that spunk, will he?

"Rawlins, for the ten o'clock," I grunt.

"Doctor will be out in a moment. Take a seat." She smiles and waves to the blue plastic chairs lined up against the wall. Only two others are waiting, both with their heads down, eyes on their damn screens.

I take the closest seat, and Reed drops into the one beside it, pushing his legs out. He tugs the ball cap down and closes his eyes before knitting his fingers behind his head.

"Worn out, gunny?" I mutter.

The grin splitting his stupid face tells me everything. I can only imagine the antics my little brother and his wife get up to. Ruby's been his godsend. He's the family and the loving arms she never had. It used to be hard not to be jealous of them both.

My thoughts drift to Grace. I need to get back to where I was. I refuse to be anything but whole. I won't let her settle for anything less than a brilliant life and family. Meaning I need to man up and get this recovery done.

"Mackinlay?" the white coat says from the end of the hall, chart in hand.

Reed groans and sits up.

"Stay down. I got this. You look like you could use the nap."

"Sure could," he says with a shit-eating grin.

I shake my head at him and push to my feet. The corridor is short. I turn into the first room on the left and sink into the leatherette seat on the opposite side of the desk. I've been here before. Been through the motions. This time 'round, I have a clear path, and the desire to power through this as soon as possible.

"How's the pain?" the doc asks.

"Fine, nothing I can't handle. When can I start the physio?"

"Let me check your most recent X-ray and your mobility, and we'll see." He shoots out of the chair he just sat in and pads to the light box hanging on the wall. So goddamn old school, like Lewistown was left behind when the rest of the medical world went digital. He plucks the pen from his pocket and taps the film with a hum.

Okay . . .

"The fractures are healing nicely. That's good."

"So, I can lose the support?"

"Should be okay, as long as you don't exert yourself. Up on the bed and I'll check your range of motion."

I make a point of not using the cane and slide up onto the bed. A lance of pain travels down my hip and leg. I lay back and the doctor grips my calf, bending my leg up, to the side, rotating it in the ball and socket joint. I hold my breath.

He does the same on the other side.

"Hmmm. Roll onto your side, facing the wall."

I roll and stare at the wall. His cold hands press and explore my lower spine. When he says nothing, removing his hands, I roll back over and sit up. "Well, when can I get back on a horse?"

His eyes widen before tightening with concern. "Mackinlay, your injuries may be healing, but I'm afraid riding is not recommended. Not anymore."

"It's not optional. Comes with the job description," I snap.

Like hell I'm standing around watching my family pick up my slack.

"If you fall from a horse again, you run a considerable risk of permanent damage."

"So I don't come off. I'm not going to be a burden to my family."

He shakes his head and sinks into his seat, as if defeated. He slides the chart across his desk and steeples his fingers. "Have you considered another line of work?"

"Have *you*?"

His lips purse together. "All I can do is educate you on the risks and facts. What you choose to do with the information is up to you."

"Are we done?" I snatch up the cane.

He simply nods, and I'm out the door like the room is on fire. Reed stands when he sees me. I blow past the receptionist, heading for the door.

"Mr. Rawlins?" she calls from behind me. "Ah, your account?"

"Send it out!" I slam a hand onto the door and burst onto the sidewalk. Fresh air sinks into my lungs and I fight to keep it there. Fuck.

FUCK.

Jaw clenched tight, I stalk for Reed's truck.

He rounds me at a jog and pulls the door open for me.

Fuck my life.

I clamber into the truck as Reed slips around the grill and slides into the driver's seat.

"Take me the fuck home." I release a breath.

He starts the truck and pulls away from the curb. We break the town limits before he speaks.

"Not great news, I take it?"

"Nope."

"What did he say?" He glances from me to the road, alternating his gaze like a skittish gangster.

Sweet Jesus.

"Gettin' back on a horse is not recommended. Overdoing it, is not—FUCK!" I punch the dash.

"You'll come back. You did last time. If anyon—"

"What if I can't? Don't? What then?" I'm yelling. It's not his fault. But this feels like the last fuckin' straw.

"Then we'll figure something out." His brows are pulled down. A far cry from the cheeky bastard who was full of himself thirty minutes ago. "Grace will know what to do."

Instantly my anger fades, replaced by the worry that was gnawing at my gut before I walked into the doctor's office. The overload of emotions has my blood invading my skull at a rapid rate. Dizziness creeps in. "Drive faster, gunny," I choke out.

The F250 bursts into a roar. We fly down the highway until we turn onto the gravel road. He sends the truck along and every minute that passes ratchets up the tension in my body. Muscles tense to rigidity, molars grinding. I grip the door handle, willing the ranch to come into view. Reed sends her round the corner and sideways into the driveway, and I let out a breath of relief. No white Volvo.

He skids the truck to a halt, and I fly out the door before the engine splutters out. Reed is hot on my heels.

Then I see it.

Tire tracks.

Not Reed's.

Not Blue's.

Fuck.

I pray it was Rubes or Adds paying Gracie a visit. The

sinking feeling in my gut knots and grows. I fling the cane to the ground and Reed jogs ahead, bursting in through the front door.

"Gracie? You here?" Reed yells. I make it up the porch, cursing my useless body, anger growing like a damn wildfire on summer winds.

"Check her art room. I'll check the bedroom!" I holler.

I lengthen my strides until the pain splinters through my lower back. Ignoring it, I swing into her room. It's empty. Void of Grace or any trace of her.

A strangled curse echoes down the hallway. Then, "Mack!"

I scramble toward the sound. Reed steps out of the art room, his face wrecked. His shoulders heave.

Oh god, no!

His gaze drops to the floor. I falter to a stop before the doorway. Blue paint is swiped over the doorjamb as if someone had hung on for dear life, the remnants of a smudged handprint in blue. Her favorite color.

Short, ragged breaths burn their way through my lungs as I step into the space Grace loves the most. It's destroyed. Paint pots on their sides. Furniture disturbed. Her stool toppled over. The easel Huddo made is the only item not ransacked. A canvas lies at its feet, a huge rip through the center.

She put up a fight.

"Mack. The paint's wet."

I spin back. His finger is held in the air, blue paint smeared over it. "It's still wet. We can catch up."

"Go, now!" I roar.

We fly from the house. I'm running with a disjointed gait. Numb from the adrenaline, I don't feel the pain I know should be lancing through my body right now. Reed fires up the F250. We leave gravel streaking through the air, shooting for the highway.

Chapter Thirty-Three

GRACE

The car pitches upward. I slide into the rear wall of the dark trunk with a thud. The only thought I allow through my mind is this: I will run. I will find my way back to Mackinlay. I have done it before. I will do it again.

The small dark space around me is studded with the lone bullet hole from Louisa's rifle and the slim beam of sunlight shining through. I stare at it. My beacon of hope. My last connection to Mack. To the love of my life. To the life I am so desperate to keep.

The Volvo hits a pothole. My head slams into the side of the trunk. My paint-marred hands are bound with duct tape. The tears I cried for the first hour in this freezing, cramped space have long dried on my face. The fear that rendered me helpless after I fought them off for a second time at the gas station is now replaced with calm. With determination.

I'm not the same girl I was in Mississippi. No, no longer a girl. A woman. The last months have seen me forged through fire. From one grand realization that I am worth more to finding my worth. My place.

I will fight.

Every day, with every breath.

I will not be subdued, ever again.

I will not give up the freedom I have found.

Nor the person I have become.

No matter how much they hurt me.

The thought of Mack coming home to find me gone, the destruction that ensued when Joel and Timmy overpowered me, sends fresh panic to my heart. Dammit, I was so stupid. Headphones blaring, brush in one hand, and oblivious to the outside world. I didn't stand a chance. They had the element of surprise. They shouldn't have. But the stress of worrying about Mack's appointment drove me to need the escape. The music gave me that.

On cue, a rhythmic beat starts up in the car, echoing through the hollow metal. Music. The thumping beat tells me it's techno. Ugh. As if my containment couldn't get any worse. I close my eyes against the obnoxious noise and make a start on running through every scenario, finding the out in each one. Planning to run.

The Volvo careens downward.

Downhill.

The engine noise lightens. We must be traveling over the mountains. Away from Montana. Heading for the River State, most likely.

The temperature in the trunk cools further. I shiver. My teeth rattle in my head. I grit my teeth, and my puffy eyes burn. A wash of goosebumps floods my skin. To ward off the cold, I fill my mind with memories of Mackinlay. His arms wrapped around me. His warm breath against my neck, the shell of my ear.

"I will find my way back, Mackinlay," I whisper to the void. "I promise."

The darkness that has swallowed me whole since the trunk slammed shut drags me under.

I lose sight of the hole and the single beam of watery sunlight.

Exhausted, I let go.

Chapter Thirty-Four

MACK

"**F**uck," Reed drawls.

"What?" I snap.

"Need gas." He swings the truck into the gas station on the outskirts of Lewistown.

I run my hands through my hair before dragging them down my face. "Make it quick, gunny."

He nods sharply and flies out the door to the pump.

Across the parking lot, a figure is striding toward us. Morley. I flick my gaze to anywhere but him. Reed pumps gas into the tank, telling the thing to pump faster. As if that will do anything.

"Rawlins!" Morley waves a hand. He's dressed up in jeans, a denim jacket, and a white hat that makes him look like cowboy Ken.

Fuck off, Morley.

"Not now, buddy." Reed tries to wave him off. He walks over to the passenger door.

"Sure, but I thought you might want to know I saw your girl before. Was getting gas but forgot the paper and had to come back. She was with two guys. Wasn't happy about it either. Sending fists into the skinny one. He shoved her into the back seat before locking her in."

Reed stares at him. The pump gurgles and clicks in his hand. "Fuck."

I'm out of the truck faster than humanly possible. "Speak, Morley."

A stupid smirk crosses his face, as if he's happy he has something we want.

"Swear to god, Morley, I will rearrange your fuckin' teeth." My words are barely more than a growl.

He holds his hands up in surrender. "Simply reporting what I saw. She was upset. They put her in the back seat. She was covered in something blue. They had it on them, too. They bought smokes and screeched their way out of here, heading south." He nods to the highway running south.

"Is that all?"

"You could say 'thank you.' It's not like she's anything to me."

Goddamn asshat.

The outside temperature is cold and dropping as the clouds overhead shift. I pray to god we find them before they make it too far.

"Not today, Morley."

Reed jogs for the truck, clearing the station's automatic door. He fires the truck up and we head south. Morley watches us from his truck. About time the waste of space did something worthwhile.

I snap my gaze to the asphalt. Reed guns it, the roar of the V8 rattling my bones.

"We'll find her, Mack."

His words are soft, though. He's worried.

I'm devastated.

The minutes drip by like molasses in winter. Fuckin' torturously slow. Reed pushes the truck as fast as he can. The old, busted Volvo isn't going to push more than seventy miles per hour. Hell, by my math, we should catch up with them sooner rather than later. Still, it's as if time stands still.

Fuck you, time.

The F250 shifts gears automatically as we ascend a hill.

"Come on, baby," Reed mutters. His hand taps the wheel. He's as strung out over this as I am. There has never been a day when Reed hasn't made my life better. Peas in a pod and all that. I stare at the man behind the wheel. Such a big fuckin' heart. Behind the charisma and tongue-in-cheek, he's all soul.

I train my focus on the highway, grabbing the handle above my head as we nosedive over the first rise. A long descent stretches out before us, and I brace my other hand on the seat. My muscles are painfully tight. I grind my molars, letting only the slightest of relaxation pull at me. We dip out at the base and roar along the flat stretch of road heading toward the township of Moore.

Something catches my attention on the horizon. A flash of blue.

"Reed!" I point to the oscillating lights.

He cranes his neck, squinting as if it will help him see better across the vast distance between us and the tiny, flashing speck of blue. Without a word, he sends the truck faster.

Please let it be Grace.

Please let her be okay.

Maybe someone called it in after seeing them at the gas station? Why Morley didn't, I'll never know. Then again, I never thought to ask if he did. The state trooper vehicle comes into focus, and I shift on the seat, leaning forward to get a better look. I flick Harry a text, hoping like hell this is the white Volvo. Praying even harder she is in one piece. If that motherfucker so much as laid a hand on her . . .

Morley never mentioned them doing so. But I imagine if she was putting up a fight, Joel would have manhandled her. Two troopers get out of the car, hands stretched out in front of them. They have their weapons out.

Jesus Christ.

The Volvo is pulled over on an angle. Like they stopped in a hurry.

Dammit.

If he has so much as—

"I don't see her." Reed flies along the highway closing in on the scene. I fling Harry a drop-pin to our location and toss my phone to the dash. Both men step out of the car, hands over their heads.

Still no Grace.

They turn and lean on the car as one officer holds his weapon to them and the other cuffs them both.

The officer closest moves to the trunk.

We are merely yards away.

The trunk pops, and the trooper bends down.

I hold my breath, heart thundering lightning through my veins. A visceral rage sends my body shaking when Grace climbs out of the trunk.

Hands bound.

Mouth covered in duct tape.

"Jesus fuckin' Christ," Reed breathes, pulling the truck to a screeching halt. I'm out the door before the vehicle rolls to a stop. Grace is nodding at the trooper. He cuts her binds, and she tugs the tape from her mouth.

She sees me seconds before I am in her space. We falter backward on impact.

"I'm okay," she rasps, her voice cracking on the last syllable.

I'm shaking, the explosive combination of rage and desperation sending my head spinning. Grace clings to me and I wrap my body around her, still needing to protect her, even though I wasn't there to do so when it counted most.

I groan into her hair, and she pushes from my arms, catching my gaze. "Breathe, Mack. I'm alright. I was alright."

I grip her arms. "No, Grace, you were so far from alright." My jaw feathers.

A high-pitched chuckle comes from by the Volvo. I straighten, pushing Grace behind me. Joel smirks at me. An arrogant, cocky piece of shit, even in cuffs. The trooper who helped Grace from the trunk dips his hat and heads for his SUV.

I take that as my cue, and with three long strides, I'm in the asshole's face. One fist gripping his ratty shirt, I slam him into the side of his busted car.

"If you ever come within three counties of her again, I will fuckin' end you."

My hand curls to a fist by my side. My height and muscular frame dwarves his gangly, thin junkie build. He nods slowly. His eyes are half glazed over.

Is he goddamn high?

Staring at me, his eyes narrow further before I decide he's not worth another second of either of our lives. I turn back to Grace. She is hugging her arms around her body, now tucked under Reed's arm and into his side. The protective brother pose. Same as the time with Addy when Morley tried his luck.

Harry's silver Chevy pulls in behind the F250 as I walk for Grace.

"Fine by me if you take my sloppy seconds. Trashy piece of ass is all yours. Enjoy my seconds, retard." The words are acid. I stop mid-stride. Before my brain overrides my head, I'm on him, fist smashing into his face with one hand gripping his shirt. He sways on his tiptoes where I have him shoved up against the side of the car, again.

Something gives way as I slam another punch into his stupid face. He smiles as blood trickles down his chin, pouring from his nose and split lip. I sink another and another into him. He goes limp in my hold. I slam my stinging fist into his face. The sickening crunch tells me I should stop.

I don't.

Another punch.

Another messy crunch, and something slides under my knuckles.

"Mackinlay." The word is almost ethereal. Grace's voice floats past my anger, sinking into my chest and touching my heart.

I hesitate.

I see her close in beside me in my peripheral.

A light touch comes to rest on my forearm holding this lousy waste of oxygen upright. "Enough, Mack."

I haul air into my lungs as if someone could steal it

away at any second. I finally turn to find her gorgeous face.

Grace gives me a sad smile and tilts her head. "Take me home?"

My grip loosens and Joel slumps, sliding to the hard asphalt. The officer from before appears at my other side, checking for a pulse.

Fuck.

He nods before waving us away.

I stagger toward my waiting family by Reed's truck. Harry pulls Grace into a long hug. He checks her over at arm's length before he and Ma return to the Chevy. How is it my father can communicate so much without a damn word?

Reed adjusts the cap on his head. "I'll give you some space." He rounds the vehicle and climbs into the driver's seat.

I lean my side against the truck and pull Grace into me. "Sweet Jesus, Gracie, I've never been so terrified in my entire life."

I cup her hands with my face, tilting her face up to mine. It's there that I find calm. Strength.

My knees give out and I slump to the ground, arms wrapped around her waist. I groan into her stomach, ugly sobs slamming into her as they leave my tightened throat. Her hands push through my hair, and she kneels before me.

I meet her gaze, and she whispers, "I knew no matter

what happened, or where they took me, I would get back to you. I would never stop trying."

My face breaks.

This woman.

I can't breathe.

"How—" I start, and the air in my lungs disappears.

"Because we are the tough ones, remember? We will do this together. This is where I am meant to be."

She's not talking about herself now. Always so damn selfless. I steady myself against the F250. When my nerves have settled and my breathing returns to some semblance of normal, I clamber to my feet. Grace follows, opening the door for me. "Home sounds really great right now."

"Yes ma'am" is all I can say. I am in awe of the woman in front of me. Tossed into a trunk, bound and gagged, yet she comes out the other side fighting. I've never been so proud and so awestruck.

"Miss Weston?" the officer says from behind her.

She spins back. "Yes?"

"Once you're settled, you will need to come down to the station to make a statement and press charges."

"Okay, can it wait until tomorrow?"

He nods and gives her a brief smile. His gaze finds mine, lingering for a moment. He tips his hat and walks back to his vehicle. Apparently, a little cowboy justice is tolerated in these parts. Neither he nor his partner made any attempt to stop me flogging the living daylights outta the sack of shit. Guess they saw nothin'.

Grace climbs on in and slips between Reed and me. She's shivering. I peel off my coat and wrap her in it. As we drive back down the highway, she crawls into my lap, head nuzzled into my neck, her trembling hands tangled through the opening of my shirt. The adrenaline of the last thirty minutes has worn off.

"I love you, Mack." The words are no more than a whisper as they float past my ear, almost drowned out by the engine's roar.

"I love you too, gorgeous girl. Always will."

A few miles later, she is asleep in my lap, her body still and relaxed. My arms are set around her in an iron grasp. No way in hell am I ever lettin' her go.

Chapter Thirty-Five

GRACE

With the trip to the police station done and dusted, I slide my hand into Mack's as we walk down Main Street, heading for the Arts Center. I want to check in before I come back next week. Don was good enough to let me have a few extra days. Lord knows I could use them. But I don't want to stay home—I have something I need to do.

"Can you come with me somewhere?" I ask.

Mack dips his head, catching my gaze. "Anywhere, gorgeous."

"Pennsylvania?" I pull a cringy *please* face.

I know my parents left my birthday party and never so much as looked back. Or sent even a text. Despite that, my gut tells me to try again. For Mama.

If there's any part of my relationship with my parents I want to salvage, it's what lies between my mother and me. If Dad doesn't want to listen, that's fine, he doesn't have to. But I'm not losing her. I refuse.

Mack stops, gripping my hand. I turn back to face him. Worry creases his face. "You sure?"

"I mean, I've done harder things . . ."

His hand is behind my neck instantly, my face smushed into his chest. I curl my fingers around the opening of his coat. "Yes." I glance up into those dark blues. "I'm sure. I can't lose her, Mack. I won't."

"Alright. When?"

"Is tomorrow too soon?"

He smiles, pressing his forehead to mine. His signature move, and one of my favorites. "Sounds perfect."

We settle into the hug for a moment before continuing on toward my work. Mack isn't using his cane. His gait is a little wobbly, but there's no telling him otherwise. So damn determined, this man. The front door chimes as we push through. Don greets us with open arms.

"Miss Gracie! How wonderful is it to see you." He has me in a hug before I have the chance to object. I guess I gave everyone a scare.

Small towns grow on you. Lewistown feels like home to me.

"Careful, Don," Mack says, "wouldn't want to start up the old rumor mill."

Don pats my back, making space between us.

I roll my eyes at Mackinlay. "You'll keep, cowboy."

He bends down, his lips by my ear. "I most certainly hope so, captain."

I give him a quizzical look. I never did ask what the captain thing is all about. Shaking my head, I walk to the front desk. The computer is on. The bookings sheet is open. Every last spot is filled for the art classes for the next six months. The small group I started with has grown to twenty-four per class. "What on earth . . ."

Don slips into view, his hands in his pockets, a grin stretching his kind face. "Thought that might cheer you up."

I stare at him. He did this?

"I—"

He holds a hand up. "Told you all this town needs is new blood. You, Gracie, are the new blood. We are excited to watch you liven this old town up."

My mouth gapes.

"Also, some of the patrons have suggested artist retreats out at R & R. I trust you can run it past Mrs. Rawlins?"

He means Ruby. I chuckle. "Yes, I can absolutely do that."

"Excellent. I'll leave you young ones to your morning. I'll see you Monday, Grace." He walks out the back with a smile and a wave.

I turn to find Mack leaning on the front counter, happiness etched all over his handsome-as-hell face. "Have I told you lately how proud I am of you?"

I groan at him. "Yes, Mackinlay."

"Good. Better get used to me lovin' on you, gorgeous girl."

"What's that supposed to mean?"

He winks at me.

"Okay . . ."

With a chuckle, he holds out a hand, and we walk back through the front doors. One last duck to find and usher into the steady row I now have.

Mama.

The undercarriage squeals at contact with the runway. I grip the armrest with one hand. Mack has the other encapsulated in his. Large and warm, his hand grounds me. The captain turns off the seatbelt sign, and I grab my carry-on from above. Mack grabs his before commandeering mine as we disembark.

You can do this, Grace. Look how far you've come. After everything that happened with Joel, explaining a few things to my folks shouldn't be a big deal. My throat closes with emotion. I want to talk to Mama. Seeing her for less than an hour at my birthday was like being given the one thing you needed most, only to have it ripped away seconds later.

Mack folds in around me. His heady scent is an instant comfort. He transfers both bags to one hand and laces his fingers through my own. The cowboy hat on his head is out of place. It makes me giggle. But I love it. Love him.

No place on earth exists that I wouldn't go with this man. A lifetime of hell with him would better than a day spent in heaven with anyone else. I thank god every day we found each other at the exact moment we did.

It forged what we have.

Sowed the seeds so deep nothing could have stopped them from growing, breaking through the surface, unfurling under the sun's warm rays, and blooming to a fully-fledged, imperfect, living thing.

We pass through the terminal and Mack hails a cab. I regurgitate my childhood home address, and the cab pulls away. Twenty minutes later, we pull into the drive of the home I haven't seen since I turned eighteen. It's remarkably the same as I left it. Mack leans forward, paying the driver. He pushes out of the cab and takes the bags. I sit on the back seat, hands gripping the edge of the cracked vinyl seat, focus fixed on the front door. Breathing, taking one breath after the other, requires all my concentration.

"Gracie, we do this together, remember?"

I break my gaze from the door to find a gentle smile and a hand held out. I take his hand, It's warm and steady. Strong and unwavering. I step out of the car and shut the door. The cab backs down the drive and speeds off. We round the hedge and the garage door is open. Mama's car is not there.

Dad's is.

"I can't do this." Spinning backward, I stalk back the way we came. At the curb, I pace up and down the quiet suburban street. What was I thinking? They don't want me here. Don't want any part of the life I made for myself. Not after I imploded the one they so carefully curated for me.

A knock rattles the front door. The bags are by the hedge. Mack's black hat is all I see over the hedge. The front door whines open.

"Hi, Mr. Weston." His hat slides from his head. It must be in his hands or by his side.

Nausea floods in when I listen to my father's stern voice. "Last I recall, I wasn't welcome at your residence. You are also not welcome here, Michael."

"It's Mackinlay. And I apologize. Things got heated. But—"

"You've wasted your time, and now mine. Good day."

The door slams.

A hushed curse. Another knock.

Oh no. Leave it, Mack.

Please.

He doesn't. Another knock. Persistent, longer, louder.

The door opens with a heavy sigh. "You slow, son? Take a hike."

"I ain't leavin' until you've heard us out." Mack's voice

has dropped an octave. It's what I imagine he used as a soldier. Harsh. All business.

Shit.

I run my hands through my hair and decide if I'm part of this team, the Mack-and-Grace team, I should be by his side, not cowering behind the shrubbery. I stride across the lawn, coming to Mack's side. My father's face turns to stone.

Mack flicks me a look. The *go get 'em* face.

"I would like to speak to Mama. Please."

My father stiffens in the doorway. "She's not here."

"When will she be back?" Mack asks.

My father pays him no heed, his eyes trained on me when he spits, "She isn't coming back."

The door slams for the second time since we arrived. I glare at it. This time, my fear is replaced by disbelief and annoyance. What does he mean, she's not here? What the hell?

A soft voice clears to our right. I drag my gaze toward the sound. Old Mrs. Barton leans over her fence, gloved hands holding her pruning shears. "Grace, that you?"

With a huff of a laugh, I cross the grass and hug her over the fence. "Hey, Mrs. Barton."

"Well now, didn't you grow into a fine-looking woman." She studies me over. I fight off a blush. No matter how hard I try, I will never have the Ruby Rawlins confidence. "And now." She nods behind me. "Is this your husband?"

Mack steps in behind me. Leaning around he offers her a hand. "Mack. Nice to meet you, Mrs. Barton."

"He's not my husband," I mutter.

She rears back playfully as if slapped. "Honey, you've got to lock this one down. And fast. Man in a hat. Bet he has a horse, too." Her face is ridiculous. Her curly grey hair is twisted into a floral bandanna on her head, her over-rouged cheeks pop with her toothy grin. I can't help but chuckle. The woman has a point. But I'm not here for love life advice, so I glance around the street before asking, "Where's Mama, Mrs. Barton?"

Her face falls to seriousness. "Oh honey, she left. They'd been fighting on and off for years after you went. After their quick getaway out west, your mother packed up her things and I haven't seen hide nor hair of her since. Good for her, if you ask me."

"Oh" is all I can say.

She left him. After decades of being the dutiful house-wife and mother, she packed up and walked away.

"Where can I find her, then?" I ask.

"She lives over on the other side of the river now. Westwood Village, Betty from bingo told me. Working somewhere over there. Maybe at the college . . . At least, I think that's what Betty said? Good luck, honey."

"Thank you."

She nods and winks at Mack before turning back to her plants.

"I'll get an Uber," Mack says, tapping on his phone already.

"Westwood . . ." I mutter to myself. "Central Penn is over there."

"She's teaching there?" Mack asks, sliding his phone into the back pocket of his Wranglers.

"I wouldn't think so."

The Uber arrives five minutes later. We zip through the burbs, over the river, and head north for Westwood Village. But it's gated, and we can't get in.

"Try the college," I say, hanging onto the back of the driver's seat. A few minutes later, we wind through campus roads. Driving past the huge triangle building, I can't wait any longer.

"Stop! Here, please." I burst from the back door and stalk my way across the concrete parking lot, homing in on the cream-colored three-story building. The administration lady startles as I rush through the doors.

"Hi, are you alright?" she asks.

"I'm looking for someone. Helena Weston."

"Does she go here?" The lady raises an eyebrow.

"I don't know." I know what she's going to say.

"I'm sorry, I can't give out student or staff information. You can't text or call?"

"I—" I straighten. "I don't have her number."

She wouldn't have mine. I never gave her my new number when I replaced my phone after a year of being in Mississippi. Never imagined I would ever call her again.

Not after Mack smashed that one, either. The glass doors swish, and I can tell it's him. The air around me changes as he comes to stand behind me. My chin wobbles. I should have tried harder. Should have kept her updated, even if I never got a reply. Should have held up my end of the communication.

A hot tear streaks down my cheek as students pour from a room down the hall. I swipe it away. "You sure you can't help me? I'm trying to find—" My voice cracks. My shoulders are shaking, but warm hands come to rest over them.

"As I said—"

"She's my mama. I'm trying to find my mother . . ." The words fade out.

A huffing sound echoes through the foyer, and I feel Mack turn toward it.

"Gracie?" a soft, so very familiar, voice gasps.

Chapter Thirty-Six

MACK

History repeats itself. That's what they say. I never would have put much stock in the phrase until lately. But after hearing Helena's story, the pieces of the puzzle come together. Grace grew up watching her father control her mother. It's what she thought a successful relationship was. And it was her greatest downfall.

Until the day she decided for herself.

God knows how very grateful I am she did.

I sit in silence as the two women share stories at a lone park bench somewhere in the suburbs of Harrisburg. Tension racks to an all-time high as Grace relays with somber words what happened since the day she left their family home. Her mother's face works through every emotion possible. As does mine. I know Grace's story.

She's shared it with me, in snippets and long talks. Hearing it again is no less painful than the first time.

A fresh hell.

Although it's over, and she is safe, my heart breaks for every day she needed someone to look out for her and didn't have them. I have to divert my gaze when Grace tells her mom about the night she fled Raymond. Helena's face is plain fuckin' heartbreaking.

I want to kill that motherfucker so bad it hurts.

With any luck, he'll be holed up in prison for a long while. And when the day comes he's released, I'll be waiting for him to step foot on the ranch. He'll be buried under one of Harry's precious damn fence posts. Deep inside the stone-cold earth. Only thing he's good for is compost, anyhow.

Overdramatic—maybe. Luckily for the idiot, Grace has a restraining order on him. If he decides to ignore it? He'll end up on the wrong end of my wrath.

". . . kinlay?"

I shake my head, refocusing on the women in front of me. "Yeah?" The word is raw.

"I was wondering if I could put Grace and you up for the night." Helena looks at me with a hopeful gaze.

"Grace?" I ask, studying her reaction.

"I would love that, Mama." She hugs her mother.

Right there—the moment that makes this entire goose chase worth it. What we came for. We make our way through the park and down a street. The entrance to Westwood Village comes into sight, and Grace bumps into my side, squeezing my hand. I glance down at her, finding the biggest grin on her face. The happiest she's been in days.

"What?" I ask quizzically, kicking up a lone brow.

She pushes up on her toes, tiptoeing as we walk. Her mouth brushes my neck as she tilts her head up. "How am I going to keep my hands off you in Mama's home?"

I turn my head and nip her ear. "I have ways of keeping you quiet, gorgeous girl, while you come around my cock. And can promise you multiple orgasms while I'm at it." I wind my arm behind her neck and slide my hand over her mouth. Her head tosses back with a laugh that warms my soul. Brown locks sway over her back, tussling over her shoulders.

"I'll see you keep that promise, Mackinlay Rawlins."

Our luggage is still hanging from my other hand. How far have I toted these bags today? The symbolism of the whole day isn't lost on me. I'll carry Grace's baggage 'til the end of the earth, with my last breath. To say I'm the savior here would be a grave misconception. If anyone saved anyone, she saved herself. And dragged me up along with her on the way.

"Oh." Grace turns back, arms outward like she set to spin around. "I've been meaning to ask you something for weeks."

"Yeah?" I chuckle. "What is it?"

"What's the deal with the captain thing?"

My fingers dig into Grace's throat. Her eyes flare, telling me she wants more. She wants my hands rough on her body. Her way of showing me her strength. Added bonus, it turns her on faster than a grass fire in a lightning storm. Her back arches, knees dug into the picnic blanket I laid under the tree. At the base of the mountain, Trigger and Sergeant are tied to the closest old shade tree.

I'm not one hundred percent comfortable on a horse yet, but I trust Trig. Always have. We took it steady. Besides, there is no way I'm passing up the only day off Grace has had for the two weeks since we came home from Pennsylvania. Her hips roll and my cock twitches. The tight grip her walls have on me sends me higher with every move she makes.

"Mack, god, I have missed you." Her words are raspy. Her eyes close as her head tilts back. I loosen my grip on her throat and clamp my teeth over a nipple. A whimper rattles past my palm.

"Fuck, Grace. Sweet Jesus. When you do that with your hips . . ."

Heat pools low in my spine. Electricity concentrating,

I'm set to explode. I send the most errant thoughts into my head, desperate to hold off. Today, this picnic, is special.

Like life-changing special.

"Oh god, Mack. Ohh—" She's out of breath. She's close.

I run my tongue over her nipple and tug it with my lips as I send my fingertips to brush over her clit. The sweetest moan turns to a breathy cry. Her walls clamp around me.

"Fuck, gorgeous . . ." I hiss.

Her head dips, hands snapping onto my jaw. Eyes lined up, she comes, wrapped around me. Eye contact. Hearts, souls, and every other part of her, and of me, joined.

"I love you," she rasps.

The sensation is too much. My heart is loved too well. The heat in my spine runs directly to my balls, and I explode inside her. A long, heady growl slips past my barely parted lips as I thrust up into her. She rides every wave between us, her orgasm spiraling along with my own.

Her hips slow. Brushing her hair back, I study every detail of her beautiful face. Her shoulders heave, those stunning breasts brushing against my sweaty chest. Four positions and three orgasms for Grace, and we are spent. In the best way possible.

"So, I've been thinking . . ." Grace dots a kiss to my

forehead, one to my nose, and one to each cheek before trailing tiny kisses along my jawline.

"Should I be worried?" I say with a chuckle.

"I figured out the captain thing."

I suck in a breath, leaning back with my hands planted on the blanket behind me. "Oh yeah, what do you think it is?"

She leans back a little, one fine finger tracing the peaks and valleys of my chest. "So, Louisa is Harry's captain. Addy is Hudson's and Ruby is Reed's."

She's got it, alright.

I smile at her, but she frowns. My smile slips a little and I wait for what's coming next.

"So . . . I was thinking tha—"

"Grace, wait."

Her face falls. I sit up and grab her shoulders. The disappointment on her face is a knife to my heart. We are not doin' this naked. I want to ask *her*. Kneel down on one knee and all that shit. Make it a moment she will treasure. Not some post-sex conversation, akin to a chat about what goes on the damn grocery list.

She moves off my lap and gets dressed.

Silently.

I clean up the best I can and pull on my jeans. As I tug on my shirt and pop my head through, she is packing up. *Fuck.*

Well, now I know where her head is at, at least.

Makes this next part a little easier.

She's putting the plates into the basket as I squat down and rest a hand over hers. "Stop, gorgeous."

"It's fine. I know I'm too young. You're more than ten years older than me, Mack. You've probably never thought about me like th—As your wi—You know what, it's—" She sinks onto her heels.

"After everything you and I have been through, you really think I would do this life with anyone else?" I turn her face toward mine.

Silver lines her eyes.

Dammit.

She sniffs. I tamp down the smile that's threatening to turn up my lips. It's not funny. But seeing her riled up over the possibility of not being Mrs. Mackinlay Rawlins is so damn sweet. Honestly, it's goddamn adorable.

Like everything else in our life, the moment I have been waiting for since her birthday party is turning out a little imperfect.

"I don't know." Her gaze turns harder.

There's my girl.

Give it back to me, Gracie. Don't take my shit.

"Reckon you can readjust the girths before we head up the mountain?" I ask.

She sighs and pushes to her feet, heading for Trigger. I follow a little way behind. Once she tightens his girth, she moves to the other side of Sergeant. I slip a hand into the saddle bag behind the fender. The small blue velvet box sits snug in there, waiting just like I am.

"All done," she says, appearing at Trigger's head. Her palm rubs his head, and he leans into her. "I'll grab up the blanket and stuff." She disappears.

"Still a lost cause for her, I see. Guess that makes two of us, buddy." I rub his neck. The blanket and basket are bundled away, and I wait for Grace to mount before swinging up onto Trigger. My old work shirt is tugged by the chilly wind as we ride home at a steady walk. I pull my hat down. The sun is low, with winter almost here.

Down on the flat, we wade through the swaying golden grass. The same grass Grace paints. The homestead comes into view, and the golden rays of the day's dying light splinter over the horizon, framing the ranch where we have lived, loved, fought, picked up the pieces, and weathered our storms together. I pull Trigger to a halt and swing out of the saddle.

Grace rides for home. Standing in the grass, I wait for her to realize I'm not following. A handful of heartbeats later, she twists in her seat, a hand on the back of her saddle. Her head is tilted, eyes squinting against the fading light. The darkness behind me is a stark contrast to the setting halo that has backlit her. I drop the reins and rifle through the saddle bag until I have the velvet box in my hand. I push it into my back pocket.

"Mack, what's wrong?" she calls back, turning Sergeant around and pushing him into a fast walk.

I meet her in the middle. "Might be stone bruised. You should check Sarge."

"Oh shit." She swings down, her hair flying over her shoulders, worried eyes following the hand she runs down Sergeant's front leg. The light turns almost orange, and the first star pops in the sky.

I drop to one knee behind her.

"Gracie, gorgeous, he's fine."

"No, I need to check him. He might—" She spins back and freezes. The horse plants his hoof back to the ground. "Mackinlay . . ."

Her eyes widen, and I swear she stops breathing.

"Wha—what are you doing?" she rasps. "I thought . . ."

I smile up at her and take her hands in mine. "Grace Elizabeth Weston. You have brought color where there was only black and white, grey at best. Breathed life into a broken and very lost man. Filled his heart so full it grew exponentially, so much it can never return to what it was. I don't ever want it to."

"Mack," she breathes.

"Gracie, there is only one thing I would change about you."

She frowns. "Oh?"

I tug the box from my pocket and hold it out to her, flipping the lid on the ring with the princess cut sapphire framed with diamonds on a titanium band.

"Yeah, gorgeous. Your last name. Will you marry me, Grace?"

Her lips parted, her face is part stunned, part twisted

with something I can't place. She sucks in a breath, and her face breaks. I push to my feet, heart hammering into my rib cage, my gut sinking like a stone. As I fold myself around her, she nuzzles my neck. Her safe place.

Fuck.

This is supposed to be a memory for us to treasure, and instead—

"Of course I will marry you," she whispers, lifting her head. Those blue eyes meet mine. "But Mack?"

I hold her at arm's length and study her face.

"My heart will always belong to Trigger." She breaks into a laugh, tears streaming down her face.

"Sweet Jesus, Grace. Give a man a damn heart attack."

She grips my coat, laughing into my chest. I smack her ass and drop to my knee again. This time I'm not gettin' up until my ring is on her pretty finger. Her laughter dies out and her face pulls with emotion. I take her hand and slide the sapphire onto her finger.

Perfect fit.

The ring on her finger.

Her heart in mine.

The captain to my ship. The woman I love. Who loves me so much she moved my world for me, giving me the chance to live again.

She tugs me to my feet. I groan against the ache blooming in my lower back and hip.

"Time to get you home, my love." Her hands brush over my jawline. Her lips cover mine. I close the space between us and kiss her with every part of me. The good, the bad, and the parts she fixed when she didn't have to. She opens for me. I claim her.

My Gracie.

My wife.

Chapter Thirty-Seven

Mama walks beside me, flowers in her hair. We walk toward the double doors of the huge barn at R & R Ranch. The stars glimmer above us, only outshone by the extravagant amount of fairy lights Ruby strung up over the barn's entrance and through the trees. Cars line the driveway. One in particular, Blue, sporting tin cans on white ribbon tied to the bumper set to drag behind her.

Something old, something new, something borrowed, something blue.

My old—Blue.

New—the sapphire on my finger.

Something borrowed—Ruby lent me an expensive looking pair of silvery-blue Roger Vivier heels. She insisted. Something about pumps being an aphrodisiac. Not sure I want to know . . .

They are under my floor-length lace designer gown, my wedding gift from Ruby and Addy. It's absolutely stunning. Too much for a gift, but stunning nonetheless. A strapless sweetheart neckline with an illusion bodice, stitched floral motifs scattered over the long flowing A-line tulle ending with a scalloped-trimmed, crystal-studded hem.

Something blue—the brooch Louisa gave me as part of our engagement gift. It was her mother-in-law's. She told me, as she handed it over, she saw a very similar strength in me that Harry's mother had. "An ability to weather any storm" were her words before she hugged me tighter than ever.

With my little pops of color over the ivory lace dress, the train glides behind me, albeit over the gravel right now. I tighten my grip on Mama's arm. A bouquet of creamy flowers rests in my sweaty palm.

Everyone is inside. The warm June breeze floats over my arms. I pull my hair around my neck and let it drape down my chest. The string quartet plays their first note and goosebumps flood my skin. It's ethereal.

I must have been rooted to the spot, staring at the barn doors, because Mama tugs on my elbow.

"Walk with me, Gracie?" she whispers.

All I can do is nod.

I hang from Mama's arm as we cross the threshold. Inside is another world entirely. It's not structured rows and formalities. Two large clusters of white chairs, with satin ribbons tied up in bows at the back, sit on either side. The enormous space is candlelit. As I pass the four musicians, the entire room stands.

White petals litter the floor. I let my gaze wander, taking in the stunning beauty of what Addy and Ruby made for us. My heart thunders as I find each face I recognize. People from work, some friends of Mack's. I search for family.

I see Addy first. Then, Hudson.

Reed and Ruby right next to them. Harry and Louisa are in the very front row with Lawson. He beams at me, and I tamp down a chuckle. I've missed having him around. He was my sounding board for a while there. And I owe him my sanity in those early days. Always with the level head. He's like the big brother I never had.

I break my gaze from Mackinlay's family, and he's there.

Standing tall to the right of the preacher. The dark suit and black hat swallow my attention. I force my eyes up. Deep blues burn into mine.

Tears swell, threatening to flow over with every step I take down the aisle.

"I'm so proud of you, Gracie," Mama whispers as we close in on the end of the aisle. I glance at her. Tears have streaked down her face. She pats my hand, and we stop. "And I love you, always." She scrunches up her face as if trying to stem the emotion.

I hug her tight. "I love you too, Mama."

She releases me, and I turn back toward the preacher.

"Oh shoot," Mama mutters, snatching the bouquet from my hand. Chuckles bubble up behind us. I step forward, my focus on the man in front of me. The angle of his jaw that feathers as I close the space to him. His eyes, like the furthest depths of the ocean, are now silver-lined and studying my face. "Hello, gorgeous."

"Hey, sweet man."

His mouth tips to a warm smile as his hands open and move between us, palms up. I slide my own into them and they close, thumbs tracing circles over my knuckles. "You ready?"

"Probably should have asked me before everyone got all dressed up."

Another swell of chuckles.

"Yes," I breathe.

"We can make a start?" the preacher man says, dipping his head.

"Fire away," Mack says.

Fire away, indeed. Louisa gives me a wink that I catch in my peripheral. Everyone goes quiet as I shift my gaze to find the preacher looking at me, waiting.

I give him a nod, and he opens his book.

"We are gathered here today to witness the union in holy matrimony between Grace Elizabeth Weston and Mackinlay Samuel Rawlins . . ."

Sergeant moves under seat as I adjust the easel secured across my back. I double-check the clasps on the rolled-up tent and supplies I tied to the back of the saddle.

Clothes—check.

Paints and brushes—check.

Food for three days and nights—check.

Trigger and Mack trot up by our side, packs strapped behind his saddle.

Handsome-as-hell husband—check.

The black hat on his head tips as he leans over, planting a kiss on my cheek. My own hat bunts up my head. I went for a white Stetson like Hudson. Black has never been my thing. Plus, it's such an awesome contrast with my long light brown hair. Everything in my life comes back to color. My work. My daydreams. The intoxicating deep blues of the love of my life's eyes. Which are now full of cheek.

"What are you thinking, Mackinlay Rawlins?"

"Ah, nothin', Gracie Rawlins."

I roll my eyes at him. "You realize you are going to be bored out of your skull, watching me paint for three days straight holed up somewhere up there." I point at the blue monster of a mountain we have aimed our horses at.

"Yup, and there is no way in this world I could ever get bored of staring at you, gorgeous."

I pull a face at him and cluck Sergeant forward. We walk at a steady pace toward the mountains, through the wispy, waving green grasses of summer. The buzz, hum, and clicks of the insects in the warm sunshine fills the silence between us. I stare up at the mountain. I've traveled some tough terrain in the last few years. We both have. The hard work, blood, sweat, and tears were worth it. Because it led me here.

It gave me Mack.

And I would walk through hell over and over to have this sweet man by my side.

"Wanna lope?" he asks, still gazing ahead.

"Okay, but we rein it in the second you feel it's too much."

He grins, turning his head. Two fingers press to his forehead. "Aye aye, captain."

Trigger bursts forward into a lope. I laugh, hearty and free, the sound rumbling through my chest and bouncing up my throat.

This is real happiness.

Real love.

The kind that makes you whole, no matter how broken you were when it found you. It stays. It sees your worth. It comforts you through the worst days. It lives for your happiness.

Just as I live for his.

I push Sergeant fast and fly after him. I have a good feeling about this little adventure of ours.

I'm breathless.

I was expecting pristine beauty, but this—this is simply serene. I stand on the peak of the mountain I have been gazing at since the day I arrived on this ranch. Nothing will ever compare to the pure exhilaration of standing on one of Mother Nature's finest creations as the sun sets, leaving its brilliant beams trailing over the vista of peaks and valleys, aqua waters and deep green forest.

The crunch of earthy ground cover closes in. "That's some sunset," Mack whispers against my neck, arms wrapping around my waist.

"It's stunning. So stinking beautiful."

"Sure are."

I turn briefly, pressing a kiss into his tousled dark hair. "Still, it's been a long, long day. We should rest our weary bones."

"Gorgeous girl, the last thing I plan on doing tonight on our mountain honeymoon is sleepin'."

Releasing me, he spins me around, planting his mouth over mine.

"Three days isn't really a honeymoon, Mack."

"Quality over quantity. Plus, Reed & Rubes have something planned for us when we get back."

"Oh god, should I be worried?"

He chuckles. "Only if Reed planned it."

I can't help the laughter spilling from my lips. It echoes through the mountains; the sound amplifies as it travels. Mack takes my hand and leads me back through the wooded trees. I negotiate my way over the forest ground to the clearing. Trigger and Sarge are tethered to a long, low tree branch, free of tack, already half asleep. The tent is up. A campfire blazing away.

"Isn't it too hot for a fire?" I ask.

"The nights are much cooler up here."

He settles on a fallen log and pulls me onto his lap. The last of the light fades out as I sink down, straddling him, fingers splayed over his jawline. The wind changes, sending the flames crackling and warmth against my back.

"As much as I love looking at your handsome face, sitting on your lap isn't going to cut it."

I push off and grab his shirt, tugging him to follow me to the tent. The cream flap gives way, and he crowds in behind me as I stop short. The inside is all blankets, two small lanterns, and a plate of food. It's heaven.

I turn back around, tilting my face up. "I don't think I ever want to leave," I whisper.

"If that's an order, cap, we can live up here for the rest of our days . . . I have everything I need right here."

"You gonna hunt while I gather, Mackinlay?" I give him my best bratty smile.

"I would do anything for you, Grace."

"Anything?" My heart flings, giving my ribs a beating.

"Say the word, captain."

I drag his mouth down into a kiss. He claims me. Tongue over mine, tangling together. I break away as fire courses through my veins, sucking in a breath. "Then, I want you. The unrestrained, raw Mackinlay. The version of you who takes what he wants."

I do. Nothing turns me on more than seeing him feral for me. His rough hands working my body. Pushing my limits. Because I trust him.

He studies my face for a moment before running a thumb over my bottom lip. His eyes darken, sending a surge of heat to my center. Need ignites.

My body vibrates with the sheer desperation I have for him. His hand lightly closes around my throat with a brief squeeze, sending lightning skittering down my spine.

"Take it all off," he finally demands.

His voice, all raw and visceral, takes my breath away. I strip down, sliding the coat from his shoulders before my fingers fly through each button on his old work shirt and it hits the blankets we stand on. When we are bare as the day we were born in front of each other, he tips his head, signaling to the hat he still wears.

"The hat stays," I whisper.

A strained growl slips out, and his top lip curls a little.

He pushes me to my knees and runs his hand through my hair before his fist tangles in my locks, tightening. His hard length is in my face. Temptation never felt so incredible. I slide a hand around it, taking him all the way into my mouth.

"So fuckin' pretty when you take my cock like a good girl, Gracie."

My eyes flutter shut as I work him up and down. Need pools in my belly, wetness coating the inside of my thighs. God, this version of my husband will never get old. I swirl my tongue over his velvety tip. Saltiness meets my tongue. It hits my core like a freight train—I do this to him. This unbreakable man, who's all heart and soul.

He groans, and his other hand brushes under my jaw, tilting my head up a little. Thrusting in further, he hits the back of my throat. My eyes water, stealing the last of my breath. I ache for him. My breasts bounce with the movement, my hard peaks desperate for touch. I slide my hand over one, rolling my nipple between my fingers. The whimper rattling up my chest vibrates around him.

"Fuck, Gracie. Touch yourself."

I trace my hand down my body until my fingertips brush over my clit. A muffled cry leaves me, and Mack's face wrecks. The warm, tingling spiral of bliss starts to form as I work my fingers around in small circles, massaging my throbbing clit. My body starts to shake. Mack's thrusts slow. He pulls back, leaving the tip of him between my lips.

"Spin around, on your hands and knees." His words are short, harsh.

Desire skitters down every nerve. I'm so strung out with need, I move automatically. My hands sink into the soft blanket. He kneels behind me, dotting kisses from the base of my spine to the space between my shoulder blades. My breasts swing as I roll my hips, desperate to find him. The blanket rubs across my nipples. It's too much. I whimper. I'm a writhing, needy, wet mess.

"Fuck me, please, Mac-kin-lay . . ." Every short, choppy breath burns.

A hand slaps my ass, hard. The sting spreads. "Don't fuckin' beg. It's beneath you."

"I don't care, please. Fuck me. So fucking hard."

Another slap to the other cheek. Wetness gathers again, re-coating the inside of my thighs. God, when he talks to me like that . . .

His hands grip my hips. He slams into me before the next heartbeat. My moan turns to a whimper with the stretch. The bliss of being so filled. So well. He pauses for a second, letting me adjust.

"You want it rough, gorgeous girl?" he rasps.

I nod.

"Say it, Grace."

"I want you rough."

He pulls out so excruciatingly slowly, my mouth waters. My center aches. My clit throbs like it's about to implode. His hand finds my hair, twisting it until it's wound over his wrist and tight in his grip. I look back. His face is feral. His chest heaves. Mine caves in at the sight of him.

"Hands," he barks.

I rest my cheek on the blanket, chest pressing into the softness, which sends my reddened ass canting up toward him as I move my hands behind my back. His free hand grips my wrists together at the small of my back. His knee nudges my right leg wider. Then my left.

I'm burning up for this man. And he's taking his fucking time. He nudges my legs wider still. So wide I can barely hold the position. I'm spread open for him.

As if he read my mind, his lip curls into a smile. "You're mine, Gracie. To fuck. To love. To protect."

"Do it already," I growl back.

He thunders into me.

I cry out. Uncontrollable bliss spirals with every thrust, flailing each time he takes it away. He pounds into me hard. Fast. My aching center is alive with electricity. His moves turn choppy, and his hands release me as he pulls out.

"No!" My gasp turns to a growl. "Mackinlay, no."

I turn back, but his hands work me over. Flipping me to my back, he grips my hips in a bruising hold and pulls my wet center up to his glistening cock. Without a word, he rams it home. I grip the blankets, shoulders digging into the blanketed ground.

He's wild.

And exactly what I asked him to be.

My breasts bounce, ratcheting up the insane sensations he is giving me. Release barrels toward me. I slam my eyes shut.

One hand disappears from my hip. Two fingers pinch down on my clit. "Eyes on me when you come around my cock." The words are pure command.

I snap my eyes open and meet his darkened gaze.

His hair is ruffled, his body so tense every line of every muscle shows. His jaw is set. His chest, covered in a sheen of sweat, still heaving.

"Milk my cock, gorgeous girl. Come for me." His fingers swirl over my clit.

I explode around him, my back arching. Hips bucking. His eyes burn into me.

His head drops backward as the veins in his neck bound. With the first hot stream of his release, he throws his head back down, dark blues trained onto my face. He roars as his cock pulses, sending liquid heat into my core, so deep in me it's hard to tell where he stops and I begin. Or maybe we've melded together. There is not one without the other. Two halves, having finally found each other.

It's hard to believe my life has changed so much in the last year and a bit. What my time with Mackinlay so far lacked in length has been more than made up by intensity. We lived through it all.

I realize he was right.

Quality is absolutely better than quantity.

But I never want this to end.

Give me forever, Mackinlay Rawlins, because that's exactly what I am taking.

Jesus fuckin' Christ, I'm old. And that ageless wife of mine, who is sound asleep beside me, doesn't look like she's weathered a damn day. She's practically glowing. Never saw the big deal with birthdays, except Ma's. Not until Grace came along. For me, I'm another year closer to forty.

Yip yip fuckin' hooray.

I roll over, burying my head into her hair. The smell of it still mesmerizes me and sends me hard as fuck, every single time. I should let her sleep, she's been so exhausted lately. I untangle myself from the best thing in my life and slip out from the covers.

I pull on my boxers and head for the kitchen.

Coffee time for this old man. I set the coffee maker up and flick the button over. The gurgling and sweet tang of fresh beans being scalded floats through the kitchen. I check my phone, still charging on the counter from last night.

Birthday messages from Ma, Reed, and Huddo. Never miss a beat, my family. Wouldn't have it any other way. Grace's phone vibrates beside my own, also charging.

Helena.

Those two are closer than ever now. After the shitstorm that was their family years ago, I'm glad Gracie got her mama back. I can't imagine not having Ma in my life. Soft footfalls snap my head from my daydreams.

Grace wanders in, wearing the tiniest sleep shorts on the planet and one of my old t-shirts that is so baggy on her it almost covers them. The same one she's been wearing for a month now. A vision that would send even the toughest man to his knees. She runs a hand through her messy brown hair, eyes homed in on the coffee pot.

"Hey, Mackie."

I wrap my arms around her as she reaches for a mug in the cupboard overhead. The charm bracelet on her wrist slides down her arm a little way. A permanent fixture on her body since the day Ma, Rubes, and Adds gave it to her. My name is on one charm, the ship's wheel on the other.

I sink my face into her hair, letting my hands wander under the baggy t-shirt, a finger brushing over her nipple. Her hand releases the mug, and it clinks back down onto the shelf. Her head falls backward to my shoulder.

"God above, Mackinlay, how does this need for you never wear off?"

I slide my hands down her side, over her ribs, and into the front of her shorts.

She's bare.

No panties.

Good girl.

I growl over threadbare breath. "Pretty damn sure you were made for me, and I was made for you, gorgeous."

She moans as my finger finds her clit. She's fucking soaked already.

The coffee hisses. It's done.

Her head snaps up. Her body goes rigid, and she turns in my hold.

"Shit," she gasps, clamping her lips down, face twisting. She wriggles out of my arms and takes off down the hallway.

I raise an eyebrow. "Okay?"

I take down the mug she was handling before I distracted her and fill it with coffee, adding the cream. I take another mug from the cupboard and pour myself one, too. The first sip is delectable. Almost as heady as my incredible wife.

A few minutes later, she reappears with a sheepish smile. Her hands are struggling to hold up a large box behind her back. Which makes her perfect tits push out. They're all the birthday present I need. Maybe without the t-shirt. My teeth clamped over them as she writhes on my lap—

"So, I know you don't like birthdays. But . . ." She pulls the bulky box around to her front, almost dropping it. "I still *had* to get you something."

"Gorgeous girl, you're all I need."

"Well, you might change your mind when you see your present."

I tilt my head, giving her a quizzical look. Okay, I'll bite. "Give it here, then."

Arms outstretched, she hands over the gift. I take it and pad to the sofa. This sounds like a sittin' down gift. She drops onto the seat behind me, arms wrapped over my shoulders and face beside mine as I lift the lid. She worries her bottom lip through her teeth as I glance at her.

"Mack, open it," she rasps.

I pull back the tissue paper. A black cowboy hat sits in the box. Pristine condition. Not like my old one that's more than earned its keep over the last decade and is now sporting a more battered appearance. I lift it out. Another layer of tissue paper rests under it, over something smaller, but still bulky. I reach for it. Grace's hand lands on mine. "Try the hat on first, please."

"Gracie, just the hat is enough. You work hard, I don't want you spending your money on me."

"I like giving you things. It makes me happy. So, deal with it."

Her face is ridiculous, and I couldn't love this woman more.

I push the hat onto my bed hair and turn on my seat to face her. "Better?"

"Better," she breathes, studying the hat.

I adjust it a little to lean in and kiss her. Something pokes into my forehead. *What the?* I pull the hat from my head. Grace rests on her heels, gaze stuck on my face, hands wringing in the old t-shirt she wears. I drop mine to inside the crown. An envelope is tucked into the brow band. I slip it out.

Bottom lip running through her teeth again, she whispers, "Open it."

I slide a finger under the back flap. My heart cracks up a storm as I pull out a small black-and-white image.

Is that?

"Fuck," I rasp, staring at the sonograph photo that shows something akin to a few swirls. I have no idea what's what.

"Happy birthday, Mackinlay." Tears stream down her face now.

"Gracie, you're—"

She nods, swiping her face with both hands, trying to dry it off. "You can open the next part now."

"No, wait," I draw her onto my lap and smother her into my chest. I'm going to be a father. Like a full-on Harry. *Fuck me.* Tears burn and flood my cheeks.

Grace pushes out of my hold. "Are you happy?"

"Hell, Grace, you have no idea how much."

She smiles, though emotion wrecks her face. She waves a hand to the gift behind me. I turn back and lift the last layer of tissue paper up, tossing it to the floor. What else could this amazing woman give me?

Another black hat is tucked in the center of the box. A tiny version of the one she just gave me.

"Turn it over, Mackinlay." The words are soft, breathy, too raw.

I rest a hand on the crown of the small hat. It fits in my palm. Goddamn. So fuckin' small. Emotions clamber up my throat. My hand trembles as I pry it out, turning it over. Another envelope.

"Grace, is this?"

I'm assuming whatever is in this one is something pink or something blue.

"If you don't want to know . . ." she starts.

I tear the envelope open like a little kid at Christmas. Blue hearts explode from the cream paper, scattering everywhere.

Blue.

A boy.

Holy fuck.

I'm going to have a son.

Grace's weight settles in my lap. She leans into my side and takes my hand, resting it over her stomach. I manically brush the tears marring my vision.

"We're having a boy?" I choke.

"Actually . . ." Her pretty blue eyes hold my gaze as she smiles and stands. She holds the tiny hat up and it pulls apart, shifting it—no, them—into two small black hats.

What the . . .

My throat closes over, my vision blurring instantly. "Shit."

"We're having twins. Say hello to daddy, boys." She rubs my hand over her belly. It's only now I see how it's swollen low between her hips. How did I not notice this? It seems so obvious now. The thought that Grace swells with my baby—my *babies*—takes my breath away, sending my cock instantly hard.

"Gorgeous girl. Come here."

She sinks onto my lap.

"God, I thought you would never ask. Pregnancy has my hormones hopped up on something hard. I'm horny. Swollen. And so desperate for you. All the damn time."

"Is that why you stopped wearin' panties to bed?"

Honestly, I thought the long floaty dresses she'd been wearing lately were her latest thrift store finds. She tends to have phases of wearing her finds continuously.

God above, I'm daft.

"Took you long enough." She giggles, grinding over my lap.

"I was too busy watching you bloom into the incredible woman you are."

"You're welcome," she whispers, shifting my boxers

down. I strip the T-shirt from her body, and she stands, pushing two fingers into the waistband of those tiny fuckin' shorts. They shunt down over her hips. As they hit the floor, her belly takes all of my focus. I palm it, caressing the woman I love. Who has given me so much. When I trail a finger down into her center, she's soaked. Wet need slicks her inner thighs.

"Come on. Sink that sweet pussy onto my cock."

She doesn't need to be told twice. Not my Gracie.

Knees pushed into the sofa on either side of me, she lowers onto me. Torturously slow. Like she's trying to lull me to a sweet, sweet death by ecstasy.

I would gladly follow her anywhere she cared to take me.

Any-fuckin-where is better with Grace.

After all, I'd still be an angry, lost, and wandering man without this incredible woman.

She was, is, and always will be my saving grace.

Need more Mack & Grace?
Grab the BONUS SCENE now!
https://BookHip.com/CDAWSCG

Continue the Rosewood Ranch series with

Harry & Louisa's story,
True North!

Sign up to the newsletter to make sure you never miss an Alexandra Banks book!!

SAVING GRACE
playlist

SKINNY LOVE
Birdy
3:21

MESSED UP AS ME
Keith Urban
3:16

A LITTLE PAST LITTLE ROCK
Lee Ann Womack
4:16

I HAD SOME HELP
Post Malone
2:58

SHE'S MY KIND OF RAIN
Tim McGraw
4:16

TOUGH ONES
Cooper Alan
3:13

NEW NORMAL
Cooper Alan
2:47

WAKE ME UP
Danielle Bradbery

LOSE CONTROL
Teddy Swims

FIX WHAT SHE DIDN'T BREAK
Nate Smith

NEVER GONNA BE ALONE
Nickelback

THE PAINTER
Cody Johnson

BONUS SONG
GRACE
Jelly Roll

TRUE NORTH

ALEXANDRA BANKS

Acknowledgments

Mack and Grace's story broke my heart and pieced it back together again. I've never cried so much writing a book in my life! This one was hard. But strangely, I loved every second, because I knew they would find exactly what they both needed. Even if it took a little while.

As always, thanks to my editors, Lindsey and Zainab. Your input and guidance is always wanted and appreciated.

To every ARC reader who volunteered to read this book, thank you!!

And lastly, but most certainly not least, my family for putting up with the endless country music playlist that I made them endure during the writing process to get into the zone ;)

Alex xx

About the Author

Alexandra Banks is a romantic at heart, and an optimist down to her very bones. Her love for everything romance sees her writing HEAs all day long.

But don't be fooled, there will be angst along the way, possibly heartbreak. But her fierce heroines can handle just about anything!

For more heartwarming reads, follow her on socials and join the mailing list so you never miss another heart throb!

www.ingramcontent.com/pod-product-compliance
Lightning Source LLC
Chambersburg PA
CBHW011052190726
48290CB00011B/3116